PARTIES

Tom
Lappin

Published by Two Ravens Press Ltd
Green Willow Croft
Rhiroy
Lochbroom
Ullapool
Ross-shire IV23 2SF

www.tworavenspress.com

The right of Tom Lappin to be identified as author of this work
has been asserted by him in accordance with the Copyright,
Designs and Patent Act, 1988.
© Tom Lappin, 2007.

ISBN: 978-1-906120-11-5

British Library Cataloguing in Publication Data. A CIP record
for this book can be obtained from the British Library.

Designed and typeset in Sabon by Two Ravens Press.
Cover design by David Knowles and Sharon Blackie.

FSC
Mixed Sources
Product group from well-managed
forests and other controlled sources
Cert no. SGS-COC-2953
www.fsc.org
© 1996 Forest Stewardship Council

Printed on Forest Stewardship Council-accredited paper by
Antony Rowe Ltd, Chippenham, UK.

About the Author

Tom Lappin grew up in England and now lives in Scotland. He has written about books, music, sport and travel for numerous publications including The Sunday Times, The Scotsman and The Modern Review. *Parties* is his first novel.

Parties is a work of fiction. All characters are creations of the author's imagination, and bear no intentional resemblance to any person, living or dead.

For H and I

A Party In 1987

Another June, another party. As always, at Liam's. Down familiar streets, up the same stairs, delivering the same heavy knock on the black door, paint blistered by a myriad fists, from a thousand and one similar parties.

It was one of those timeless corners of Edinburgh, summer leaves rustling in the breeze coming up off the Forth. You could stand on a cobbled corner and look all the way down the hill beyond Trinity and Granton, see the grey water and Fife beyond, and know little had changed there in centuries, save the murmur of the traffic edging down Broughton Street, and the muffled buzz of the television sets lighting up Georgian drawing-rooms.

You could find Liam's flat nestling there in a forgotten corner like a bad tooth, spreading quiet corruption. Here was a dwelling whose occupants were unwelcome at the local residents' committee meeting, bitterly begrudged possession of the key to the communal garden; who were a permanent challenge to the patrician liberality of the neighbourhood.

The flat was a two-storey affair, its degradation increasing by degrees the further you ventured into its bowels. Its filth was artfully accumulated: the result not so much of deliberate slovenliness as of the luxury of too much space. The place had six bedrooms, but the flat rarely had more than four occupants. So they had developed a system whereby residents moved from room to room whenever their own quarters became too squalid.

At any given time there were usually two rooms lying fallow to recover their integrity. Unfortunately, these were the quarters where surprise guests would be accommodated. They would wake the next morning and look around them in horror. Staggering through to the kitchen, they would murmur apologies. 'Listen man, I'm really sorry about the room. I'll clean it up before I go.' 'Don't worry,' they would be told, 'it was like that already'.

There in the hallway was an array of grubby photographic equipment: stained chemical trays, tripods, alchemical flasks for mixing the fluids stored in glass vials. Behind one of those doors, a Swede called Patrick is most likely peering critically at his latest shots: dark studies of angular nudes, all shadows and stark grimaces. But leave him be…

1

The next door along, a sandy-haired male in his early twenties, Leonard – never Lennie – is freeze-framing a clunky old VHS recorder on an image of a Mexican having his hand sliced off in a sawmill, tutting at the flicker and the two white parallel lines obscuring the picture, clicking on frame by frame until the definition is satisfactory...

Down the stairs, along the corridor. There, by the kitchen door, a couple just out of their teens are kissing, their shoulder-length hair entwining, mingling into one clump, to be reclaimed by the owners later on. Their hands feel around blindly, searching for erotic clues. The girl looks over her lover's shoulder, stares on into space, briefly settling into a default blankness, before turning back to contrive excitement. Belinda and Gary. No, not them...

Past the lovers, turning right, pushing open the door, looking into a living-room, filled with the smoke, sweat, perfume and drunken aftermath of predictable defeat. Nobody looks up. There we have them. The four of them sit in a comfortable tableau, slumped in various poses of disconsolate acceptance, together still after four years, linked by some imperceptible understanding, but still not quite appreciating they'll be pinned together for so many more.

Beatrice is the first one of them anybody would notice, and in many cases, the only one who would be noticed at all. Stretching out in her black linen shift dress, her arms and legs fall into positions of smooth, symmetrical grace. Black hair in an unfashionable round mop frames a face that is English in all but its slight hint of Mediterranean colouring. The grey eyes flicker tiredly, and Beatrice is softly biting down on the bottom lip, staring at the silent television screen. It is distraction more than anxiety. She looks across at the others occasionally, and Richard smiles back at her. Beatrice is the most beautiful woman any of them will ever see, although here again, they are still a long way from knowing that. They are still of an age where hope can wrestle back the sighing bleakness of experience.

Richard might have a suspicion of Beatrice's unvanquishable beauty, although the way he grins at her is companionable rather than romantic. One of Richard's constant sorrows is that he has not the looks of a lover. His roundish face, wide blue eyes, fair brown hair that made the decision a while back that it could not be bothered with the presumption of becoming blond ... everything suggests comfort rather than exalted passions. Except Richard wriggles around, shifts in his seat, taps his foot edgily to the barely discernible beat coming out of the cassette machine, looks like he would rather be anywhere but here.

Next to him on the filthy sofa, Gordon throws him the occasional irritated look. Gordon has a newspaper unfolded in front of him, is filling in with a ballpoint pen the results that flash intermittently across the foot of the screen. Gordon is mapping the scope of the defeat, fleshing out the details, looking for clues, indications, the small subtexts lurking within the greater story. You would look at Gordon's plain, hollowed face and see calculation, see a planner vexed with the desire for more information. And if he caught you looking he would flash back an embarrassed grin that would make you feel guilty for being suspicious. Gordon is in a constant struggle to prevent his thought processes showing on his face. Experience will make him more adept.

Gordon occasionally lifted a hand from his paper and, half-affectionately, half-proprietorially, draped it over the shoulder of Grainne. Grainne sits, a study in misery, pale face propped in her cupped hands, long thin strands of brilliant red hair falling across her eyes, down her cheeks, halfway down her back: red rain. Grainne, green-eyed, nervous, hugs herself into a ball. Grainne was the image lexicon compilers have in mind when researching the description 'voluptuous.' When she slumped back in the sofa with a bleak cry of despair, if Richard failed to glance at her cleavage then it was because four years of opportunity had taught him discretion.

The television sound was turned down, the radio cassette machine rattled tinnily, playing the first Pretenders album at slightly reduced speed, so that Chrissie Hynde's voice took on additional masculine overtones. The four of them stared at the freckled face of the defeated leader making what was apparently a concession speech. 'Should we listen to this?' Beatrice whispered, but nobody moved towards the volume control.

Gordon crushed a lager can in his fist, and skimmed it gently into a corner where it settled in the foothills of a sierra of detritus. Gordon grinned fiercely and indicated the slightly out-of-focus picture on the screen. 'Look at the expression on his face,' he spat. 'He looks as if he's eaten a bad pie and is looking for somewhere to spew.'

'Don't,' Grainne said. 'I feel sorry for him. It's not his fault the nation is full of selfish idiots.'

So it had been for the last two hours: morose scrutiny of the screen, fatalistic tallying of the score, desultory acceptance of a story that had taken a quick narrative twist away from a happy ending too early to allow for suspense.

Liam came into the room clutching a four-pack of lager under one elbow, and caught Grainne's words. 'Can't blame the people, Grainne darling. They've been seduced by the promise of free shares for all, no taxes and no more bloody immigrants being let into the country.' His words were greeted with a series of unenthusiastic grunts, but Liam was a showman who didn't need to feed off audience response.

'More than that, Thatcher has promised that if Johnny Foreigner even sniffs round anything that used to be British, she'll send another task force. How can the great British public resist that offer? More lager, anybody? Might be a bit warm, but what are you gonna do? It's June and the fridge in this place just isn't up to chilling one hundred and eight cans to the correct degree of iciness.'

Liam, at twenty-six, affected the demeanour of a man ten years older. He had worked on the look conscientiously and with attention to the crucial details. He had the receding hairline and the slightly overhanging belly already, but he also had the maroon cardigan with the stains and cigarette burns that sang of a slovenly bachelor. Liam's favourite role was that of host, bringing disparate elements together, blending them in the punchbowl of his festering flat. He saw himself as the catalyst, flitting from group to group, providing connections, building bridges, allowing the party to simmer into one cohesive whole. It hadn't ever worked. Liam's parties always devolved into close-knit, mutually hostile groups who took advantage of the flat's out-of-the-way spaces to avoid each other.

Still, Liam was necessary: a conduit who spliced together connections with an enthusiasm and inefficiency that recalled Latin wiring. Liam would lay claim to being Irish when he wanted to, whipping his London vowels into some approximation of Hibernian roguishness. He would muscle into holes in conversations, abhorring a verbal vacuum, filling it with verbiage that spilled out and oozed into all the cracks like loft insulation. Liam had a morbid fear that a conversational chill might settle over his parties. He threw a lot of parties, never very successful. Somehow, though, people kept coming back. Liam encouraged belief in a world where hope conquered experience.

So Liam would scatter words to the winds indiscriminately, sowing conversational seeds, knowing that if only five per cent of them sprouted he would have fulfilled his function. Finding a room so steadily quiet was a challenge to him, an affront.

'Why are you kids all sitting in here?' Liam asked reproachfully. 'There's food in the kitchen; everybody's in there.'

'You mean there's a bunch of nationalist wankers in there,' said Gordon. 'All rabid kilties happy to see Labour lose, because they're all secret Tories underneath.'

'Harsh words, Gordie,' Liam said. 'Besides, they've finished singing *Flower Of Scotland* now. Come on through and have a baked potato.'

'That's another thing. It's hot as fuck through there because you've had the oven on all night. Whoever told you that baked potatoes were suitable for a party in June?'

'What do you mean?' Liam said in a tone of mock outrage. 'Potatoes are the Thomas More of vegetables. Suitable for all seasons. Besides they are the only thing I know how to cook. Must be the Irish in me. Every now and then I get an urge to bake a shitload of potatoes in case there's another famine round the corner. I will retire hurt by your cruel words.' Liam lingered, though – mainly because he liked looking at Beatrice. She was the only woman of his acquaintance he hadn't tried to get into bed, shying away from that minatory look in her eyes every time he said something flirtatious.

'Leave the lager,' Gordon said.

'It's him, really, isn't it? The Celtic boyo,' Richard was saying. 'If there's one thing the English can't stand, it's a cocky Welshman.'

'True,' Liam agreed, 'except there's a lot more than one thing the English can't stand, and that boy seemed to have most of them.' Liam pointed at the crestfallen, freckled face still staring out of the TV screen, the chin rising with each word delivered to the silent TV speaker. 'Freckles, bald head except for the red hair – sorry, Grainne darling – intelligent wife, passion, willingness to look an idiot occasionally. Righteousness, that was his biggest mistake. You know – sounding genuinely upset when Thatcher announced her latest plans to shaft anybody who didn't live in a semi, drive a Rover and have their own share portfolio. Not very British, righteousness. They prefer cynicism, you know: acceptance. It's a passive thing, your British conservatism. They think everything is going to be pretty shitty in the end, so why try to avoid it?'

'Right,' Gordon said. 'But you can use that to your advantage. What they need is someone as ruthless as her, only smarter. Somebody who will point out that a lot of her most vicious schemes are economically unsound or unnecessary. The electorate might not understand cold logic, but they know it when they see it.'

'They can't get rid of him, can they?' Grainne asked. 'Who would they get? Cook? Smith? Not Fattersley, surely?'

'No chance,' said Gordon. 'He'll hang on for a while, be the fall guy, until someone younger is ready. Has to be Brown, doesn't it? Young, cool, good-looking, Scottish...'

'Trouble is, he's called Gordon,' Beatrice said, languidly stretching out an arm to collect a beer from Liam, and giving him a radiant smile that momentarily confounded a man who hadn't been bashful since his fourth birthday. 'Nobody would vote for a Gordon, would they?'

'I get the impression that nobody would vote for anybody wearing one of those red roses, whatever their name was,' Richard said, hearing himself, feeling he sounded peevish, going pink with self-awareness, but ploughing on. 'I always wondered what it would have been like living in Spain under Franco. You know, looking around at a Europe that had fought against the fascist dictators and got rid of them. And there you are in Valencia or Barcelona or Seville, and it's getting to the end of the 60s, and then it's the 70s, and Franco is still there, still telling you what to do, and you're going, "yoo-hoo, over here, there's someone you've forgotten about." Now I know. It's a bit like this.'

'That's the bloody problem, Rich,' Gordon said, angrily cracking the ring-pull on his lager. 'People have all this romantic ideology stuff. They go round bleating, nyah, nyah, Thatcher's a fascist. Not the way to do it. See, drawing the attention to all her union-bashing, warmongering stubbornness, ruthlessness, not-for-turning, hate Europe, hate foreigners, love America ... that's just highlighting all the stuff people like about her. What they have to do is point out that, actually, she's not all that competent; that the economy is going down the tubes, that having all that many unemployed is inefficient. It's pointless bleating on about the indignities of being jobless, you have to point out that it's bad management.'

'And that she's a loopy old bitch with a face like a zombie,' murmured Grainne.

'You mean you have to accept that the only possible political language is the Conservative one?' Beatrice said quietly.

'If you like, yeah. Got to have a bit of realism. They've defined the battleground. Might as well accept it, and get down to working out some decent tactics. Hey, hey, hey, Grainne.'

Grainne sobbed gently, and the other three turned and saw the tears cascading down her cheeks. She sniffed soundly and scrunched her face into a watery grimace.

'Sorry. It just seems so hopeless, you know? We can sit here and be all smart and cynical about it, but what's going to happen in the next five years? What else are they going to do? It's frightening, isn't it? I'm sorry. I just can't help it.'

'We're all doomed, doomed I tell ye,' Liam said, reappearing in search of his cigarettes. 'And I've only got three years left to finish my fucking PhD.'

But Grainne was sobbing furiously by now, and Gordon held her, stroked her hair, made soothing noises, as if to a cat or a baby. Liam wasn't happy with these kinds of scenes, and looked around him awkwardly. Beatrice glanced at Richard, gave him a signal.

'Maybe we'll check out what's going on in the kitchen,' he said, getting up.

Beatrice stretched, and got out of her chair. 'Me too.'

'I'm sorry,' Grainne moaned, her voice muffled by Gordon's embrace.

In the kitchen, Beatrice and Richard had a peek at the conversational menu, and had the choice of a discussion led by Leonard and Liam about whether Sam Raimi was kitsch or revolutionary, or a debate in another corner about which of the Ewings was the most sexually alluring. 'Do you think they're talking about Dallas or the SNP?' Richard asked. They were left to themselves.

'So what happens now?' Beatrice asked, and Richard knew she was asking about his own future rather than the country's.

'I hang around, try to get a bit more freelancing work, and

7

eventually there might be a staff job. The problem is, there's too much competition. For some reason there are quite a lot of people who think that writing snippy reviews about pop music beats working in a bank.'

'Have you thought about London?'

'Yeah, but the trouble is there's ten times as much competition down there, and it costs five times as much to live. What about you? Are you going back home?'

Beatrice could look up at Richard and the greyness of her eyes could express more than he quite wanted to know. Not for the first time, he was a little afraid of her. He knew that she knew more about him than he would ever know about her. He had spent four years in her company, had told her things about his life, his feelings, which he had barely acknowledged to himself. Beatrice had taken it all in with a quiet nod, an occasional phrase that broke down all his years of convoluted introspection into a clear and embarrassingly reductive description. Beatrice could look at you, listen to a couple of sentences, and turn it all into a short and demoralisingly accurate chapter that summed up your failings. So, he liked to turn the conversation around whenever he could. 'All sorted for the postgrad, are you?'

'Depends, really. Depends what I get in the finals. They've said they'd be keen for me to stay, but then there's the money to worry about. I really don't know if I can afford to commit myself to this kind of life for a few more years.'

And she looked around, and Richard followed her gaze. Across the table littered with empty Bulgarian wine bottles, a baking tray crowded with wrinkled potatoes, a bowl full of sweating orange cheese, an overflowing ashtray. He looked around the callow faces of men and women in their early twenties, standing in their studied poses, holding out their experiments with facial hair, radical hairstyles, tentative body-piercing for approval, offering their opinions in the same way. *Here is what I am, what I might be, what I aspire to.* Richard shuddered at the breeze of adulthood running through the room on this June evening in 1987, when the British Labour Party had lost its third successive election, when a little life cul-de-sac was completing its arc and returning them to the highway. No U-turns.

'You're bound to get a first, though, aren't you?' he said. Beatrice looked quickly at him; sharply, for her.

'What do you mean *bound to*?'

There was information they both knew, and Beatrice was wondering whether Richard was being malicious.

'I didn't mean it like that,' Richard stammered, mortified that she would think so. 'I wasn't thinking of … no … Oh fuck, you know what I mean. You're ten times cleverer than the rest of them.'

Beatrice laughed at his confusion. 'Thanks, Rich. You're so sweet, but there are no guarantees. And it might be more hassle than it's worth, you know. Because you might not be thinking it, but there will be plenty who are. Someone is bound to say the Morelli tart got a first because she was shagging half the department, don't you think?'

Beatrice put everything in elaborate quotation marks, but Richard was still surprised to hear the blunt words emerge from her lips. She always preferred lilting, delicate sentences, or sweetly allusive teases. He looked back at the grey eyes and saw confusion and a slight shadow over the habitual Morelli serenity.

'I wouldn't worry about it. Everyone is gone by the end of June. Who's going to say anything?'

'Ah, but if I stay here to do postgrad, I'll still be in the department. People will still be whispering…'

'Are you still going to see…'

And Richard was on the verge of being inquisitive, of asking a pointed question when normally he would prefer the circumlocutory approach. But at that moment Liam slapped both of them on the back simultaneously, forcing Beatrice to stumble forward and clutch at Richard's arm for support.

'Listen you pair, there's a bloke I want you to meet…'

With Liam, there was always a bloke he wanted you to meet. Resistance was pointless. You would meet the stranger, chat for a minute, discover mutually hostile and irreconcilable views, and agree to part and never acknowledge one another's existence again. 'Diamond bloke, old Quentin,' Liam might say of a man who had been sounding you out about joining a clandestine troop of patriotic paramilitaries. 'Bit reactionary at times, but once you get to know him…'

Liam dragged them through the kitchen, through the throng assembled from Liam's usual casting agency. There was an aristocratic voice holding forth about the joys of shooting and eating your own ducks; an American female demanding that her audience accept women's infinitely superior sexual capacity; a couple of Germans. There were always a couple of Germans, looking around hopefully for someone who will speak to them.

So it goes: another Liam party towards the end of the 1980s. And as Liam's party drifts to its gradual conclusion, move on out of the kitchen, slip past the lovers making tentative explorations of each other's underwear, fingers edging forward with the tentative mission-creep of trench-raiders from old wars. Continue past the queue for the toilet, made up of more optimists yet to be defeated by their first experience of Liam's facilities. Carry on up the stairs, past the photography equipment, past Patrick's drying monochrome prints of Nordic art-pornography, and out into a surprisingly chill Edinburgh June, where it could still be any year, any time. From there we can hold the memory of them, gathered exclusively together in that dank living-room; we can look back on them and see the little flaws – superficial enough, but still to be corrected.

Here is work in progress. The hair, for a start. Grainne's still has a few traces of the kinks left from hot irons, the crimping that killed a boring afternoon in a wet Edinburgh April. Gordon's is flicked across in what is only three bouffant degrees short of a Princess Diana. Gordon had cast a consumer's eye across various subcultures on offer in his student days, and rejected them all as somehow too exclusive. Why join a cult when you can flit opportunistically between the margins? Richard's is a messy mop that will never quite be under control. Beatrice's is perfect, but here in 1987 the difference is that she doesn't quite know it, is still prey to doubt. The thin fingers occasionally brush back a lock that she wrongly feels might have fallen out of place.

These four, on this sofa, in this place, are artists – or at least artisans – in the process of creating themselves. Like anybody in their early twenties we see the potential, but cannot miss the need for substantial work. We see them quite a good way along the path, but not yet committed to their final drafts. Still looking at the colours, wondering at the vigour of their brushstrokes. If they could stand out of time, outside, in the breeze of a new Edinburgh morning, look through Liam's murky windows, gaze in at themselves with the clearness of hindsight – if they would want to tear up this picture, screw it up and throw it beyond recovery, it would be because of more than just the details.

Each would want to deny something different. With Grainne, it would be her helplessness: the power of the most distant and third-hand events to reduce her to tears. She would cringe at the emotional switch that would flip at the first sight of a victim swept away in the world's torrents. With Gordon, it might be the callousness: the way his mind immediately rendered calamity as opportunity; the way his thought processes flipped impatiently past pain and regret, and moved on to future possibilities. With Beatrice, it would be the glimmer of uncertainty: the suspicion, however vague, that she was vulnerable, that her carapace of self-reliance wasn't quite complete. With Richard, it would be words – failing him again, when he wanted to say something pithy and memorable.

Or with Richard, it might just have been the music. The music was oh-so-wrong. Even from outside on the cold dawn street, Liam's kitchen blares to contemporary pop, laden with the hollow drumbeat that sounds as if a beast has been eviscerated, its hide shellacked to a shiny finish, and then battered ceaselessly in a railway tunnel. This is the sound that will eventually force all eighties music into a cellar where posterity will decree it unlistenable.

But they don't know that. Richard and Beatrice in that kitchen listen to the Pet Shop Boys and Big Country. Richard feels the hiss of the syndrums in the soles of his feet, and it seems modern and shiny enough to him, the enhanced sound of electronic technology filtering art into commercial brightness. Oh, there was so much that none of them knew, in that decade that was so splendid in its ignorance.

Back inside, the television cameras are lingering on the defeated leader. He is looking defiantly into the lights, but is already beginning a gradual crumble into history, already scurrying towards the footnotes. His deputy has the same grey, lost look over the camera's horizon, a thousand-yard gaze of acceptance and contemplation.

Nobody is there to see it. The politicians' stares fall on a sofa occupied only by an unheeding Belinda and Gary carrying their own mini-narrative towards a happier conclusion.

Gordon and red-haired, red-eyed Grainne have drifted through to the kitchen and are sitting at the table drinking Liam's bad supermarket whisky. Grainne sips long, coughs a little, sips more, and occasionally a stray tear escapes and she shakes it away with impatience.

Gordon reclines in his seat and shakes his head, slowly and amusedly, at the words of Callum, a black-haired poet sitting opposite him. Callum becomes more and more infuriated by Gordon's complaisant smile; waves his hands excitedly.

'Maybe now the voters will realise that the Labour Party is never going to get them out of the clutches of the fucking Tories,' he said with a certain relish. 'Maybe they'll realise that only the SNP can deliver an Assembly.'

'Yeah, and maybe they'll remember that it was the SNP that delivered them into the clutches of the fucking Tories by voting against Callaghan in '79,' Gordon replied in measured tones that carried more hostility than any shout could have achieved.

'Children, children,' Liam interrupted, spreading his arms in an avuncular embrace of the whole room. 'This is a general election party. Let's not spoil it by talking politics.'

Grainne sipped her whisky and hiccoughed. Nobody paid her any attention. 'What's going to become of us?' she whispered, and reached for the crisps.

Crisps

Beatrice

Bay-a-tree-chay. That's who she had been for the first seven years of her life, the seven years when she had been too unformed to enjoy the sweet cadences of those Emiglio Romagnan syllables. Now, every time she remembered them, they came with their own sensory accompaniments: the ancient tang of a Mediterranean tobacco, background garlic notes, a memory of slightly yellowed teeth, menacing indigo eyes, and a voice that even then she knew was trying to lay a claim to her.

Then her father had gone away, one Christmas: on a train that said Victoria, but that disappeared over the gap between the decades.

Afterwards, in the 1970s and beyond, she had been Bee: the simple, single English syllable whispered from the soft lips of a peach-skinned simple English mother who smelled, always, of Simple soap, tea and of promises that would be kept. Hers were the milky-blue eyes that spoke of loyalty and honey sandwiches, and a group of Roberts, Charlottes, Emilies eating crisps and cake once a year on English Bee's birthday.

Bee she had been at eleven, tripping reluctantly over the threshold of her secondary modern, already thinking that she would have been happy with that place in the world, that eternal B-dom, finishing a comfortable second, getting by without having the disturbing attention of those who aspired to A-ness. And Bee she would have been happy to stay, but at eleven she could form literary arguments more sophisticated than the A Level students she watched through the Common Room windows jigging listlessly to *Hunky Dory*. At eleven, she could recite French irregular verbs without needing to think. At eleven, she was reading Muriel Spark and Hemingway, and finding the American tedious. At eleven, she was becoming aware of the misfortune of living in the English suburbs, of approaching her teenage years ten years after English pop culture had planted a flag at its zenith and began its steep descent. At eleven, she was denying herself Bee-ness, and being asked to assume the duties of an A...

'Nadine reckons that with a name like Morelli you must be a dago or a wop,' Jacqui Francis had said to her two days after they had started at the new school. 'But you look pretty English to me.' That it was meant kindly, Beatrice had surmised from the subsequent offer to admire Jacqui's collection of David Cassidy pictures taped to the inside of her desk, and share her break-time bag of crisps.

It was a miraculous intervention, a Jacqui-shaped bridge to the rest of the school, to teenage existence. Beatrice felt as if a Streatham-born guardian angel had reached out a protective wing. At twelve, Jacqui had tree-trunk thighs and a squint that should have brought down on her all the derision and pubescent wrath of which her peers were capable. But Jacqui was blessed with a steely ferocity and confidence that daunted all but the bravest from pointing out her deficiencies. And all who associated with Jacqui shared her immunity.

At thirteen, Jacqui had the largest breasts in the school – sixth-formers and teachers included – and presented them to the world as sturdy defences from hostile scrutiny. Beatrice could hide behind them, meek in her pink-framed National Health glasses, those thick lenses hiding eyes that darkened a shade with every one of the rare letters she received from her father.

As Beatrice turned thirteen, Jacqui's divorced mother (known as Doreen to her daughter and to Beatrice) took both girls to the beach at Worthing for a week. While Doreen smoked in promenade pubs and looked hungrily at balding men gulping pints of light ale, Beatrice and Jacqui lay on the beach drinking Cokes, eating crisps and cooking in the hottest summer anybody could remember. Jacqui's pale yards of flesh soon flashed angry red signals, until it looked just like the watery bacon they faced every morning at the breakfast buffet.

Beatrice discovered a hidden olive skin under her English paleness, and caught the intimidated sidelong glances of freckled English boys in bright nylon swimming trunks. If she looked back they flushed, averted their gaze. If they looked too long, Jacqui would yell insults, harsh and contralto and always enough to send the boys chastened into the sea, like a motley landing force turning away from the defenders' machine-guns.

In their bed-and-breakfast bedroom, as they washed off the sand by the cracked sink, Jacqui made Beatrice compare their pubic hair, and squealed her envy at Beatrice's delicate black fronds, while lamenting her own springy ginger coils.

At sixteen Jacqui had razor-blade earrings, purple hair with a jagged white lightning flash running through it, and a boyfriend called Stan. By then, school had filtered them in different directions: Beatrice towards the 'O' Level elite, to Racine, to *Poems of Faith and Doubt,* to precocious arguments about spiritual weakness; Jacqui down distant corridors where Beatrice's imagination couldn't follow. They met at breaks and at lunchtime. Jacqui couldn't tell Beatrice a thing about school, so instead offered information about sex, about amphetamines, about the fight that Stan had got into with a bunch of anachronistic but violently-inclined Teddy Boys in Soho. Beatrice listened and envied, and stored up the words as treasures.

On their last day of the fifth form, Jacqui and Beatrice drank Babycham and cider under the trees in Norwood Park, a brilliant British June sun beating down on their foreheads. On this afternoon Jacqui was, for the first time Beatrice could recall, the sadder of the two. Beatrice was a month away from receiving a discreet envelope telling her that she had eight grade A 'O' Level passes: not a B to be seen. Jacqui was three months away from sitting in a pub toilet, seeing a chemist's testing kit turn as blue as the sterilising blocks in the urinals.

That afternoon, Jacqui had drunk most of the cider and all the Babycham, and had rolled over gently but deliberately so that her breasts pressed against Beatrice's slight form, and had raised her head and crushed her full, black-painted lips against Beatrice's in a kiss that seemed to last until a cloud stealthily covered the sun. There was a stillness there, a cool pocket in the June heat, and Beatrice could hear the birds, could hear the buses straining at the hill, could hear the charter planes coming out of the stack above Gatwick. Her lips were numbed with the pressure and she could feel the heat coming off Jacqui in waves, the sweat, sweetness and the alcohol tang.

When it ended Beatrice had grinned, uneasily. She could see a tear forming in the corner of Jacqui's right eye, but knew it wasn't because she hadn't responded. It went further than that. Beatrice was looking nervously down the hill towards the playground, where a group of twelve year-olds were gathering round a third-hand copy of *Penthouse.* Jacqui sighed, a mixture of defeat and frustration. Jacqui kissed her harder this time, trying to mould her face to the bonier shape of Beatrice's. Jacqui's tongue tasted of apples and salt and lipstick, and Beatrice struggled to breathe. When Jacqui's hand reached under Beatrice's skirt, and her fingers brushed against bare skin, Beatrice had squirmed away, her knees clamping together in an instinctive piece of chaste self-preservation, an old Italian trick that evolution had killed off in South London. Jacqui was left looking down at her own hand, wondering what to do with it. Beatrice felt the breeze this time, heard the shouts and taunts of the kids down the hill, smelled the cider on Jacqui's breath.

'I love you Bee, you know that. Stan's nothin' …'

Beatrice had smiled, had licked her own black-stained lips, and shook her head gently. And Jacqui had smiled too, and then started to giggle, and the two of them had laughed loudly at what they were: a couple of sixteen year-olds who knew, although both would deny it, that they had parted forever on a summer afternoon in 1979. The tears were streaming down Jacqui's face, forming long and ludicrous black streaks, turning her plump cheeks into damp mint humbugs.

To Jacqui she had been Bee, and to her mother she was 'little Bee,' and to herself she was 'plain old Bee,' but around the beginning of December each year she would allow herself to be Beatrice and, just occasionally, permit herself to pronounce it the Italian way. That was when her *panettone* would arrive in the post from Parma, sent every year by her father's family, with a card addressed entirely in Italian. Her mother could read the language perfectly but would invariably refuse to tell Beatrice what it said, offering instead a disapproving précis along the lines of: 'It says Happy Christmas, plus a lot of flowery stuff that amounts to nothing and is just there to show off.'

By the time she was thirteen, Beatrice had taught herself enough Italian to read her grandmother's messages for herself and to understand that her mother had been truthful; but that, in Italian, the words "To our darling English lily whose face we never forget and carry into our dreams every night, perhaps with a little tear and a little prayer that we will be allowed to see her again soon, before another cherry harvest, before this year's grappa is ready," had a force that their translation could never approximate.

Every year, Beatrice would cut into the *panettone* and offer the first slice to her mother. Every year, her mother would say the same. 'Not for me, thank you. It's really quite tasteless. Doesn't know whether it wants to be cake or bread. Give me a good English fruit cake with marzipan any day.'

So Beatrice would hoard it for herself and Jacqui, and they would sit in her bedroom listening to Roxy Music, The Damned, Patti Smith; moaning about their mothers, giggling: a pair of fatherless girls at Christmas. Beatrice, out of superstition, made sure the cake was finished by Twelfth Night.

When she was fifteen, the *panettone* arrived as usual and Beatrice, already imagining herself a European literary sophisticate – her room full of Fielding, Rossetti, Gide and Camus – went through the ritual of offering a slice to her mother.

In their living room the gas fire had sucked all the moisture out of the air, South London rain was pattering on the grimed window-pane, tea-time street lighting was glinting on the tinsel of their three foot-high artificial Christmas tree. Beatrice's mother's eyes weren't as reassuring as they used to be. Instead, they signalled nervousness, a wariness of her intellectual daughter, the tired ache of too many years trying to keep her to herself.

'You really need something to wash that down,' she said, when Beatrice proffered the slice of *panettone*. And she headed off to rummage in a cupboard crammed with forgotten debris. She returned, dusting off a bottle containing an amber wine.

'*Vin santo*,' she said. 'Your father and I brought back a case of the stuff a few years ago. But you know how it is. It doesn't taste the same if you take it away from its own country. Too sweet, really.'

The words came out awkwardly, and her hands were shaking. But she opened the bottle, and they drank a glass each, and Beatrice's mother ate her *panettone*, and the next year Beatrice was allowed to fly to Italy to visit her other family.

She was given only a week, and only because her mother realised that Beatrice's preparation for her mock A Levels was somewhat redundant, given that her daughter could have passed the examinations three years earlier. In Parma, Beatrice was met by her grandmother and her two aunts, who veered between rhapsodies about her beauty and tearful outbursts of regret that they had missed the stages of its arrival.

Her father (who she had seen about once a year) was there too, the tobacco cloak still hanging around him, the eyes troubled by his second divorce, this time in a country where it still bore a moral sting. Her aunt Ofelia told her the details after the *grappa* that followed her grandmother's assault course of a meal.

Vincenzo hadn't been satisfied, Ofelia griped, in a comically aggressive whisper. After he had returned to Italy in disgrace from his English divorce, and without his lovely *bambina*, he had been lucky to find Antonia, a wealthy widow, only two years older, elegant, thin – almost aristocratic, really. She had the restaurant and the bar, and Vincenzo hadn't needed to worry about money.

But … she was two years older, Ofelia went on, and Vincenzo had always been weak. Theresa had been twenty-two and had been working in the bar, which is not a job for a modest girl … and ah, these things happen if they are meant to happen. So Vincenzo, a forty-five year-old man, was at home with Mama, and was wondering if he would have any money after the divorce. Antonia was making all these hurtful accusations that Vincenzo had been siphoning money out of the businesses; she was threatening to go to the police if Vincenzo tried to contest the conditions of the separation.

Beatrice had listened, wide-eyed, thrilled. She had never been allowed to be privy to this kind of scandal. Her parents' divorce had happened before she was old enough to pay proper attention to the important details. Her mother would not answer direct questions, and all Beatrice's information had come from sporadic, oblique asides. 'It was a crime to take him out of Italy, like uprooting a vine,' she had said once, on a still, dusty London Sunday afternoon. Then, 'They all need their mothers. I think they are breast-fed until they are thirty,' she had observed, seeing an Italian footballer writhe on the ground in agony as mother and fifteen year-old daughter had watched an England-Italy match on TV in 1977. It was the only time Beatrice had ever known her mother to watch football.

In Parma that December a cold wind blew in from the mountains, cutting in and along the streets. Parma wasn't Beatrice's idea of Italy. Where were the excitable kids on Vespas, the old peasants selling olives? But then it wasn't England either: the grey wet sprawl of southern suburbia. Her father took her walking, initially amused by her enthralment with the city, her fascination at its foreignness. But he wanted her full attention. He had taken her into a bar, ordered a couple of coffees, lit a cigarette, looked at her.

She didn't know him. Couldn't know him, not when she had

only seen him six or seven times since he had left; not when he lived in a foreign country; not when he had written just twice a year, terse best wishes on birthdays and at Christmas. But she could see something in his eyes that was beyond the blandness of sadness or guilt.

'Ofelia has told you, I think, about what is happening?'

Beatrice had nodded, and looked down at the froth on her coffee, wanting to be a kid again, not wanting to have to pretend to understand.

'I am too old for this, I know. I should have stopped being a boy a long time ago. Should have been a man when I was with your mother, but...'

But Beatrice had switched off by then, seduced instead by the surroundings, by the sounds, smells and tastes of Europe, by the flowing Latinate rhythms of the two old women yelling intimacies at each other at the next table. Her father had continued in his defeated English, telling her about the financial problems of the bar, the failure of the restaurant, the scarcity of customers that year, and it seemed a half-hearted sort of confession, a wish to present her with the tattered fragments of his manhood so that she might smile, and redeem him. But she was lost in her own excitement.

Her attention had only been reclaimed when her father reached out and seized her hand, had looked at her in an imploring way that had inspired a very English blush of embarrassment. He seemed desperate that she should hear him, understand him.

'I have written to your mother,' he was saying. 'There are things that I can explain that will mean, perhaps, that she will see things differently. Perhaps it is not too late.'

Beatrice looked back at him, not knowing what he meant. When she looked into his eyes, he cast his own downwards, fumbling with his cigarette packet. Then he looked up quickly, urgently.

'You know I love you, my Beatrice. This Theresa is nothing...'

Beatrice remembered the moment only in retrospect, and forced herself to trim away the extraneous details. At the time they had absorbed her: the sharp, smoky, adult taste of her coffee, the sweet escape of the unending list of *gelati*, the incongruous tones of The Clash's *London Calling* that emerged from the café transistor and filled the air with a cautionary London familiarity.

Afterwards, she had to dredge her mind of all this interference,

21

had to identify and erase each distraction, to focus on those words, on the fractured syllables of her father's voice – forgetting his English with each month away from its shores. Her name had been alien on her tongue, her twisted memory making it sound like a reproach to her. Beatrice was Italian for betrayal, surely.

It was the last time she saw her father.

Her mother broke the news three weeks later. It was the first Tuesday of the Eighties. Landsdowne Hill was covered in a jagged coating of filthy ice, England was still moaning its way through the remnants of a New Year hangover. *London Calling* still blared from every other radio.

Beatrice had returned from a depressed trudge round the West End sales to find her mother, wet-faced, shivering, staring into the gas-fire. When she spoke to Beatrice, it was if she was demanding forgiveness.

'They found his clothes on the beach...' her mother had said, in a voice drained of will, devoid of purpose. There was no ambiguity. There was only one 'he' in their lives. Beatrice had enjoyed three seconds of romantic speculation, three seconds to run the tightly-edited scenes through her mind: her father buying a forged passport, her father growing a beard, her father folding his clothes with a conspiratorial chuckle, her father in the immigration queue at some Australian or South American airport, her father with a suitcase of banknotes to finance his new existence, her father's cryptic but comprehensible letter fluttering onto her Norwood carpet inviting her to visit him, sending an air-ticket. Three seconds.

'The coastguard pulled his body out of the water. All he was wearing was his wedding ring.'

Beatrice had cast around her immediate feelings, searching for one that would hide the pain of knowing that her father, who had left the 60s on a slow train to Victoria, had left the 70s on a beach just north of Rimini.

She didn't want her mother to comfort her; couldn't face the picture of the two of them slumped on their faded London sofa, breathing the gas-scorched air of the suburbs, trying to fabricate a too-late intimacy over the loss of Vincenzo Morelli: womaniser, failure, suicide. She didn't want to know what her father had written in that letter to her mother, certainly didn't want to know if her mother had replied and how. What was the use? What would come out of it, but hate and blame and guilt and separation?

Instead she picked up a bag of crisps, opened it carefully, looked inside, then, looking up at her mother, selected the tiny glimmer of bitterness, polished it, and held it up to the light.

'Really? Which one?'

A year of London lingering crept by, Beatrice measuring it in her mother's smiles: three in total. The plan was to study for the Oxbridge examination, but Beatrice couldn't face another three months of school. 'You should go there,' her mother had said. 'You're clever enough, why not?' But Beatrice made her own decisions by then, and she was still Bee enough to want to avoid the self-satisfied world of medieval cloisters, gowns and pointless secret societies. Besides, Oxford and Cambridge were both a little too close to home. She needed more distance. With every mile, she felt she would come a little closer to Beatrice.

In October 1983, with her two suitcases and her sensible handbag, she struggled into a taxi at Waverley Station and asked for Nicolson Street, the flat assigned by the University. Three hundred yards and three minutes later, she got out.

She stood in the middle of the tiny kitchen, looked at the three of them, still uneasy with each other, hugging their chunky coffee mugs, and she felt the relief emanating from them, the gratitude that there was a fourth to share their awkwardness. The Scottish boy had spoken first. 'Well, you must be ...'

She knew she couldn't ever be *Beatreechay*, but at twenty she couldn't be a Bee again, either. She had looked around at those nervous smiles, had seen their uncertainties in a glance, and had felt a flush of sufficient strength, independence and freedom to choose her own name.

'Hello everybody,' she had said, letting her cases drop with a confident thud. 'I'm Beatrice Morelli. You can call me Beatrice.'

Gordon

Childhood was the taste of half-chewed cheese-and-onion crisps swimming in warm Coca Cola. On Glasgow August afternoons at the start of the 1970s, the three of them – the Hendrie brothers – would be sitting in the dust on Dumbarton Road, watching the traffic go by; a line in descending order of height, like an old variety-show comedy sketch. Gordon, Denis and Paddy, in short trousers, with their green-knitted tank tops protecting them against the caprices of a Scottish summer.

If children are unformed, then at least they are not without substantial clues as to their eventual shape. With the Hendrie brothers, the family could always look back at the childhood pictures and spot immediately who was going to be who. Outside that pub, probably Heraghty's on that particular afternoon, they could almost have been posing for posterity.

Their expressions gave a clue to the pecking order. Gordon, wavy brown hair swept back, stern blue eyes fixed ahead, had half an air of authority already, and was looking to increase it. Denis beside him, brown hair flopping greasily across his eyes, seemed to be plotting some devious and sleazy spot of mischief of his own, putting up with his siblings' presence unwillingly, impatiently. Paddy, wet-mouthed, freckled, with ginger spikes jutting at mutually hostile angles from his scalp, kept casting sideways glances at his brothers, looking for a lead from them, unwilling to take on any vestiges of independent thought.

Further up the road they could see pockets of other kids waiting outside other pubs, but the groups rarely mixed. Once you had selected your pub you stayed loyal to it, whether you were the drinker inside or the eight year-old waiting by the gutter. The kids were the camp followers of the Saturday afternoon drinking campaign. Their mothers might only be over the road in the butcher's or the mini-market, but neither kids nor mothers would acknowledge each other. Saturday afternoons were when the offspring became their fathers' responsibility, which meant lingering for hazily-defined stretches of time outside one of Dumbarton Road's seventeen hostelries.

The groups would look each other up and down, occasionally booting a stone obligingly up the street back into the field of its desultory kickabout, a courtesy acknowledged with a terse nod.

Inside Heraghty's or, some afternoons, Drummonds or The Thornwood, their dad would be taking in pints steadily and purposefully, like a lorry refuelling for a long stretch to Carlisle and beyond. Uncle Paul or Uncle Michael, or Uncle Brian – never their dad – would emerge with the cokes and the crisps. The Glasgow policy was to behave indulgently to other people's kids – never your own. Although their dad didn't seem to obey those rules. He would ignore his nieces and nephews with the same determination he brought to disdaining his own children.

'These'll keep you quiet,' Paul or Michael or Brian would say, throwing a few playful shadow punches. 'We'll be along in a wee minute.' The wee minute that would stretch until a quarter to three, the final bell, and the hoarse shout of an always irate landlord.

Gordon would swig his coke quickly while it was still tepid from the pub shelf, enjoying the luxury of knowing he had further supplies at the ready. Paddy and Denis would hoard theirs, untaught by experience, crooking their elbows in an over-optimistic protective gesture, as if such feeble concealment would deter Gordon from launching his imminent raid. Otherwise they would make a show of chewing soggy balls of crisp and spitting them down the neck of the bottle, shaking it like a Christmas snow scene, holding it up to the weak sun and watching the flecks of potato saturating the brown liquid.

Gordon didn't care. He enjoyed the fight more than the drink, and at eight, felt obliged to assert his authority over his brothers, to make them feel the power of his ten-month head-start on Denis; twice that on Paddy. He knew it was a lead that was diminishing in significance with every birthday; but he was already enough of a precocious mathematician to know that an eight year-old still held a considerable advantage over a seven year-old, while baby Paddy was a mile down the track.

So, first he would grab Denis in an arm-lock, then slowly throttle him until the coke was released. Swigging the noxious brown soup with one hand, he would fix the apprehensive Paddy with his most threatening stare, stretching out his open palm like a Roman emperor demanding tribute. Paddy would put up a feeble fight, spitting tears and phlegm onto the street in frustration. Then he would hand over his drink with the glower of hatred in his eyes. Towards the end of summer Paddy's spirit would be crushed. 'Jus' have it ya big bastard!' Paddy had said one afternoon, and Gordon and Denis had cracked up.

Some Saturdays there would be football. Their dad and their uncles would come out of the pub a little before closing time, reluctant at the surrender of an extra pint, but already talking about the game and maybe a few more pints afterwards. They would catch the bus east, through the city centre. The bus became a magnet trawling through iron filings, picking up a few more at Hope Street, Argyle Street, St Enoch's, the Tron – until Gordon couldn't believe it could carry on with this huge a cargo. The air was thick with smoke and beer and August sweat, some old jakey playing random notes on a mouth organ and demanding a contribution in cash. Gordon and his brothers would cling to their seats, look nervously across and get a reassuring grin from Uncle Paul or Uncle Brian, or Uncle Michael.

Then the ground. Gordon could only ever remember it swathed in sunshine. Looking back, it seemed to him as if Parkhead had basked in some localised climatic ideal in which the pitch was always a lush green lit by the rays of a beneficent sun. In later years, at the end of the news, he might catch a clip of a football match and see mud and rain, and hear the commentator telling him it was Parkhead. It left him dissatisfied, disbelieving, as if his childhood certainties were being dismantled.

Even at eight, Gordon was still being swung across the top of the turnstiles, shoved into the heaving mass of fat and sweat and green and white beyond. In the future Gordon would read about war, read about fear and confusion and a great mass of panic-stricken men screaming their torments at the sky. Reading the descriptions, Gordon could never quite dismiss the picture of Celtic Park in the 1970s: a pall of smoke hanging over the stand and the smell of warm piss everywhere – men urinating onto the concrete terraces casually, while continuing a screamed conversation with their neighbour – and the barely comprehensible clamour of the songs and the swearing.

There would be a time when Gordon could put to use these childhood football matches, would spiel off the details with relish, exaggerating and polishing them, highlighting the glint of masculinity like a conscientious jeweller. He knew by then that the games gave him a retrospective credibility in certain quarters, would round off a mendacious picture of proletarian humanity. Going to the football as a kid could score the sort of points that academic qualifications never equalled. But at eight, Gordon would stamp out a space on the terrace, and hug himself in hate and disgust and fear.

Denis and Paddy at least had the consolation of being interested in football. 'See that McLuskey, some player, eh?' Denis would yell to him, and Gordon would nod disconsolately, unwilling to admit that the men in the hooped shirts were all the same to him, that it took him twenty minutes to work out who was attacking which end, and unable to confess that he was secretly rooting for the opposition, the spindly Aberdonians in the red, the Hearts in their cheering maroon, or Airdrie with their startling red Vs. He liked to see the despair and anger in the crowd when their team went behind, enjoyed the demoralised peace of the still silence that descended, interrupted by solitary forlorn cries of frustrated obscenity. In those moments he saw the masses crushed by an arbitrary instant, reduced to seething surrender, studded only by isolated outbreaks of outrage.

At eight, Gordon only liked football for its power. It seemed to him like an additional force of nature, like a hurricane or tidal wave that could sweep in and make a mess of people's lives.

Gordon remembered the following summer, when his English cousin Benny had come to stay for a fortnight. His first instinct had been to feel sorry for the wee bastard.

He first saw him at his granny's flat in Scotstoun. Benny was there with his parents and his sister Angela, up on a visit from England. Gordon's Uncle Davie had headed south when the shipyards started to lay men off. He had found a job laying cable in Kent or somewhere and, about the same time, found this big blonde Cockney wife, introduced as Auntie Maggie.

Uncle Davie already had slight but perceptible differences from his brothers. He seemed to be wearing Brylcreem or something like it, was smooth-shaven and crisp-jawed while they all seemed to have permanently pocked and stubbled jowls. Uncle Davie's voice had softened a notch, as if the Partick burr had run up against some southern sanding machine. The accent was the same Glaswegian on the surface, but with a smoothness, a prettification of the consonants. Gordon admired it, copied it in secret.

Angela was all bows and ribbons and clean pink knees and a look of cold hauteur and barely-disguised disgust at having to be polite to her northern relations. It was Maggie who was the fascinating one. She had the sort of pink femininity you saw in films or in TV comedies, but never in Glasgow. In Glasgow, women were mothers or aunties or grannies, sharp-toothed, squinting and tutting as they leaned in with a spit-moistened finger to scrape dirt off your cheek. This Maggie was different. She had no authority, none of that necessary air of being likely to deal out unpredictable and spiteful punishment at any moment. Her hair had the yellowy gloss of butter, and when she spoke she seemed to breathe perfume into the room. She looked nervous. Even Gordon could see that she was smiling despite herself, unsure what to make of his grandmother's teasing remarks about Sassenachs and Bannockburn, and wee Jimmy Johnstone.

Gordon had stared at her for a while, entranced and repelled by the thick powder, the crimson lipstick, the Englishness of her every word. Then she had caught him staring and grinned back; so, abashed, he had turned his attention to Benny.

Benny was small, but tough-looking, with none of the bony fragility of Denis or Paddy. Benny's face looked almost fat, but avoiding softness thanks to eyes that Gordon, in the first pang of familial recognition he had experienced in his entire life, realised were the image of his own.

His cousin didn't look happy, piling his grey mince into a minor range of hills, with white outcrops of potatoes. 'D'ye no' like yer mince and tatties, son?' his granny enquired. Gordon immediately felt resentful. Why the tender tone, when Gordon knew that in the same position he would be treated to a clipped ear and terse order to 'eat yer tea and stop playin"?

'Oh, it's just that he's not used to the Scottish food,' Auntie Maggie had explained with a grin, and Gordon noticed that her plate was still pretty full as well. 'Ach, would you rather have a piece an' jam?' granny asked kindly. Benny stared at her in bemusement, and Gordon sniggered.

'Take the boy out for a wee while, Gordie,' his granny said. 'Show him round the place. Here's two bob for the icie.' Gordon pocketed the cash, with no intention of spending any of it on the English invader, wincing at being called 'Gordie' in front of his cousins. He could see the disdain in Angela's smile.

'Granny's mince is shite, is it no'?' Gordon whispered on the stair, by way of introduction. 'We say shit in England,' Benny said matter-of-factly, and Gordon felt like smacking him in the mouth. Instead, he suggested a game of football. From his earliest years Gordon had heard that the English had no idea how to play football; that the World Cup had been fixed for them by a Russian referee.

So Gordon, Paddy and Denis took Benny to play football, away from the tenement flat crammed with its startling religious ornaments, its lingering spiritual odour of sausages boiled white in their casings. They took him for a kickabout in the back close.

The problem was that Benny could play. Even at eight, he was pretty useful. Gordon was nine by then, and couldn't get the ball off his cousin. He saw the grins on the faces of Denis and Paddy when they witnessed their big brother being made to look an idiot by the cocky little English kid. Gordon soon tired of the effortless way Benny swerved past their lunges. Gordon felt his authority being challenged, knew he had to find a response.

He met Benny again a couple of days later. It was a black-and-white memory now, like old TV footage from the very beginning of the 60s, before The Beatles. No – black, white and red, like that touched-up film of a grey Geoff Hurst blasting a crimson football into the roof of the German net, that clip they never tired of showing you.

In this memory the sky was grey, the tenements at the edge of Partick were greyer, and even the clothes were dirt-coloured. The red was the cinder pitch where Gordon's plans were laid.

'How, Benny; you want a wee game with my pals?' Gordon had said with a grin. 'They're no' that good, mind. Maybe you could show them a trick or two?'

He loved that feeling, the omnipotence he felt hurling that grin at his wary cousin, feeling the reassurance slipping between the words, like the silver coins his uncles would offer him as an inducement to run down the shop. He loved the broadness of his influence, knowing that out at the pitch he had already prepared Benny's reception, and now only had to persuade his cousin to walk into the trap.

On the cinder pitch they would play with such an assortment of miserable freaks that, decades later, Gordon could no longer trust his memory of them, half-believing they had been replaced by some images he had picked up from sociological portraits of 30s slum children. Eyes that wept yellow matter, sleeves caked with dried mucus, knee joints where the bone pressed against scabbed skin, rotted milk teeth occasionally spat into the wire behind the pitch – types who seemed only to be waiting for the opportunity to play extras in horror films.

The English kid had quickly earned himself the nickname Cliff Fuckin' Richard, and it wasn't bestowed kindly – all the vowels tortured so the 'i's mutated into hoarse phlegm-filled 'u's. Little Benny was a quick learner, and soon knew not to open his mouth, because the accent that came out seemed an invitation to physical torment. His cousins weren't about to protect him.

Gordon wanted to see Benny's face ground into the cinders. Everybody here had been made aware that the newcomer was foreign. These were kids who regarded a gang from Whiteinch as exotic; a true English boy was a prize from heaven. All felt obliged to trip him, shove him, and spit in his face at every opportunity.

When they could catch him. He was fast. Too fast for the mostly undernourished Partick crew, especially those sophisticated ten and eleven year-olds who were already shrinking their lung capacity with a five-a-day smoking habit.

It was just a matter of being patient, though. Gordon remembered that game for years, with a glow of illicit pride. He could remember the smell of Glaswegian sweat, the rancid breath of the kids, the hoppy whiff of the air wafting in from the brewery, the acrid scent of the cinders, the sour taste of the Clyde coming in on the breeze. Gordon could see those clouds of filth and smog hanging over the shipyards, and most of all he could still see his nine-year-old self, a leader. Calculating, orchestrating, staying away from the front line, Gordon ensured his plans were carried out.

Not that his followers needed much encouragement. Wee Benny seemed designed to provoke them, skipping away into space, into empty air, with that too-soft, torn football at his feet and a snarl of tenement frustration filling the space where he used to be.

They had to get to him in the end. It was a big lad they called Gowk who caught him, one of those kids whose growth hormones had been dished out in one job lot to save the bother of parcelling them out in regular doses each year. He was the biggest, the slowest and the ugliest of the bunch, and lurched around the park with straining muscles unwilling to carry his lumbering frame. Benny simply hadn't seen him, had jinked away from one outstretched foot, skipping over the scuffed black school-shoe that was thrust in his path, rolling the ball under his own sole, when the shadow of Gowk simply swallowed him up and rolled him into the cinders. Benny skidded along for several feet, feeling the skin of his calf leisurely peel itself away in a neat curl, reminding Gordon of the way his mum carved a potato, preparing chips.

It was perfect in a way; an injury that could be presented as a genuine footballing mishap, where a black eye or a smashed lip might have been trickier to explain. Gordon galloped over, biting back his grin, putting on a solicitous frown, but feeling vindication at the sight of English blood running in a fine stream down his cousin's shin.

Little Benny lay in the midst of a gape-mouthed ring of grotesques, most of them grinning, Denis and Paddy looking at each other, a little uncertain about how they would explain the maiming of their wee English relative later on, but enjoying the moment all the same. The only one who looked vaguely upset was Gowk, who, at length, reached down an apologetic arm. 'Sorry an' 'at, wee man,' he mumbled.

Gordon saw Benny's eyes were filled with tears waiting to erupt, but had to admire the kid's reaction. Everybody was looking at him, waiting for Benny to break. It was one of those heady summer moments, still with expectancy. That stink from the river was like the sting of salts, you could hear the bronchitic rattling of the older kids, feel the strain of their breathing.

The weakness in Gowk's words had been enough encouragement for Benny. He had hauled himself to his feet, put his face an inch from Gowk's neck, which as near as he could get to his facial features, and delivered a broadside of all the swear words he had ever heard his Glaswegian uncles and his cousins employ. Plenty of them he didn't understand, some of them he could only render as furious approximations, but their syllables, their consonant pairings, and elongated, guttural vowels carried all the hatred he needed at that moment. Gordon watched, and although there was comedy there, in the tight purple ball of fury that was Benny's face, in the incongruity of the Partick language mauled by the English palate, Gordon couldn't laugh. Language, he saw – even at that age – was more powerful, violent, more capable of inflicting lasting damage than any jagged Glaswegian football pitch.

Gowk just stood and grinned back at him. The rest of them laughed, impressed by Benny's vocabulary. Gordon hauled him away, patted him on the shoulder. 'Steady there, wee man. Y'all right?'

The coup hadn't quite had the devastating effect on Benny that Gordon had anticipated. His cousin was uncowed. But it had been exhilarating enough to watch his plan unfold, to see the end result of the previous evening's quiet word, to watch those innocent, grimacing faces, none of them looking askance at Gordon, seeing the blame dissipating into the rank air, floating away over the Clyde.

The game continued. Benny played on, although every touch of the ball sent sharp agonies racing up his scalded calf. Nobody called him Cliff Fuckin' Richard again. He started to speak, to yell for the ball, demand it as his well-earned right. Gordon quite liked the little guy now, happy in the knowledge that if he felt like it, he could make them skin that other knee, black that eye, smash that lip. 'Watch out for that Gowk,' he said, with a knowing grin at Benny. 'He's a clumsy big shite.' Gordon held the pause for a moment, then turned back. 'Sorry. A clumsy big shit.'

And Benny, who was a smart enough kind of eight year-old, looked back at his cousin and could read that smile as easily as he read his infant school storybooks. Gordon kept on smiling, stopping just short of succumbing to temptation and nodding his head.

Childhood was the wash of warm Coca Cola, and mashed-up cheese-and-onion crisps; the smell of piss, beer, smoke; the quick thrill of hatred, and the first, always sweetest taste of power.

Grainne

B ack then, she would always know when they were laughing. Then it became just a question of confirming that they were laughing at her. It seemed more than likely, and it would be for the obvious reason. They would have absorbed the unusual name when the teacher made her write it up on the board, made a quick comparison with her size, and enjoyed the sort of simple irony that even the dumbest of teenagers could appreciate.

Sometimes, if she had half an hour in the morning, Grainne could even enjoy the examinations that she indulged in. Could find something fascinating about tugging the white flesh, clasping it between the four fingertips and the flat of her palm, pulling it out until she had, oh, a Merchant of Venice's helping, and wondering whether it would be possible just to slice it away, trim it off like the butcher did with the belly of lamb, toss it, white and red and quivering into her bedroom wastepaper bin with the Clearasil-soaked tissues and the empty crisp packets, to be emptied by her complaining stepmother that afternoon.

At sixteen, Grainne had read enough American feminism, had snorted at enough inane teenage magazines, to believe that she was nothing out of the ordinary – just another case study, a girl oppressed by patriarchal expectations under decadent Western capitalism. She liked the important sound of the syllables, but she knew that they were referring to the everyday. The quotidian, she said to herself.

She looked at herself in that full-length mirror, her white bra and pants only the finest shade lighter than her skin, and saw what she was: a teenage girl who was slightly overweight, cursed by an inch of flesh that was there only because Grainne didn't exercise, because she found all forms of exertion embarrassing. Because she preferred to lie on her bed, staring at a book or listening to a record; couldn't bring herself even to catch a bus into a city still unfamiliar to her.

Meanwhile, the only people who knew her – well, they would have been laughing – or wanting to. Because Grainne felt that she knew enough about teenage girls to be aware that they had sensitive antennae for that extra inch: could discern its presence under the baggiest sweatshirt, despise it as weakness.

It might have been bearable if it were all she had to worry about. But she had seen the looks they had given her in the sixth-form common room when she had turned up in September. She knew they knew her story; knew that an over-solicitous teacher would have filled them in with a discreet whisper, a Miss Brodie aside. Grainne knew that teenage girls found curiosity and disdain far easier than compassion, and they had looked at the new girl's clothes, hair and figure rather more carefully than they'd looked for tragedy.

Grainne knew she had been a disappointment. There had been no time, or thought, for turning a girl from Mull into a sixth-former fit for the capital. So Grainne had sloped in with the same outfits she had worn for her 'O' Grade year.

Tobermory had been a town unwilling to let its daughters grow up too soon. The gales coming in off the sea, the icy squalls twisting across the sound, bringing spray from Loch Sunert to disperse across the island, had discouraged anybody that might have been inclined to wear a skirt above the knee, or expose any flesh at all beneath the chin. Catriona Morgan had brought a boob-tube back from Blackpool the summer before last, but as a holiday novelty rather than an addition to her wardrobe. It hung on a hook beside her dressing-table, her friends giggling and holding it up to compare. Grainne had blushed when Catriona had said, in awed admiration, 'you'd only squeeze one of yours in there.'

Grainne knew about wool and tweed and the heavier synthetics, but Lycra had not made great inroads into the island by the time she left it. In August she had looked in the shop windows on Princes Street, with the promise of her father's money ('not too much, mind') if she had seen anything that took her fancy. But she hadn't even seen the ra-ra-skirts, the ruffled blouses, the garish slips of electric fabric. She had seen her own reflection in the windows, staring back with alien eyes, looking like a European refugee adrift in an alien city. Only refugees might be a bit thinner, she told herself.

She hadn't wanted to take her father's money, anyway. She was still trying to come to an understanding of what she had seen in the hospital on a sunny May afternoon in Edinburgh.

She had stood in the ward, outside the room, looking through the glass, hot and out of breath from running from the bus stop. She had felt embarrassed because she knew she had rings of sweat forming under her arms, and the nurse was standing beside her.

The nurse's arm was resting on her shoulder. It had been put there at first as a gentle signal not to enter the room. Her mother was only allowed one visitor at a time, and her father was there. But the nurse's arm had stayed there, and the fingers were digging into her shoulder in a clenched caress. Grainne wasn't sure why, but wasn't up to wriggling away.

Looking through the window, she couldn't hear what her parents were talking about, but her father seemed impatient. He would lean into her mother's face, say something quick and urgent, then lean back, get out of the chair, pace a few steps to the end of the bed, then turn, sit down again, wave his hands about. He made a thrusting gesture, with parallel palms, like a farmer shoving a recalcitrant cow through a gate, then leant back and shook his head as if the world, and his wife, were beyond his ken.

This went on for twenty minutes or so and Grainne still stood there, getting hotter and hotter in the hospital's clammy atmosphere and in the nurse's possessive clutches until her father, shaking with irritation, turned away from the bed and marched towards the door. Only then did he see his daughter peering in through the window.

'Ah, you're here, are you? She's not so good today. Don't be too long or you'll tire her out.'

He delivered the words petulantly, dumping them in her face. Then he marched off in the direction of the car-park, already pulling out a packet of cigarettes. As she turned to go into her mother's room, Grainne caught a look of flickering contempt cross the nurse's face.

Grainnes's mother was dying, slowly, excruciatingly and, her father once let slip, expensively, of cancer. They had brought her from Tobermory a couple of months ago. There had been surgery, the extent of which Grainne could never guess at, because she only ever saw her mother wrapped in hospital sheets with a couple of drips fed into her wrists. Her mother didn't want to speak of medical detail; sometimes couldn't speak at all. Instead, Grainne told her about 'O' Grade revision, the weather on the island, the antics of Aunt Bryony's Yorkshire terrier. Grainne would see her mother smile occasionally; other times she would grimace. 'It's the painkillers,' her father would say brusquely. 'She's not all there.'

That afternoon she was all there. 'Your father asked me to reduce the medication just this once,' her mother said. 'He had something important to tell me and he wanted me to take it in, properly. So I'm sound of mind, only not too comfortable.'

'What did he want to tell you?' Grainne didn't know if her mother's tears came from the pain or what her father had been saying.

'Best let him tell you in his own time. But don't be angry with him. You must understand your father, Grainne. He's doing what he thinks is best. Really, it's probably the right thing to do. Should have done it sooner, really.'

'But what?'

Grainne couldn't push the matter because her mother was writhing under the sheets – not dramatically, just in a very slow and remorseless twisting.

'Tell me about school, Grainne. Must be torture for you, stuck inside there when there's all this lovely weather.'

One Saturday afternoon in the June of 1980, Grainne's mother died. Grainne had been sitting on the Meadows in the bright sunshine, reading Bertrand Russell, finding each one of his crisp sentences strangely painful in their inexorable logic. Grainne's father had collected her outside the Golf Tavern, pushed open the door of the Escort and said, matter-of-factly, 'It's over, Grainne dear. Your mother is no longer with us.'

Grainne had sat and stared out of the window for the rest of that journey back to Balerno, seeing the city slip away from elderly grace into the colder patterns of the new suburbs, the gap-teeth of the building sites, the contractor's boards offering executive-style residences. She looked out at a world that had changed in an afternoon; that had altered its colours forever while she was trying to read philosophy. She thought it wrong that the sun seemed to shine all the harder.

Lynne was there, and Grainne knew that the look on her long equine face had been studied in the mirror, practiced, honed, and finally rendered thus: anxiety tinged with tenderness, and not entirely clear of irritation. Lynne was an actress, or at least had been in a couple of Fringe productions at the Churchill that she never tired of talking about. Must have been quite a thespian challenge, that one, though: greeting the child of your married boyfriend an hour after the death of his wife, and her mother. Grainne was too numb to notice how much conviction Lynne brought to the part.

Grainne had her own room, a polished, curtained, pristine escape that she filled with books, a photograph of her mother, and another of her mother and Aunt Bryony on the waterfront, the multi-coloured house fronts of Tobermory making the scene seem almost European. It was comfortable, peaceful, and Grainne was suitably oppressed by every tiny detail of its 'traditional modern' furnishings.

Grainne spent two months reading in her room, fielding the concerned looks of her father and Lynne. She found family meals painful, both for the sporadic silences and for Lynne's occasional attempts to flirt with her father – a Lothian Doris Day trying to be playful. Like all fifteen year-olds, Grainne found the idea of a thirty-eight year-old coquette both absurd and offensive.

They worried about her eating, but in her room Grainne would steadily munch her way through a family-sized bag of crisps, trying to absorb herself in Angela Carter, Doris Lessing, Dostoyevsky. When the bag was finished, she would meticulously fold it eight times into a tiny cube of greasy plastic and place it at the bottom of the bin, where it would escape Lynn's inquisitive eye.

She would read Russian at university, she had decided. She wanted to feel the exotic consonants of the Cyrillic alphabet sticking in her throat like dry crisps, wanted to read works with the texture of mile-thick snow drifts, wanted to crunch the words underfoot with fur boots, wrapped in a mantle, with her luminous white cheeks poking out from beneath a mighty bearskin cap.

She wanted Russia to take her away from this dismal western suburb, Balerno, with its name that was a whispered lie that promised the Mediterranean or Adriatic. Now this was supposed to be her home: this dreary executive quarantine, six miles and an infuriating forty-five-minute bus ride out of a city centre where at least there were enough people to make you anonymous.

'Bit of peace from the hurly-burly out here, isn't it?' Lynne would say brightly. 'I used to live in Stockbridge, when I was a bohemian thesp. We had some times, of course – did I ever tell you the time I made it into the *Scotsman's* festival gossip column? Ah, the Sixties! – but eventually you want a little seclusion. Am I right?'

'Am I right?' was Lynn's personal mantra, delivered in a rising scale, accompanied by a challenging thrust-out jaw. In Grainne's opinion, Lynn used it to protect sentences that were patently wrong.

Grainne knew it was a cliché to dislike her father's girlfriend, that it was beneath her, but could hardly resist it.

'I worry about you, dear,' Lynn would say, distracted, looking up from her morning sherry. 'It's the essence of tragedy, of course: a pale young thing like you left without a mother at such an important age. And I can never be a substitute, although I hope I won't be such a wicked old stepmother.' Lynne cackled, showing her back teeth, and Grainne was reminded of a wildlife documentary about wolves.

'But still, you know, *in loco parentis* and all that. If you need to ask me about anything … well, you know, I might look like an innocent sort of thing, but I've been in the theatre and I've seen a lot of stuff that we'd best not tell your father about. So, girls' stuff, come to me, yes? Am I right?'

Grainne had looked back at her, aghast.

'Any boyfriends on the horizon? Pretty thing like you, well-developed as well – would kill for a bosom like that myself, would keep your father happy, I know – anyway, there must be a few admirers. I know, you're keeping it secret. I always did, but don't worry about it. If you need any advice about, well, you know – family planning and all that – I'm sure I could be very discreet. Your father need never know. I've got a very sweet gynie myself. Gentle hands, very important. I'm sure I could make you an appointment. Just say the word.'

Grainne, not a religious girl despite what they said about islanders, silently prayed for a white-hot hail of meteorites to strike Balerno. She was offered the compromise solution of the phone ringing, and Lynne being called away to a forty-five-minute debate on the Jenner's sale.

When she returned, Grainne asked tentatively, 'What do you mean about being my stepmother?'

'Oh, has your father not said? Silly me, I suppose I should have let him tell you. But well, we're all family now, and it's just the same coming from me. We're going to be married just before Christmas. Nothing fancy, of course, what with the recent bad news. Registry office in Victoria Street.'

Grainne couldn't trust herself to say anything.

'We had been planning something bigger. I know it's second time around for both of us, but we had thought, well, that's not any reason to be all low-key, is it? We wanted to get it sorted out before the end of the year. That's why your father asked your mother to sign the papers. No, we had some big plans. You'll laugh, but I was even thinking of getting one of those fancy frocks. In cream, bit of padding, you know; try and be glamorous for the big day. But alas, not to be.'

'Sign the papers?'

'Mmmm, dear. The divorce papers. All very distressing, I know, but it had been on the cards for a couple of years, and really there was no need to delay it any further. Am I right? But as it turned out – well, there was really no need in the end, was there? So sad how it all ended, but the registry office will have to do. And between you and me, I think your father is quite relieved. Didn't want too much of a fuss. And we'd love it if you'd be a bridesmaid or something. We'd ask you to witness, but John and Marie Gallagher are down for that already.'

'He asked my mother to sign divorce papers when she was in the hospital?'

Lynne looked a little anxious. 'Yes, dear. Well, we didn't know how long ... and our plans had to be firmed up ... and ... Oh dear, you'd better speak to your father about this. I think I might have said too much.'

But Grainne couldn't speak to her father about it. She hadn't been able to look him in the eye since; found it hard being in the same room with him. Instead, when he returned from work, she would prop *The Brothers Karamazov* on her knee, and wonder how long she had hated him.

Was it when he had taken her aside, back when she was a serious thirteen year-old, and begun the conversation that started, 'Grainne, you know how your mother and I haven't been getting along...?' Was it when her mother had told her, quietly, that her father had gone to live with another woman whom he'd met on the ferry one Friday night and had been visiting once a month for the last year? Was it when it was revealed that he'd organised a new job for himself in the company's Edinburgh office, that he was moving in with Lynne, that a furniture van would be collecting his green-covered, entirely-unread collection of Walter Scott, his Dizzy Gillespie records, his tweed fishing jacket, his golf clubs? Was it the tone she had heard in his voice the time she had phoned to tell him that her mother was very ill, and had to go to hospital immediately?

Not really, Grainne thought. None of those had been real surprises. It must have been before that. Might have been the time when she was eleven, and wolfing down her birthday cake, and he had grinned and said, 'Want to watch it, Grainne: don't want to turn into a little porker.' Might have been when she was seven, and she'd run to show him her dancing dress and the new shoes, and her mother had been grinning behind her, proud and maybe tearful. 'Been hammering the cheque-book again, have we, Mhairi?' he had said, angrily lighting a cigarette.

Grainne put herself into cold storage for a year in that room in Balerno, piling up books as winter insulation. Lynne she learned to filter out: learned to absorb her stepmother's patter, blot it all up and empty it, folded away tidily in the wastepaper basket in her room. Her father wasn't quite as easily suffered.

The following summer she delivered what she wanted to be an ultimatum that she hoped would hurt him.

'I've thought about it,' she said. 'I'm going to ask Aunt Bryony if I can use her address to send my university applications. If I apply to Edinburgh from here they might think I'm going to stay … in Balerno, when I'm a student.'

She couldn't make herself say 'at home.' That would have been too ridiculous.

'You mean you won't be living here if you manage to get into Edinburgh?' Her father's tone indicated that he was trying to be surprised, at least – not having the nerve to try to sound disappointed. Instead, the words came out comically hopeful.

'I don't think it would be a good idea. I need to have some independence. Besides, you and Lynne wouldn't want me around.'

'Nonsense.' But he didn't pursue the matter, and there was obvious relief in his voice. 'Will you write to Bryony, or should I?'

'I'll do it.' That would be best, seeing as Bryony held Grainne's father in some considerable disdain, had exchanged about three icy words with him at the funeral, and hadn't deigned to reply to the wedding invitation Lynne had insisted on sending.

Bryony obliged, Edinburgh accepted, and Grainne could look at Lynne and her father with the resignation of a prisoner whose parole date had been named. Grainne counted off the days until she could escape six miles north, to lose herself in the wynds and the cobbles of the old city, shake off the suburbs and Lynne, and her own old self.

She wouldn't make the same mistakes this time, she told herself. Wouldn't allow the island girl to live beyond the beginning of October. She would enter the university as an undergraduate in the Russian department clutching an air of mystery around her: west of Scotland innocence converted into Slavic enigma. She would pronounce Grainne in an airy, poetic manner, with a St Petersburg 'ya' for a final syllable, look into the distance, bury herself in books.

That August, she had a summer job in a hunting lodge in Perthshire, helping out in the kitchens. Early one morning, four hours before she was required to start scrubbing vegetables, she walked out to the banks of Loch Tay. She was alone, and the sky was beginning to light up just for her, grumbling at the necessity of revealing its beauty earlier than it should.

Grainne felt warm, comfortable. She stripped down to her underwear, shivered with sensual anticipation, took off her remaining clothes and lay naked in the shallow water, feeling her hair stream out behind her. Laughing at the cold cleanness of the water, she sat up; stretched the damp long red strands of her hair until they reached down and clung to the underside of her breasts. She stared down at herself, white and pink and red and young, and realised that, from now on, she might almost be happy with herself. She tugged at the white roll of flesh at her middle, felt it squirm under her fingers, then let it go – and she laughed. At herself, at the remains of her family, at the knowledge that Perthshire summer had turned at that moment into Scottish autumn, and she could feel big fat raindrops on her bare breasts.

Not so bad.

Richard

A turn on the forklift would at least have made it more interesting. But that wasn't to be. One of the multiple dark rumours that went round the factory concerned the time one of the local kids had been trusted with the keys to the forklift and had impaled a fat girl called Sheila who had been standing in front of the salt 'n' vinegar stack at the wrong moment.

It wasn't true of course. One of those stories created in the quiet hours, around three in the morning, passed on, and embellished with each telling. 'Bloke was called Nick, mate of my brother's. He was in a mental home for a while, but the thing is, afterwards, him and this Sheila started going out together, and they're getting married next month. She's still got a big hole in her side where the fork went in.' That had been Richard's contribution to the oral tradition, passed on to a newcomer. 'Fuck off, Richard, you haven't got a brother,' had been the eavesdropping Marcus's response, but he had laughed all the same.

The forklift remained unattainable. The company had a limit to how many stupid risks it would take, and stopped short of trusting the workers with the transport. Their policy of pushing their luck reached its furthest extreme by employing Joe to drive down to the Blue Boar just before closing time and fill his van with six underage drinkers to do the nightshift.

It had always been this way. It had been an accepted part of growing up in the town. You knew, at sixteen, that if you needed some extra cash, you drank in the Blue Boar, and waited for closing time, when Joe, always Joe, and the crisp van, would come round. The company had a tacit agreement with the unions, who overlooked the nightshift casuals. Everything was conducted in a clandestine manner that gave the job a shallow air of romance.

Nobody ever saw Joe come in the door. He would appear at the bar like some astral presence (or as Marcus put it, 'like Mr Ben coming out of the changing room, except it's always the crisp van driver episode').

Joe's expression was always the same: firm, businesslike, but strangely fatherly. With a few sharp gestures of his finger, Joe would point out his select half-dozen. He made it seem as if you were being selected for the England youth team, and that the opportunity to pack crisps for six hours overnight was an honour that was bestowed only after careful and detailed scrutiny of your talents, or after perusing the reports of his scout network. In truth, he picked the youngest and least inebriated kids in the bar. Anyone older than seventeen was more trouble than they were worth, given that they might be less than enthralled at the £1.50 an hour they were paid, and didn't quite have the younger kids' ability to stay lively throughout the night.

Richard was always picked, because he was tall, looked stronger than he was, could hold his drink, and wasn't as lippy as Marcus, who couldn't resist the occasional mutinous grumble at working conditions. Still, Marcus was picked more often than not. The Blue Boar's juvenile labour pool simply wasn't deep enough for Joe to afford to be too selective.

On an industrial estate three miles out of town they drifted into familiar corners and started work. They listened to badly-tuned pirate radio, to Caroline or Luxembourg, because the rest of the stations were off-air, or filling the time with the sort of soft jazz that wasn't conducive to staying awake. It was an appropriately industrial soundtrack: wisps of melody interrupted by howling interference. Every time he ate crisps for years afterwards, Richard was doomed to an internal reverie. Doomed to hear again the crackle of feedback, the sudden power surge that would bring The Jam or The Bee Gees into clear focus, the echo of a crunching chord or harmony briefly flaring like a match, then fading away into a melée of interference mayhem.

On their first visit Joe had given them a ten-minute seminar in the art of crisp packing, a skill worked out over the decades until it had attained a crucial choreography. Individual bags were given a tiny shake to allow them to settle. This allowed the empty top of the bag to be rested against the full bottom of the neighbouring pack in an overlapping pattern. 'Less crushing, but more packs in a box,' Joe explained, allowing himself the only note of brightness that ever crept into his voice. It was a sweet theory, but you were supposed to get forty packs into a small cardboard box, and by pack thirty-eight everybody was giving their bags a surreptitious squeeze, enough to render the crisps pliable. The radio provided cover from the crunching, although Joe knew full well it was going on.

The crisps were already in their plastic bags, but somehow the smell still crept through. Richard was invariably assigned cheese 'n' onion. 'Think yourself lucky, pal,' Marcus reassured him. 'At least it smells of onion, which is a recognisable food product, although I grant you not the most seductive aroma on the planet. But try the chicken shift. I'm not sure what that smell is, but it has nothing to do with poultry. I think they boil up tramps' pants and then just distil the liquid until all that's left is pure rankness. It seeps into your skin. My own mother won't come near me after a night on the chicken, so you can imagine what it's doing to my pulling power.'

Richard would look at Marcus, in his grey cardigan, with the sweat-soaked hair hanging in clumps over hunched shoulders, a couple of spots always congregating around the lips, glasses flecked with stray specks of deep-fried potato, and would wonder exactly what Marcus's pulling power amounted to. But then you never knew, exactly. Any given Saturday in the Blue Boar you would see worse gargoyles than Marcus accompanying striking examples of female pulchritude.

'Gift of the gab that one, innit,' Joe would say begrudgingly. That might have been it. Marcus would talk rubbish without even the excuse of being stoned (although Richard knew that Marcus laced his Mars Bars with hash, could see the gouged holes in the chocolate where Marcus would shove little chunks of resin).

Gift of the gab was one of the attributes Richard envied in Marcus. Richard preferred the security of silence. He knew it was a defence mechanism, willed himself to have the flair and inventiveness to say what occasionally flickered through his mind, but settled for the flat-line of silence, rather than risk ridicule.

He hadn't realised quite how much of a character trait it had become, until one of his sister's friends pointed it out at the wedding reception a month earlier. His sister's wedding had been a thirty-minute registry office affair followed by a buffet lunch and, later, a disco with a predominantly Two-Tone theme.

Richard, three years younger than everybody else there, had felt decades older. He had stood by a speaker, clutching a can of warm lager, staring at the strobe lighting like the victim of psychological torture, wincing as the saxophone breaks imitated the sound of fairground rides; a panicky madness orchestrated to a ska beat. The lack of colour had made the place seem like some early-sixties newsreel: the dresses stark – chequer-boards or geometrical slashes

– and the only flash of colour the fat DJ's pink face as he peered at his records under a green spotlight.

'You're the quiet one, entcha?' It was one of his sister's friends looming up beside him, or at least attempting to loom given that she was five feet one in her high heels. In a black and white mini-dress, white lipstick, and cropped blonde modette hair, she looked as if she'd made a determined attempt to erase every trace of colour from her life, but Richard honed in on the greenness of her eyes, a detail that made all the rest of her seem absurd, even if he hadn't known that she had been a David Bowie freak a month previously.

'Never say a word, just stand there with that smile on your face, as if you're finding us all very amusing.'

He looked down at her and cast around for something to say that wouldn't be incriminating or embarrassing or just feeble, but couldn't come up with a word. Because what she had said was essentially true. He couldn't feel a part of this, didn't like discos, didn't even like the music much. Had nothing to say. All he knew was that he liked the feel of the bass booming through the soles of his feet, and liked the greenness in this girl's eyes, knew it didn't belong here and wanted to take it away from here and study it in more detail, without all the distractions of the black and the white.

'Want a drink?' she was yelling.

'Got one,' he mimed, holding up his can.

'Please yerself. Don't yer love this record, though?'

He had nodded acceptance.

'Madness,' she screamed.

'One Step Beyoooond.' And she yelled right in his ear, and he quailed, and thought silence wasn't quite such an evil. And then she went away and took her tiny hint of green promise with her, and he was left with the knowledge that the only words he had said to her were 'got one' and he hadn't even bothered to vocalise them. The movement of the lips had been enough.

Somehow he knew that Marcus would have dealt with the situation more impressively. Marcus simply had the ability to fill in spaces with his own verbal pastures, long verdant acres of amiable enough rubbish that was invaluable on long nights in the crisp warehouse.

'You think crisp manufacturers have some sort of sinister Masonic agreement where they aren't allowed to use the word 'and'?' Marcus would begin, to a muted chorus of groans and sighs. 'It's always 'n' isn't it? Cheese 'n' onion, beef 'n' onion, salt 'n' vinegar...'

Richard was happy to play the foil. 'Actually, Marcus, I think you'll find there was bacon *and* tomato flavour a couple of years ago.'

'Exactly, but where are they now? Answer me that. Or better still, find me a packet. Could fetch a pretty price at a Sotheby's auction, I reckon: a genuine packet of bacon and tomato. Bacon and tomato died a death because they didn't obey the holy crisp law that prohibits the use of 'and.' Makes you wonder if crisp people – you know, the really big crisp magnates, Mr Walker, Señor Golden Wonder – ever use the word 'and' at all. Out shopping at Marks 'n' Spencer, taken ill, rushed to Accident 'n' Emergency. Heart attack due to all the ducking 'n' diving at the office with the secretary. Fancy a bit of slap 'n' tickle, Miss Jones? How about you strip down to your bra 'n' pants...?'

Marcus could go on like this for an hour or so, or until someone lobbed a well-directed crisp packet at his ear.

Richard would listen to Marcus, and Marcus would be suitably grateful because his spiels were not always greeted as tolerantly. Richard believed Marcus knew more than he would admit, and hung around in the hope of picking up stray information left floating on the breeze. At seventeen Richard felt like a scavenger, hunting through massive piles of distracting rubbish for the treasures he needed: a joke, a song, a pair of green eyes flashing in a cheap strobe.

They went to London to see The Clash at the Lyceum. Richard was surprised that every song seemed to last six minutes at least, extended into meandering dub codas. This was confusing. 'Not exactly punk rock, is it?' he yelled at Marcus above a bone-shaking skank.

'Punk was four years ago, Rich. That's a lifetime.' Marcus had an assurance in these matters that Richard accepted, even if he wasn't keen on the affected off-hand tone in Marcus's voice. He started to appreciate the textures in the music, to relax into the bass running through his soles again.

On the train back Marcus was unusually quiet, so Richard said something he had wanted to admit for a while. 'It's all right for you, Marcus, not having to worry about your parents giving you all sorts of shit if you get in after midnight.'

'Yeah, I suppose having a lesbian prostitute mum has its advantages.'

'Prostitute?' Richard, despite himself, couldn't help but sound aghast and at the same time excruciatingly interested.

He knew Marcus's mother Cheryl was a lesbian, because Marcus had told him pretty much the first time he visited Marcus's house, when they were both eleven years old. They had been playing an extended Subbuteo World Cup in Marcus's garden shed, and rather than make the tiresome trip up to the house, had urinated into glass Corona bottles. Cheryl had shrieked her disgust when she brought them down some cake.

After her sustained invective, Marcus had simply sighed and said, 'Come on Mum, leave it out, or I'll have to tell Richard what you and Auntie Jean get up to on Sunday afternoons.' Cheryl shook her head, turned and stormed off. Richard, forgetting the fact that he was 1–0 up in a semi-final, immediately demanded to know what Cheryl and Jean got up to on Sunday afternoons. Marcus obliged with the sorts of details that Richard had to wait a couple of years to appreciate fully.

But prostitution was something Marcus had never mentioned before. Richard tried not to look too eager for information, but he was staring at Marcus with the sort of prurient impatience that was impossible to ignore. Marcus sighed.

'Think about it, Rich. We live in a nice semi, despite the fact that I have a non-existent father who disappeared pretty much after lighting the post-coital fag. My mum serves tea in the library café. How much do you think that pays? I'll tell you, not a lot more than loading cheese 'n' onion into a cardboard box. So yeah, the cash has to come from somewhere, and my Mum keeps herself in decent shape, dyes the hair every month or so, stays off the chocolates. And every week, usually on a Tuesday, she gets a little phone-call, pays a little visit, and gets a little pocket money. After all, somebody has to keep me in Doc Martens and tickets to see The Clash three nights in a row at the Lyceum.'

Marcus turned away and stared out the window.

'Is this West Horndon, or Upminster?'

'Right,' Richard replied, ashamed of his own lack of sophistication.

'Right? What do you mean, *right*? Is it West Horndon or Upminster?'

'Er, Upminster. I meant right, about your Mum.'

'Oh, I see. Well, thanks, Rich. We had been kind of hanging on waiting for your approval, but now we can continue our sordid but strangely lucrative lives without a qualm.'

And Marcus was silent for another three stops before he relented.

'Actually, you'd be surprised how many hookers are lesbians. They come up with all these theories about it: that prostitutes are so disgusted by men that they look for affection elsewhere, but I think it's simpler than that. If you do something as a job, then you don't do it as recreation, do you? You need a bit of variety. So after a hard day's graft shagging blokes you want to come home to a bit of something different. I mean, professional footballers don't go for a kickabout on their days off, do they? Same with prostitutes. When you clock off, last thing you want to look at is another naked bloke. That's the way I see it, anyway.'

Richard nodded his acquiescence. As the train approached their stop, he was still thinking about it, and concluded that, lesbian and prostitute notwithstanding, he still envied Marcus his family.

'See ya later then, Rich,' Marcus said. 'Oh, and don't even think about it.'

'What?'

'Phoning my mum up for a date. You couldn't afford it, anyway.'

There was a family, Richard thought.

He thought about it again, looking out from the eighth floor of his sister's council flat, watching the lights of a couple of boats out night-fishing in the estuary. Nothing as gloriously unsettling and romantic as traffic zig-zagging in and out of the lights over the Westway; no desirably alienating thrill there. All you could picture was a couple of blokes in anoraks, smoking Embassy and gutting eels.

This was a town he had never grown into, like a shirt that always remained one size too large until one morning you woke up, tried it on and found it straining at the seams, throttling you. Richard had never felt he had been comfortable here, never had half an hour even when he had fitted in, when he hadn't felt they were waiting for him to make his inevitable mistake. Now every day became a matter of getting through, of surviving without cutting across the estuary tide, being tugged into its tenebrous depths.

People would ask him about his family, and he would struggle to come up with even an adjective, a glimmer of description. He found it easiest to deflect inquiries with second-hand stories borrowed from others or from books, and attribute them to his mythical brother.

He half-believed in the brother; had named him Ryan. He remembered when he was about eight, his sister was eleven, and a babysitter called Janet had become bored with Friday night television. Janet, her acned friend Mel, Richard and his sister had dimmed the lights and assembled around a makeshift ouija board consisting of twenty-six Scrabble tiles placed in a rough ring around two scraps of paper marked 'yes' and 'no.'

They had placed their forefingers on an upturned wine glass, Richard had been told sternly not to laugh, and Janet had intoned in a serious voice: 'Is there anybody there?' When the glass had started to move in slow, lazy circles, the teenage girls had started to shake, and stifle giggles. Eventually it had spelled out a name – 'RYN' – that made no sense. Asked if it was related to anybody, it spelled out 'RICH.' He had just smiled, thinking the babysitters were trying to scare him. When the glass started to speed up and lap the board in a swift, smooth pattern, Janet and Mel shrieked, leapt up, and rushed for the front door. His sister had followed them, in tears. Richard had sat there, looking at the toppled glass, wondering what had happened. He had been the one to start the pushing, finding it easy to guide the glass without being detected. Then it had got out of control.

He still wondered about what had happened that night. The following morning his sister had looked up from her breakfast and said, 'You ever have an abortion, Mum?' His mother had looked down from her customary stance frying bacon, and said absentmindedly, 'No dear, what makes you ask?' His sister had chewed on a piece of fried bread, and thought about it. 'Well, what about a miscarriage?'

So Richard had invented Ryan, the brother they never had. That was their problem, he thought. Theirs was a too-balanced family: two parents, one daughter, one son. They either needed a fifth

49

element, or to lose one of the principals, to set up a little tension, a little conflict.

They had lost his sister to cheerful single-parenthood in a council high-rise when she was seventeen and Richard had been left to his own devices, to his records and his books, interrupted only on Wednesday nights at eight, when his mother would bang on his bedroom door to tell him Benny Hill was on the television. She could not countenance anybody missing Benny Hill.

Eventually, it was time to escape. One cold morning in September, with the light just appearing behind the industrial estate, Richard went through to the back office to collect his last pay packet. Putting the money in his back pocket, Richard felt he ought to make some attempt at a farewell.

'Well, see you, Joe.' Richard stuck out a hand awkwardly, uncomfortable with the stilted adult gesture.

'Yer what?'

'Won't be back, Joe; I'm off to university.'

Joe thought about this, weighed it up, then gave a slow nod, acknowledging the possibility that someone might just contemplate giving up a part-time career in food packaging.

'Well, bully for you, son. You'll learn fuck-all there, except how to screw, take drugs and get pissed all day.' Joe indulged in a theatrical pause. 'Hold on a minute, don't sound too bad. Think they'll take me?'

And, on the last occasion Richard would ever see Joe (although Joe would be working there as long as the world still needed crisps) he saw him crack a smile so beatific, warm and radiant that Richard realised why he didn't do it more often.

'Here, son: leaving present.'

Joe idly stretched out a foot, and booted over a box of rejects. Cheese 'n' onion.

A Party In 1985

How did we get here? Nobody would ever remember, but there had to be a first time, a beginning: Liam's first party.

Did he send out invitations? Announce it on faculty notice-boards? Was it some collective mass hallucination that gathered Edinburgh's jaded optimists that summer, brought them down Dublin Street, up Broughton Road, along Scotland Street, pilgrims following a star, not quite knowing what spiritual enlightenment awaited them across that grubby threshold?

Well, no. Liam had just phoned a few keystone guests, said: 'Having a bit of an end-of-term bash. Bring some mates and loads of booze.' A prosaic beginning, but then you cannot extrapolate initial significance from future import. Grainne, green-eyed, red-haired Grainne, could tell you that the first time isn't significant because it's the first time. It's just the first time. She would insist.

Here we are at that Ur-gathering, on a windy June evening in the early summer of 1985. There's a world outside, going about its business, its peace initiatives, its economic forecasts, its charity rock concerts – but it's a world that is checked at the door. Its languages and its currencies are no good here.

We've missed the preliminaries, managed to avoid watching Liam, in grimy lilac boxer shorts and a grey tee-shirt, cramming can after can of lager into a protesting fridge, piling three large bags of potatoes into baking trays, telling Patrick to open the tins of tuna. 'Should we give the place a bit of a clean-up?' he ponders briefly before answering his own question. 'Nah.'

We've missed Liam at his happiest, in those moments where all is anticipation, all is possible. Liam's achievements, those conquests, his erotic adventures, are manifold and impressive, but still cannot quite match the expectations that crowd his imagination as he whistles an Irish air and opens the spare can of lager that cannot quite join its cousins in the cooler.

We've arrived at midnight, just in time to see Gordon, Grainne, Richard and Beatrice coming down the stairs, their plastic bags of cheap wine, cheaper beer, clinking metronomically with each step. They are smiling. They are two years younger, and they wear it well.

Except Gordon, perhaps. This is a fatter, less confident Gordon.

He walks with a swagger that at first looks aggressive, but on closer inspection breaks down into an uneasy jig of uncertainty. Gordon's sidelong glances tell of a boy who still hasn't found what he is looking for, although he's getting closer. He clutches his carrier bag nervously, but with a certain expectation. He leads the way. He is the one who took the call from Liam, although he had only met him a couple of times before. 'Great guy, very funny,' was his succinct description to the others, but Gordon expects more from Liam's world: expects it to offer him illumination, guidance into a more substantial existence.

Here is Grainne a step behind, swathed in brown velvet, hardly a dramatic summer variation on her Slavic ice-maiden get-up. Her smile would like to be enigmatic, but actually it's June, work is over, she is looking forward to going to Russia in the autumn, she is happy, and just occasionally the smile flicks up a couple of notches and becomes radiant. She is clutching a bottle of genuine Russian vodka – not with the intention of getting completely off her face, but simply as her proper accessory.

At twenty-two, Beatrice is only gradually unfolding herself into the most beautiful woman any of them would ever see, but all the clues were there. In 1985 she is strikingly non-contemporary. In a sea of perms, flicks and shoulder-length shaggy coiffures, her simple black bob seems both antique and futuristic, her long black dress a sheath of stylish neutrality amid a Dantean array of infernal fashion. Beatrice already looks as if she had stepped off a grainy cinema screen. Liam's guests all turn aside for a brief moment, and blink at her passing.

Richard wants to look like Robyn Hitchcock, Nikki Sudden, or any other obscure exponent of the new psychedelia, but realises he would probably need to develop a heroin habit. Instead he's a cherubic seditionary, the baggy shirts and floppily spiked hair never quite preventing him looking like the scruffy boy next-door. One problem is that he smiles too much, smiles to cover up nervousness, smiles instead of saying something smart. He practices moodiness in the mirror, but always finds himself smiling back at his own unthreatening homeliness.

They are all smiling now, because it's a party, because it's a Friday night, and because they have never seen anywhere quite like this before.

'Quite a flat,' Richard is saying.

'Yeah, in a really filthy sort of way,' Beatrice offers. 'Who is this Liam, again?'

Gordon replies but then, and forever, can't quite do justice to Liam in words. 'You'll see,' he says, and immediately they do.

'My, my, my,' Liam is saying, arms outstretched at the foot of the stairs. 'Gordon, you sly bastard, you never said you were bringing a harem.' And something about the way Liam grinned, the parodic manner in which his eyes goggled at them, stilled Beatrice and Grainne's capacity to be offended. Liam too was out of time, for this was an era of stern ethical dictates, at least in their straitened campus circles, where any word of admiration or comment was assumed to be cloaked in prejudice, contempt and misogyny. Liam had somehow managed to contrive an eternal exemption.

'Beer in the fridge, wine on the kitchen table, coats and anything else you'd like to take off over there, in my bedroom,' Liam was saying with a clownish grin, and Beatrice laughed out loud.

Liam had been in the flat for two weeks, but had already started modelling it into a New Town speakeasy, a place of social engineering. Liam needed two conversations with a stranger before they qualified for his circle of intimates. In a city where suspicion was the prevailing social mien, Liam was a benign virus, a necessary catalyst.

'Come and meet Patrick,' he said. 'He's even more disgusting than me, but because he's Swedish he gets away with it.'

Richard went over to browse with increasing disbelief through the cassette collection. AC/DC. Joni Mitchell. The Mamas and The Papas. Cream. Richard looked over towards the doorway, half-expecting to see the flickering waves that always signified a time vortex on cheap TV shows. Gordon took up position by the fridge, where he was quickly embroiled in a fast-drinking, bullshitting circle with Liam and a bunch of fellow Glaswegians, vying to outdo each other in the deployment of tough, masculine expletives and edgy cynical asides.

Beatrice and Grainne were left with Patrick. Patrick had a serene expression that Grainne attributed to a Scandinavian temperament, and the worldlier Beatrice identified as marijuana-derived. He had the fair hair and bland expression of a mid-west American farmhand. Patrick flashed a quick smile and looked at them sidelong, turning his head sideways and eyeing them critically.

'You look really good together,' he said in an English that, because it was accentless, seemed all the more foreign. 'The contrast is very stimulating. Olive skin, white skin, red hair, dark hair. Oh, yes; I think it would work. Perhaps you – Beatrice, is it? Lying in your friend's arms, looking away to the left. Yes, very good.' Patrick stared off into a distant tundra of his imagination, then smiled brilliantly again and spoke with a spark of excitement. 'Tell me – are either of you shaved?'

Liam came over at that very moment and dragged them off towards the wine. 'See what I mean about Patrick?'

'He asked us if we were shaved,' Beatrice said, still disbelieving. 'I don't think he meant our legs. It was about the fourth sentence he said after being introduced.'

'Yeah, well, sorry, but he's Scandinavian. And, not to put too fine a point on it, a pornographer. Calls himself an artist, but I tell you I learned a few things just from looking around his room when he was out one afternoon. Gave me nightmares. Although I must admit I had another shuftee yesterday. I presume you're not, by the way. If you are don't tell him, or he'll be pestering you all night. Red or white?'

And so they were introduced to Liam's world. Liam is an adept in the politics of attraction. His parties, even in these unformed, preliminary incarnations, are untidy ballets of sexual display, roughly choreographed by the host. Liam, a director who likes to make Hitchcockian walk-on appearances, provides plenty of the action himself, his eye alighting on promisingly impressionable undergraduates or frustrated academics in their thirties, according to his opportunistic mood. But his own appetites never allow him to forget his duties as host, facilitator and encourager of all romantic intrigues.

The times and the place demanded his presence, and Liam rose to the challenge. This was Edinburgh before the fall, a city looking from the margins at the brashness of an economic flourish, wondering whether it would look foolish if it joined in.

In the next decade, all those hallowed financial institutions would ship their employees out to suburban warehouses, and the prime city-centre buildings would be turned into 'exclusive' wine-bars, the exclusivity being purely fiscal, in the form of extravagant prices.

Tellers' counters would be turned into bars, economic civilisation's form of beating swords into ploughshares. But until then, Edinburgh huddled in its suspicious crouch. It was an assiduous follower of fashion in a permanent ten-year time-slip. Behind the scenes, of course, it was embracing the voguish trends of AIDS and drug addiction faster than most European cities, but it kept its decadence to itself, was unwilling to advertise.

Down here, though, hidden on the corner of Edinburgh's most demure quarter, lurking beneath the flagstones, was a happening of sorts. Liam was a party alchemist, mixing the fluids to come up with his potent tonic. Liberality, alcohol, informality and an ambience that encouraged filthiness of mind and deed to emulate filthiness of furniture and carpets became the base ingredients.

For the next seven years, Liam's parties were an underground microcosm of what the city above was a little too douce to acknowledge as its own. Representatives of most of Edinburgh's subcultures drifted through in a democratic throng, from the jaded academics to embryonic politicians, drug-dealers, filmmakers, acned bass-players, part-time psychopaths, thugs, dreamers, losers, liars. All went away muttering 'shit party,' but most returned for the next one.

They came because of the erotic promise. For hours Liam's parties would seem dry pockets of tired debate, but in the interstices, in the little cracks between the verbal posturing, was a veritable Sodom. It was estimated that twenty percent of the people came to Liam's parties looking for a sexual pick-up. The other eighty percent, in Liam's view, just didn't know that was why they were there. These were fair game for Liam's own powers of persuasion, his own whispered insinuations.

Not that his guests need much encouragement. Two first-years, Belinda and Gary, who would gracefully disgrace Liam's parties together for another four years, had brought a case of Portuguese beer and had occupied a corner of his battlefield of a living-room. They were working their way assiduously through their twenty-four bottles, oblivious to the obvious truth that trying to drink beer from the surface of each other's tongues wasn't the most efficient method of consumption. When the twenty-fourth bottle was drained, they would rise, fulfilled, soft smiles on their faces, and head off into the night, as if the consumption of this eight warm litres of Superbock had been the entire purpose of their erotic connection.

A middle-aged American woman, an Eliot expert with a correspondingly sharp eye for masculine deficiency, was looking for an undergraduate she didn't teach, in order that her sexual adventures shouldn't be compromised ethically. 'I guess I'm just a bit of an old-fashioned girl that way,' she explained, dipping a finger into the tuna mayonnaise. A fellow faculty member, Lleyton, sipped malt whisky from a chipped mug and talked about the 60s in an irritated way, listing counter-culture heroes in a tone of increasing contemptuousness. 'Hey, chill,' the American told him. 'Abbie Hoffman was an asshole: get over it.' Lleyton's gaze drifted over the room, looking for victims.

Two Germans, who had arrived separately, had edged through the crowds, separating the throng with their Teutonic vapour, had found each other, and were now delineating all the common ground between Munich and Aachen in a methodical but slightly depressed manner.

Then there was Patrick, observing Liam's world through an imaginary viewfinder, seeing carnal combinations in every configuring of limb, lip and breast. Occasionally he would ask questions, the sort of questions that made their objects drift off hurriedly. Except for some, and Patrick knew this – some who would stay, and raise an eyebrow, and ask questions of their own, and a week or so later emerge dripping from Patrick's development tray, their angles and shadows captured in brutalist monochrome.

Our foursome comprises suitable cases for treatment. Two years after being thrown together by a quirk of the student accommodation agency, they still clung together in a platonic cluster, still pretended that the secular ties of flatmate status were infinitely preferable to anything erotic.

Yet, you didn't need to be as acute as Liam to see the yearnings. Richard was a lost soul, afloat on a sea of self-consciousness, still to grow into his own personality. Beatrice's steely confidence suggested she was about ten years older than everybody else, and yet there was a querulousness there, an impatience with the very pointlessness of these kinds of parties. Gordon wanted to look older, desperately needed to be taken seriously, so he drank and swore and tried to talk about football, looked around distractedly at every female that passed by, but mostly at Grainne. Grainne seemed on the brink of hysteria, or perhaps just drunk, hugging her vodka bottle proprietorially.

Liam looked at Beatrice with a certain longing himself, as he had every time he had glimpsed her in the English department that year. Something told him that Grainne might be a more catchable quarry, judging by the manner she was putting it away. He had made a mental note to this effect, but by the time he looked around, in the early hours, she was ensconced in a corner with her Stolichnaya and Gordon, and, reading the hand gestures and Gordon's glassy-eyed gaze of adoration, they wouldn't brook interruption.

By then, Richard had bonded over the music collection, with a curly-haired girl from Dundee. Beatrice had gone looking for her coat, and Liam went after her, he told himself, to help her find it.

'Beatrice, darling, not leaving us already?'

'Sorry, Liam, it's been lovely, but I've got to write a tutorial paper tomorrow, you know.'

'Don't want to worry about that. I give some of those bloody tutorials, and I've never listened to a paper yet.'

'Mmm, but unfortunately not everyone shares your liberal approach.'

'How's it all going?' Liam put on his serious tone, the one he used when he didn't have a wider audience. He wanted to keep her talking, to hold her there for a few minutes. Nothing more. 'Lleyton tried to get into your pants yet?'

'I think so. At least he too took me for a drive to the seaside. But listen – I'll tell you about that another time …'

'It's the academic curse, you know,' Liam said, rallying words that might hold her for a few minutes more. 'You might not believe this from my generally dissolute appearance, world-weary demeanour and casual air of being completely fucked, but I'm only in my mid-twenties. This was my first year of teaching. And I've looked around at my distinguished colleagues in the department. For them October is like feeding frenzy. They are vultures in the desert circling overhead, spotting a fresh batch of corpses on the sand. That pretty much sums up their attitude to the undergraduates. Female undergraduates, of course, although you won't need me to tell you the faculty member who takes a solicitous interest in the problems of young lads fresh out of the more old-fashioned public-schools. What makes me laugh is you hear all the girl students complaining that the Union discos are a cattle-market. They're actually a lot safer there than in the first week's lectures in English literature one.'

Beatrice was buttoning her coat but she was smiling, so Liam ploughed ahead.

'You know what it's like. Seventy of you crammed into a lecture hall, and there's the lecturer looking out over the sea of faces. And at eighteen you think he's offering the bond of learning, seeking out intellectual understanding, a spark of literary empathy. Actually he's just trying to figure out who's got the biggest tits and who might be a goer.'

'You're a cynic,' Beatrice smiled, because she knew he was right.

'That's my strong point. How about the teaching? In despair of us yet?' Liam still didn't want to let her go.

'It's fine. Everyone seems slightly disappointed, though. It's like they're all trying to be *post*-something-or-other. They're all desperate to distance themselves from what has gone before, and trying to pretend that their absorption of previous theories and regurgitating them in a rearranged form represents a new strand of critical theory in itself.'

'Ah, Beatrice, you've just dismissed the whole point of academia in a single sentence. It's not about the texts any more; it's about using them to back up your own viewpoint. Academics have become the equivalent of blokes arguing in the pub saying, 'listen if you don't believe me, ask my mate Tommy Eliot'. Listen, can't I tempt you to another drink? There may be a half-finished bottle of Canadian whisky under the bed.'

'Oh, Liam, that sounds so enticing, but I really have to go.' Beatrice gave Liam one of her looks, and, the first night he met her, Liam realised that Beatrice was substantially stronger than he would ever be. But he was a resilient soul, and didn't let it deflate him. Plenty of others to chase after all.

And then there were three. Liam was left to wander back to his kitchen, to slap Gordon on the back and give him an encouraging word. Gordon looked at him in surprise, then smiled. The boy would be all right.

Richard had found a Dubliners tape. *The Leaving Of Liverpool* was blaring out of the living-room, and Richard and the curly-haired girl from Dundee were sharing a look of condescending hip disdain, a bond that a romantic observer as astute as Liam could see would last them a month. A month that each would regret, that each would remember five, ten years hence and wince and think, 'How could I?' Liam knew, because he had already accumulated a substantial back catalogue of such moments himself. Still, he congratulated himself on a success. He had met Richard for the first time that night, and somehow Liam's talent had instantly reaped rewards. Temporary rewards of course, and less subjective interests might have thought he would be better off going home chaste and alone, but those interests were not invited, not welcome.

So it goes. The 80s would drip away in a series of such parties, in a sea of cheap booze, bad music, the occasional life-enhancing flash of possibility. The cast remained substantially unchanged, occasionally reinforced with fresh blood. It was a four-act drama: the anticipation, the dullness of sluggish plot development, the sudden spark of attraction, concluding with the early hours comedown, the retreat into the practicalities of taxis, phone-numbers, sleeping arrangements, contraception.

Another party began to die. Lleyton was asleep in an armchair, wet snores confirming that whisky had conquered libido. The American was arm-in-arm with a bright-eyed girl with brilliant black hair that reflected light at startling angles. 'Mel's going to give me a crash course in the works of Sappho,' the American called out to Liam, waggling her tongue at him lewdly. 'Hey, you're never too old, right?' Liam waved them off with a grin.

The director went back to the concluding scenes. Liam was pleased with his new recruits. They had potential. A naïve juvenile lead, a femme fatale, a bittersweet supporting actress, and a confused boy with the makings of a villain; they would fit into his continuous production, would expand their roles with the years. They were callow, sure; unformed still, with too many contradictions, too many of the clichés of impressionable kids in their early twenties. But that was hardly an insurmountable problem. They just needed direction.

Around five, Liam peered into the living-room. Grainne and Gordon were gazing at each other, smiling, the distance between them measurable in fractions of a centimetre. Richard and the curly-haired girl from Dundee were about to get their coats. It was a comfortable scene of fresh intimacy. The only jarring note was

Patrick, who was sitting in a dark corner, looking over at Grainne, and smiling with all the chillness of a Stockholm November.

'I'm making some coffee,' Liam said. 'Anybody interested?'

Coffee

Beatrice

C offee: the full, bitter, adult bite of proper Italian ground coffee.
Beatrice would roll it over her tongue, savour its foreignness
and allow herself half an hour of Mediterranean romanticism in
the mornings. She isolated it, a fragment of personality, swilled
around in dark strands at the bottom of her deep blue mug. The
others would bite into their bacon rolls (Gordon), slop their cereal
bowls full of milk (Richard), frown a little grimace of disapproval
that the coffee wasn't Nicaraguan (Grainne) but they would leave
her to it. After those first few weeks of well-meaning enthusiastic
conversations, it had become accepted that breakfast was a meal
to be survived rather than enjoyed.

Once a week, Beatrice would creep just a tiny bit self-consciously
into the Italian delicatessen on Elm Row. Once a week she would
deflect the gazes of the shop assistants, all looking at a face they
seemed to recognise as one of their own. It was disconcerting.
Edinburgh people would never stare; that was regarded as among
the worst of solecisms, like swearing in Jenners. The Italians looked.
They looked so hard that Beatrice would reach swiftly, grasp her
coffee in a quick hand, forbid herself to inspect the shelves full of
Italy, full of forgotten family, and hurry to the till, where she would
emphasize the flat, dead South London vowels in her 'thank you.'

The shop assistant would seem briefly disappointed, but then
he would smile: the grin of somebody who knew a secret, but
wouldn't tell. Beatrice would scurry out of the shop vowing that
next week she would make do with bloody Gold Blend. But the
following Thursday there she was, lurking on the pavement for a
few moments before stumbling into those smells, that heady wall
of Italian ambience, packaged up in brown boxes and shipped to
the north. She would breathe it all in, replenish the vestigial Italian
lurking within her, grasp her green-foil carton of coffee, cast her
eyes downward and return to life. As a student of literature she
liked to laugh at Proust, but at these moments she would allow
him a little gift of insight.

'We measure our lives in coffee, don't you think?' she said to
Richard one night, when the two of them had been left amid the
debris of a Friday night kitchen, eking out the thin hours of post-pub
Edinburgh. These conversations would spin off into tangents, wheel

around on themselves, congeal over the table like the forgotten washing-up.

'Coffee at breakfast. Meet people for coffee in the union after the first lecture. Coffee in the afternoon. Tutors talk to you about your essay over a cup of coffee. Then someone chats you up in a club and asks if you want to come back for coffee. It's like some sort of obligatory social lubricant. Mother's milk for grown-ups.'

'It's because you're a girl,' Richard said. 'With blokes, it's lager. Pint at lunchtime. Quick one in the afternoon. Session down the union in the evening. Then it's "last pint anybody?"'

Beatrice loved the ritual, delighted in the quick familiarity of the rhythms of being a student. In her first week, in her first year, rapt in the self-consciousness of learning, with her reading list, her textbooks, her foolscap notebook, her eager eyes, she began by being assiduous, and could never quite bring herself to let that initial conscientiousness lapse. Her essays became smooth, precise constructions of impeccably restrained arguments. In tutorials she would make obliquely incisive comments that would be greeted by the tutor's look of agreement tinged with what she often thought was annoyance.

After a month she was in love. In love with the dust and decay of an ancient library, with the quaint, reassuring patterns of academic bureaucracy, with the heavy thud three forgotten critical works from the 1930s made when you planted them on a desk in preparation for an afternoon of dismissing their effete arguments. She loved the torpor of Wednesday afternoons looking out from the third-floor library desks over the wet November of George Square, stripped trees shivering in the breeze, while teenaged optimists scurried along the stones.

She never learned to keep the love out of her eyes, and there were always those who would misinterpret it. This, after all, was a faculty that existed only to give alternative readings of plain enough texts, to see metaphor and opportunity where the author only intended statement. There were plenty who wanted to make a study of the stories behind Beatrice Morelli's grey eyes, wanted to claim their narrative for their own. It's the academic inclination: to render the work of others unto themselves.

For two years they came after her. Not the younger ones. They admired from afar, smiled at her, occasionally talked with her about

Larkin or Lessing over coffee, tentatively, looking up regularly for a shade of agreement or approval, thirsting for it. Liam had been the sweetest. A couple of years into his postgraduate course he had a few traces of boyishness still hanging about him. Over a pint in Greyfriars one Friday afternoon he had leant back in his chair and declaimed 'Beatrice, darling, I'm probably a little too fat, degenerate and perhaps unhygienic to have a chance of us ever being lovers, but if your standards should ever plummet alarmingly, you will let me know won't you? You've got my number?'

Beatrice had smiled assent.

The older ones had a hungrier, haunted look in their eye. Beatrice was a challenge, and one that had to be reduced to a level where they could understand her. The head of department tried gravitas, a fatherly hand on the shoulder, a frank gaze of appraisal. She had been selected, his eyes told her, and she should not be over-awed; these things occasionally occurred in the worldly environment of a twentieth century university. Beatrice demurred in a manner calculated to suggest she had no intention of acknowledging the true nature of the offer, and awkwardness was avoided.

The enfant terrible of the department, Lleyton, now forty, with a brilliant book on Lawrence three years behind him and a future of disillusionment and dialysis looming over the horizon, had tried a more flamboyant approach. They had driven out to North Berwick in his open-topped sports car, as Edinburgh autumn dusk had retreated into a chill night. There, by a beach hung with black cloud, they had looked over to the hulking Bass Rock, and down the coast to the power station. Lleyton had tried to involve Beatrice in some moonlit skinny-dipping. Beatrice had smiled her unwillingness, had hugged her scarf to herself, had sat in the car, and giggled at the sight of his thin pale buttocks clenching against the cold as he ran down the beach. He returned to the car wet and unabashed and drove back into the city. They sat looking at each other over acrid pints of real ale in The Green Mantle.

'What do you call your organs of reproduction?' Lleyton asked her suddenly, peremptorily.

'What do you mean?' Beatrice said, startled, although she knew Lleyton's reputation. 'Do I have a pet name? Like my flower or something? In which case, certainly not. I'm twenty-one years old.'

'No, woman. I mean the everyday word. The noun you employ if you want to identify that area.'

'Well, it doesn't come up that often in my daily conversation, but I suppose I would say vagina.'

Lleyton snorted. 'Typical middle-class gentility. The word is cunt. Call it your cunt and have done with it. Perfectly good word.'

He said it loudly enough, and with such an aggressively sibilant accentuation of the final *t*, for Beatrice to be briefly alarmed. She looked over at the barman steadily polishing his pint tumblers, but he merely offered a half-shrug. Lleyton was a regular. They knew his habits.

Beatrice felt a quick reluctance to reply with anything that would offer her own opinion, wanted to relinquish nothing of herself to this preposterous wreck. Instead she borrowed from a militant friend of Grainne's. 'It's a word that has been too heavily politicised. We can't use it until it has been freed. Shouldn't take long.'

Lleyton's disappointment was expressed in the sag of his chin, the dullness that crossed his eyes, the slight nod to the barman and the brandishing of his empty glass. 'Could I invite you back to my place for coffee?' he said, but the voice was colourless. 'Only it's okay because my wife has left me to do a three-month stint at a peace camp…'

For a couple of years, Beatrice measured her academic life in her increasing talent for administering diplomatic rejections. She would look at what should have been clever, subtle men, and see their defeats etched in their faces, see them clutching the tattered mantles of intellect around them and trying to piece together the shreds of dignity.

She wanted only a little of what they had. She craved that confident disdain of theirs, that ability to snatch an entire philosophy, a strain of thought developed over decades, and throw it to the wind of academic dismissal, like scattering dead ashes from the stern of a ship heading inexorably in another direction.

The dryness of their literary insights she gathered, and pressed between the leaves of her foolscap collector's notebook. When she looked back at them, they never quite retained the magical hubris of their initial delivery.

Still, every middle-aged male on the faculty pursued her. When they became damp with temporary desire, began to offer parodic glimpses of youthful ardour, she backed away, frightened by the desperation in their eyes, repelled by the cloying eagerness of their hands on her arm. It seemed like a loss of control, a demolition of their cool confidence.

Men her own age drifted around her orbit, unable to come close because of the counter-tug of her own gravity. They would see Beatrice Morelli, see the eyes and cheekbones and hair and lips of the art-house heroines they would worship at the fifty-pence Wednesday matinees in the Filmhouse. Beatrice was the same as the continental drama divas: a projection on a screen to be admired, desired, but destined to belong to somebody as stellar as herself.

So they would blush when she said hello, trip over daily nonsense in their stilted conversations with her, not gaze too long at her lips lest it damage them, like staring into the sun. If she had faltered in tutorials, if she had occasionally forgotten to read the books, if she had mistaken the name of a minor character: that might have provided a chink ... But no. Beatrice was there to quietly correct the tutor's errors, to offer a qualifying interpretation of a scene, or an insight that they would all write down assiduously in their own notebooks. Sometimes three of them, privileged to sit close to her at the first lecture of the morning, would argue afterwards. 'She smelled like almonds,' one would assert. 'Not almonds, it was vanilla,' another would suggest. The third had travelled a bit. 'Neither of those. Beatrice smells of coffee. Italian coffee. Espresso.'

Richard was a little different. It had taken three months, but Beatrice had eventually managed to establish something like a normal friendship between them. He had been the only one of her three flatmates she had told about her father. He had seemed almost envious, as if childhood tragedy was an accomplishment, another piece of Beatrice's collection of achievements. Richard had passed on the information, delicately, to Grainne and Gordon, as Beatrice had rather hoped he would.

Beatrice would see Richard look at her strangely sometimes. She smiled when she saw him wondering where to put his eyes when she came out of the bathroom cloaked in her towel. On Saturdays he would sometimes bring her coffee in bed, and she would see his gaze chasing itself around the room, not wanting to linger on the bareness of her shoulders, or the underwear hanging over the chair, instead settling on the chaste neatness of her bookshelves. She liked Richard because he was more complicated than the young men in her classes, but she liked him in a way that didn't come close to the idea of hauling him under the bedclothes with her on those wet winter Edinburgh Saturday mornings, when the seagulls sailed around the rooftops crying out in boredom.

'You're attracted to older men, aren't you?' Grainne had said accusingly, over another of those coffees in the arts faculty basement. Grainne had watched wide-eyed while Beatrice conducted a flirtatious five-minute banter with the drama tutor, who had sashayed off towards the lifts in a flurry of musk and a garish tie, and a fleeting happiness that Beatrice had spoken to him.

'Who, me?' Beatrice had said. 'No. Well, not him anyway. He looks like a member of Deep Purple.'

'Tanya told me you were having it away with half the faculty,' Grainne went on. 'Which I know isn't true, because you're too smart for that. But I do think you're attracted to the older type. I suppose it's inevitable really, considering…'

Beatrice had laughed out loud. 'Of course, of course. My father died when I was a kid, so I'm getting over it by lusting after tweedy academics with terrible hairstyles. It all makes sense now. Thank you so much for your insight, Grainne dear. And to think you only did Psychology One as your extra course. Forget the Russian, dear. Lucrative Freudian practice awaits you. Can't wait until next year. You'll be able to give me complete therapy, find out all my neuroses for free. Agreed?'

Granne had smiled, and sipped her coffee, still thinking she was right.

Grainne had smiled again, for longer, by their third year, when Bryan arrived.

He arrived as that rare creature: a new appointment to the faculty. An elderly lecturer had died (mysteriously, in a Greek discotheque), everybody had shuffled sedately along the hierarchy and a vacancy had appeared, to be filled by Bryan. Bryan was from Liverpool, had made a sufficiently intimate scrutiny of that city's reputation for laconic wit to be able to perform a creditable enough imitation for the undergraduates whose pub tables he would gatecrash. Bryan's nasal vowels and understated air came as sweet relief from the verbose desperation of most of the faculty. Bryan wore a leather jacket that he had weathered himself by driving his car over it a couple of times three years previously, when he had looked around his Wirral semi-detached and decided to build himself an academic personality.

Bryan made out he knew George Harrison, and skilfully backtracked to make a joke of it when he realised he was talking to people whose sketchy notion of George Harrison's identity inclined them towards hostility. Bryan would buy drinks generously, and then in an effort to reclaim some credibility, would beg cigarettes off everybody, munificence crossed with the affectations of student poverty, but nobody ever questioned the contradictions.

Bryan was married to Barbara, who would appear at faculty parties occasionally, looking like the dark-haired singer out of Abba, except for one misguided Christmas when she looked like the blonde-haired singer out of Abba. She would position herself with easy reach of the department's red wine hoard, and look on, sadly, at the eighteen year-olds smiling shyly at her husband as his voice travelled the uncharted country between John Peel and Jimmy Tarbuck.

The professors and the senior lecturers and the fellows would gather in small clutches and smile to each other, or at least would crinkle their thin lips at each other, eyes darting from the husband with his Hamelin of nubile admirers to the wife, pink-eyed in chiffon. Then they would always look around anxiously in the hope of seeing Beatrice. Except that Beatrice never came to these affairs.

How these two – small, dark calculating Bryan; languid, divine Beatrice – ended up together is one of those sour mysteries thrown up by the cryptic equations of attraction. 'How could she?' discerning women hissed at each other. 'How did he manage that?' envious men spat in bile-soaked accents.

Beatrice couldn't have answered them. She could have showered them with a series of truths that still wouldn't have provided a convincing case. Bryan made her laugh (although never in the way he intended). Bryan was clever enough to have constructed himself in a manner that set him apart from the rest of the department, so had at least the recommendation of novelty. Beatrice found it attractive that Bryan was smaller than her, that he had no claims to any form of masculine beauty.

But mostly Beatrice felt a need to surrender, to come back into the fold. For a couple of years she had wandered high plains where the air was pure but thin. She was finding it hard to breathe all by herself up there. She had been looking down into the valleys and wondering at the untidy frolicking that went on there, but after a while she was overtaken by the curiosity to trip down and find out for herself.

So, at one of Liam's parties, she had found herself listening to Bryan talking about the brutalist strain in modern poetry, and had been touched when she had heard his voice retreat from its Scouse inflections, settle back into the comfortable drawl of a middle-class academic. And because Beatrice had been drinking Liam's Canadian whisky, and because Bryan's hair was falling over his eyes, and because the dull light of the room, and the wormwood blast of the whisky made him look like a twenty-two year-old poet, and just because it was time, Beatrice had kissed him. And Bryan had been afflicted with the inevitable effects that every man Beatrice would ever kiss always experienced, beginning with gratitude, and moving on to a sudden and rational belief in the existence of a benevolent deity.

They became what department gossip bleakly rendered as 'an item.' It was a relationship conducted in the brown language of infidelity, the beige wash of adultery, the ochre drudge of an eternal plotline. Barbara, despite hints from Bryan, proved unwilling to head off to the peace camp to join Lleyton's wife. So instead, he took out a permanent loan of the infidelity guide-book, studied its chapters on duplicity, pre-cooked excuses and the necessity of taking timely showers. 'Beatrice and Bryan' was not quite a conjunction that would be writ, star-crossed, along a romantic's indigo sky.

They snatched at love, or at least intercourse, according to convenience. In a reversal of the normal patterns, Bryan would moon after Beatrice, write her little notes, contrive to make their paths cross 'unexpectedly.' Beatrice would sigh, make half-promises, point out the urgency of her work commitments. And yet she continued, even as the whispers of 'how could she?' found a crescendo.

Bryan. Beatrice knew that their union was a flimsy construction. In truth, she knew that it hung together by the flimsiest cartilage of that *y*. If he had been a Brian, she knew that would have been the detail that toppled the whole ludicrous heap of cliché and contradiction into the dust. A *Brian* could never be a lover, although

70

she supposed there may be thousands, perhaps millions of women out there, perfectly contendedly snuggling into their Brians. But the *y*, the Hellenic-looking unenthusiastic half-vowel had softened the name, had brought a raffish, quietly bohemian air into the middle of that prosaic prole-name, and saved him. Beatrice could cling to that *y* and hope it would be influential, would stretch out its promise and be Bryan's saviour.

A year and a half later, she knew it hadn't. She lay naked, sleepy and salty in the bed of Bryan's out-of-town friend. Ah, he was a useful acquaintance, this one, with his flat on the Meadows and his job that took him out of town so often and his spare key and his double bed and his washing-machine to cleanse all the afternoon's evidence.

It was a Friday afternoon in term time, after a drunken lunch. Bryan had to go back to his wife. Beatrice had to go home and make up an excuse to her flatmates to explain why she wouldn't be going out with them tonight.

She looked through half-closed lids at one of those prints of a tough American and a past-it blonde sipping dark green cocktails in a half-impressionistic after-hours bar, and felt the aftertaste of bourbon and Bryan. He was rustling around in the kitchen, and then he came through the door.

She looked up at him, his ruddy face cracked in a welcoming grin, that hirsute, mottled chest of his puffed out in mock-pride, the torso hanging out bare and bold over the grey boxer shorts. He was forty-two years old, and a boy, and Beatrice saw him in the light filtering in through the window and felt maternal, but like a disappointed mother realising that her darling child is never going to be a Michelangelo or a Richard Burton. His arm held out the mug, his voice was puppyish, eager-to-please.

'Coffee?'

Richard

Two things kept him alive, or three if you counted Beatrice's eyes as separate entities.

First, as always, there was the music. In the future, when he had grown into a knowing, retrospective cynicism, Richard could divide his student years into pop groups. At the time, of course, he wouldn't use such a reductive description. Shying away from the crassness of 'bands' or 'rock groups,' he would struggle for descriptions that could convey gravity, intellect, sensitivity, all the attributes he wanted to wear vicariously when he put needle to vinyl.

1983, that initial, tentative year of first impressions, shaping together an identity from surface detail, had been New Order. Those crystalline beats, the anonymous vocals conveying banalities with the ennui of the truly enlightened, had seemed a perfect enigmatic soundtrack, avant-garde without being overly expressive. Richard would find himself tapping out the rhythms of *Blue Monday*, *In a Lonely Place*, *Hurt* and the rest of the songs with titles that hinted at depths, at an art house intelligence at odds with the opaque lyrics. They were muscular, digitally aggressive, but modern, European, distanced from sweat and passion. The swaggering bassline of *Age Of Consent*, the way the singer offered a parodic 'whoo-hoo' in the middle of his customary deadpan delivery, made Richard's stomach lurch with suppressed exultation every time. It was suburban white-boy soul, exuberant in its very cold, suppressed parody of dance-music. 'You play this album all the time,' Grainne had said once, in a rare tone of complaint. 'They sound like Nazis,' she said. Richard had smiled triumphantly.

1984 had been The Psychedelic Furs. Richard was sufficiently narrowly-read, attuned to the currents of voguishness to know that these were beyond the pale, critically reviled, and slightly ludicrous in their scuffed approximations of 60s and 70s attitudes. But he found the tinny, synthetic rhythms, whining keyboards and keening, off-key groans of high romantic sadness, unbearably irresistible. He could hear the guitars heading off towards middle America, and his *NME*-reader's intellect would sneer, but the rest of him was away, chasing that heart-tugging chorus. And the singer was called Richard. Until his flatmates told him not to, Richard would wear purple shirts with pointed collars, mess his hair into a sugary mop, talk in a cross between louche aristocrat and South London drug dealer. 1984 was a year for being impressionable, its Orwellian numbers an excuse to be stupid in your individuality.

1985 had been the year for being confused. It began with the Jesus and Mary Chain. Richard had already tormented his flatmates with the feedback howl of their first single, *Upside Down*, played at life-threatening volume though his cheap stereo, so the speakers, the window-frames, the furniture would rattle in sympathy with the trebly attack of East Kilbride guitars. Richard found the noise emotionally upsetting, and listened to the record all the more for that. One afternoon, the clatter of its toy drum sound kicked in for the fourteenth time, and Grainne had burst into tears.

When the LP came out, Richard played it as devotedly, but if anything it was too tuneful. Richard needed the noise to flush out his head, to wipe out the possibility of reflection. Instead he found himself humming melodies, instinctively piecing them together from the bombsites of feedback, constructing something positive from the wreckage. This wasn't right.

So he found himself listening to Prefab Sprout's *Steve McQueen*. He would be mortified in future years to find it described as a 'student classic,' to see a summer of his life reduced to cliché, to a common mass experience. But for months he had lived between the notes of the record, savoured its precise, tasteful delineations of romantic failure. He could gulp down great chokingly sweet draughts of regret during the chord changes on *Desire As*, could nod his twenty-one year old head knowingly to the very adult confessional of *Horsin' Around*, offer a weary sigh at the failure of non-existent affairs. For once he had found a record nobody disliked. Even a one-night stand with a fireman's daughter from Hawick had been punctuated by her repeated demands to hear *Appetite* one more time. That night, for him, the song turned into an exhausting, arm's-length lament about female insatiability.

Richard felt as if he had been prescribed contradictory drugs. He would attempt to flush his head clean with bracing Scottish feedback, but the Jesus and Mary Chain's nihilism left gaps, where creeping regrets could crawl back in, and demand to be fed some muted, minor-chord melancholy. May to September, Richard felt mood swings at 33⅓ rpm.

The problem was his other lifeline. Beatrice of the grey eyes and the smile, and the devastating ability to read character from a five-minute appraisal, had edged herself between every floating, muted phrase in his music. When he heard *Desire As,* when he imagined the ephemeral, reproachful, disappointed, other-worldly heroines of this music, they all turned out to be Beatrice-shaped.

This shouldn't be. About a week after meeting her that first time, Richard had accepted that he and Beatrice could never be together on anything other than a term's rental agreement. He had recognised the exalted, seen the gaps between them, pulled back with a case of romantic vertigo. But that hadn't prevented him adoring every fold of her blouse, every eyelash, every cool, clever word she bestowed upon him.

But something as gossamer as a summer love song needed to be populated by the listener's imagination. For loved ones he could see no further than Beatrice Morelli; she claimed the role every time. No other could give grace to the part. Two days after the fireman's daughter, Richard couldn't remember that honest Borders face, could barely recall if the hair was black or brown. But with Beatrice… 'haven't seen that dress since February,' he would say in May, and Beatrice would smile at him, looking as if she could taste his sweetness on her tongue.

He knew he had to play a supporting role, and he wanted to cast himself as confidant. Those evenings, spent in that student kitchen, sipping coffee and Grainne's vodka, she would talk despairingly about her family. Richard wasn't entirely fooled. He saw she was embellishing the details, corralling truth into a more interesting fiction. Her mother, her father, aunts and grandmothers were being developed as characters. The more often Beatrice brought them up, the more vivid they became, and yet more fictionalised. Richard felt privileged to be allowed to witness the expansion of her imagination, but would have preferred to have been privy to some more obviously truthful confessions.

Because whatever he told to her quickly wriggled out of the flimsy wrappings of pretence and artifice he applied, and Beatrice could hold it up to the light in its unvarnished awkwardness. She could see through each evasion and knew Richard's meaning as soon as the words were freed. It was unnerving.

'Are you in London at all over the summer?' Beatrice had said

74

that June. Richard hadn't planned to be, but as the words flowed from the ether to his mind, that changed. 'Mmm, probably, why?'

'You could come and stay with us. I'm going to be bored rigid with my mother. Sometime in August?'

So it was settled. London, maybe all of Britain, was dusty that summer, great clouds of dirt floating on squalls, stopping briefly then moving on, making London's summer heat grimy and oppressive. Richard hadn't been there for any length of time since the summer before he headed off to Edinburgh. It seemed changed to him, dirtier, louder, less ready to offer a quick answer to every question. He looked around as a stranger, and wanted to see it through another's eyes.

Sometime in August, Richard got off the commuter train at Tulse Hill, and there she was. He hadn't seen her for a month and a half, and he realised with a start that he felt like a husband coming home from the war, that he was looking at Beatrice for signs of change. She looked sadder, tired perhaps, almost ill-at-ease.

She held his arms, kissed him on the cheek with a sort of choreographed exuberance, as if this simple action had been practiced so fervently that she could do it in one effortless, divine swoop. Richard went pink, and wished there were more people on the platform to witness this moment. But it was mid-afternoon, and nobody goes to Tulse Hill on an August afternoon.

They went back to Beatrice's flat, and Richard was introduced to her mother. She looked at him quizzically, disapproving almost. 'I've heard a lot about you Richard,' she said. 'Well, relatively speaking. Beatrice never tells me what she gets up to in Edinburgh, do you dear?'

Beatrice rolled her eyes and said nothing, and Richard caught a glimpse of tension and sadness, and exasperation. It was a shocking novelty to see Beatrice's assurance dented, to see that someone could get past that veneer of competence. He looked back at Beatrice's mother.

She was as tall as her daughter, but the hair was fair, a pale blonde with white threads that could have been age, or an attempt at platinum sensation. Her expression was querulous, her eyes following her daughter's every move, milky-blue eyes that had the thrilling clear flash of shaded ice. Eyes like that should have been motherly, Richard thought, but there was little maternal in them.

Beatrice's mother looked at Beatrice like a rival.

'Let's go to Croydon and look round the shops,' Beatrice was saying, standing by the window, hands fluttering. 'I need some new shoes.' Richard nodded, quickly cutting off a train of thought that found him standing obediently as Beatrice emerged from changing-rooms in summer dresses, silky tops, bikinis...

'Shall I cook?' her mother said.

'Don't worry,' Beatrice replied. 'We'll go into town later. Get a curry or something. Can't keep Richard cooped up in the suburbs all the time.'

So for three days they had dusty London to themselves. Beatrice treated him like a tourist, and Richard obeyed. She knew he had grown up forty miles from the city, knew he was hardly a stranger, but she wanted to show him her London, her refuges, the bolt-holes she had found from her single-parent suburbs. Here were her 70s: the galleries of the British museum, the Tate, National Portrait Gallery, the brightly anachronistic floors of Selfridges, a basement café in Kensington, a wet bench in Green Park.

They sat on that wet bench and looked at a damp, blue English sky, the colour of Beatrice's mother's eyes. 'I don't like London any more,' Beatrice said. 'It's not as big as it was. Even when I head into the centre, that suburb seems to follow me everywhere I go. The people have changed as well. Nobody smiles any more, nobody has any time.'

Richard saw a different Beatrice, a woman who would sweat in the grimy heat of London, a woman who looked ill-at-ease offering him toast and jam in the morning, who would ask him how long to boil an egg, who always seemed to be on edge when her mother appeared.

Those South London mornings were tense affairs. Beatrice would gaze out the window in mid-sentence, would offer embarrassed apologies to Richard at the meagre offerings for breakfast. He didn't care, but he could see that she did.

'How many spoons of this coffee do you use?' Beatrice would say, resentfully holding up a Nescafé jar.

'Er, just one I think,' Richard said, 'unless you like it really strong.'

'I like it really Italian,' Beatrice said with some asperity. Beatrice would sip her instant coffee and wrinkle her face at its smoothness, at its bland brown Englishness. 'I'd buy some proper stuff, some espresso, but mother wouldn't like it,' she said, and Richard understood.

Beatrice's mother came into the kitchen, a lilac robe hanging loosely around her sparse frame, and looked at them suspiciously. 'What time did you get in?' she asked, but lost interest in the answer. She would make more coffee, despite Beatrice's protests, and Richard would politely take another mug, feeling the stretch of South London through the grimy panes, the fringes of the great city turning milky-brown with every sip.

They would walk out along the suburban streets of Dulwich, Norwood, Sydenham, Tulse Hill, Beatrice pointing out the pubs where the Saturday night fighting would keep a couple of Black Maria teams occupied, the polite terraces where 1950s moral values still held sway, the antique shops and estate agents of South London's property-obsessed marches. 'This is the city of the dead,' Beatrice said, and Richard told her it was a Clash song. 'Isn't everything?' Beatrice replied.

On the last day of his stay, they took a boat out on the lake in Crystal Palace Park. The rain was falling in the half-hearted warm spit of a dying summer, and they had the lake to themselves, watched from the bank by jaded parents and small children who shared the same expression of English disdain at the folly of young adults.

'The thing is, she hasn't called me *dear* since I was seven,' Beatrice said. 'It's all for your benefit. To give you the impression we're a sweetly devoted mother and daughter. Whereas I've long been of the opinion that she is a sour manipulative old witch who's ten times smarter than me, for all my O Levels, A Levels and class prizes.'

There was a wobble to Beatrice's voice that made Richard slow his rowing, made him look across at her, just to see her vulnerable. He saw that steady lip tremble, saw the little tears in her eyes, saw them break, and trickle in fast lines down her cheeks. He looked again to make sure it wasn't a trick of the rain and the watery sunlight, but Beatrice Morelli was crying, and all he could do was reach over a hand and hold her wrist, tentatively but tenderly enough. He would have embraced her, but he thought it might capsize the boat.

'I'm sorry,' Beatrice said with a grotesque sniff that almost made his heart break, there on the water. 'Only I feel I should be responsible for her, because there's only me. It's bloody ridiculous. She's my mother, not the other way around. But she looks at me sometimes as if I should be able to tell her what to do.'

Beatrice drank port in a Victorian bar two hundred yards from her front door. She drank it with a purposeful grace, each glass offering her a little more ruthless distance from the remnants of her family. Richard sipped his pints and looked on, nodding when he needed to, listening, basking in the sensation that at last he was getting the raw material, lush and thick and fast-flowing, before it had been refined and edited and packaged for external consumption.

'I feel a little ill,' Beatrice said after her seventh port, her voice still unslurred, her vowels stretched a little. 'Perhaps we had better go home.'

She had taken Richard's arm and he had led her back up the anonymous street, up the dingy staircase, into the flat, where Beatrice's mother had taken her in hand. They disappeared for half an hour, leaving Richard in the living room, watching *News at Ten*, and a report of a famine in Africa. Richard looked at the pictures and supplied the requisite adjective 'harrowing,' but he was already learning, from Beatrice, the art of fabricating an emotional response by the medium of words.

'She's gone right off,' Beatrice's mother said from the doorway, and for a brief, surreal moment it was if Richard were her husband, and she was talking about their baby, troubled by teething pains. 'But it's still early. Would you like a drink?'

Richard thought she meant coffee, because Beatrice's mother drank the stuff by the gallon. But no, she was reaching into a cupboard, and hauling out a long, thin dust-coated bottle with a clear spirit in it. 'Grappa,' she said brightly. 'Had it for years, but it's not like the stuff is perishable, is it?'

Richard sipped the viscous fluid and felt it was an anaesthetic, felt his thought processes, his nervousness slip away into a warm cloud of numbness. Beatrice's mother was talking in a low voice, her lilac robe shifting with the words.

'She tries to hide it, but I know she's not happy here,' she was saying. 'I don't know if she's any happier in Edinburgh. She's not as tough as she makes out, but she thinks she has to put on a brave face all the time.'

Richard couldn't think of anything to say, so he fixed Beatrice's mother with what he thought was a solicitous, adult gaze, looking back into pale blue eyes that returned his stare.

'You know about her father, I suppose? It was a few years ago, but it must still affect her. I think she's tried to use her work, all her books to stop herself thinking about it. And yes, she's very clever, and I'm very proud of her, but I just wonder if it's healthy, you know? There might be problems further along the line.'

'Beatrice has always seemed very together,' Richard said tentatively. 'Of all the people we know, I think Beatrice seems the most sensible.'

'You think so?' Beatrice's mother didn't seem convinced. 'Ah, but I still think of her as my child, that's the difference.'

And she stood up, one pale thigh pushing through her robe, and beckoned to Richard. 'Come and have a look.'

Richard followed her down the corridor, tiptoeing for some reason, as if he were stalking some highly-strung deer. Beatrice's mother swung open the door to her daughter's bedroom, and there she was, lit by a watery moon lurking somewhere over Herne Hill. Richard thought about that vision for years, decades afterwards, trying to understand where it belonged. At first he had thought it a watercolour from an illustrated Victorian children's story, later a still from a silent melodrama, later still an ancient Greek mosaic.

She was lying on her back, one bare arm reaching out towards the wall in an uncomfortable and incongruous gesture. The mouth was slightly open, and Richard could see her tiny teeth and the chin rising slightly with every breath. The maroon blanket was pulled up to her white neck, making her look small, childlike in the big bed. But the most important detail was the eyes, tight-shut, extinguished. For once they weren't there to reflect back knowledge, insight and perception.

'You see,' Beatrice's mother said sadly. 'Still a child, really.' And she ushered him out of the door and closed it silently, softly behind her. Richard still numb, although whether it was from grappa or the vision he couldn't decide, stood still for a moment, then turned to head back up the corridor towards his guest room.

He felt a light hold on his wrist. 'She's a beautiful thing, isn't she? I'm not sure how. More beautiful than either of us, that's for sure.'

Later Richard realised that her mother meant herself and
Beatrice's father, but at the time he thought she had meant himself,
and nodded sagely.

Beatrice's mother held on to him, nodded in the dark and
whispered, 'This way.'

He followed her past the bathroom, to the end of the corridor,
through the doorway. He followed her into darkness, and heard
the door click shut behind them. Then he felt purposeful hands on
his back, felt lips finding his own. He felt a thrilling shock that he
thought was fear, but that within seconds turned into arousal.

'My name is Alice,' she said. 'Like in *Through The Looking
Glass*.' As she spoke she was untying her robe, and Richard felt her
naked skin, smooth and chill in the dark, and saw the quick angle
of her cheeks as she leant into him again. Then they were on the
bed, and midnight came and went, and they said nothing more for
an hour or so, except the half-formed words, fragments and gasps
that pass for language in these affairs.

'Was that all right?' she murmured at last, half-asleep, and in the
same tone of voice she had used to inquire whether his coffee was
strong enough. 'Only I haven't done this for fifteen years.'

It was fine. Finer than one-night stands with firemen's daughters
from Hawick, finer than his month-long relationship with a nurse
from Broxburn, finer than a two-month sojourn with a curly-haired
sociology student from Dundee ... not as fine as his imagination. His
mind wanted to tell him he was a victim, that he was a sacrificial
offering to a succubus in her forties. But in the half-light Alice
looked translucent, or at least like a collection of brilliant white
highlights shaded with monochrome valleys. It was an English kind
of beauty, lacking charisma, but comforting, seductive. Richard
asked himself how this had happened. The first time might have
been dismissed as an action spurred by surprise and grappa. Second
and third times were more concerted decisions.

That Richard lay awake wondering what this meant might have
been an indication of some guilt, of some awareness of an act
of classical drama betrayal. That Richard lay awake for only ten
minutes proved he was twenty-one; that the complications were too
entangled to allow intimate reflection; that he was exhausted.

He was woken by a soft deep voice a few hours later. 'Best

go back to your room now, dear,' Alice whispered, as dawn slid through the window. 'Wouldn't want Bee to see us. I'll go and make some coffee.'

He drank his coffee, smiled at Beatrice groaning at him over the breakfast table. A couple of hours later, he bent awkwardly to kiss her at the railway station. 'See you next term,' she said, and he heard in her words that she was looking forward to it. He looked at her quickly and saw what had changed. Those grey eyes weren't omniscient any longer, there was doubt in them. Richard knew something she didn't. She must never know. He didn't think he could bear to look into those eyes and see that knowledge lurking in there with all the rest.

1986 had been *The Queen Is Dead.*

Grainne

No, she didn't like the taste, but she told herself that wasn't the point. It was about creating a little personal ripple of positive effect. Grainne would look at the boxes stacked up in the office, see all the labels with the addresses of the various university outlets and feel, briefly, that she was a revolutionary.

In moments of colder honesty she would admit to herself that if it hadn't been Campaign Coffee it could have been anti-vivisection or CND. Grainne, at eighteen, had been shopping for a cause. She had turned up for her Freshers' Fair still nursing the notion of Slavic aloofness, wanting desperately to become a mysterious campus femme fatale, a Karenina from an island in the West or, ignoring the auburn tresses, she wanted to be a Natasha Rostov, flighty and exotic. But some of her aunt's homely advice had been absorbed: she realised it might be an idea to make some friends, to have an interest that would justify not having to see her father and Lynne at weekends.

So she wandered the stalls like a market browser trying to buy a life. She looked and laughed at the student politicians, affected twenty year-olds already embracing the pomposity of party structures, already finding comfort in committees. She rejected the outdoors and sporting crowds, all of them offering alcohol as an inducement, and who seemed somehow too hearty and sensibly-dressed to be appealing to a potential aesthete.

She gazed for a while at blurred pictures of puppies with electrodes attached to their shaved skulls, but drew back, scalded by the intense stare of the green-haired girl minding the stall. She felt the girl was trying to send telepathic injunctions to her, compelling her by emotional force to pull a stocking over her head and liberate some Dalmatians. As she turned away she felt the stare turn to a glare, as if Grainne herself was flipping the switches, shearing away flesh.

She looked longer at montages of mushroom clouds settling over London and Washington, listened to an earnest boy called Mark McGuire reciting statistics, telling her about the crusade against mutually-assured destruction, adding that there was a subsidised bus trip to Grosvenor Square lined up for November. She wavered, and he followed up with a quick resume of the various developments in biological and chemical warfare. 'Terrifying really,' he said, with a certain cool relish.

But she had moved on, and met Janice. Janice had grinned at her and given her a cup of coffee with cream and lots of sugar and, encouraged by Grainne's gratitude, had given her the soft sell. Janice didn't know much about Nicaraguan politics, but she knew the Sandinistas were under threat from American-financed forces, were being undermined by a CIA conspiracy, and for some reason their very survival depended on selling large amounts of their only cash crop, this coffee. 'It's not the greatest coffee in the world,' Janice said, 'but if just a few people give up their Nescafé, it could make a real difference.'

It had appealed to Grainne, because it didn't seem to involve striking a moral pose. Grainne wanted to do good without having to read all the attendant literature, subscribe to a complex political theory or assemble a wardrobe of sloganeering tee-shirts. Janice, plump, pale, in what looked like a Chilean poncho, gave her a vanilla slice to go with the coffee. 'Are these Nicaraguan too?' Grainne asked. 'No, they're from Crawfords, but they're scrummy.'

So Grainne had signed up as a volunteer, her name was put on the roster for the tiny shop in Nicolson Square, and she was given a free sample bag of coffee with which to woo converts. She went away feeling as if she had made the first step to establishing herself as an independent, free-thinking adult.

'This is disgusting, Grainne,' Richard had pointed out, mildly enough, as she looked on anxiously while he sipped from his Dark Side mug.

'Well, no, the instant stuff isn't great, but if you've got a percolator, the Rich Blend is supposed to be really aromatic. Besides…'

'…It's for a good cause. Yeah, well, I bought *Sandinista!* so the least I could do is drink their coffee. Only not very often.'

'Think I'll stick to my Italian stuff thank you very much, Grainne,' Beatrice said, swilling her cup down the sink with a friendly grimace. 'But best of luck with it.'

Only Gordon had been entirely positive. 'Tastes fine to me. Put me down for a bag a week. Have to support anti-Americanism, don't we? Besides, don't Nestlé murder babies or something?' Grainne had smiled gratefully at him, and he half-blushed.

Mondays and Wednesdays, Grainne would spend the afternoons

in the shop that doubled as an office. Visitors were rare. Edinburgh consumers were instinctively conservative, and if they wanted coffee they would pull a jar off the shelf at the supermarket. Grainne spent a desultory hour or so filling in labels, tidying the shelves, drinking coffee, finding that by the third cup her taste buds were sufficiently desensitised.

Occasionally she would talk to Joachim. He was tall, pink-faced, with dyed blonde hair, a couple of earrings, and a strange penchant for garish flowered shirts, hanging in loose crumpled folds. Sometimes he would wear beads, sometimes metal chains wrapped tightly round his wrists. He would come around to collect a couple of boxes of coffee to deliver to the Union shop. She recognised him from her Psychology class. He was shy to the point of neurosis but eventually would speak more than the few words needed to arrange the delivery. She thought from his name he would have a foreign accent, but he spoke in a neutral, middle-class English voice.

'My mother is Swiss, so I ended up with this name,' he explained. 'And giant bars of Toblerone from Berne at Christmas.'

After a month Joachim would sit and drink coffee, and tell her about the gigs he went to see. It turned out he knew Richard vaguely, they were always at the same concerts. Grainne said she found Richard 'very sweet.'

'Is he your … er …'

'He's my flatmate.'

'Oh, I see.'

They talked about Janice. Janice was having an awkward affair with Martin, who was a big noise in the Latin-American Solidarity campaign. Martin was from Greenock, but insisted on his name being stressed on the second syllable. He was married to Begoña, whom he claimed was a refugee from Allende's Chile, although Begoña herself, badly-briefed by her husband, acknowledged that she came from Lima. Martin had grown what he had hoped would turn out to be a Zapata moustache, but had come though a virulent ginger. Martin was dissatisfied with home life. Instead of fomenting kitchen revolution, Begoña had invited two brothers, a sister and a cousin to stay indefinitely while they searched for people willing to marry them and provide British passports. At a Campaign Coffee salsa party, Begoña had asked Grainne, perfectly pleasantly, what she thought of her brother Teofilo. 'Seems very nice,' Grainne had murmured. 'Ah, then perhaps you could marry him,' Begoña had beamed. Grainne hid herself in a corner for the rest of the night while Teofilo sought her out, looking for a partner to jig to the pan-pipes music, and beyond.

Martin and Janice would have half-hour carnal flings behind the coffee boxes in the office. When Grainne turned up for her Wednesday shift, she would see Martin emerging from the office, rearranging his cardigan, covered in fine brown dust. She would find Janice eating a doughnut, a dreamy post-coital look on her face. 'He only married Begoña for the politics, you know,' she would say. 'This is the real thing.'

Grainne found them sweet; Joachim was harsher. He would laugh a little, then turn serious. 'The thing is, the sad thing is, she really loves him. I'm sorry, I'm all for the good cause and helping Nicaragua and everything, but you look at someone like Martin, with his alpaca and his little beret and his Mar-teeen, and his big ginger 'tache, and you think: twat.'

'Mmmm,' Grainne agreed. 'I can't see the attraction myself.'

'That's different. That's love. Love has a wicked sense of humour. Look at couples walking down the road, or on a train wherever. You can always think, 'What does she see in him?' You hardly ever see a couple of beautiful people who have found each other. More often perhaps a couple of freaks who have bonded, but usually it's one perfectly acceptable specimen of humanity and one complete gargoyle.'

Where do I figure in this? Grainne asked herself, suddenly abashed by Joachim's critical scanner.

'It's love having a laugh at our expense. Don't you think?'

Grainne held love in some degree of contempt. Her parents' love had dissipated around the time of her own first memories, and she had found herself in a childhood where marriage seemed to be a series of minor disputes about money and responsibility. Whatever existed between her father and Lynne still seemed closer to obscenity than emotion, a classic case of blackened souls finding each other in the abyss. Even Aunt Bryony's husband Stuart had left her, running away one weekend to live with the proprietress of a fish and chip shop in Oban. 'Dumped for haddock in batter,' Bryony would say, and laugh, but the laugh always seemed to choke her.

At school Grainne had pretended to be interested in boys only as a means of fitting in. She had written 'Duane' on her foolscap folder, the name an imaginary construct explained to her friends as someone who 'goes to the high-school.' Humiliatingly, she had kept her old notes for her first year at university and had left the notebook on the kitchen table. 'Grainne and Duane? Has a ring to it,' Richard had said, 'if you could get him to pronounce it "Dwonya"', and Grainne had sworn at herself for being stupid.

Things changed. Grainne had arrived in Edinburgh caught between two conflicting urges. She still wanted to be the Slavic enigma, casting icy looks all about her, disappearing over the steppes with nary a backwards glance, hearing only the howling of the wolves, the hiss of the sled's runners. Oh that would be fine, to be an ice princess. But then she didn't want to be a little Tobermory virgin any more.

Which is why she started to look at Joachim and wonder. But she saw the earrings and the dyed hair and the beads and the chain bangles and she thought he was probably gay.

'People look at me,' Joachim said one day, 'and they see the earrings and the dyed hair, and the beads and the chains, and they think I'm probably gay. Not that I mind. In fact it would probably be a lot easier if I were gay, but it's surprising, isn't it? You know, we're at a university where the theory is that people here are of above average intelligence, well-educated, and yet they still prefer to obey all those prejudices based on external images.'

'It's shocking,' Grainne had murmured.

They started to go out for the occasional drink. Grainne was a little taken aback the first time she saw Joachim in his evening guise. It used his afternoon get-up as a starting point, but the hair had been teased into a vertical mop, the eyes lined in thick black, the innocuous ear-hoops replaced by vivid red dangling ornaments that Grainne couldn't help thinking looked like the sort worn by a barmaid in a popular TV soap. Grainne couldn't be sure if Joachim was wearing lipstick or whether it was just because he was drinking snakebite and blackcurrant. There was something in his eyes: a distraction, an impatience.

People would look at them in bars. Subconsciously, Grainne took to wearing the most sober clothes she had in her wardrobe for these evenings out with Joachim: black pullovers, sensible skirts, flat shoes.

It happened in February, midway through Grainne's first year. She thought she would laugh at an Edinburgh winter after the island, but there was something relentless about that wind in the morning, the rain teeming into your face, the smell of wet wool on the top deck of a number 23 bus as it climbed Dundas Street, its gears groaning with relief when it saw the art gallery on the Mound.

They had been drinking in the Café Royal, but had sneaked out giggling when they noticed Janice and Martin huddled over two pints of Guinness in an alcove. 'When he's with Begoña he only drinks rum and grapefruit,' Joachim had whispered. 'It's like a double betrayal, really, isn't it? Erotic and alcoholic.'

They had ended up in the Royal Oak, where they had been told to shut up by a stern old man in an Aran sweater. A fat woman had started singing a song of the isles in a wavering nasal accent, and the whole pub had frozen in fearful impatience while a few old-timers and German business students looked on enthralled. 'Shall we leave?' Joachim had mouthed, and Grainne had nodded, desperately trying to avoid laughing.

They had fallen into a taxi, and Joachim had continued the mime act, mouthing 'Coffee?' at her. Grainne had laughed and agreed.

In a large, cold damp flat in Stockbridge they huddled in front of a gas fire, heard the wind rattling the loose window frames. Grainne was startled by a sudden high howl. Joachim laughed and pointed at the old ventilation fan high up in one of the corner windows. The room smelt musty, the carpet felt clammy under her hand. 'I'll fetch the coffee,' Joachim said, 'or would you rather have tea? The Sandinistas can get by without us this once.'

They sipped tea. Joachim dimmed the lights and put on a Smiths tape. It was like a parody of a seduction scene, and they both laughed, Joachim's earrings glinting in the half-light. She saw him, pink and nervous, and knew that he would never make the first move. So she leant over, grabbed his wrist, and moved her lips to within an inch of his. He laughed and they kissed, and things fell into place.

Not right away. The removal of their clothes was awkward, Grainne struggling with a conflict between urgency and demureness. Her tights snagged on the buckle of her shoes. Joachim struggled for a minute to undo her bra, until she laughed, and helped him out. He stepped back as her breasts were revealed, as if he was worried they might crush him. Grainne realised he was feeling even more anxious than she was. By the time she was naked she was also freezing, and leapt beneath the bedclothes. As they huddled together, she whispered in Joachim's ear, still adorned with its ludicrous accessories, 'I'm a virgin.'

It had an unfortunate effect. Joachim suffered from an attack of nerves. He stopped kissing her neck, looked at her in the dark.

'Wish you hadn't said that,' he murmured. 'It sort of puts a lot of pressure on me.'

'Why?'

'Well, you always remember the first time don't you? Can't help it. So it's like this big spotlight is shining down, and you're taking notes, and everything is going into the scrapbook.'

'That's stupid, but if you'd rather … well, we don't have to do anything…' Grainne said, not meaning it.

'What difference does it make? It makes none,' Joachim replied.

'What?'

'Sorry, just singing along to the tape.'

And that night they hadn't done anything very much, although they tried, but snakebite and fear of posterity proved a lethal combination. In the morning they woke around the same time, and found each other naked, and so did pretty much everything in the grey light of an Edinburgh February Saturday, with the rain on the windowsill and the occasional shriek of the ventilation fan as the soundtrack for the time that Grainne was supposed to remember forever. Then they had coffee, and Joachim slipped back into shyness until Grainne pulled on her clothes and headed off to her flat to have a shower, read the papers, wonder what had changed.

All that had changed, it turned out, was Joachim. For a couple of weeks their conversations in the shop dwindled away into politeness, a cool formality. Grainne, not disturbed, not overly upset, merely curious, confronted him.

He looked shifty. 'I'm sorry. It's just difficult, you know. The thing is, I really like you, but I was worried. You know – about the virginity thing. It's like a responsibility.'

'Well, it had to happen eventually.'

'Yes, but, well, I'm not really all that reliable, you know. Not the most conventional…' Joachim's eyes were everywhere except on her.

'Well, I wasn't thinking of marriage quite at this stage,' Grainne said drily, but Joachim didn't seem to appreciate the joke.

'Look, maybe it's best if we just stayed as friends. I'm not sure if anything else is a good idea.'

'That's fine by me.'

And for a day or two Grainne suffered the familiar anxieties, wondered what she had done wrong. Was she so terrible? Well, she had told him she was a virgin; what did he expect? When she caught herself staring in the mirror, clutching a little roll of white flesh between her thumb and forefinger, she laughed at her own predictability.

'How's your pal the speed-freak?' Richard asked one afternoon. 'The German guy with the New Romantic fixation.'

'Swiss. English, actually. What do you mean, speed-freak?'

'You must have noticed. He's always rubbing his gums, and speaks at a hundred and forty miles an hour. I think he's started dealing, actually. I saw him in the Sorbonne surrounded by a bunch of lowlifes.'

'Er, yeah. What are the side-effects, Rich, do you know?'

'Speed? Well, from my own experience: mild depression, headaches, listlessness – although actually I can feel like that without any chemical assistance at all. At the rate he's doing it I'd suspect he's into psychosis, bleeding gums, and complete loss of libido by now.'

'Oh.'

'Ah. I get it. Loss of libido. Didn't know you and he were…'

'We're not. We're just friends. Only he acts strange sometimes.'

'It'll be the speed. Cheap, effective, but unfortunately it has a downside.'

So Grainne and Joachim became just friends, and his visits to the Campaign Coffee office settled into amiable chats where Grainne would look at his yellowing eyes, his trembling hand, and wonder what she had escaped.

By now, Gordon was becoming more attentive. Somehow they had got into a strange ritual whereby Richard would bring Beatrice coffee in the morning and, about an hour later, Gordon would do the same for her. He came in one morning just as Grainne was stuffing herself into her bra and, in a scene straight out of a bad

Doctor In The House film, dropped the mug all over the carpet while his jaw gaped and he flushed a bright crimson. 'Oh my God, Grainne, I'm really sorry. I knocked, but you couldn't have heard me.'

'Don't worry about it,' she said, but she was blushing too. For some reason Gordon couldn't look at her for weeks without pinkening, and Grainne realised that he was summoning an image of her bare breast every time he saw her. She thought she should find this nauseating, but instead found it funny, and intriguing.

Gordon had terrible friends. Whenever she saw him with Andy McInnes she tried to avoid them. Gordon would attempt to adopt this breezy man-of-the-world air which, considering he looked barely sixteen, was faintly ridiculous. She heard the words Andy used: 'bints,' 'sorts,' 'seeing-to,' and winced, but Gordon seemed enthralled.

She ran into Joachim in Bannerman's early one Friday evening, and he persuaded her to have a drink with him. She had a pint of Tartan while he drank coffee. 'It's filter stuff,' he said, 'not Nicaraguan. I'd join you in a pint, but I've just been on a three-day binge in Glasgow.' She looked at him and believed it.

'It's good to see you,' he said, heaving the words up from some mine deep in the bowels of his consciousness. 'Good to see someone who is relatively sane.'

His voice was wrenched with hoarseness. His every movement seemed a battle against fearsome forces. He was wearing what looked like a fake leopardskin tee-shirt. The chains were there again, but underneath them she could see grubby scars on his wrists. She was reminded of a girl in the sixth-form, Andrea. But self-mutilation was just an adolescent girl's thing, surely?

'You know what, though, Grainne?' and his voice cobbled together a temporary clarity. He sounded like a judge imparting flat information that was of no personal relevance. 'You're really a very beautiful girl.'

And he drank his coffee, and smiled at her, the brilliant smile of someone who has discovered a simple truth, a smile only partly weakened by the fuzzy emptiness in his eyes.

Gordon

This was love of a sort. Gordon just wondered why it had taken him so long to find it. The words themselves had gouts of eroticism hiding in between the syllables. *Executive Committee.* That would suffice for a start: a classic 4–3 syllabic combination; the poetry of bureaucracy.

Gordon sat third from top of the committee table, a position he had worked out had a strategic advantage, being more or less in the middle of any debate, allowing him to make contradictory or meddlesome interjections into any argument that came his way, whether from top or bottom, left or right. One of the first lessons he had learned was not to bog yourself down in doctrine, or else your contributions became formulaic, obvious, and most dismaying of all, unheeded.

That was the problem for the nationalists and the communists. They delivered their doctrinal sentences, everybody sniggered, and business moved on without them. You needed to be flexible, prepared to be obstructive on any issue, regardless of how well-meaning it might be. So Gordon would get to meetings early, claim his middle seat, and look expectantly for the smoke of battle from any quarter. Andy had told him it was the equivalent of being a midfield playmaker, and Gordon had nodded, impatient with the Scottish male's determination to reduce everything to a football simile.

But love, yes. Love for the badly-typed, roughly-photocopied order sheet, love for the eleven items that were the fecund seed for extended argument and posturing. Love for the notion that all eight of them sitting around this table had a title, a wordy honorific to encapsulate their duties as students' representatives. Gordon was happy enough for the time being with the Vice-Convenership of the External Relations Committee, but there were more illustrious prizes to aim at, more committees to annex.

Gordon had become an obsessive reader of notice-boards, an avid consumer of the posters that were dotted around the university. Visiting speakers, support groups, protest rallies, ideological invective, all these had replaced beer as his support system. Gordon wandered between departments with a clipboard under his arm, to mark him out from the scruffy masses with their Scotmid plastic carrier-bags. At lectures he sat dreaming of querulous points to raise at meetings, of counter-arguments he should have used a month previously but could use again soon, as the same debating points came around with reassuring regularity. This was love by any definition, the first flush of love, when every waking moment is spent pondering the glories of the object of adoration.

Gordon even felt a faint love for Andy McInnes there, standing up in his role of Executive Committee chairperson – although, like most loves, it was tinged with envy, resentment, and occasional loathing. But Andy had brought him here; Andy had the undeniable distinction of introducing Gordon to the love of his life.

'First item on the agenda,' Andy was saying in that self-satisfied demotic boom of his, 'the renaming of the swimming-pool. The shortlist is the Mandela Pool, the Biko Pool, the Daniel Ortega Pool, or the, ahem, William Wallace Aqua-Sports Centre.' To Gordon's left, Aonghais Og-Urghainn flushed proudly above his black beard. 'Could we wait for the coffee to arrive before we start?' drawled Karen, a crop-haired Socialist Worker from Maidstone, Admin Convener, in a bad mood because she was unable to smoke her thin roll-ups during meetings.

Gordon rustled his papers, settled back in his chair, and prepared for action. This, he believed, was what they called the big kick-off.

It had taken him nearly three years to discover this pure thrill. He put his tardiness down to his background. The way he saw it, the Scottish working-class male was inculcated with the idea that executive committees are not for the likes of him, that he must be content with the holy trinity of beer, sex and football.

His first year had been devoted to the two of those that interested him, and to overcoming the daily flush of shame and inadequacy that threatened to engulf him every time he saw somebody as insouciant and smart as Beatrice Morelli. Beatrice was pleasant and friendly, but a daily reminder of his uncouthness. Gordon would stay in the shower for twenty minutes, spray himself with half a gallon of deodorant each morning, stare in the mirror trying to look less Glaswegian, but whenever he emerged to see her sipping her Italian coffee, smiling brilliantly, he would feel a little smaller.

So he would go drinking. Occasionally with Richard, although the Englishman was too quiet, a little too fond of slow and ironic half-comments to be a satisfying drinking partner. He discovered Andy: a brutalist from Govan who was studying politics, shared some of Gordon's history classes, had a flair for rhetoric.

'It's your duty, you know,' Andy said one afternoon in Bannerman's while they sat over their fourth pints and cast up only the slightest of regrets that they had missed a lecture on the root causes of the First World War. 'This town is full of upper-class bints who thought they were coming here to do art history or English literature, but subliminally want to be shafted by big ugly Scotsmen like ourselves. We're only fulfilling our class obligations.'

It was one of Andy's fixations. His family had expected that Andy would be going to Glasgow University, would be within reach. Instead, he had opted to go forty miles and several worlds east to Edinburgh, lured by an erotic fascination for upper-class Englishwomen.

'Their names are like a taunt,' he would say. 'Like inbred aphrodisiacs. Emma, Charlotte, Sophie, Camilla ... What's that flatmate of yours called?'

'Beatrice, but she's not upper-class.' Gordon was surprised to find himself sounding protective.

'Eminently fuckable, though, wouldn't you say? Have you tried?'

Gordon couldn't even contemplate ever occupying a realm in which the concept of trying might not be utterly ridiculous, so he changed the subject. Andy taught him to drink, taught him to expand the idea of a session in the pub well beyond its accepted Friday night/ Saturday night parameters so that Monday lunchtime required a 'face the week' session, Wednesday afternoons were 'half-day closing,' Thursday nights involved a few games of snooker, and Sunday nights were a chance to 'kiss the weekend goodnight.'

Andy tried to teach him womanising as well, but Gordon was a slow learner. Then, just as he was beginning to pick up a little confidence, Andy had deserted him, softened by the love of a communist from Buckie. Andy gave up his relentless chase of willowy Pimms-sipping Home Counties girl and surrendered to ideology, studying Marxist tracts in order to whisper sweet doctrine into the ear of his disdainful beloved.

Gordon was left with Grainne. In truth, he had adored her from the start, had softened at the sight of that pale skin and red hair, had thought of her as some quiet Gaelic princess out of ancient history. Gordon might have revealed his fondness earlier, but Grainne had been quiet, sensitive, wrapped up in dense volumes about Turgenev or Gogol. When she spoke it was to spin out fantasies about Mother Russia, about the eternal tragedies of a cursed country, while he had tried to inform her about Chernenko, Gorbachev and Shevardnadze and the new reformist streak of *glasnost*. Grainne wasn't interested in the distinction between ideologies. She was hanging around with an ecological crowd, working in the Campaign Coffee shop, seeing imperialism in everything. Romance had never quite sparked.

They would drink vodka together occasionally, on those nights when Richard had dragged a compliant Beatrice off to see some ludicrous band with effeminate haircuts. Then Grainne would knock back her iced spirit with a joyless determination, and its effect was to make her more solemn rather than playful. Gordon would look at her pale sternness and wish himself down the pub with Andy, cracking coarse jokes.

Still, he lived in hope. Towards the end of the first year, Andy had caught Gordon looking at her tenderly in the union bar, had overheard a half-intimate conversation between the two of them. Andy had dragged Gordon to the bar and made him drink another pint, too quickly. 'Don't shag on your own doorstep,' Andy had admonished him in the voice he used for imparting romantic truths along the lines of 'Catholics go like a train,' or 'Crieff is full of lesbians.' 'Gets a bit awkward if you have to dump the bint and she's living in the room next door.'

So he had obeyed, although he had his suspicions that Andy was trying to clear the path for his own attempts at seducing Grainne. She hated Andy, of course, looked straight through his crude jokes, his hectoring banter, his determination to give her lemonade with her vodka.

It was at the end of the second year that Gordon and Grainne finally got together, began to be able make those gentle jokes about always being destined to be a couple. Andy had cut back on the drinking, tried to interest Gordon in the lacunae of student politics, the committee meetings that had muscled in to claim Monday lunchtimes, Wednesday afternoons, Thursday nights.

Gordon wasn't quite ready for that love, although he was progressing there. Instead, he was talking regularly to Grainne

– about Bolshevism, the Soviet empire, about the great snow-blanketed stretch of Old Russia – and she was leaning towards Gordon, looking at him with a new light in her green eyes, a gleam that made him feel occasionally guilty, occasionally unworthy, but more often gave him the glow of anticipation. This was right, he would think; more right than anything else he had ever done before.

It had happened at one of Liam's parties, towards the end of their second year. They both knew that Grainne would spend most of her third year in Russia, that they were short of time if they were going to make a move. Perhaps neither would have had the courage if it hadn't been for the complicated chemical ambience of Liam's parties, occasions where the most unsuited of lovers found each other, where the generous geography of that New Town flat allowed opportunities that would otherwise be slender. Liam prided himself on romantic alchemy, on witnessing the flourishing and flowering of countless affairs. 'Sometimes I think I should just stick a red light in the doorway,' he would say proudly.

That night they were hogging a slim bottle of Stolichnaya, and for once it was flushing Grainne's cheeks, exciting her. Grainne spoke about Russia, about the trepidation that vied with impatience to see the place. Summer stretched in front of her, another daunting three months of trying to avoid family responsibilities.

'I don't know what I'm going to do,' she said. 'I can't face seeing my Dad, and Tobermory gets pretty dull after a week or so.'

Gordon nodded. 'Know what you mean. Glasgow just means hanging around with my brothers, which means a choice of a criminal or an idiot. And this place is just full of tourists all summer.'

They got back onto their favourite subject, delineating the various failings of their family, concluding with what had become a ritual exchange.

'My Dad's an alkie in Partick.'

'My Dad's a bastard in Balerno.'

And they had clinked their tiny glasses, emptied their vodka in quick, hot swigs, and she had smiled at him, smiled with her whole face, her whole body, and Gordon thought fancifully (it was one of Liam's parties and whimsy was encouraged) her whole soul. The Stolichnaya was finished, but something had begun.

Gordon went into the kitchen looking for fresh drinks. Liam slapped him on the back while he was finishing the dregs of a bottle of Bulgarian Cabernet, and grinned at him leeringly. 'Bad idea, old son. Don't want to mix the grape and the Grainne.'

Suddenly Gordon saw it though an outsider's eyes. They were an item, a couple waiting for consummation. He had returned to Grainne, handed her a plastic cup of red wine, waited for it to stain her lips an eastern European shade of purple, and kissed them, tentatively, half-apologetically, but in a way that would brook no misinterpretation.

Grainne leaned forward and he felt the power of her, felt her breasts crushing against him, and realised, exultantly, that there was no turning back. Later still, they agreed to spend a month in August on an Interrail trip round some of Europe's less obvious cities. Gordon realised he would have to stop drinking throughout June and July to save enough money, and he knew it then. This was a love, of sorts.

That August they slept in German railway carriages, lived off black bread and sausages, smiled guiltily at the poverty of Poland, but smiled more selfishly when they realised it meant they could live for days for the zloty equivalent of five pounds. Gordon felt himself turning into a romantic. He lost his faith in dry intellect for an evening. He was lying on a hotel bed in Cracow with a half-empty bottle of Bison Grass vodka at his side, and Grainne stepped into the room in her towel, shivering from a Warsaw Pact shower, goose pimples breaking out over her upper arms. When she dropped the towel, damp strands of hair hung over her breasts, the red not quite long enough, almost reaching the red patch between her legs but falling just short. Gordon felt he could have kept his eyes lingering on that white gap between – that perfect blankness – for an eternity, but Grainne shivered and hopped under the covers, clung to him. He didn't deserve this, he thought, in a rare moment of lucid self-appraisal.

They spent a month weaving chains that could hold them together, compiling a mental scrapbook. Then Grainne went off to Russia, and Gordon came back to Edinburgh looking for something to fill this new-found void, head haunted by the vision in Cracow. Changed.

In third year Grainne had returned for the third term, back from a Russian winter to the remnants of a Scottish one, and nothing had been forgotten, everything remembered. Except she found a new, slimmer Gordon: an enthusiast who babbled of committees and motions and elections and posts and battles that confused her, but she smiled because he had a passion, and they moved into the big double room together. Beatrice and Richard groaned, and warned them not to be 'too bloody couply,' but for once there was no blight on the horizon. Gordon relaxed into a new life: one that offered direction, purpose, love, sex, recognition at last.

Here he was, around the table, sipping his Nicaraguan coffee, and not quite managing to suppress the wince that came with the bitterness in every cup, an acrid taste that familiarity could never soften. Anthony Jeffreys, Conservative Students' representative, laughed out loud, dunking his tea-bag in his cup. At the first meeting of the term, Jeffreys had registered a personal motion recording his determination not to drink the coffee as a gesture of protest against the imposition of Nicaraguan products on the free-market rights of committee members. Gordon occasionally envied him.

A desultory argument was going on between Andy and Karen as to whether Mandela or Biko had made the more decisive contribution to the 'South African revolution.' 'Sure, Biko died and that,' Andy was saying, 'but Nelson would have too, if they'd let him. Except the poor bugger's been locked up on that island for the last twenty-five years.'

'Best place for him,' Jeffreys mumbled, and was shouted down.

'Comrades, I agree with a' that,' Aonghais Og-Urghainn said, 'but do you no think we should look a wee bit closer to home?' Aonghais really wanted to say 'hame,' but they had laughed the last time he had, and he was still a little uneasy in a committee that refused to spell his name the same way twice.

'Please,' Gordon said, and he held a pause for a second to savour the way the word had emerged, the way it had sidled into the debate and made a substantial space for itself. 'It seems to me we already have the Nelson Mandela Union, the Mandela Square, the Steve Biko Peace Garden, and last time I was up Stirling way there was a dirty great monument to William Wallace, although in times of struggle like these I wonder about the wisdom of glorifying divisive nationalists, but…'

And in the midst of a storm of outage from Aonghais, Gordon

continued, 'but in the spirit of plurality, I believe we should support the motion in favour of the Daniel Ortega swimming pool.'

'Yeah, right, except Ortega is a macho misogynist who is probably siphoning half the Soviet cash in Managua into his back pocket,' said Karen, although she seemed to be speaking to herself. Nicotine deprivation had weakened her capacity for righteous argument.

And so it went on. Gordon looked through the union building windows to a grey Edinburgh, to the tower of the arts building, across to the library where he knew Beatrice would be piecing together one of her forensic dissections of Pound or Auden, towards the trees of the Middle Meadow Walk. Gordon remembered that Grainne had told him she had been sitting on the Meadows when she heard the news of her mother's death. Just for a moment, Gordon felt a pang of love for the second most important part of his life.

Forty-five minutes later, after a fruitful discussion on the dangers of the cult of personality, of the pitfalls of exalting individuals ('especially when they're men,' Karen mumbled) and a ten-minute rhetorical cul-de-sac in which Aonghais tried to make a case for the 'Margo MacDonald Water-Sports Facility' until a point of order reminded him they could only discuss short-listed candidates, they came up with a compromise. The Sandinista Swimming Centre it would be, at least until next year's committee had their chance to change all the nomenclature.

'Right. Item two,' Andy said. 'The establishment of a working group to look into the correct wording for a message of solidarity with the People's Republic of North Korea.'

'Oh for fuck's sake,' Jeffreys responded in a delighted aristocratic drawl. Gordon looked over at him and realised that Jeffreys loved all this as much as he did. And he looked round at all of them – at Karen, Aonghais, the pink-faced Liberal whose name he could never remember, at Andy, at Mark McGuire, the tight-lipped Labour Soc convener – and he saw the love in all their eyes, the distinction that brought them here while outside in the Edinburgh rain mere mortals were going to the pub, playing football, heading to classes, frittering time on those ephemeral pursuits outside the oak-panelled corridors of power.

'Could I have a word, Gordon?' McGuire said to him in those characteristically neutral tones, after the meeting. Gordon was surprised. He thought McGuire despised him, thought him a dilettante. McGuire's Labour crew were a dour bunch, oppressed by electoral misery, carrying around a collective futility like zombies enslaved by the voodoo of Margaret Thatcher. 'Let's get a coffee,' McGuire said, and followed up the invitation with a significant look. For a fleeting moment, Gordon wondered if he was being recruited for MI5 or the KGB.

As it turned out, he was being recruited for the Labour Party. 'You're the type we need, Gordon,' McGuire said with a singular lack of enthusiasm. 'We're gradually weeding out all the Trots and the Militants and the tankies and the crazies with beards, but the trouble is, that means half the membership is going down the river. We have to replace them with somebody.'

'And you think I'm the sort of amenable fodder you can persuade to toe the line,' Gordon said.

'It's not like that. It's just we need less … well … windbags. And more pragmatists. Neil is going to reshape the party into a more modern image. We have to start embracing post-industrial realities…'

McGuire continued in this vein for a while, Gordon still smiling at that casual use of the word 'Neil.' He stopped listening, though. Politics for him wasn't about this dreary sort of reasonableness; it was about fiendish Machiavellian plots, about the manipulation of others, the deployment of principles merely as a tactical gambit rather than as a driving force. It was about fun, and the thrill of power, however slight. They were talking to the wrong man. He heard McGuire tailing off with a '…so how about it? You interested?'

'I don't think so, Mark. No offence, but you look like a bunch of losers to me. And at the moment there just doesn't seem to be much point in the Labour Party. Christ, it's not even as if you've got any good-looking women.'

McGuire offered a small snort, and shrugged. He finished his coffee with a grimace and stood up.

'It's a party, Gordon. In the end, everyone needs a party.'

A Party In 1989

The momentous days should be marked by some peculiarity, some distant chiming of significance. Instead they are punctuated by the same ticking of the clocks, the same patter of raindrops on dusty windows, the thick popping of champagne corks, the occasional snort of laughter.

The end of a decade, the decline of the dayglo 80s into the new brown austerity of the 90s was approaching. The slope could be seen, the deep incline pulling them a little nearer to the millennium, the date which they had all separately and privately made the watermark of their middle age. Ten and a half years away, it seemed a distant horizon, shaded with uncertainty. They were in their mid-twenties, a time designed by genetic expedience to allow only the most contemptuous idea of what it would be like to be in your late thirties.

Yet none of them could deny that this event was a staging post of sorts, a formal tallying of adulthood, supposed maturity. Even if it had seemed to take the familiar form of getting drunk and listening to bad pop music.

'Where were you?' Beatrice was asking, stressing each word separately, looking as close as she ever came to being exasperated. The sentence spun across a few feet of space and reached Richard. He was already confused, and wondered whether she was really interested in where he had been, or whether he had missed out on some particular duty that only he could perform. She reached out to a passing waiter, collected a couple of glasses of warm champagne, and passed one to Richard.

'Sorry, sorry, sorry. Only I was out with this band until four in the morning, and I left it a bit late getting ready.'

'You look a disaster,' Beatrice said, but it wasn't entirely true. Richard had found a small serenity, these days. He wasn't quite as susceptible to reproach, not quite as ready to shrink into the background. Richard had begun to patch together a world of his own, a place where he felt comfortable.

Beatrice and Richard had grown closer by knowing each other less well. Richard would disappear into a world of tours, album launches, strange elongated interviews with slick-haired guitarists that stretched over weekends in Amsterdam. Beatrice was lost

100

in nineteenth century letters, the crumpled afterthoughts of late Victorian social realists whose names had failed to ring down a cruelly superficial century. They saw each other about once a month, were always delighted in each other, always at ease. But Richard couldn't be as unnerved by the occasional flicker of Beatrice's gaze, felt that she couldn't quite read his every thought, and smile at its paucity of nuance. Beatrice had heard of his romantic disasters, been encouraging, told him they were all wrong for him. She had offered a few sketches of her own in return, brief glimpses of bedroom melodramas, but her more illuminating passions were for prose, the graceful curve of narrative, and this was more difficult to make amusing.

Richard thought he preferred it this way, although at times he had pangs for a past when he hadn't needed to provide all the detail because Beatrice had known it instinctively. He never asked about her mother, although Beatrice would occasionally mention that she had asked about him.

'It was the wedding of two of your best friends. You could at least have tried to be on time, looking semi-respectable.' Beatrice, though, had softened the reproaches. Richard looked over at Gordon and Grainne, shuffling around to a Phil Collins song about an acrimonious divorce.

'Look, it's fine. I was there, I saw everything – well, I saw them signing the register, and that was really exciting. Anyway, it wasn't as if I was best man or anything.'

'Oh, I see: that's it.' Beatrice was smiling. 'You were just sulking because Gordon picked Andy instead. Come on, I don't think you and Gordon were ever best buddies, were you? And you know what he's like. He'll never miss a chance to smooth his path. You know Andy's an influential face in the Party these days.'

Beatrice said the last few words in the sort of eager drawl Gordon often employed, and Richard laughed, reaching out for a fresh glass of champagne. 'Yeah, I know, and no, I don't care a bit about not being best man. It's just I can't get excited about a wedding. I don't even know why I'm drinking champagne. I hate the stuff. Anyway, how come you managed to get out of the purple satin frock? I thought that was always the deal with the bridesmaids. To humiliate them, just to give the bride something to smile at when she's signing herself into lifelong slavery.'

Beatrice was wearing a grey off-the-shoulder silk dress that managed to be both startlingly elegant and yet subdued enough for her not to be suspected of trying to overshadow the bride.

'I wasn't a bridesmaid, I was a witness,' she said. 'Although that McInnes bloke seems to think we have some duty to snog each other, at least.'

'Yeah, I saw the way he was looking at you in the registry office. Witness. Sounds as if it were a crime. Have I told you what Liam likes best about weddings...?'

This was the last April of the 80s, and if the party had a more subdued air, it might have been down to the fact that Liam had a bit part in the cast rather than directing, and that the presence of Grainne's father and stepmother and Gordon's posse of Glaswegian relations cast a certain pall over proceedings.

Grainne and Gordon were married and, for those few hours after the ceremony and before the ritual send-off to the conjugal bed, they were forced to relive their childhoods. Smart clothes, proud families, dancing and cake were to be suffered, and the two of them were still grinning fixedly in a combination of mania and shock.

'What is it with wedding DJs?' Richard asked. 'Just because it's supposed to be the happiest day of their lives, does he think the couple aren't going to notice that he's playing the worst kind of sententious shit?'

But at that moment, Grainne came up and screamed at them. 'Come on, you two – it's *Dancing Queen*.' They were hauled onto the dance floor, Beatrice shuffling elegantly if distractedly, Richard hauling his feet backwards and forwards, mentally composing a piece for the magazine about the tragic melancholy of cheap music, the misery lurking within the time signatures of a disco rhythm track.

He had made it just in time, stumbling into the registrar's on Victoria Street, lurking at the back behind Liam, who had whispered a genial 'nice fuckin' entrance, Rich.' He had seen it done, watched Grainne and Gordon lean over, heads almost colliding, signing the register, Beatrice following suit with a controlled smile, Andy McInnes signing at the same time, glancing sideways with a complicit grin at Beatrice. 'Not a chance, sunshine,' Richard had thought, dry-mouthed.

He had looked around at the scene, smiled at its familiarity, the

102

looks of tight impatience on the faces of the scrubbed uncles, the sentimentality of the aunts, the thin smiles of the young women who knew they were a mere chorus on this day, the peculiar glares on the faces of Gordon's intimidating brothers. It had all been over in fifteen minutes.

'Love a good wedding, me,' Liam said to him as they headed for the door. 'Puts the women in the mood, and the piss-up is usually free. Normally pull, always get hammered; other people's matrimony is a wonderful thing indeed.'

Then they had stumbled out into brief, moist sunshine on George IV Bridge and milled about aimlessly for a few minutes, being gaped at from the tops of buses heading towards the University. Nobody seemed to know quite what was happening next. Gordon and Grainne looked suddenly sheepish, conspicuous.

They were all young; all trying to deny it. Gordon managed to look about fifteen again, with his tidy haircut, pink face and a smart Burton's suit spotted with dandruff-like confetti. He was being cooed over by his mother and aunties. Grainne, in cream, with a veil and a bouquet of wilting violets, seemed briefly confused, looking around her as if longing for that number 23 bus to carry her away to Tollcross, Brunstfield, Morningside ... over the hills and beyond. Lynne, with the hat and her actress's mother-of-the-bride expression, said something to her, but Grainne's gaze went right though her. Perhaps it was the after-shock, a belated acknowledgement of the significance of those two neat signatures on Edinburgh District Council's ledger, but bride and groom both seemed to need a dose of smelling-salts.

Cars had appeared, carrying the couple and close families down to Queen Street Gardens. The rest had followed down the Mound in an unruly procession, like a peculiarly well-dressed crew of football hooligans, talking loudly and making oncomers cross the road to avoid them. By the time they had arrived at the gardens, Edinburgh's April rain was falling on the bridal party, and Gordon kept gazing skywards as if he could somehow persuade the clouds to briefly let up, give them a respite. Grainne, shivered, her bare arms pimpling in the breeze.

Richard had seen the last few photographs taken: uncles, cousins and infant nieces crowding in, hair flattened by the drizzle, ears reddening in the spring breeze. Richard leaned against a tree and thought of that first year summer, when the four of them had borrowed a key off a friend with a flat on Queen Street, had sat under the trees eating shortbread and drinking sherry. The sherry had been Beatrice's idea. She thought it the stuff of academia, the scent of common-rooms, the oloroso lubricant of learning. It made her girlish, which was remarkable enough: made her crack silly jokes and slap Richard around the neck when he refused to laugh. Five years later he thought, with a surprised smile, that for such a miserable nineteen year-old, he had been remarkably happy that afternoon.

He looked at Grainne and Gordon and was surprised by how unchanged they seemed, even in their costumes of adulthood, looking up in hope with a background of the banks and financial institutions of the capital, promising lives of stern probity, with the sensible fiscal offers broadcast over their Georgian windows.

'Enough photies,' Gordon yelled, lapsing into a forgotten raw Glaswegian for the benefit of his assembled family. 'Let's get stuck intae the bevvy.' The cheers were widespread, Liam's loudest of all. Liam had already smiled alarmingly at Gordon's seventeen year-old cousin Linda, and her father had already started to look murderous.

Then they had found their way to a cheap hall in Broughton Street. Through the week it was used as an Unemployed Workers' Centre, the walls decorated with Marxist slogans, posters advertising left-wing rallies, the language of righteous denunciation gate-crashing their wedding. Gordon's aunties sat nursing their vodka and oranges underneath a mural showing the British police attacking a picket line of striking miners. *Asturias 1935–Orgreave 1985* read the slogan, over a logo of clenched fists bonded and the words *International Workers' Solidarity*.

One of Gordon's uncles stood at the bar, reading from a list he had scrawled on the back of a cigarette packet. 'Hey, hen: three vodka orange, four pints of heavy, a Bacardi and Coke and a Jack Daniels.' Grainne's friend Janice, roped in to help out with the bar, shrugged helplessly as she poured half a pint of froth into a pint glass. 'Fuckin' Edinburgh,' Gordon's uncle murmured with satisfied disgust.

'You made us proud, Grainne dear,' Lynne was saying, holding her step-daughter firmly by the elbow lest she slip away. 'Oh, I had a tear in my eye, didn't I, Petey? You know, Victoria Street, the cream dress ... couldn't help but be reminded, could we?'

'You looked very nice, Grainne,' her father told her in the same tones he had used to ask whether the champagne was French, and the same expression of controlled confirmation he had adopted when he had been told it was Spanish. Grainne hadn't heard Lynne call her father Petey for a long time. She was reminded of how much she hated it. It made him sound like a rich old malt whisky, a rare variety from one of the quieter islands. With a start she realised that this was how Lynne saw him, as a luxury brand, an aromatic old character from the West. Perhaps this is what she had to look forward to. Perhaps marriage was the beginning of the slow erosion of intelligence and discernment.

'Why did they do it, do you know?' Richard asked Beatrice.

'Why does anybody? They were in love, wanted to be together through all eternity, couldn't bear the thought of spending another night apart, wanted to cherish each other in sickness and blah de blah.'

'Mmmm.'

'Or Gordon wants to get on a candidate's shortlist for a winnable constituency in Houghton-Le-Somewhere, and Andy McInnes told him he would improve his chances one hundred percent if he had a fragrant young wife with flashing green eyes and an ample bosom. Although I suspect Andy might have used more proletarian language.'

'Really?'

'Oh, you know Gordon. He needs to have a substantial amount of advice from several informed sources and consult a wide range of opinion polls before he decides what flavour yoghurt to buy. I think he adores her though, all the same.'

'She looks beautiful,' Richard said, quietly.

'Oh yes. She does have a very nice bosom, too,' Beatrice said. 'I really love that word. I think I will make a point of slipping it into every chapter of my thesis. Subliminally, just so the lecherous old external examiner finds himself nodding in approval without quite knowing why.'

'You look beautiful,' Richard said to Grainne half an hour later, and she smiled at him, half-blushing from the compliment and from the champagne. 'How are you feeling?' It was a stupid question, he knew: the sort of line he would never dream of throwing at an interview subject.

'Tired, relieved, bit pissed. Why do we put ourselves through so much ridiculous ritual? Why can't we just sign our names, drink a toast, throw the glass on the floor and walk out?' Grainne had given up most of her notions of being a Russian princess by now, but a few details lingered still.

'I couldn't ever imagine it,' Richard said. 'Any of us getting married.'

'Me neither. You know what I said when Gordon proposed? You know what word just slipped out? *Why?* He asked me to marry him, and I said *why?* He wouldn't talk to me for about twenty minutes after that.'

'Did he ever tell you?'

'He told me he thought women were supposed to know why. He said it was up to men to get to the point where they knew they wanted to marry you, and up to the women to explain all the reasons. He said something about it being one of the few areas where gender responsibilities remained unalterable.'

'Always was a bit of a sloppy romantic, our Gordon.'

They both looked over at him, dancing with his mother, a look of stoical suffering on his face. Looking over her shoulder he caught their eye and gave a long-suffering grimace.

'This is all hell for him,' she said.

'Where's the honeymoon?' Richard asked. 'He told me, only I've forgotten.'

'Cyprus. Cheap.'

'Listen I know, I'm supposed to ask all these grown-up things now. Where's the honeymoon? Are you going to buy a house, or rent for a while? What about your job? Are you going to start a family? All that sort of stuff. But you know, it just wouldn't sound right coming from me, so I'm not going to bother. Is that okay?'

'I know,' Grainne said with a sigh and a smile. 'It's mad, all this.' She was beckoned over by her Aunt Bryony, and squeezed Richard's arm. 'I need some more champagne,' she said. 'I've only had a bottle and a half so far.'

'Andy thinks I'm in with a chance,' Gordon said to Beatrice, after despatching his mother to tell his brothers to go easy on the whisky. 'It's a winnable seat so the shortlist is going to be packed with high-flyers, but my advantage is that I'm the youngest. The last bloke they had was this fat old union bastard who did nothing for years and then lost the seat in '87, so they're looking for someone who's fresh-faced and dynamic.'

'But you think they might still consider you?' Beatrice said. 'Sorry, only teasing. Go on.'

Gordon smiled uneasily. 'Yeah, well, Andy says most of the others are straight out of the Policy Unit, all these Cambridge PPE sorts with steel-rimmed glasses and radical economic theories. And they might not go down too well with all the phlegmy old pit-face types. Whereas, if I play up my proletarian roots, don't use too many long words, I could be the right blend of young and working-class.'

'Young, dumb, with a hint of scum. That's the new face of Labour, is it?' Beatrice asked, gently.

'That's what Andy thinks.'

'Ah, well it must be true.'

'That's what I love about you, Beatrice,' Gordon said, with the boldness of Spanish champagne. 'We can never have a conversation without you taking the piss out of me completely.'

'It's good for you, Gordon. Think of me as a consultant, here to keep you aware of what might otherwise be ridiculous. Once you're MP for Houghton-Le-Fuck-Knows-Where, you can pay me a small retainer for my services, to supplement my meagre academic stipend. Oh, and Gordon?'

'Yeah?'

'You looked so sweet when you were signing the register. I thought I was going to cry.'

'Piss off.' But Gordon was laughing.

There was dancing. The swaying of uncles, balanced by the ballast of a lager can and a cigarette, mouthing choruses, the bored jigging of young women, the self-conscious swaying of aunts dragged away briefly from their involved discussions of family history. Lynne and Grainne's father offered a little half waltz to an Eric Clapton song, and Richard nodded subtly to Beatrice to point them out.

'You know what?' he said, breath hot with champagne bubbles and lager chasers. 'That little scene in itself encapsulates everything I hate about this country. The perfect suburban couple, the skinny bit-on-the-side who has become the respectable second wife, the sleazy middle-management type, doing their little shires shuffle to that old bigot Clapton droning on about the way you look tonight. Is that not the most nauseating thing?'

Beatrice just raised an eyebrow and smiled. 'Oh Richard, I love it when you're vitriolic,' she said, giving him a peck on the cheek to calm him down.

Grainne and Gordon disappeared in a cloud of confetti and drunken, coarse encouragement. The Glaswegian crew piled into their bus for the trip back along the M8, away from the alien temptations of the capital, sending back one of the young cousins to pile a dozen lager cans into a plastic bag for the journey. As they milled about on Broughton Street, waiting for their bus, one of the uncles raised his arm to wave goodbye, forgetting that he had wedged a last bottle of champagne under his elbow. It exploded on the flagstones in a froth of glass and bubbles. He looked down, bereft, and started to laugh, a manic cackle that proved infectious. As the bus pulled up, the raucous laughter of twenty Glaswegians drowned the hiss of the brakes, as dusty champagne ran down the gutter towards the Belle Vue church.

Beatrice and Richard were left with Liam. Liam had lost his seventeen year-old prospect to an over-protective Catholic father, and was consoling himself by pouring the remnants of the empty wine bottles into a pint glass to produce his own personal blend of Rioja, Shiraz and Cabernet Sauvignon, which he sipped contemplatively.

'Nothing quite as sad as the aftermath of a wedding reception,' he said into the stillness. He paused, as Richard and Beatrice looked at him. 'Unless it's the aftermath of a wedding reception where you haven't managed to sort yourself out with a shag. Ah, I'm getting too old. I'm losing it. Time was, I would never let a willing teenager slip away into the night like that.'

There were the wedding pictures lined up on the tables, propped against black and white posters showing gaunt groups of miners' wives. The damp smiles of the bride and groom were brilliant daubs of garish colour against the grey trees of an Edinburgh April. In one, Gordon and Grainne looked through a shower of confetti, mouths open, expressions of vague fear on their faces.

In another, Grainne crouched down, her dress spreading beneath her, looking up at the camera with an expression that blended hope and relief and, in her eyes, provided a green to make the trees sag with envy.

In most of the pictures Gordon seemed stoical, obeying the social imperatives, accepting the camera. In one or two you could see the smile, see on his face the awareness of the occasion, forcing itself into what he thought were the accepted facial patterns. They came out grotesque, as if he had pulled on a mask.

'It's funny,' Beatrice said, looking down at the pictures. 'It must be a trick of wedding photography, but it seems to make everyone appear younger than they really are.'

She was right, except in regard to herself. There at the edge of the pictures Beatrice remained ancient, if ageless, a presence apart from everybody, her sideways smile an offstage gaze of acquisitiveness, her eyes picking out the details, storing them up.

Champagne

Beatrice

'Hey, Beatrice! These are the Nineties,' Jayne Holland-Patrick said, loudly and inaccurately, lighting another Marlboro. 'Listen, I'm sorry about the fags, but I've only got three more days before I give up forever, and I feel like I'm on Death Row, you know. You've finished eating, haven't you?'

Beatrice looked down at the remnants of her salmon salad, and nodded. She let her gaze wander around the pin-striped suits lunching West London Laura Ashley girls, saw the spritzers and the chard and the desperate modernity of the stripped pine, and felt strangely nervous.

'You're very quiet, Beatrice. You're not unhappy about this, are you? It's a pretty good deal for a first-timer, and really they are very keen. There is no way anyone in the publishing industry would make a deal over Christmas unless they were shitting themselves that someone else might get in there first.'

It was December 28 1989, a bright crisp afternoon in Fulham, and Beatrice was being bought lunch by her literary agent. Jayne had brought a contract for Beatrice to sign, confirming that Beatrice's first novel would be published the following spring in paperback original; that she would receive an advance that, while not threatening to change her life, was substantially more than she was earning from teaching George Eliot to undergraduates. Jayne had given her a biro with a chewed end to sign, and Beatrice had written her name, neatly, at the bottom of the page. It already looked like somebody else's.

All in all, she thought, this should be a landmark moment. Jayne, with her lipstick and her hypertension and her worried stare, was right: she should be very happy. Beatrice pushed the lettuce around her plate and wondered why this was such an anti-climax. It was what she had wanted for years, she knew, and yet it seemed unremarkable, another meeting in another voguish restaurant off the King's Road. People said you were supposed to measure your life in these kinds of moments – little breakthroughs where you became someone different. But everything seemed too prosaic, too straightforward.

She had met Jayne twice before. The first time she had wondered whether Jayne's parents had been dyslexic, or merely fond of what they thought was Olde Englishe spelling. She had thought Jayne was what the sketch would look like if you asked someone to do 'literary agent' in one of those modern parlour games that appealed to people reluctant to surrender their childhoods. The second time she had wondered how Jayne kept her blonde hair in such a gravity-defying bouffant crash-helmet without the aid of scaffolding. She had found herself unconsciously echoing Jayne's staccato conversational style, which managed to seem both abrupt and strangely intimate. The third time, Beatrice realised she was growing to like her.

'So how autobiographical is it?' Jayne was saying, leaning forward. 'People like to deny it, but everyone's first book is about themselves. They can't help it. So let's see. Your heroine, Isabella. Academically-inclined girl? That's you all right. Half-Italian? Well, that surname of yours doesn't sound very English, does it? Single? Check, although God only knows how, with that face. Uncovering a sinister conspiracy involving Opus Dei, the Middle Ages and a philosophical Italian hit-man? Is that what you do in your spare time, Beatrice?'

'Well, everybody says write about what you know, don't they?'

'Yes, yes, yes. And look – I think they loved it. I know they loved it. But you know it's a two-book deal, don't you? They usually do that just as an insurance policy. You see, despite all their pontificating, they haven't really got a clue what is going to sell. So just in case you become a surprise bestseller they have to cover themselves. Wouldn't look very good if you sold a hundred thousand and then swanned off elsewhere for a bigger advance. So, what I'm getting around to asking is, are you working on anything else?'

'Yes, actually I am. Very different to the first one.'

'That's good. Do you mind if I tell you something? Not a criticism.'

'Go on.'

'If there was something missing from the first one, well...'

'What?'

'And really it didn't show; not a problem...'

'What?'

'Sex. You see, we have a single girl in her twenties. Now, I might be being cynical here, but I know the reader is going to flick to the inside back page and see that full-bleed author portrait, and that's how they're going to picture their heroine. And they're going to wonder where our Isabella Torcini, academic super-sleuth, wisecracking, smart cookie that she is, gets her fun. It's not a question you ever answer.'

'Well, it wasn't that kind of book.'

'No, it wasn't. Of course it wasn't. But what I'm saying is, it wouldn't be a big disappointment to any of us if the next one *was* that kind of book. Nothing trashy, of course. I think the shopping-and-fucking thing is running out of steam, and your style is a little more elevated anyway. But the truth is that it is the 90s, and publishers, slow little souls that they are, want to catch up with the 80s. They want to be brash and commercial and out there in a shoulder-paddy, big-hair sort-of-way. The new word they all want on the jackets is *provocative*.'

Beatrice made a face.

'Look, don't get all prissy on me. It's a business, in the end. They want you to sell. I want you to sell. Even you want you to sell. Publishers want authors who can be what they are still a bit embarrassed to call "the whole package." Marketing is the buzzword, and because of the wickedly shallow world we live in, it's rather easier to market an extremely attractive – don't blush, darling – girl in her twenties than a gargoyle like Rushdie. So yes, there will be the full-page author picture, and their PR department will try to get you into the right magazines. At first it'll be easy enough to sell the "clever chick with the PhD" angle, but later on they are going to need to get a bit sexier. Oh, look at your poor face. I can see this is not what you want to hear. But don't worry about it. The important thing is getting published. Everything else is detail. And I'll look after you, don't worry about that. Let's have brandies. It's still bloody Christmas after all.'

'Yes, let's,' said Beatrice. 'Oh, and Jayne?'

'Darling?'

'When do I get the money?'

'I love you, Beatrice. You're my kind of girl.'

The afternoon drifted away, Beatrice's mood lightened with her brandy, and Jayne started offering titbits of literary gossip while snow began to fall on Fulham. I'm a writer, Beatrice thought. With a two-book deal. Having lunch with my agent. I can afford to go to a private dentist. Except her teeth were perfect.

Out of superstition and reticence, she had told nobody. She had left her mother's house that morning with vague words about a meeting to do with her work, maybe a quick look round the sales. Her mother hadn't asked any questions, smiling in the watery, weak way that had become her habit.

Christmas had been a mostly joyless affair, her mother over-anxious to please, Beatrice wondering whether the publishers would get around to giving her a decision, and so being too distracted to be fully responsive. They had never quite summoned up the energy to snap at each other, instead sitting in front of the television, dehydrating in the thick heat of the gas fire. Beatrice was surprised to be reminded how silent London could be over Christmas, everyone retreating behind their front doors as if war had broken out. She would look down their suburban street, see the tattered, recycled tinsel in people's windows, know it was the same gilded paper that had been glinting at her all her life, more indestructible than the scattered families behind the doors.

On Christmas Day, Beatrice's mother had made roast goose, and they had smiled at each other across the kitchen table at the surfeit of food for the two of them. Her mother had chilled champagne, and they chinked their glasses together and said 'Happy Christmas' simultaneously, while the Queen's clipped vowels drifted towards them from the television set. 'Awfully greasy, this goose,' Beatrice's mother said. 'Mmm,' Beatrice replied. 'That's something Dickens never mentioned. How much bloody fat there is on a Christmas goose.' Her mother had looked fondly at a daughter who had turned into a fount of literary reference. Beatrice felt guilty and piled Brussels sprouts onto her plate.

They had sat together companionably on the sofa, sharing a box of chocolates, watching *The Sound Of Music*, laughing at the same bits. 'One of your cousins is a nun,' her mother had said, offering up another snippet of information about her Italian family. Each year, another tantalising little fact would emerge. By the time her mother was eighty, Beatrice thought, she would have revealed everything, each revelation gift-wrapped, and handed over at Christmas.

'Are you still heading back to Scotland for New Year?' her mother asked.

'Yes, well there's a party and I said I'd be there and...'

'Of course. They do New Year so much better up there, don't they?' her mother said blandly, and that was it. They drank sherry.

When did her mother start drinking sherry, and why did she have a case of it under the stairs? They watched a repeat of Morecambe and Wise, and Beatrice looked surreptitiously at her mother laughing, glancing at her sidelong. 'I always thought the little one was funnier,' her mother said. It was a sentence delivered every Christmas, and just for a moment Beatrice felt seven again, remembering that Christmas twenty years previously – the first Christmas when it had been just the two of them. Beatrice had always preferred the one in the glasses. No, that wasn't really true: she found neither of them very funny, so she sat, sipped her sherry, watched her mother. Beatrice hadn't seen her for six months. Seeing her smiling, softened by her sherry, the habitual anxiety temporarily forgotten, she seemed very beautiful, and very old. It was nonsense, of course. She was middle-aged and well-preserved, the soft adjectives of the middle-brow newspapers her mother favoured. For the first time, Beatrice found herself wondering whether her mother would remarry.

Beatrice left her the next day, hauled her suitcase onto a packed train at Kings Cross, and stared out the window at a Britain growing colder by increments. It was as if affluence had found a way to keep away ice. Through the Fens and Lincolnshire the fields glistened with dew, whitening only above Newark, taking on the jagged aspect of the north past Doncaster, turning into mud and slush by Newcastle, the black and white local colours.

At Edinburgh, there was snow on the ground and a long queue for taxis, so Beatrice staggered up to the bus stop on Waverley Bridge, revelling briefly in the skyline of a city she had known six years, had allowed to shape her adulthood. In St Giles, the tall thin tenements of the Old Town, the Scott Monument, she read sentences of freedom, escape from a mother, a room, a London that still only seemed to stretch to the paper shop at the end of that suburban street.

'Look at the state of my fridge,' Beatrice said a couple of nights later, swinging open the door. Inside was a slab of dried-up cheese, a strawberry yoghurt, a box of Belgian chocolates that Richard had left her before Christmas, and two bottles of champagne.

'We can drink one of these bottles now, and take the other one round to Liam's. Actually, there's something I haven't told you about. Something to celebrate.'

'Oh, Christ, you're not getting married too, are you?' Richard said quickly.

'No! Why would you say that?'

'Sorry. What is it, then?'

And Beatrice told him about the novel, about Jayne Holland-Patrick, about the two-book deal, about the full-page author portrait. Richard looked back at her with a smile.

'So, what do you think?'

'What do you mean, she spells it with a Y? How do you spell Jane with a Y?'

Beatrice hit him.

'No, it's brilliant.' Richard raised his glass in a toast. 'But you can't expect me to be surprised. We always knew that this is what you would do. It was just a matter of time. But really, it's brilliant. Congratulations.'

'I know, I know,' Beatrice said, prising the foil off the champagne bottle. 'But you know what's strange? I just can't get excited about it.'

'Yeah, but you're probably not used to the idea. Once it sinks in, you'll appreciate it. It's not like it's easy. You know how many first-time manuscripts get rejected?'

Beatrice knew. It was the sort of cold fact she had nursed while waiting for the publisher's decision. She poured champagne into glasses.

'I know you hate this stuff, but drink it anyway. No, it's not that. Or rather – it's more than that. It's something to do with me. I think I'm immune to happiness.'

Richard looked at her, not sure if she was being serious. The words had been delivered in a flippant, matter-of-fact tone, as if she had been telling him her blood group.

'I know, it sounds stupid. But look. Gordon gets a great big grin on his face every time he manages to persuade some branch committee to accept his amendment to the minutes. Grainne is sort of serene every time one of her leaflets helps out some old biddy who's got a complaint about the post office. And you seem to be able to become blissful just hearing some adenoidal American groaning over a totally anti-social racket. What are they called, again?'

'Dinosaur Jr. But those are just passing fancies, aren't they? You must feel the same … I don't know … writing a particularly trenchant critique, or coming up with some snappy dialogue.'

'Snappy dialogue? Listen, Rich, when the bloody book comes out, don't read it. You'll be disappointed. No, but the thing is, with you and Gordon and Grainne, okay, those moments of happiness might be fleeting – but for those instants I can see the look on your face. Even my bloody mother – who would be the big picture in an Observer magazine Miserable Cows' Miserable Cow feature – I was watching her this week, and she was in a state of nirvana watching Ernie Wise trying to sing a song. Didn't last, of course, but for that minute and a half, or whatever, she had buried her eternal melancholy in some bizarre empathic connection with ...'

'Ernie Wise. Right. But what are you saying? You must get satisfaction from something ...'

'Before you even go there. No. With that stupid Scouse bloke I knocked around with when I was in third year. I was never really happy about it. It suited me. It diverted me. It filled my days. It seemed the sort of thing a twenty-two year-old should be doing. But at no moment did I ever pull back the curtains, whistle a merry tune and think 'Fuck, I am so lucky'. I'd have to think for a bit before I could tell you his name, to be honest.

'It's the same with this book thing. You see, I keep telling myself that this is significant, that it's an achievement to be celebrated, that I'm finally doing what I want with my life. But then I think it's just a bit of fun. You know, having lunch with Jayne with the Y, seeing my name in print, seeing that picture of me with moony eyes, doing interviews. I think I'm enjoying it at the same level I enjoy a joke, or a nice meal, or taking the piss out of Gordon.'

'Well, that's good, isn't it? It shows you're being level-headed. After all, very few writers make a great deal of money, do they? From what I've heard it's even worse-paid than being a music critic. And you don't get the opportunity to snort cocaine off naked teenage Thai girls.'

'No, it's more than that. It's as if I'm wrapped up in that polystyrene padding you get in parcels. As if nothing really strong can get through. All I feel is a gentle nudge, a tiny ripple.'

'You sound like some of the musicians I interview. They've done so much coke or smack or crack, or whatever their deal is, that they have to take huge doses just to feel normal.'

'Yes, yes. It's like that. Anaesthetised, I suppose. Except it seems unfair, because I've become desensitised without actually having the overdose in the first place.'

'Is it really such a bad thing? Sounds almost enviable to me.'

'Enviable? Really? But what does it amount to? What I'm saying is simple. Nothing makes me happy.'

Richard looked at her, but she looked back at him bright-eyed, sipped her champagne. She didn't seem distraught. Quite the opposite. She seemed almost satisfied that she had identified such a key aspect of her own character.

'Mmm, that's a shame. Because I was going to suggest we watch the Rikki Fulton Show on BBC Scotland,' he said. 'There's nothing quite like bad parochial comedy at a time like this.'

Beatrice smiled back at him. 'You watch it. I'll phone my Mum, wish her a slightly less than completely miserable New Year, then we'll go to Liam's. You'll have to tell me about those Thai girls.'

'Hasn't happened yet. But the possibility is the only reason I'm still in this game.'

Her mother's phone was engaged, so Beatrice slumped on the sofa, sipped champagne, and asked Richard why the entire Scottish nation should be so enthralled by the sight of an elderly man dressed as an elderly woman.

'Beats me. Perhaps it's some collective delusion that afflicts the rest of the population. Ernie Wise syndrome.'

Beatrice reached into the fridge for the second bottle of champagne. They headed down the hallway, towards the stairs. Richard swung on the banisters. Beatrice looked back into her flat with that customary moment of anxiety, that fleeting thought that she may have left some lethal appliance running, that she could return and find her life altered by mischance. Then she swung the door shut, hearing the satisfying click of the Yale lock fastening itself, slamming on the last of the 80s. They headed off into the crowded Edinburgh night, another party awaiting them, straddling the years and the decades, but otherwise just the same as all the rest.

Next door's cat woke Beatrice up around midday with its piteous mewling, a combination of reproach and sexual yearning, that drowned out the quiet buzz of the kitchen radio. Beatrice drank coffee and orange juice, and only when the unimaginative DJ played *New Year's Day* by U2 did she remember that this was a new decade, the beginning of the last decade of the millennium. Through the champagne hangover she felt strangely optimistic.

It must have been half past twelve when the phone rang, and only a sense of virtuous optimism, a feeling that she wanted to start the 90s properly, made her pick up. The voice at the other end was nervous and formal. 'Miss Morelli?'

'Yup?' Beatrice was surprised by how upbeat she sounded.

'It's Croydon Royal Infirmary here. It's about your mother.'

This time there was no three–second respite. No three seconds in which Beatrice's mind came up with its defence, gave her another world in which she was told her mother had been a bit scared but it had just been a gall-stone twinge and she was feeling a lot better now and they would keep her in for a couple of days, and Beatrice could be at her bedside with a box of chocolates, a bag of grapes and a reproving wave of her finger. Perhaps the last ten years had killed that little bunker of hope in her mind, or perhaps Beatrice just knew her mother better than her father. Before she heard any more words in the receiver, she had seen the jar of pills, the bottle of sherry, the television flickering in the corner, the gas-fire turned up full, the phone taken off the hook. Maybe her mind preferred the neatness of it all, the chronological symmetry. Her family had been unable to make it over the bump at the end of the 60s, her father hadn't been willing to see the end of the 70s, and now her mother had determined that the 90s could do without her.

'... The worst possible news, I'm afraid. There was really nothing we could do. But we are sure she wouldn't have suffered at all. We're really very sorry. This time of year ... There will need to be an inquest, of course.'

'Thank you,' Beatrice heard herself saying: 'thank you' – politeness seeming the only way to end a conversation that had fulfilled its purpose.

She sat in the kitchen, the cat still mewling outside, her hand still resting on the phone as if it was the last viable connection to a living parent. She looked over at the champagne bottle, still a third full of flat wine. Really, she thought to herself, she knew Richard hated champagne. She should at least have made the effort to get some beer in.

Gordon

There was ice on the fields past Dunbar, bright wet sunshine spearing down from over the North Sea. It was one of those December mornings where winter seemed beatable. Gordon ate his bacon sandwich, sipped his coffee, looked out over the edge of Scotland to the sea's horizon, and felt a brief thrill of exultation. He was going places, at a hundred and twenty-five miles per hour on a British Rail express. The eighties were ending, and Gordon, just twenty-six, felt for the first time that his life was on track; that after too much hesitation, too much cowardly delay, he was seizing his chance.

In the seat opposite, Andy McInnes swore and clunked his portable phone heavily on top of his copy of the Times. 'Tried to get Peter, but this bloody thing won't work. Soon as you get above walking speed the bloody signal cuts out. No infrastructure, that's the trouble. This country is so far behind it's unbelievable. Anyway. I thought he might be able to help, but it's no big deal. Peter's very good at those little phrases, *sound-bites,* he calls them; got the word off the American media during the Bush campaign. They're the simple little lines that you slip into the interview to get everyone rigid with excitement. Still, we'll have to do without them. But not to worry, they are going to love you.'

Gordon was heading back to the grim Tyneside town for a second interview in front of the local Labour party's selection committee. The first interview had been little more than a hand-shaking session with some local councillors and a tour of the constituency. It hadn't been the most pleasurable of afternoons. He had looked with concentration and the right expression of concern at high-rises covered in spray-paint, wastelands, empty factories, canals clogged with waste and supermarket trolleys. All of it had reminded him of home. Involuntarily he had said so, and the councillors had looked at him with a certain shrewd regard. He had said a few familiar words about industrial regeneration and they had yawned, so he had talked about football, community spirit, not throwing the values of old socialism away with the outdated ideology. They had smiled. One of them had even put his arm around Gordon's shoulders as he pointed out a huge brick chimney scheduled for demolition. Gordon had done pretty well, and knew it. He had very little desire to come and live in this shabby backwater, but it was a staging post, as Andy and Mark McGuire assured him: a first step. 'Distinctly winnable, as well,' Andy said. 'It was only boundary changes that let the Tory in last time, and we've got every chance next time.'

Gordon looked over at Andy, who had decided against the bacon roll and was sipping a coffee with skimmed milk. Andy looked up inquisitively from his Telegraph.

'Is that Armani?' Gordon asked as the train pulled out of Berwick, leaning forward as Andy self-consciously tugged at the sleeves of his jacket. 'Christ, it is. Fucking Armani. Who do you think you are?'

Andy flared up briefly. 'So what? You think designer suits are just for the Tories, do you? Think the trappings of the free market are not for the proles? We all have to plod round in sackcloth? Listen, sunshine, I bought this as my contribution to the peace dividend, to mark capitalism's bloodless victory over the misguided forces of communism. While those poor buggers are pulling down the Berlin Wall, I am wearing Italian. Besides, we're all Europeans now. Oh, fuck off, it's just a nice suit all right. Peter's got three of them. Even Kinnock's thinking of going bespoke. The days of the boiler-suit and the fag behind the ear are gone. The seventies are as dead as Keir Hardie. Remember that. Remember that this afternoon when you're charming the pants off those sooty-faced old gits.'

Gordon grinned at Andy's obvious discomfiture. 'Armani. You big poof.' Gordon laughed. 'How much did it cost?'

'Don't even think about it. You're in your grotty Burton's number until you get elected. Don't want to push your luck just yet.'

The train rattled on through Northumberland, getting the scenic stretches out of the way before they reached the sort of economic bombsites that, Andy promised, were going to witness the rise of a new, sleeker Labour movement. 'Where there is misery, let us bring a new reality,' Andy said in a mock-Thatcher accent. 'In every dream-home bought off the council, a heartache waiting to be soothed by a softer socialism.'

'You make it sound like we're selling bog roll.'

'It's not that dissimilar. Listen, Gordon, you did fine the first time,' Andy continued, adopting his businesslike tone. 'Kept your eye on the ball, kept it tight at the back, stuck a few in the back of their net, no mistake. But we have to take a subtler approach this time around, okay?'

'How do you mean?' Gordon liked everything to be spelled out in detail, didn't trust himself to be able to improvise. Behind his back, Andy, Mark McGuire, even Beatrice would say 'How do you mean?' in a mocking imitation that each of them, in their different ways, thought was affectionate.

'Well, these people aren't sure what they want, exactly. They feel at home with the horny-handed son of toil, because it's what they've always understood. The previous incumbent was one of them: factory hand who became a shop steward because he was more gifted with his mouth than with a spanner. But the thing to remember is that they realise that they are supposed to be disenchanted with that. They realise those types aren't going to be listened to any more. They know they need a bright young thing with a couple of letters after his name, and the sort of smartness that is going to get noticed in Westminster. When I say they know, I actually mean they've been told, but they have a keen sense of party discipline. Not many of your long-haired Militant beardies up this way.'

'So how do I play it?'

'Not too strong on the prole-ish roots, Gordie. Sure, the occasional oblique reference to having it tough, understanding the problems of a working-class community. But go a little stronger on the thrusting young pragmatist with a sharp streak of ruthlessness, this time. They've had decades of the decent old soul who'll buy the pensioners half a mild down the Working Men's Club. They want to be swept off their feet by the sexy young face of the future. And seeing as he ain't here, Gordie, you'll have to do.'

'You sound like Beatrice.'

'Mmm, Beatrice. Still can't get over her failing to fulfil her duties as bridesmaid at your wedding. I've heard all the rumours about her working her way through the English department, but I'm not convinced. Sure she doesn't play lacrosse for the ladies' team, if you know what I mean?'

'You can be very Old Labour at times, you know, Andy?'

'Yeah, I know. It's a failing, but what can you do? Peter keeps pulling me up about it. *Unreconstructed* is the word he uses. Listen – I'll see if I can get him on the phone again. Seeing as we're in England, the technology might have caught up with the 1980s.' Andy picked up his apparatus, and started pressing keys.

Gordon looked out of the window at a half-demolished Victorian factory and started practising his lines. His lips moved soundlessly as he ran the phrases across a mental monitor: 'Coming to terms with the reality of a service economy,' 'Developing a sense of social inclusiveness,' 'Turning the scrap-heap into a seedbed for the future,' 'Grasping the exciting opportunities of the new technology.'

'Fucking phone,' Andy said, throwing it down with disgust. 'They'll never catch on.'

Two hours later, Gordon was looking around the eight faces on the panel, mentally classifying them into Labour party types. There was the Ruskin College sort, living proof of a little knowledge being a dangerous thing, dying to ask Gordon a couple of questions about French socialist theory. There was the treasurer, an abstract bureaucrat, who appeared to be estimating the price of Gordon's shoes. There were the old union sorts, wanting to be unimpressed. They had calibrated their careers in sardonic snorts, nasal articulations in response to derisory management offers. Gordon thought they would have been more comfortable conducting the interview in bronchial sounds instead of words. There was the constituency secretary, Barbara Green, steely grey eyes looking him up and down, making him feel like a schoolboy again.

'Recently married, I see, Gordon,' she said. 'Is your wife in the Party too?'

'No, she isn't a member. She works for the Citizens Rights Office in Edinburgh.'

Gordon, briefed by Andy, left it at that, although he attempted to convey with a respectful smile that Graínne was on the frontline of the battle for justice for an oppressed underclass, and simply too busy with the struggle to be able to join a political party.

'You've a lot of committee experience; done some time as a researcher,' Barbara Green continued, flicking through her notes. The rest of them nodded, as if they had been ruminating on weighty matters rather than wondering if they could get this over with before the last race from Catterick. She was apparently the voice and brain of the selection panel, the one he had to convince. 'Obviously, our concern is that here you will have to be much more high-profile, will have to lead from the front. We're dealing with a lot of people who have been victims of this government, people at the sharp end of what's happened to industry ...'

125

Blah de bloody blah, Gordon thought, allowing his eyes to wander around the impassive faces of those provincial stalwarts, determined foot-soldiers in the people's cause, the scruffy, pie-fed cannon fodder who kept ploughing up the hill, kept pounding the pavements, stuffing letterboxes, calling the meetings, kept on keeping on. Losers, all of them. He wondered about his own expression, wondered whether his expression of quiet respect was holding firm, or whether that internal grin was beginning to creep onto his lips. Barbara was finishing off.

'... So our candidate will need to have a deep-rooted understanding of these people's experience, be able to relate to what they have gone through, and to address their concerns in their own language. How do you feel about that?'

Gordon swivelled his gaze back to Barbara, held her eyes for a few moments longer than necessary, until they were looking at each other with the uneasy flirtiness of bored marketing conference delegates longing for excitement after three cocktails. 'She's pushing fifty, and she fancies me,' Gordon thought.

He stayed silent for a minute, heart racing with the sheer nerve of that silence. He felt like a performer, on stage, in the spotlight, pushing his sense of timing to the limit of his courage. One or two of the old union boys cleared their throats rheumily. Someone sniffed. Then Gordon began to speak. He lowered his voice, emphasised the Glasgow accent.

'If I may, I'd like to tell you a story about my father,' he began, looking around for a few moments as if seeking permission. They stared back at him. 'My father was a riveter. Worked on the Clyde, in the John Brown's shipyard, which of course, you'll all have heard of. My father wasn't an overly ambitious man. He took pride in his work, though; came home with a bit of a glow about him, in the knowledge that he had made a contribution, however slight, to some of the vessels that would still be knocking around on the high seas for decades to come.'

Vessels sounded a bit pompous. Was he spooning it on too thick, Gordon wondered? But then, looking around, he realised he'd struck the right note, said something resonant about the dignity of labour. They still believed all that shit, he thought with mild surprise.

'In those days, there was a community spirit in the shipyards.

These were tough men, and the work was pretty hard, and the pay not that great, but still there was a sense of it being worthwhile. And there were characters. I tell you, I could write a book full of the stories my Dad told me about the people who worked in Brown's in the 50s and 60s.

'1967, this was. The shipyards were already in serious decline, simply wasn't the global demand any more, and the yards were looking for any excuse to lay people off, and in the meantime they were cutting too many corners. So one afternoon, my Dad's working on a riveting job with his pal Archie Rees, a great wee guy from Dennistoun. My Dad takes one look at Archie and says, 'You cannae work in they boots, Arch; you need steel toecaps.' Arch says the company won't supply them, and told him just to wear leather shoes. Which of course, is against all Safety Regulations...

'So Dad goes off to the foreman, tells him that they can't do the riveting job until Archie has the right equipment, and knowing my Dad, he probably quoted the paragraph from the appropriate act. Either way, he got short shrift, and was told to get on with the job or face the consequences. Now we've got a word in Scotland – don't know if you've ever heard it – *thrawn*. Means stubborn, or that's as close as you can get to it in English. It's a particularly Scottish kind of stubbornness. Either way, my Dad and the foreman go at it for an hour, and meanwhile the supervisor's come over to ask why there's no riveting happening. So Dad explains, quotes the paragraph again, and the supervisor gets a bit peevish and agrees to sort out some boots for Archie.

'So Dad thinks no more of it until the end of the month, and there's the foreman, can't look at him in the eye, and he hands Dad his cards. Now Dad had been working at Brown's for thirteen years. He knew there were redundancies on the way, but he thought he was a long way down the queue. 'This is about that stushie with Archie, entit?' he says. The foreman can't look him in the face, turns away, says, 'No such thing, Rab. It was a lottery; your name came out.' Which was rubbish, of course.

'Dad's sick, naturally enough, but he figures a riveter with thirteen years experience has a better than average chance of getting taken on elsewhere. There aren't so many yards, and not many are hiring, but at each one they just shake their heads as soon as he mentions his name. He finds out later that he's on a blacklist, strictly unofficial of course, but a list of potential troublemakers. No way around it, because there was nothing official to fight. So that's how my Dad never worked in a shipyard again.

'I was only wee at the time, of course, but as I was growing up I'd notice how my Dad would never go past the shipyards, even if it meant taking a half-hour detour out of the way. We'd be on a bus going along by the quayside, and I'd watch him, and he'd turn his head away. Couldn't bear to see where other men might be building ships. I don't want to get dramatic, but I think it killed him inside a little bit, just the simple, easy way they took away his livelihood, just with a word, you know.'

Gordon had allowed his voice to falter a little, to get quieter, so that they had to sit forward in their seats to catch his words. Now he gave them the pause again, longer this time. There were no coughs, no sniffs.

'So, yes, if you ask me, I suppose I can understand what it's like to be in that position.'

Gordon looked around at them, registered the changes in their expressions, saw the reluctant arrival of respect, and knew that he had them. Good job nobody was likely to ascertain that Robert Hendrie was dismissed from John Brown's in 1967 after turning up for the afternoon shift under the influence of six quarter-gills of Bell's and had dropped a white-hot rivet on the boot of his workmate Archie Rees, burning a neat, rivet-shaped hole through Rees's non-regulation boot and searing off the middle toe of his left foot. It was true about Gordon's father being blacklisted, though. Archie held no grudges, still bought Rab the occasional pint, and if he was in the mood, would pull down his sock and show you the brown stump where his middle toe used to be. 'Could have played for Celtic if it weren't for that bastard,' he would cackle.

'But listen,' Gordon continued, 'that's about the past, and the problem in this party is that we've spent too long dwelling on the iniquities of history, however recent, and not looking into the practical demands of the present...' and he was away. He dropped some names, threw in some half-understood theories, arrayed all the phrases into a neat column and pushed them forward like a bloodthirsty marshal. He pulled on the dress of a modernist, but he knew they were still remembering the little naked glimpse of a soul, the brief story they could understand.

Gordon felt it again, that visceral thrill of allowing words to be a lever, to tip them just a little and watch the results. He was glowing. He smiled at Barbara Green, and she positively beamed her approval back at him.

Andy was waiting at the bar in the railway station, nursing his portable phone in one hand and a pint of Guinness in the other. 'I asked if they had champagne, and nearly got decked,' he said loudly. 'I think it is in the bag, my son. I don't know what you said to them in there, but they're tumescent for you, Gordon. Or they want to have your babies.'

'You really think so?' Gordon was flushed with excitement.

'I really think so. Martin the treasurer thinks it is assured; old Davey Richardson gave me a hint of grudging approval, and the lovely Babs told me to be very bloody optimistic.'

'Yeah, well, the interview went well. I laid it on a bit thick, but they seemed to go along with everything I said. You know, it's just like being a salesman, you just have to persuade them that you're giving them everything they need. I started...'

But Andy was smiling complacently.

'What?'

'Look, I'm sure you played a blinder, Gordon, but the truth is we were halfway there before you even stepped in that room. I believe in giving my boy a two-goal start before he runs out of the dressing-room.'

'How do you mean?'

'Thank me, Gordon, for I have gone beyond the call of duty in your cause.'

'What did you do?'

'See that Barbara Green? She may be pushing fifty, but she can't resist a smart-dressed man. A man with an Italian suit, access to some of the party's chief movers and shakers, and a sexual technique that combines modern sensitivity with the robust directness of the labour movement down the century.'

'You didn't?'

'I certainly did. I've been giving her one – no, make that giving her two or three – on odd weekends since the first interview. Actually, it wasn't such a chore, you know. I've always had a thing about older women, and she keeps herself pretty fit. See, the thing about these Geordie women is...'

'I do not fucking believe it,' Gordon said. But looking at Andy, he did.

They drank four pints of Guinness each; Gordon told Andy the story about his father that he'd delivered at the interview. Andy shook his head admiringly, raised his glass, and slurred, 'To the dignity of labour,' and they waddled off to the train.

They continued drinking.

'Oh, you'd better have this back, while I remember.' Andy was rummaging around in his wallet. He pulled out a wedding picture of Gordon and Grainne. It wasn't one of Gordon's favourites. It showed the two of them grinning sweetly, like children from a Victorian fairy-tale, stooping under an archway of arms sprinkling confetti. Grainne was caught in mid-laugh, Gordon in a look of blithe youthfulness.

'I nicked it out of your album while you weren't looking a couple of weeks ago,' Andy said. 'I took it to show Barbara. See, if there's one thing a middle-aged woman appreciates even more than a regular rogering from a young stud like myself, it's the belief that she is about to give a break to a sweet, innocent young couple, with the glint of fresh hope shining out of their eyes. You really should have seen her face when she looked at this. Beautiful, Gordon, beautiful.'

Gordon threw an empty lager can at Andy as the train went into the tunnel above Morpeth, carrying them north at a hundred and twenty-five miles per hour, speeding them on into a new existence.

Grainne

S o now she was Grainne Hendrie. It had a middle-aged ring about
it, she thought, not unhappily. Grainne Hendrie, twenty-four,
wife and mother. Except for the mother bit. That wasn't about to
happen any time in the near future. She looked through the double-
glazing at the affluent young Mums ushering their smartly-dressed
kids into the backs of the estate cars, school lunches packed into
plastic boxes, and felt a vague fear that this might happen to her. It
was something she was supposed to crave, according to what she
read in the magazines. Instead, it brought up a lurching flutter of
apprehension.

Sometimes she wondered how she got here: how she came to
own this coffee-table, this magazine-rack, these polished champagne-
flutes waiting for another celebration. There had been a lot of
celebrations already that year.

Six weeks into the 90s, they had been sitting around the dinner
table back in the flat in Edinburgh, the four of them, just like old
times. Except there was a thick tension in the air because Grainne,
Gordon and Richard simply hadn't known how to talk to Beatrice
without using the soft, anodyne tones they thought proper for
addressing the recently-bereaved.

They had chewed their way through vegetarian lasagne, poured
back Tuscan red with the determination of people wanting to chip
away at the ice in the room. Richard, the most nervous of any of
them, had told them a story of a loutish Edinburgh rock group who
had been in the middle of a photo-session down by the Water of
Leith when they had felt obliged to break off the posing and hurl
sexual innuendo at some passing schoolgirls. The anecdote began
as an amusing diversion, but then Richard had felt constrained to
turn it into an angry lament about the intellectual capacities of the
people he had to deal with. Beatrice had laughed, and then frowned,
obligingly. Grainne had looked at Beatrice carefully, half-hoping
for bags under the eyes, some unhealthy thinness, greasy hair. But
Beatrice had been as serene, as impeccable as ever. The tiramisu
plates sat around the table like embarrassed witnesses.

Grainne had bustled off to the kitchen to make coffee. 'I'm not
drinking it if it's Nicaraguan,' Beatrice called after her cheerily.
Gordon brought the plates through, pulling the kitchen door closed

behind him.

'How do you think it's going?' she asked him.

'Fine. She seems perfectly okay to me.'

'That's what worries me. It can't be normal. It's only been six weeks.'

'Well, obviously, she's either bottling it up, she's in shock, or else she just wasn't that fond of her mother.'

'Gordon.'

'Well, come on, let's not get too bloody sentimental. If your Dad popped his clogs in a freak DIY accent, or mine woke up one morning just in time to feel the twinge of his final liver functions, well we might shed a token tear or two, but by the afternoon I think we'd be down the supermarket frowning over the price of baked beans. Maybe that's what it's like for Beatrice.'

'That's a terrible thing to say.'

'True though. Anyway, even if it's not the case, all you can do in times like these is just be around. Maybe she doesn't want to talk about it. You know her better than I do, but from what I remember, our Beatrice has never been one for spilling her emotions all over the carpet, has she?'

Grainne took the coffee through, Gordon following behind with a bottle of brandy. Grainne poured coffee self-consciously. This was the sort of occasion when she felt so much older. The four of them had shared countless meals before, but previously there had been a level of equality, a desultory squabble about who was doing the washing-up, a few derogatory remarks about the cooking. Now it was all tense smiles, too many 'thank-yous,' the polite passing of the sugar. Grainne felt like a 1950s hostess, looking to impress her husband's business associates. She looked over at Gordon to see if he felt the same, but saw he was unchanged, that marriage hadn't cracked that air of distracted anticipation he habitually wore. He was reading the label of the bottle of Spanish brandy as if it was a breakdown of an opinion poll.

The phone rang about ten o'clock. Gordon grimaced, and picked it up with an irritated sigh. They could only hear his end of the conversation. Beatrice cast a questioning glance at Grainne, mouthed 'Is it ... ?' but Grainne didn't know.

'Yeah. What?

'Fuck. Are you sure?

'No. Fuck. If you're winding me up.

'When did you hear?

'Fuck, and you waited a couple of hours, you bastard.

'Are you sure? No mistake? Absolutely certain?

'I know. Christ.

'Tomorrow? Sure. Fuck.

'Yeah. Sorry man. Thanks. Fucking thanks.

'She's here. Yeah, Beatrice and Richard.

'Fuck.'

He hung up the phone. Grainne looked at him. Beatrice was smiling. Richard looked puzzled. Gordon had turned to them, and this time his face had changed. There was exultation, impatience, near-hysteria there.

'I got it,' he yelled. 'I fucking got it!'

Grainne hugged him. Beatrice, grinning broadly, leaned over and kissed his cheek. Richard laughed and tried a manly clap on the shoulder that was a bit too vigorous, and knocked Gordon slightly off-balance.

'Woo-hoo, you're going to be an MP,' Richard said.

'A candidate. Just a candidate,' Gordon said, trying to sound down-to-earth, but missing by a mile.

'It's brilliant,' Beatrice said. 'I'm so happy for you.'

'Incredible, more like,' Richard added. 'You're twenty-six years old. You can't do this. You only joined their bloody Party a couple of years ago. You're supposed to be pushing leaflets through doors. You're not allowed to be the candidate for a safe seat. Come on.'

'Yeah, except for the boundary changes, and the various bribes the Tories...' and Gordon might have been about to give them a lecture on the political intricacies of his prospective constituency, except that he caught sight of Grainne's warning expression. 'Sorry. Shit. I think we've got some champagne in the fridge. This calls for a celebration.'

'Gordon.'

Grainne looked at him in exasperation, and cast a sidelong glance towards Beatrice. Gordon looked a little awkward.

'Ah, Beatrice, I'm sorry. Didn't think...'

But Beatrice just smiled back. 'Don't be silly, Gordon. It's a big occasion. Of course we should have champagne.'

'Still don't know how you did it,' Richard said, breaking in to try to gloss over any awkwardness. 'Don't they have people who have been in the Party for twenty years and still haven't had a sniff of a winnable constituency? I reckon you must have made some pact with Satan.'

'Yeah, aka Andy McInnes,' Grainne said, softly.

Six months later, Grainne looked out over the flat lawns of her suburban housing estate and wondered what she was doing here. Wondered how easily she had smiled and complied when Gordon had told her they had to move south into this anonymous streak of north-east England, told her they had to pitch camp in what he called 'the locale,' told her they had to woo the community.

She had given up what she thought of as her job, although Beatrice had told her it was her career. Grainne, try as she might, couldn't quite bring herself to feel wronged by that. The Citizens' Rights Office had always seemed another step along from the Campaign Coffee shop, another philanthropic organisation that gave Grainne a dry sense of doing right without ever convincing her it was where she belonged.

She had been recommended for the post by Martin, a Martin who had gradually dropped his Hispanic affectations, had left Begoña for Janice, had set up home in a bungalow in Davidson's Mains. Martin wore a look of defeat or resignation, had become crushed by political realities.

Grainne had looked around her and seen people growing old in quick instalments. Gordon, always desperate to be mature, had started to dress smartly, talk responsibly about pensions and fiscal prudence, and was more irritated than abashed when she laughed at him. Richard's innocence seemed to be turning into a kind of detached cynicism. He had by then retreated from the world with his beloved Sarah, the two of them developing a detached existence of their own, all private jokes and obscure pop references. Only Beatrice seemed unchanged, unbreakable almost, still wiser and smarter than the rest of them, still unfathomable. Grainne found that she could hate Beatrice sometimes. But only when she wasn't there. She could hate the idea of her. But one look from her could melt her heart.

Around her, Grainne saw defeat. Or at least, surrender to unwelcome reality.

The CRO headquarters was full of similar types, the prevailing mood one of futility, of anger eroded into a refined sadness.

When she had started, she had been stirred by a notion that information was power; that she would be on the frontline of a campaign of dissemination, providing facts as weapons against a totalitarian state. Citizens' rights were being infringed every day, she told herself, and it was up to the likes of her to fight every battle.

What she hadn't envisaged was that the battles invariably took the form of guerrilla skirmishes with bureaucracy. Too many of the people coming through the doors had similar tales of lost Giros, of pension books that had been cashed by unscrupulous relatives with a talent for counterfeit signatures, of housing benefit cheques sent to old addresses or confiscated by landlords in lieu of rent arrears, the small print of economic suffering. A regular client was a well-dressed woman from Morningside who claimed that the post-office assistant would make a point of giving her the filthiest pound notes every Thursday in a form of humiliating vendetta.

'What am I supposed to do?' Grainne asked her boss, a wearied Dundonian called Jamie, one afternoon. 'Phone them up and tell them to iron their cash before they hand it out? I don't exactly feel this is the most heinous social injustice going on in this city.'

'Ah, Grainne,' Jamie said with a tired sigh. 'We have to pay attention to the details. Like with the Irish, the revolution starts in the Post Office.'

She had left the job without any pressing regrets. They had promised her freelance work to do at home, which involved writing leaflets instructing claimants how to fill in benefits forms. She looked over at her coffee table, piled high with bureaucratic pamphlets, legal text-books, pink errata forms, and wondered again how she got here. She didn't have the stern moral discipline to be a socialist crusader, couldn't summon up the correct degree of righteousness to make anger work for her.

Instead she re-read Turgenev. She kept a copy of *First Love* in the original Russian, because it was short and bitter-sweet, and because running though its Slavic cadences became a mental work-out, kept her language at a minimal level of fitness. Otherwise she knew it would slip away, knew the declensions and conjugations would skip out of sight over the lush green landscapes of the north-east executive belt. Sometimes she would read a passage aloud to herself, feeling the satisfying thickness of the vowels against her palate, the guttural 'sch' sounds drying her throat. Then she would reach for the green-labelled Moskovskaya, fill a glass with tonic, and kill a cold northern afternoon trying to dream up the dimming astral lights of St. Petersburg.

After two drinks Grainne found she could laugh at herself, could see the comedy in a romantic escapist falling for a youthful marriage to an ambitious, boyish hero, who had taken her all the way to the Crawheaton estate, had given her fitted carpets, and one of those new CD players that Richard's friend Stephen had recommended.

She had been deserted, she would pretend to wail, watching the rain blown in off the North Sea clattering silently against the double-glazing. Really, she should get herself some Valium and find a window cleaner to seduce.

Gordon could commute, whizzing up the A1 to the print company in Dunbar. Grainne had never really known what he did there. Plant manager, he told her once, but had then described his job in terms of its Labour Party identity, as *light-industrial executive, rooted in manufacturing, but with a forward-looking white-collar, stripped-down flexible aspect.* 'It means the bastard never has to get his hands inky,' Andy McInnes said.

She knew him less now, she realised. Certainly she saw less of him than when they were students. Since that phone-call back in Edinburgh, his face had settled into a fixed expression of genial confidence. He had been told he wasn't allowed to show signs of nerves or uncertainty as a prospective parliamentary candidate, and like a method actor living his role every off-camera minute, Gordon brought his breezy optimism home with him. 'We're rebuilding him as the model of a '90s Labour MP,' Andy said, and it took Grainne weeks to realise he wasn't joking. Andy or Mark McGuire would be on the phone constantly, giving Gordon advice, or orders. Gordon kept a notebook by the phone to jot down their instructions. Beatrice would glance at it, try to make sense of notes like 'hair?', 'soften accent,' 'get angry occasionally,' 'look emotional.'

Occasionally it would snap into irritation. He would talk to Grainne seriously about the need for her to 'make inroads into the local left-leaning community,' 'make herself an asset' in areas where Gordon's own influence couldn't reach. She wasn't sure what he meant, although she suspected he was asking her to make friends.

He snapped at her too for her inability to speak to Andy or

Mark McGuire in the right way. He had winced when she had asked Mark how the CND was getting on. Mark had merely looked at her in surprise.

'You know, I remember you running the stall in Fresher's Week,' Grainne said brightly, trying to make conversation. 'All those posters. I nearly joined, you know.'

Mark just looked faintly contemptuous. Gordon had rolled his eyes. 'Ancient history, for fuck's sake, Grainne.'

'No, no,' Mark interrupted. 'It's true. For a while, the unilateral road did seem the best policy. But the world changes, you know, Grainne. You have to adjust to the little seismic forces on the world scene. The Russians stayed in Afghanistan, the Iranians and Iraqis were slugging it out, the Falklands thing had happened, opened a few eyes back here, made us realise some of the priorities for the British voter. Then the Wall came down, Warsaw Pact fell apart, rules of the game changed. You have to move with the times. Multilateral is the word on everyone's lips now, and we've made some real breakthroughs.' Mark smiled at Grainne with a coolness that infuriated her.

'But the nuclear weapons are still there, aren't they? Still pointed at us. What were the words they used to use? Mutually Assured Destruction.'

'Sure, Grainne, but it's more complicated than that. A lot of the people in CND were well-meaning, nice people, but then a lot of them were the sort of agitators and propagandists who have turned out to be the real enemy. They were the ones who stopped us having any chance of a Labour government.'

'Grainne,' Gordon said, with exasperated pointedness. 'This is all old stuff. Try to keep up, will you?'

With Andy McInnes, she simply found it impossible to go along with his banter. She looked at his round, rubicund face and saw the stuff of golf-club lunches, company directorships, the easy camaraderie of the gin and tonic set. Andy would try to be flirtatious. The words he used wouldn't be too different from the ones Liam would employ, but somehow Liam could spin them with charm, and an ironic shrug. There was a meanness about Andy's lips that disturbed her. 'Gordon's been looking a little bleary-eyed lately,' Andy would say. 'Been making unnatural demands on him again, have we, Grainne? I know you're still crazy about each other and all that sickly stuff, but go easy on him, will you, darling?' He would laugh hollowly, leer a little, and Grainne would have to hurry out of the room.

There were other changes. Gordon would get back from a meeting around eleven some nights, find her half-watching Newsnight, trying to get a grasp on the economy so she could join in his abstract conversations. He would look at her sideways, stare at her for a while, then if she turned and looked back he would smile and come and sit by her, kiss her softly.

One night he came back after a few drinks in the pub, watched her for a while, then smiled to himself. 'Grainne,' he said speculatively. 'What do you think of rubber?'

She wondered briefly it was an economic question, whether Malaysian civil war had ripped into the world latex supply. But there was a gleam in his eye.

'How do you mean?' she said.

'Rubber. Black rubber. Only I think you'd look really good in a rubber dress. You've got the figure for it.'

She laughed, but she knew he wasn't joking. Gordon didn't joke any more. Or if he did it was in a bitter, sarcastic way, the sort of jokes that only amused himself.

'Let's be adventurous,' he said, and he smiled at her, and maybe because she had drunk four glasses of Moskovskaya before he got in she nodded, laughed in a way that was easy to interpret as agreement. She would think back to that moment for years afterwards, wonder at that tiny inclination of the head that had meant so much. Language wasn't enough, the 'shs' and 'yos' of Slavic could never be quite as sad as a simple nod.

They had been married for eighteen months. Up until then there had been sadness, boredom, a little frustration, but nothing remarkable. Grainne, the sensible Grainne who still battled with the green-eyed, vodka-drinking Slav, told herself that this was a period of adjustment; that she just needed to define a role for herself. She was in a new, unpromising town, trying to adjust to a new world. Gordon had exciting matters to occupy his time.

Now, as she stood there sheathed in black latex in her suburban dining-room in the November of 1990, she realised that she had become just another exciting diversion to occupy her husband's time. She saw the look on his face, and it was nearly the same look he had when he came back from one of his successful political coups. He looked like a little boy about to devour his birthday cake. Grainne creaked and squeaked and waddled over. He said, in a parody of awe, 'fuck,' and the profanity should have been enough for her to realise that she had wandered into a dangerous country. But Grainne was still hoping; Grainne still wanted to believe.

It had taken her half an hour to get into the black rubber dress. It had arrived in the post that morning, and she hadn't wanted to ask Gordon how he knew where to send off for these kinds of things.

Now she felt it pulling her flesh around, chafing under her breasts, making her thighs sweat, puckering around her bottom. She looked at Gordon and realised a threshold had been crossed. Now it wasn't about sadness, about boredom, about loneliness or frustration. It had turned into something as black at the thick, semi-matt coating of that dress. Marital misery already smelled of the sickly artificial roses of talcum powder, the acrid adultness of black rubber.

Bent forward awkwardly over that respectable coffee table, Grainne made a slow tally of the various kinds of discomfort. The tight rubber was pushed up over the tops of her thighs rolled into a thick coil around her hips. She briefly pondered the irony of having been a teenager obsessed with having a spare tyre, only to become a housewife with a thick Michelin expanse of black rubber around her middle, bent over to please a husband who was thrusting into her with the youthful energy of a man who had discovered passion a little late in life. She wondered whether this was just the inevitable fear of the first time, whether she would grow to relish the kinkiness of it all, to share the obvious excitement Gordon was feeling. But for now she felt ridiculous, hot, in pain, violated.

Grainne stared through the couple of inches gap in the curtains, looked over the neat lawns, the discreet drying areas, the new cars parked tidily, the little flicker of dimmer-switch lighting around their cul-de-sac, the subdued buzz of televisions.

So this was what people did in the suburbs, she thought. And just for a second she had a bleak vision of Balerno, of her father in a mask, Lynne in black leather, the kitchen table rocking with their carnal frenzy. The image was so vivid that Grainne couldn't help but groan, and Gordon laughed. 'Great, isn't it? We should have done this ages ago,' he panted, pushing himself forward inexorably, clutching hands slipping on damp rubber.

Richard

I t's not her story. That belongs elsewhere, perhaps told by Richard himself, although she probably deserves a more dispassionate chronicler. All that matters is that she appeared, sometime in the winter of 1989, and things changed for him forever.

If you asked them separately how they would have described Sarah, you would have seen different reactions flickering across their faces. With Gordon, you would have watched the hesitation, seen the little smile – an attempt at man-of-the-worldliness – drifting into a rueful grin, while his mind pondered whether he would kick her out of bed or not, and quickly returned the obligatory 'or not.' Then he would say, 'posh.'

With Grainne, you would see the softening of the face to show that she liked her, a little thoughtfulness to suggest that she didn't know her, a little doubtfulness to hint that not knowing her was to be regretted. Then she would say, 'posh.'

Beatrice would seem slightly irritated, as if Sarah was a question she was still getting to grips with, and was finding it difficult to unearth the original source material. There might be a tiny hint of asperity that Sarah had stolen away some of the intimacy she had taken for granted from Richard. Then there would be a pleased smile as Beatrice found the word she needed to keep you at bay until she had a more rounded description to hand. Then she would say, 'posh.'

But, Richard would insist, they didn't know her. Long after Sarah had disappeared into the ether, Richard would swear they had never really known her, that she was unknowable. That was about preserving a vacuum where he could store his own theories. For Richard she was lethal, and by that last New Year party of the 80s, he was set on the path to his doom.

Leaving Beatrice in Liam's enthusiastic arms at the front door, he had shuffled along the hallway, eyes searching the shadows until he had seen her smiling out at him from the kitchen, tall, serene, with winter-black hair, slightly flushed cheeks, brown eyes glinting with a breathtaking happiness at seeing him. There was a space around her, as if her aura had been impenetrable until he arrived. 'That's her, then?' Beatrice said steadily at his shoulder. 'She looks like a Jane Austen heroine. One of the early ones, before they got all virtuous.' REM were playing *The One I Love*, and Richard winced at the brief, cloying perfection of the moment, enjoying the idea of his life being paced by big American chords.

They lost him for a while after that. Lost him to a compelling story of his own, as he spent a blithe Edinburgh winter kissing under bridges, lying on chaise-longues, looking out at minatory Lothian skies, understanding the meaning of French films, learning to appreciate the mysterious eroticism of Sarah's polo-neck sweaters.

Richard learnt a new language. Until then he had only known the basic vocabulary, absorbed from his music: the lexicon of romantic attachment. Until then he thought he could appreciate those swooning lyrical constructions, professions of adoration bursting out over artfully muddied guitars. But until he knew Sarah, he realised he hadn't ever understood the sweep of their intentions. She was his Rosetta Stone, the key to what all those references to love really meant.

Then fluency arrived. In bad Chinese restaurants, on wet park-benches, in cinemas and bus queues – all those lyrics came to him, now colourised, revealed in all their human glory, the perfect frailties of the world becoming apparent at last. He felt as if he had been allowed through a secret portal, could look on the rest of the world with the condescending pity of the enlightened.

He started to appreciate the art of detail. He could find himself losing himself in tiny aspects of Sarah: the folding of her skirt, her bitten nails, the plain brown Englishness of her shoes, the way her words would trip her up when she wanted to tell a funny story. There was a hidden language there, too, in the strange resonances of fabric, the troubling shift of a bare wrist, the blink of an eye.

When he was with her, there were moments when just the flow of that black hair would seem almost unbearably intense, a tiny piece of intimate theatre that made him realise why artists had to paint, write and sing about these secret glories. Richard would have to take deep breaths, laughing at his own weakness, exulting in it.

With Sarah he had plunged into an abyss of longing, a fierce love that went beyond words. He recognised only a little of it as familiar: he knew he had felt the beginnings of something similar with Beatrice, but that had been a long time ago, when he was too young and too fearful, and he had drawn back from the edge. Now he had plummeted, was lost, was still falling.

She was two years younger than him, two years that made him think with an irrational tenderness of the two years he had spent alive without her. He felt a sense of his own ridiculousness, but that didn't stop him mentally translating everything into French, smiling at the rain, hugging himself every morning with the anticipation of seeing her.

'It makes you sick, doesn't it?' Liam said to Beatrice that New Year, pointing them out in the corner of the room, their body language building a wall of intimacy against the outside world. 'Just because they're getting it regular, they think they are the chosen people.'

'I think it's sweet,' said Beatrice, who didn't understand then, but would.

Richard knew he had changed, knew that the suspicious, tough exterior had been pulverised, that he could no longer pull on his misanthropy with his black leather jacket in the mornings. That blitheness meant he found it very difficult to be around Beatrice at that time, although she needed his support. It was simply impossible to hold a suitably sombre expression for any length of time, because Sarah was floating around the forefront of his mind the whole time.

Being with Beatrice made him think of her mother, brought a guilty nausea swimming up. He saw her clearly as she had been on that night, opening her dressing-gown, ushering him forward, smiling at him with what the imagination of hindsight insisted was madness. What was worse was that one of the first things he had felt when Beatrice told him the news was a swift flush of selfish relief, a realisation that now Beatrice would never know. This had horrified him, given him a brief glimpse of his own suppressed depravity. Then he had realised he was wrong anyway. He knew about it, and so there was nothing to stop Beatrice finding out. If the information was out in the world, Beatrice could find out. One look into his eyes at the right moment would have done it.

'What's got into you, Rich?' the editor of the music magazine Richard wrote for asked one icy morning in February. Richard had drifted into the office to pick up some new albums for review. He had stood around in his usual aimless fashion, browsing through the back issues, but this time he hadn't felt inferior, self-conscious. He could feel the smile on his face, impossible to remove.

'How do you mean?'

'Well, something's changed. We're used to an acerbic, miserable bastard who tends to write off most of the stuff we give him as indulgent pap, and yet the last three albums all got four stars. Which is fine, except that one of them was by an American with a beard. Not going soft on us are you, Richard?'

'Hey, it wasn't a bad record. Maybe my tastes are just becoming a little more catholic. Don't want to be too predictable, do we?'

The editor looked at him suspiciously. 'Listen, there's a trip happening next week if you're interested. Brussels. Dave was going to do it, but he's just got back from a three-day speed frenzy and his paranoia is at an unacceptable level. Three-page feature, and the record company's paying, so the hotel should be decent.'

The magazine was struggling, and the collective mood in the office was one of bemusement that it had staggered into the 90s still solvent. They were on a slow learning curve where the final lesson was that you couldn't make a profit from a Scottish music magazine. Most of the work was done by freelances like Richard, who were paid very little in the way of cash, but on the last Thursday of every month were invited out for a drunken lunch by the editor. Afterwards they were brought back to the office and told to help themselves to the piles of unheard records, unread books, unseen videos that spilled out under the reviews editor's desk. By selling these in second-hand shops, they could convince themselves they were making an acceptable living.

It was unusual for Richard to be given a foreign trip. He would get the occasional train ticket to London to do an interview or attend a showcase. He had been to Dublin once to interview a folk-singer who was threatening to become a crossover success. Otherwise, he spent a lot of his evenings in Glasgow watching Govan kids who wanted desperately to come from New Jersey.

For a while it had seemed the only occupation imaginable, a tiny crumb of bohemia well away from the frightening adult vistas of real work. Now he looked around the office and realised how ridiculous he had been. On everyone's face was that look of supercilious hipdom, the critical mien chosen in your early twenties that is supposed to denote a kind of generous scepticism, a wariness. A couple of people working there were into their thirties, and Richard wondered about the little tragedies of their lives, about the spare rooms stocked with 'classic' albums, about their grumbling concerns over the real interpretation of Astral Weeks. He knew then that this would have to stop, and soon. He felt the exhilarating fear of someone who had made the decision to leave their cocoon. It didn't matter, though. None of it mattered. He had Sarah.

'You're on a Sabena flight out of Heathrow on Monday afternoon,' the editor was saying. 'Which means you can get the train down to London Monday morning, save us some cash, get yourself a nice cheese sandwich and a cup of tea.'

'Okay, fine.'

'And Richard? Could you review the new Siouxsie and the Banshees for us? It's the same as all the others, so perhaps you could find it in you to rediscover your critical faculties. We've been wondering what's wrong with you. Dave thinks you've discovered a source of high-concentration MDMA, and feel mellow towards everybody. I wondered if you'd come out to your parents over Christmas and they're being very supportive. Angie thinks you must be in love.'

Richard smiled and then tried to recapture that elusive critical gaze, the nihilist-with-a-typewriter mystique they all craved. Nobody noticed. The editor was on the phone trying to charm guest list tickets out of a PR girl in London. Angie, the picture editor, was sorting through colour transparencies of Annie Lennox, and Dave was treating his amphetamine-anxiety with cups of strong black coffee and trying to dispel a nightmare (later to come true in every detail) that he would end up doing the 'Set The Video' slot in the local evening newspaper's TV listings section.

Five days later, Richard was in Brussels wondering how such a provincial-looking city became the polyglot capital of the new Europe. For a couple of hours before the interview, he wandered out from his hotel near Berlaymont and marvelled at the way the Belgians would order their window displays like nineteenth century military reviews, serried ranks of chocolates and truffles in their geometrically-precise formations, craving his approval. In those few, precious months of first love, he found an infinite sorrow in the emptiness of others' lives compared to his own exalted existence with Sarah. He almost wept at the thought of a plump Flemish bourgeoise furrowing her brow because her truffes de champagne wouldn't sit straight.

He saw them, and thought fleetingly of the chocolates he had bought for Beatrice at Christmas, remembered them sitting in her fridge on New Year's Eve. 'I'm saving them for when I'm feeling miserable,' she had said. Richard wondered if they were still there, lurking behind the cheese, not quite up to the job.

The interview was with a middle-ranking, middle-aged singer-songwriter who was just relaunching his career with an album that would be successful enough for him to afford the sort of lawyers who could erase his name from such tangential stories as Richard's. He wasn't the one with the well-publicised penchant for Tantric sex. He wasn't the one with the supermodel wife.

'You see,' he told Richard, in his suite in a hotel that was chic enough not to be part of an international chain, 'what's great is that I've no idea what Tantric sex is, and I don't have a supermodel wife, unlike some of my contemporaries. If I did, I don't think I'd have ever got around to writing these kinds of songs.'

The voice was teasingly mid-Atlantic, with just a few raw traces of the provincial English town that has its anonymity protected by a subsidiary clause of the singer's lawyers. Richard preferred to interview the middle-aged artists. They tended to speak in sentences rather than declamations; they had a certain fluency in wryness, perspective and insight rather than the jamboree bag of spite, arrogance and superciliousness he would get from bands releasing their first single, bellowing their rage from a rehearsal studio under railway arches.

The established performers also had hotel suites, discreet PR women called Barbara, champagne in an ice-bucket, a silver salver of oysters on a bed of crushed ice. Richard hated champagne and abhorred oysters, but he gulped his glass of fizz down, sipped at an oyster, just to make it apparent that he was as blasé about these sorts of details as the singer and his publicist.

'The record seems to take a somewhat bleak perspective on sex and relationships,' Richard said with what he thought was a man-of-the-world raised eyebrow. Richard said 'reckid' in the sort of sub-ironic half-American way he always did, a personal quirk that he had developed because he hated saying 'album' and because 'LP' made him sound like his mother. He worried briefly that the singer might think he was taking the piss out of his accent.

But the singer was crinkling his blue eyes, looking out towards the full-length window, and cracking a well-rehearsed rueful grin.

'Richard, I'm not going to go into all the sordid details...'

That was a shame, Richard thought, because all the sordid details were exactly what his editor would have preferred.

'I'm sure you've read all the cuttings, all the stuff about the divorce, the lawsuit in America. Jesus, those American lawyers are assholes.' With brilliant inconsistency the accent tried to get more English to attack the Americans, but ended with a very Californian 'assholes.' This is why these people become stars, Richard thought: they have no sense of their own ridiculousness.

'The bottom line, as I believe I put it in the opening track, side one as we used to say, is that love fades, love dies, all the promises turn into lies. Jaunty tune right enough, but with the words I was trying to write an anti-love song. Not a heartbreak song, not an 'Oh Christ the bitch has left me' song: just a spot of realism to try to counter all the "moon in June" stuff that's out there. Be a darling, Babs, and fetch us another Moet.'

With the sun coming in through the polished window-panes, the singer sank back on his sofa and took on the aspect of a traveller spinning tales of his exotic wanderings. He started off a little abashed, throwing in self-deprecating qualifications, but with each glass of champagne he grew more confident, more expansive. Richard glanced at his tape recorder to make sure it was still rolling. This was working out better than he had expected.

'That song *Natasha*. Want me to tell you what that's about?'

'Please.'

'My first love.'

'This was back in...'

'Well, yes and no. It was a bit of a long-distance affair. I was there, but she was in Moscow most of the time. And in the nineteenth century. And in a work of fiction.'

'Ah, *War and Peace*.'

'Yep. I was a pretentious kid when I was fourteen. And I fell in love with the idea of Natasha Rostov. You know: that innocence, that transcendent spirituality. You could tell Tolstoy fancied the fur-trimmed pants off her, but he wanted to make her untouchable. Now I've read all the feminist treatises – or rather my last wife summarised them for me – and I realise that Natasha is some idealised male fantasy of the eroticised virgin or whatever, but hey, when you're fourteen, these things can leave a lasting impression.

I fell in love with Natasha, and the real thing never quite lived up to my imagination. But that's art's job. To surpass reality.'

'In the song you say you've been searching for her all your life, but you know she'll never look the same again.'

'That's not just Natasha, that's any woman you love and lose because of your own failings. That's what's great about being – hey, Babs, what's my official age?'

'Forty-six,' the publicist said, grinning at Richard and opening another bottle of champagne. 'He's just kidding. That's his real age. At least I think it is.'

'Just put that I am ageless. Anyway, that's what is great about this time of life, that sense of being able to look back and peruse your personal history as if it were a library. See, on the record before this one I was trying to sound like I was still an eager young blade, and it didn't seem very convincing, as all you bastards made a point of telling me in the reviews. So with this one, I wanted to view all that early action from a more mature perspective, try and be an adult about it. Which surprisingly few of us ever do.

'You know, they say that you never forget the first time. That's not true. I forget how I lost my virginity. I know I was fifteen; I was doing a lot of purple hearts, hanging around on the Mod scene. *Four-eyes* they called me, because I had these big black National Health specs. I'm pretty sure it happened on the seafront at Scarborough. But I can't remember the girl's name. I was trying to write a song about it, and I couldn't remember her name. I panicked for a while, thought this was some terrible failing, some indication of my shallowness. Then I thought about first love, about the girl who had made a lasting impression on me, and that's how I came up with Natasha.

'That's what you think about when you look back. The Natashas that never quite existed, because all the smiling, innocent, black-eyed beauties turned out to be dull, grasping hags who just want a percentage of what you're worth.

'You see, Richard,' he went on – and it was apparent that the singer was no longer interested in waiting for the questions – 'love affairs won't stand still. You can't keep them stalled at that moment where everything is great. It's like this bottle of champagne. First couple of glasses and it goes to your head, and you're up there on the clouds and nothing can stop you. Then you either stop, in which case you begin to feel just a little bit shit, or you carry on and the stuff starts to taste sour, and you're sick of it, want to move on to the brandies. That sounds almost profound to me, but I suspect countless other bastards have done the flat champagne metaphor. Seem to remember a Sinatra song – what was that called, Barbara?'

She ignored him.

'The thing is, after a little while, you get fatalistic. You are suspicious of being in love. Start trying to fuck up your own happiness. So even if you've got a lovely lady, you're still convinced that it's doomed. You start looking for her replacement before things have started going wrong. Which of course means that things start to go wrong. That's what one of the new songs is about.'

'Self-Fulfilling Prophecy.'

'Yeah, crap title I know. Don't know what I was thinking of. But, Robert –'

'Richard.'

'Yeah, sorry. A word of advice. Try to get them before they're twenty. Seventeen or eighteen ideally, before they've really got minds of their own. When they're still bright-eyed little Natashas, looking up at the stars and believing in a holy redeemer in leather trousers. Then you've got a chance. Straight out of school...'

'I think that's time up, Richard,' Barbara said swiftly, moving forward to switch off the tape-recorder. 'Thanks for coming. I'll be in touch.'

Richard looked back from the door. The singer was upending the champagne bottle, refusing to believe that it could be empty.

A Party In 1992

I t was the end of an era. They knew it, because Liam went around moaning 'It's the end of an era.' Alternatively, he would groan 'Feels like Napoleon's retreat from Moscow.'

Liam was leaving Edinburgh. Around the walls of the New Town flat the boxes were piled high, packed full of books, videos of surprisingly visceral horror films, notes for unformed lectures and the not-entirely-clean clothes that made up Liam's possessions. Unworldly possessions perhaps, because none of it had any practical application, and it might have been better to have burned the clothes on one of his ill-disciplined bonfires in the scrap of garden behind the kitchen.

Such an occasion had to be marked in the only way possible. So, once more, Liam, accompanied by third-generation flatmates, tripped down to the supermarket, there to load up the trolley with beer.

These were the 90s, and the beer on offer had multiplied at a similar rate to the states breaking off from the old Soviet Union. From nostalgia, Liam piled in the yellow Tennents cans and the blue McEwans. But the beer world was a pluralist affair, so jostling for attention were the tall bottles of real Budweiser from the Czech Republic, the voguish Mexican Sol (Liam knew people who would shove wedges of lime into the necks, that's how tolerant he was), French Kronenbourg, and the slabs of Hofmeister offering twelve and a half percent extra. More beer was a concept that appealed to Liam's uncomplicated aesthetic. He took two trolleys. The final party deserved a little extra commitment.

As the party edged its way towards a beginning, Liam looked around like the worst kind of theatrical showman, sighed, wiped away an imaginary tear. 'I can't believe this is happening. I feel like a pioneer loading up a wagon and heading west to bring learning and civilisation to an untamed township,' he told Richard.

'You're hiring an Arnold Clark mini-van to drive to a flat in Langside and teach Modern Literature at Glasgow Uni,' Richard said. 'Only you could try to romanticise that.'

The party was a farewell to Edinburgh, the formal closure of Liam's scene. For a few days it was planned in addition as a more significant celebration, a less affectionate adieu to Conservative government. For a few days there had been a nervous gleam in all their eyes, a tiny flicker of hope. Faith had smouldered longer than it should have.

'Exit polls aren't looking good,' Liam's girlfriend Sally had told Richard and Beatrice as they arrived around eleven. Sally's pinched face was twitching in frustration. She had a dedication to the Labour Party cause, a fondness for psephological detail that made Richard and Beatrice wonder, separately, what Liam saw in her.

What he saw was dogged persistence. Sally had stolen into his affections and refused to be discarded. Seeing the fate of so many of his dalliances, Sally had bitten deep and held on while he tried his gentle avoidance tactics. Simply by continuous contiguity she had worn him down, seen off any number of possible successors, established herself in that most unlikely of roles: Liam's steady girlfriend.

Sally followed Liam around issuing quiet orders. His face was a study in defeat. The beers went into the fridge, the potatoes went into the oven, the cans of tuna were opened, but under observation he performed all the tasks without verve, watched over by Sally, who smiled, nodded her head in a barely perceptible acknowledgement of her power. Liam's friends looked at her with respect. She had turned out to be the mighty lever who could shift Liam from his splendid torpor, move him out of the grazing lands of his Edinburgh estate. Occasionally she would go over and pat him affectionately, and friends would look away, ashamed of his humbling.

Sally was just one of the more obvious symptoms. Change had crept down Dublin Street, taken a turn, skipped down the steps, stamped its boots on the step, left its contribution on the table, and set about demolishing the fragile politics of Liam's parties. Faces had changed, the last decade had carried a few away with the tide, their replacements substandard, too young, or simply too 1990s. Liam hadn't been ready for the earnestness of the new decade, hadn't been prepared to see so many of his circle get married, find steady jobs, give up seven-day drinking, find sensible hairstyles, wash every day. He had swum against that tide for a couple of years, but now it was sweeping him up and away. Although, in his good moments, with a few cans and some Canadian whisky on board, he could pretend he was surfing. In the bad moments, he would look around at the callow faces who populated his parties, and wonder where all the real people went.

Patrick, of course, went back to Scandinavia to start a radical and influential new school of film that combined uncompromising realism with a painterly eye for the blankly erotic. He is more famous than any of them, except perhaps Beatrice.

Lleyton was rocking himself backwards and forwards in what is euphemistically called a sanatorium, occasionally sending letters to the University in which his imminent return to work is announced in cut-up form between lengthy quotations from early Van Morrison albums.

Belinda ran off with a heroin dealer who supplied her with enough free samples to make her less resistant when he suggested that she work a Saturday shift picking up clients on one of the darker junctions near Leith Docks. Gary, unamused by this development, took upon himself the sole responsibility of drinking the case of Superbock, sentimentally holding the bottle up to the light before sinking it methodically. He was supposed to be here tonight, but had collapsed in someone's kitchen in Warsaw, or perhaps Wishaw, and wasn't aware of the identity of the new government until six days later.

The American Eliot expert is here, her quietly Anglicised voice making polite points, her eyes flickering regularly and adoringly over her girlfriend Mel, a struggling poet who is working on a collection about the innocence of children. Liam says they are the staidest, most conservative couple he knows.

The Germans are still here, although they may be different Germans. They have found each other again, are sipping lukewarm Becks, are swapping bolted-together compound nouns in sad, fluid sentences. They may of course be exchanging bitterly sarcastic putdowns of Liam's latest, last party, but their faces look too innocently pleased for that. They may be merely discussing their enthusiasm for pipe music. The German soul has a strange affinity for all that is Celtic.

Gordon, of course, is not here. He has a better place to be, and Grainne is the wife by his side. Richard and Beatrice, though, have turned up together, and might be the leading candidates for the party's most popular guests.

Beatrice was being besieged by Mel, the bright-eyed poetess, who was telling Beatrice how much she adored the new novel. It is not an original reaction. In three months *Bosom* had sold upwards of ten thousand copies, which, as Jayne Holland-Patrick assured her in the relaxed tones of a woman whose ten percent now meant something, was 'fucking phenomenal for literature.'

'I loved that scene in Siena, just so romantic,' Mel was enthusing. 'I'm not normally a big fan of prose but your stuff is just so, so … limpid.'

'Mmm, limpid,' Beatrice said. 'I wonder if that would look good on the back of the jacket?'

'I know I'm being a bit cheeky, but do you think if I sent you some of my poems, you could…'

Beatrice smiled and nodded quickly, and Mel, for all her adoration of the Eliot expert's glorious American curves, fell a little in love with Beatrice's smooth lip, straight nose, the glint of the cheekbones, all the details that ten thousand readers had already spent rather longer lingering over than they had the first chapter.

Beatrice Morelli at thirty had a certain literate section of Britain in her thrall. For her, too, it was the end of an era. In her neat flat on Great King Street the boxes were piled up. Neater piles, fewer boxes, containing just a few clothes, a selection of her more obscure books, a little jewellery, the photographs of her mother and father that she never looked at.

She never spoke about them, either. At least, not aloud. *Bosom* told the story of an orphan's erotic odyssey from Venice to Naples, a summer's road-trip with enough Latin sex to make Jayne Holland-Patrick sigh damply; enough autobiographical allusion to intrigue Richard; enough dark, satirical observation to make the critics vie with one another for the right cerebral superlatives. At the end, in the Bay of Naples, the heroine … but no, you might not have read it yet.

Beatrice is leaving Europe. There is an apartment awaiting her, not quite Lower East Side but within flirting distance of the still un-gentrified quarter of lower Manhattan. There is a job awaiting her too, as the eleventh 'classiest' member of the writing team on a frank, contemporary urban comedy series for American network television. Beatrice is already polishing up the contempt she knows she will have to feel for her new job, and already anticipating the relief she will feel when she sees her first pay-check, spelled in that delicious American manner that encourages a second scrutiny of all those noughts.

She wanted to see Britain rescued before she went, although she hadn't believed the polls, hadn't accepted that the English would ever open their arms to that freckled, ginger-haired Celt whose words were too polysyllabic, whose passions were too apparent, to ever be in charge of this cold country.

Richard had believed for a while, simply because Richard's calculated cynicism, his veneer of pessimism, could never quite stamp out a belief that people would do the right thing. Richard wanted to trust in other people's goodness, although that might have been because he had lost faith in his own.

Richard was being besieged by the younger, more degenerate-looking denizens of Liam's party. These days, Richard had a weekly column in a national newspaper, highlighting promising musical newcomers. In short, this meant that in that tiny world he had a considerable amount of power. There were people at Liam's party who had come along with the sole purpose of slipping a cassette into Richard's palm and saying a few, carefully-prepared words of seduction.

A bass player called Deke accompanied his proffered cassette with a wrap of silver foil and a broad wink. Because Sarah wasn't there, Richard accepted with a nervous smile. 'Speed?' he mouthed discreetly. Deke's eyes widened, although his pupils looked like pinpricks. He shook his head, smiled enigmatically, and drifted away to put on the Mamas and Papas tape.

Richard without Sarah sometimes felt like a child that had escaped its parent. Sarah was in Normandy, on holiday with a sister who was suffering the disappointment of relative academic failure, getting a 2:2, the finals results hardly helped by unoriginal wags who kept harping on about a 'Desmond.' With Beatrice, Richard had tripped back in time a little, crossing the threshold of Liam's flat. He was already carrying an infidelity around in his head, pondering the dilemma of sealing it away as a solitary aberration or accepting it as an indication of his hopelessness, and surrendering to his own wilful inclinations.

'When is he on? We don't want to miss them,' Beatrice said, coming up with two cans of beer. Richard thought she was talking about Gordon as if he was the headliner at a rock festival.

'Not for a while. He said it would be after two.'

'I'm surprised he didn't ask us down there for his moment of triumph.'

'It was funny. Grainne called and asked if we would go down. I said sure, and then an hour later Gordon called, said there had been a misunderstanding, that it was strictly party members and campaign staff only, that he couldn't swing it, he'd tried and got the knock-back, sorry and all that. Sounded very shifty.'

'When doesn't he? You know what I think? I think he's worried about losing. Couldn't face us seeing the look on his face if he doesn't get in.'

'Maybe. Although we'll see it in close-up on the telly. But he should be all right. Shouldn't he? He told me he needed a two percent swing, and Labour's getting more than that, even in the worst forecasts.'

'Don't. You're beginning to sound like Sally. That may all be true, but you know Gordon. There's always that little bit of him that suspects someone is going to come along and wreck it all.'

'Talking about golden bollocks, are we?' Liam said, sidling up with a selection from his cosmopolitan range of beer. 'Looks like he might be one of their few bright spots. Sally tells me that Major's going to get in quite comfortably the way things have been going. Their big mistake was having that stupid knees-up in Sheffield. Nobody likes a cocky Welshman, do they?'

'Would you believe it?' Richard said. 'Look at Major, he's a middle England mediocrity all the way from the three 'O' Levels to that stupid cricket tie, right down to the sensible wife in the crap hat. Can you believe we're going to get another five years of him?'

'*You're* going to, Rich,' Beatrice said blithely. 'I'm off to the States, where I've got high hopes for that lovely Clinton chappie.'

They were interrupted by the *tsk* of a lager can ring-pull, as Liam systematically opened the beers and passed them over. He did it ritually, dispiritedly. Liam's verve was sagging already, because Sally had skipped up and demanded his presence in the kitchen where the television needed retuning.

'What will we do without you?' Richard said, looking over at Beatrice.

'Well, in your case, I suspect you will carry on living in sickening conjugal bliss with the lovely if distant Sarah,' Beatrice replied, although the slight rise at the end of the sentence implied the hint of a question.

'It's complicated, though, isn't it?' Richard said, looking away to a far corner where Deke was finding it hard to muster the necessary degree of concentration to eject the cassette.

'Is it? I don't really know. I'm a celibate writer with little or no experience of settled relationships, remember. What's complicated?'

'I don't know. The whole thing. Keeping it together.'

'I think you're trying to say something, Richard. Is there something amiss in Rich and Sarah land? I thought you were heading off for some blissful weekend in Norfolk any day now?'

'We were. We are. I mean, I'm just a little unsure on the various steps. We've been going out for a couple of years nearly. I'm just not sure where we are supposed to be.'

'I don't think there's a set time-scale. Although there probably is in America. Do you want me to look for a book in New York and send it to you? *The Love Timetable*. Something like that.'

'Yeah, I know. It's ridiculous. It's just the whole thing, you know: the monogamous relationship.'

'Oh Richard, when did this happen?'

'What?'

'Come on. I know you read my first book. Remember the thing about the heroine? Isabella Torcini, which is a name I regret, I can tell you. Her trick was being able to deconstruct people's sentences in order to identify their crime.'

'So?'

'So you said *monogamous relationship*. Unnecessary adjective, Richard, unless it has already become a false description. Which, I can see from your face, it has. So: when, who, how? Or really, considering I know the way you feel about Sarah, why?'

Richard had drunk enough beer to want to tell her, and did, and Beatrice slowly shook her head and sighed, and drank some beer herself, and picked over the tiny details, and when he was finished she clutched his arm and gave a little sad smile that was neither reproof nor consolation. Richard brought out the wrap of silver paper.

'He said it wasn't speed. Actually, you know what? I think it's coke.'

'Really?'

'Really. Rather generous. I suppose I'll have to listen to his tape. Beatrice, look, you'll be in New York this time next week, where this stuff is pretty much compulsory, especially in the TV business. So you'd better prepare yourself.'

Richard laid out a couple of lines, and Beatrice laughed at his voice and at his not knowing that she had been familiar with cocaine for a couple of years, that her editor found it a necessary aperitif before any discussion of page-proofs. She made out she was being a good sport, and they did a couple of lines and chuckled at each other with that glimpse of childlike irreverence.

In the ensuing rush, the thirty-minute buzz that held his defences down and subdued all his instinctive shame and regret, Richard told Beatrice a lot more – about a chance encounter in London, about a three-day trip to Bologna, about a girl very different to Sarah, but with a more direct way of capturing his attention. Richard found himself telling Beatrice about the curve of a naked breast, the softness of a lip, about an irresistible morning sipping black Italian coffee under a portico in Emiglia Romana.

Beatrice swallowed the details, erased Richard's instinctive deceptions, put together the story in a vault, saw all its possibilities. 'I wish you'd told me all this before,' she said. 'I could have used it in a book.' As she said the words she realised she meant them. She hadn't known cocaine was a truth drug.

Liam was watching the television. The result was being announced from a constituency somewhere in the less-defined part of the north-east of England. The Conservative total had been announced as 18, 679, and the returning officer was continuing: 'Hendrie, Gordon Alexander…' and the television announcer whispered 'Labour.' Liam looked at Gordon's face, flashed into harsh close-up on the screen. The tuning efforts hadn't been one hundred percent successful, and the features were slightly blurred, but Gordon seemed on the point of vomiting, deathly pale, with his lips failing to hold the confident smile. His eyes were wandering to the side, looking for reassurance. He looked like a condemned man on the scaffold.

'…19, 842. I duly…'

The rest of the words were lost in the whooping in Liam's kitchen. Nobody there, with the exception of Liam himself, would have gone as far as to describe Gordon as their friend, but they knew him, and he was now an MP, and that made them feel a tiny bit happier about themselves as they ploughed into Liam's beer pyramid.

'Fuck me, he's got it,' Liam said, looking around, but finding only Sally and the American watching. He looked back at the screen and laughed out loud. Gordon had the fixed grin of an escaped lunatic, and was clasping his hands above his shoulder in the triumphal pose of a middleweight champion, holding his own handshake as if unwilling to allow anyone else but himself to congratulate the newly elected member. For all the supporters and functionaries milling around, Gordon seemed to be enjoying a moment so private that Liam felt it almost obscene to be watching. As the camera wobbled around, Liam spotted Andy McInnes smiling tightly and punching the keys of a mobile telephone. Then he saw an ethereal figure float up in what looked almost like a wedding dress, and plant a chaste kiss on Gordon's cheek.

'Who's the Transylvanian princess?' the quiet American purred at his side.

Liam looked again, and saw the brilliance of the eyes glinting away miles from the surface, black hollows beneath them, saw a smile that wasn't convincing enough to survive the remorseless lens of a TV camera. He saw her laugh, and saw that she found it difficult to stop. He saw her looking at Gordon in the proudest moment of his life, and he saw something that he would struggle to define: something halfway between contempt and fear. He saw all of that before he could recognise her.

'Christ! Is that Grainne?' he said. 'It is. Looks out of it.'

'She must be sedated or something,' the American said with a certain satisfaction. The American was something of a barbiturate dilettante herself, and liked to think she had illustrious company. But Liam had his own field of expertise.

'She looks pissed.'

At that, as if she had heard his words, Grainne seemed to turn to him, to stare straight into the camera and smile a brilliant smile of disorientation, just before the station cut to a tight finish in Chester.

Liam turned around to look for Richard and Beatrice, but they weren't there, hadn't seen it. 'Over a thousand majority,' Sally was saying. 'Pretty good.' But Liam, for once, ignored her. Instead, with love and respect, he raised a can of Stella Artois and drank a deep draught in homage to the new first lady of Houghton-Le-Fuck-Knows-Where. 'Good luck, darling,' he whispered to himself.

Beer

Grainne

Winter afternoons in the north-east demanded sherry, the civilised schooner of the respectable middle-classes. Perhaps hogging half a bottle of the stuff in front of the radiator, watching a North Sea squall whipping a few remaining dead leaves off the neatly-trimmed trees wasn't quite the essence of refined living, but Grainne was comfortable enough. Sitting there in her chunky cardigan, strands of hair clinging to slightly damp cheeks, she looked out at her familiar vista.

The windows opposite were sprayed white around the corners. Grainne had never understood that idea of trying to convince passers-by that you had a six-foot snowdrift in your living room. Gold foil letters spelled *Merry Christmas* over the front door. Grainne looked up at their own minimalist green nylon tree, an afterthought next to the crystal cherry bowl, the flat Portuguese ceramic vase, the framed photograph, all three of them detritus from the wedding in Edinburgh.

Grainne propped her chin on her elbows and looked across the estate's green, now frosted white, with a muddy patch where Gordon had turned the car around. 'Why don't you pop in on the neighbours? Compliments of the season and all that,' Gordon had said that morning before heading off down the A1 for a meeting with a local councillor. Grainne had snorted to herself.

There was Marjorie over the way with the two year-old twins. Marjorie's conversation attempted to drift over international affairs and literature, but somehow returned inexorably to the relative merits of Pampers and Huggies and how the phenomenon of her babies' eyes following you around the room was a sure sign of precocious intelligence. At Marjorie's you would get one glass of lukewarm Chardonnay from a bottle that had been opened two days ago. Marjorie didn't like to drink alcohol because she was still breast-feeding. Grainne was hazy about whether it was normal to breast-feed for two years, but the idea frightened her.

Then there was Glenys next door. When Grainne had introduced herself they had laughed together about the name, Glenys had proffered a gin and tonic, and Grainne had briefly thought she might have found a soul-mate. But Glenys only wanted to talk about Gordon, wanted to know his opinions on the poll tax, on housing associations, on aid to Romania. When Gordon and Grainne had popped next door for a drinks party, Glenys had stared over Grainne's shoulder, apparently fascinated by the way Gordon was hanging up his jacket. Grainne thought she looked like a leopard spying a fleshy antelope.

Or there was Kate. But Kate was rarely in. Grainne would see her pull up in her BMW, step out, all hard geometric lines in her business suit and tight skirt, clutching her briefcase and a mobile phone. Kates's house was the only one without Christmas decorations in the windows. Kate would be mineral water spritzers, Grainne thought to herself, then an hour on the exercise bike to sweat away the evil traces.

Better by myself, she thought, getting up from her kneeling position because it had unpleasant connotations, reminded her of scraped knees, sweat and humiliation. I could finish that sherry, she thought to herself. After all, it's Christmas Eve.

She tried to summon up a Christmas memory that wasn't tainted. The best she could do was an idealised, edited version of when she was eight. There had been snow that year, unusual on the island. After unwrapping her presents on Christmas morning and squealing over the new dancing shoes and the show-jumping Barbie set, she had gone for a walk with her mother. The sun had been glinting off the fresh crisp snow. The houses of Tobermory, their various colours topped by white icing, looked like a display in a cake-shop window. In the afternoon they had gone to Bryony's and she had played with her aunt's Yorkshire terrier in the snow outside, watching the wind whip up the waves like caramel Angel Delight. Her aunt had given her a selection box and Grainne sat on the step, trying to take the wrapper off a Marathon bar without removing her wet woollen gloves. 'Don't eat all those sweets at once; you're looking a bit pudgy as it is,' her father had shouted at her, but his voice was softened by Bryony's rum punch, and the world was fresh and white enough for it not to matter that time.

They had gone home, and Grainne had sat behind the sofa galloping the equestrian Barbie over a circuit formed by lines of hazelnuts. Her mother and father had been half-watching Morecambe and Wise, half-bickering. 'The trouble with your sister is that she doesn't believe there's a world outside this island,' her father had been saying. 'She thinks the mainland is the outer circles of hell.' 'She likes it here, that's all,' Grainne's mother had replied. 'She doesn't see the attraction of Glasgow or Edinburgh. Oban once a month does for her.' 'She's a bloody teuchter, that's all, and you're just as bad,' her father continued, but in the next moment he was laughing at something on the screen. Grainne knew this was an argument that would occasionally blow up into a mighty tempest, but that Christmas, something in the air, something in that blanket of greying snow, kept the tempers subdued.

Grown-up Grainne looked out at the frost and wished it were snow. She wished she could call her mother and ask her if she remembered that Christmas. She shouldn't have thought about it. She shouldn't have kept at the sherry. Now she was getting tearful. Gordon would come back and see the red eyes and would sigh and stomp off to his study and start making phone-calls. She had come to loathe his phone voice, that staccato, laconic array of words filtered through what he thought was a manly cynicism. It made him sound twenty years older, although she couldn't tell him that because she knew he would take it as a compliment.

The Christmas break had been a strain. She had got used to him being away from Monday to Friday, in that tiny flat in Kennington, or sitting in the House, making those tiny, bland interjections that had been prepared for him in advance. She was used to the occasional triumphal phone-call pointing out how he had wrong-footed the Minister with a technical query, that there were rumours he might get a place on such-and-such a committee, that everything was going according to plan, and they would be in Government within two years.

Grainne loved these calls, loved to hear him three hundred miles away. Speaking to her, the phone voice was different: it still had that boyish enthusiasm tinged with a need for her approval. 'Don't you worry about what he gets up to down there five days a week?' Glenys asked her one morning when they met by the post-box. 'Young attractive high-flyer like that all alone in the big city?'

But Grainne knew what he got up to. Committee meetings, manifesto sessions, think-tanks, lunches with whips who might have the leader's ear, off-the-record meetings with local journalists, briefings with Shadow Cabinet member's private secretaries. Grainne knew he was conducting his love affair all over Westminster, knew he was slaking his desires every waking moment.

He would come back on the train on Friday evenings sated, full of the residual excitement of another week trying to muscle his way along the cramped corridors of power. Weekends, he insisted, were for recreation. Which is where the awkwardness began.

The rubber dress had just been the beginning. For a few weeks afterwards, costumes had predominated. Dressing up as a French maid or a policewoman had seemed so ridiculous to Grainne that it had killed any notion of desire she might have been feeling, but Gordon seemed to enjoy it. Grainne felt like a bad actress on a downslide in her career, learned to drink three fast vodkas before pulling on her fishnet stockings or her gymslip.

'Try to get into it, Grainne. It's just fantasy,' Gordon would nag. 'It's just letting go of our inhibitions. We're young, we're not like our parents, we should do this more often.' Gordon had brought home a riding crop, and Grainne had said no way, but he wasn't abashed. He asked her to dress as a dominatrix, and that was the first time it hadn't worked. Gordon had become embarrassed, a little angry. 'You can't do it, can you?' he shouted. 'You don't have a forceful bone in your body.' Grainne had shrugged, pulled off the sweaty leather catsuit, and kissed him. 'I can't pretend to be angry. I'm sorry.'

Gordon, who had taken to sending off for specialist magazines, discovered bondage, would tie Grainne to the bed with silk scarves and leave her there naked while he went off to read the paper. Grainne knew she was supposed to lie there writhing with frustrated desire, but usually she fell asleep, and only awoke when she felt Gordon on top of her thrusting away more in annoyance than passion. She wondered if all this was normal. After a few drinks she thought she might ask the neighbours. But she suspected that Marjorie would be appalled at the idea of sex without procreation, that Glenys would be far too interested, and that Kate probably got up to much kinkier stuff herself.

Gordon came back from his meeting with the councillor, pleased with some agreement they had made whereby local redundancies would be pre-arranged with a pragmatic union boss, so that there would be no unpleasantness in the local press and Gordon would not be pressurised by his constituents to raise the unfashionable matter of workers' rights in the House.

They ate an overcooked lamb casserole that Grainne had

prepared that morning, watched a little television, looked at each other during the carol service and thought different things. Grainne was thinking that hymns were implanted in your brain from such an early age that their simple cadences could still have an effect long after you had lost all faith in the words. Grainne allowed herself a brandy before she went to bed, humming 'O come all ye faithful, joyful and triumphant.'

Grainne made pancakes for breakfast and sat with Gordon, happy in a mound of coffee-cups and maple syrup as they exchanged presents. Gordon had bought her emerald earrings. 'Got them in Bond Street,' he said proudly. 'They go with your eyes'. He had bought her tiny crimson satin lingerie as well. Also to go with my eyes, she thought, but didn't say it, because this was a good morning, almost a proper Christmas.

She had bought him a leather document case. 'For when you get that Ministerial post,' she said. 'Steady,' he said, 'let's not take anything for granted.' But he was thrilled, and he kissed her, leaving maple syrup on her lips.

They walked down to the sea, held hands for a few moments, looked down from the cliffs at the wet sand and driftwood. 'Next year is going to be the big one,' Gordon was saying. 'Peter's got us all having presentation meetings every Thursday. The sort of detail we're going into, you wouldn't believe.'

Grainne had heard it before, and was listening to the screams of the seagulls. She briefly regretted not bringing the leftover pancakes to feed to them, then shook herself. She felt her long hair blowing in the breeze, and had a vivid image of herself, ageing, turning into one of those eccentrics in the stained dresses, a can of Special Brew at her feet, reddened arms reaching out to feed pigeons.

'Have you ever been to Morpeth?' Gordon was asking.

'Don't think so. Why?'

'We're going there tomorrow. Party. Somebody Andy knows. Quite prestigious actually. I think you might enjoy it.' He sounded pleased with himself, but Grainne knew not to ask too many questions. He loved his little surprises.

They had grilled salmon for their lunch. Grainne felt a full roast Christmas dinner was the preserve of families, and she and Gordon weren't a family. They were a modern late-twentieth century couple, she thought glumly, the kind you read about in the lifestyle section of the Mail On Sunday. Grainne had just one glass of white wine. But Gordon demanded Christmas pudding, and she needed port to wash it down.

They sat together on the sofa in the afternoon, while northern night gathered outside. Gordon pulled the curtains and dimmed their lights, and they watched *It's A Wonderful Life* on BBC2. 'Only Hollywood could make a sentimental anti-capitalist movie,' Gordon said, quoting Liam so faithfully that he even said movie, when it was a word he would never use.

'Ah, but Capra has a Slav's soul,' Grainne said, and she looked at Gordon and saw that his cynicism had been conquered this time, and his eyes were as moist as hers. She opened the Belgian chocolates Richard had sent. He always sent chocolates. He always remembered birthdays. She loved him for that. 'Better watch yourself with those, Grainne; don't want to get porky,' Gordon said. But his voice was softened with brandy, and Grainne didn't let it upset her.

The following afternoon, bright, windy and freezing, they drove out to Morpeth. Gordon had detailed directions on the back of a business card, but it took him a while to find the house. It was a restored manor set back from a B-road in a few acres of grounds, and Grainne couldn't help exclaiming as they drove up an elm-lined avenue. 'Bloody hell, Gordon, who lives here?' He grinned, satisfied that she was impressed. 'Wait and see.'

They were greeted at the door by their bleary-eyed host. He was wearing a too-small tee-shirt and shorts; a little white paunch hanging out. Grainne recognised him as Danny McBeth, a Geordie comedian who had been the only success of an otherwise embarrassing Channel 4 Saturday night TV comedy show two years previously. Now he had his own sketch show on BBC2, appeared as the faintly offensive guest on panel shows, and wrote a newspaper column for one of the middle-brow tabloids.

'Gord, great to see ya,' Danny said, his TV Geordie accent softened into a metropolitan media burr. Danny looked cheeky on TV, but he looked like a rodent in real life, eyes too eager, movements too sharp and sudden. His eyes alighted on Grainne. 'And this must be the much better half.' His eyes were fixed on her for a deliberately long time, until she looked back at him, and he laughed. 'She'll do,' he said, grabbing Gordon by the elbow and steering him inside.

Gathered in an enormous drawing-room was a collection of youngish people in various forms of intoxication. The room seemed to have been deliberately made to resemble an eighties student flat, all dayglo sofas, lava lamps, and casual stashes of German beer piled around the skirting boards. In the middle of the room, thin young blonde women were shuffling around in a semi-dance to bored-sounding tunes by New Order or The Lightning Seeds, smiles plastered to their faces like party hats. Grainne looked around, slightly flustered. She recognised Andy McInnes, who raised a lager can to her in salute, barely taking his eyes off one of the thin blonde women he had cornered by the window. She recognised Maddy Price, the oldest and thinnest of the blonde women. A few summers before, Grainne had gone with Beatrice to see Maddy's stand-up comedy act at the Edinburgh fringe. The jokes had been so gruesomely gynaecological that Beatrice had winced, but Grainne had been entirely impressed by the sheer élan of the woman. Here, in the harsh light coming from French windows she looked older, manic. She came up to Grainne quickly, took her by the elbow, in much the same way Danny had treated Gordon.

'You must be Gordon's...' she waved her arm airily to supply the missing words.

'Grainne.'

'Mmm, lovely name. You'll be drinking vodka, then.' Maddy reached over, lifted a shot glass from an ice-box and poured a quick measure of Stolichnaya. 'We've gone all traditional. I told Danny to make sure the boys drank beer, while the girls had the hard stuff.' Maddy gave a noiseless laugh, then fixed Grainne with an intense scrutiny.

'You're not what I suspected.'

'How do you mean?'

'Well, Gordon is so ... ambitious. I thought he'd have a hard little political wife, you know the type?'

Grainne knew the type, but didn't know what to say.

'Listen, come with me. I want to show you something.'

Maddy led her up the broad staircase, her buttocks swaying strangely in their red leather casing. She pulled Grainne into a cluttered bedroom. Maddy reached into a drawer of her dressing table and pulled out a little oak box. 'Got this in St Lucia last summer. You're supposed to keep cinnamon root in it, but I use it for more entertaining purposes. Danny says I'm a complete twat, as the box might as well have "stash" written on it in capital letters, but I think it's stylish. That's the sort of tragic old slag I am. Will you have one?'

Maddy held out her palm with some white pills on it. They were stamped with an owl motif. Grainne knew she was looking uneasy, but she was already feeling the relaxing glow of her first vodka.

'Ecstasy, is it?'

'See, I was right. Hardly the unworldly sort, are you? It's pretty good stuff; as pure as you can get these days. Only don't tell Gordon, because he would freak. He can be a bit pompous sometimes, but I probably don't need to tell you that.'

Grainne laughed, and perhaps because it was Christmas, perhaps because of the vodka, but more likely because it seemed to her that Maddy very much needed her to do this and Grainne had been brought up to be obliging, took a tablet and popped it into her mouth. 'Politician's wife in E-crazed Boxing Day orgy,' Maddy laughed a little too wildly, and Grainne laughed too.

'You're staying behind afterwards, aren't you?' Maddy said. 'Danny is looking forward to it.'

'I'm not sure, Gordon didn't say.'

'Oh, you leave Gordon to me.'

Maddy led her back downstairs and kept a careful eye on her, never letting her vodka glass stay empty for more than a few moments. Around ten, the rest of the guests started to disappear. Andy McInnes was the last to go, winking at Gordon, clapping Danny on the shoulder, murmuring 'lucky bastard.' The music had turned into The Cure, big alienating swirls of whining guitar. Grainne was still dancing, but now she felt like lying down. Maddy led her through to a huge bedroom in the back. 'There's a heated pool as well, for afterwards,' she said mysteriously.

Grainne lay on the bed, a little unsure where she was, wondering if she was back home in their bedroom, but not recognising the light fittings. Then Gordon was there, smelling of beer, undressing her, smiling, calling her his 'game little darling.' She felt her wrists being tied to the posts of the bed, giggled, sighed and murmured, 'Bit tired.'

'Can't be tired, darling; the night is young.' The voice wasn't

Gordon's. It was a soft Geordie whisper. Her mind was still sorting it out while Gordon tugged at her little red knickers and pulled them down over her ankles. She felt cool, and thirsty. Then he fastened her feet to the foot of the bed.

'I told you, Danny: had to be a natural redhead,' whispered Maddy.

'I can see that. Fire down below. I like it.'

The ecstasy had made Grainne both sleepy and hypersensitive. She would look up and see Gordon looking down at her with the pleased grin he always wore when he came back from London after another successful committee meeting. But she could feel tongues and fingers roaming over her bare body, feel her skin rippled with sensation. She tried to find the words to ask for water, but her tongue seemed swollen. Then she looked down and saw blonde hair between her legs, dyed blonde hair with dark grey roots. This, she thought, must be shocking, but the sensation wasn't unpleasant, just numbing. Then she drifted away for a few more moments. When she came around she looked over to the dressing table to see Gordon astride Maddy, her long mottled legs reaching up high to his shoulders. She could see his face in the mirror, see the redness of his cheeks, his eyes closed as he gasped for breath.

Locking eyes with Gordon's in the mirror, Grainne gave a wordless yelp and at the same time felt herself being invaded, saw Danny McBeth squatting between her legs holding her thighs apart and entering her steadily. She saw the look of intense concentration on his face, and realised she was watching him in one of his more daring TV comedy sketches, seeing him pushing back the frontiers of what was acceptable entertainment. But then she could feel him pushing inside her. It seemed real, but...

Then she awoke, shaking her head at the nightmare. Grainne stared up at the ornate ceiling, her head pounding with an ache that seemed to be moving around, looking for a place to settle. She felt herself sweating profusely, felt her throat constricting with dryness. As she tried to swallow she felt herself choking, and coughed. She looked around her and her stomach turned over in panic, shot through with bile. Next to her the comedian lifted himself with a grunt, pushing his palm onto her bare hip, painfully, to lever himself up. Grainne moaned, looked upwards but couldn't focus. 'Do you think I'm funny?' he said aggressively.

Grainne screwed up her eyes, stared at him, at his little pot belly hanging over his flaccid genitals, at the sweat running off his forehead, at the querulous tremor of his fleshy lips. How had this ever happened? How would it end? Where was Gordon? The comedian seemed to be waiting for an answer.

'No, Danny,' she said, distractedly, looking around for her clothes.

'That's the trouble,' he said quietly. 'No fucker does any more.'

Gordon

H e would walk it. Stung by a remark on the Sunday afternoon from Andy McInnes who had prodded him in the midriff and said 'Watch out for the puppy fat, Gordon: the new party is about being lean and muscular,' Gordon had decided to take some exercise. Not that Andy could talk. In his early thirties, he was already getting the jowls of an elder statesman. When Gordon pointed this out, Andy slapped his chins and said something about having too many power lunches.

That December Monday, then, towards the end of a parliamentary term, Gordon had looked out the grimy window of the flat in Kennington, looked over towards the traffic heading up Walworth Road, seen it was dry, and decided to walk to Westminster. Walking, he had read somewhere, was just as beneficial as running. He clutched at his bare abdomen, held a handful of white, freckled flesh and wondered if it had always been there or whether Peter's image-consciousness sessions had just made him more sensitive. He thought perhaps he just looked bigger because of the tininess of the bathroom. He had told Grainne that the rent they were paying for a year on the London flat could have bought them a house in Glasgow. He knew how he would rather spend his money, though.

Normally he would take a taxi. The day after he had moved into the flat in Kennington, Gordon had stepped out onto Walworth Road, held out his umbrella in his best imitation of an English gentleman, and hailed a black cab. He had felt the rush of importance as he climbed in with his briefcase, his security pass, his locker key. 'The House, please,' Gordon had said in his politest middle-class Glaswegian. 'Which 'ouse is that, Jock?' the cabbie had said. 'Only if you look out yer window, you'll notice there's quite a few of the buggers.'

Maybe he would walk every day, he thought now, feeling the novelty of a grimy London breeze blowing in off the Thames. He cut along Penton Place and headed towards the river. The buzz of London could still get to him; that adrenaline thrill of feeling at the centre of things. He thought back with a smile to the accent of his English cousin coming up to Glasgow when they were kids, remembered the instinctive prickle of hostility, the way his hackles had risen at the threat of the unfamiliar. In London wine bars now,

Gordon would bask in the Englishness of it all, feeling money rolling off the characterless vowels, power seeping out of the deliberately downmarket drawls.

Andy and Mark had both started to speak in quick, matey approximations of *EastEnders* voices. Gordon listened to them at times and thought they had learned their lines from a script, with phonetic symbols printed alongside the words. 'Alwight me old china,' Andy had greeted him the week before, and Gordon knew he was only being half-ironic.

Gordon almost resented hearing a Scottish accent down here, as if he had found refuge in a private paradise and now it was being gate-crashed by the very people he had been looking to escape.

A few of the more earnest of the new intake from north of the border had sat at his table in the Commons canteen, as they insisted on calling it. They were the ones with the sausages and chips, the steak and kidney pies. They had tried a few initial Scottish bonding overtures, suggested he get involved in some of their collective lobbying, half-suggested it was up to them to present a unified front in the enemy camp. Gordon had reverted to his broadest Partick accent and explained that he had to be careful because he was representing an English constituency, and with the devolution debate about to get into full swing, he didn't want to be a liability. Gordon could be persuasive. He knew it was the reason he was here. They had nodded respectfully, chewed on a bit of gristle, washed it down with a slug of beer, clapped him on the shoulder and told a few anecdotes of Paisley or Irvine or Cumbernauld, as if he were thirsty for Caledonia. Gordon had smiled and tried to get a wistful look in his eye, but it was a struggle.

He would avoid them after that, but needn't have. After a few months in Westminster, London had killed them too, and if they found themselves next to him at the bar would swap details of drinking dens on Old Street, night-clubs in Hackney, the seductions of the capital, the outrageous price of a decent glass of Merlot in the Aldwych brasseries.

Gordon headed along the Embankment, climbed the stairs to Lambeth Bridge, and joined the stream of office-workers, secretaries, post-boys and clerks filtering over to the north bank. After more than a year as an MP, Gordon still smiled at the constant temptation to yell, 'Hey, I'm a Member of Parliament. I get to decide the laws of the land. I'm in charge of all you people.'

It wasn't enough, though. Gordon yearned for a tiny piece of recognition. As an opposition back-bencher, and moreover, one sworn to loyal obedience to whatever the reshaped party line was that week, there was little chance for attention-grabbing. He wasn't even in demand for local radio station or TV discussion shows, so orthodox were his views. In his moments of candour Gordon accepted that he was a drone. A drone with such a conventional buzz about him that he was in danger of becoming invisible.

This is what he hoped his morning meeting was about, the chance to raise his profile. Andy was sitting on the steps by the Victoria Embankment with two polystyrene cups of coffee and a couple of croissants. 'Working breakfast, sunshine; it's what the Americans do,' he said by way of greeting. 'Why are you sweating? Doesn't look good, Gordon.'

'I walked here over the river. Thought I could do with the exercise.'

'Possibly true, but the thing to remember is that, like several other activities I could mention, exercise should not be done in public. You can't be seen to care about that sort of thing.'

'So what was it you wanted to talk to me about?' Gordon said. Andy hadn't been quite as attentive of late. He had his own ambitions to attend to. Andy had a job as a Shadow Cabinet aide, preparing speeches and coordinating research. He was still liaising closely with Mark McGuire who was involved with what was called, in the requisite hazy language, the *policy unit*.

'Your future,' Andy said, sipping his coffee.

'I know, but what exactly?' Gordon said. He still liked to have the details spelled out for him.

'Next year is going to be the big one,' Andy said. 'That's when the real players will be shaping up, because '95 and '96 are going to be one long campaign. Next year is when we have to get into our starting positions. And if you aren't in the team for the friendlies, you won't make the World Cup squad.'

Always the football analogies, Gordon thought.

'Meaning?'

'Meaning, you have to get yourself attached to a department. Foreign, Home, Trade and Industry. Except we think we may have the perfect place lined up for you. Ahh, here's Mark. He'll tell you more.'

Mark had acquired a jacket with no lapels, a lot of hair-gel and air of importance. He had brought his own coffee. He brushed the step fastidiously and took a seat with a grimace. 'Sorry about the alfresco, Gordon, only we needed a little privacy and waitresses have ears, apparently.'

'How's the policy unit?' Gordon said politely, although he only really wanted to talk about his own prospects.

'If I told you I would have to kill you,' Mark said benignly. 'The stuff we do in there could destabilise British democracy.'

'Really,' Gordon said, wide-eyed. He loved this stuff.

'Well, not really, but it's non-stop amusement, I can tell you.'

'Go on, Mark, tell Gordon what you do,' Andy said, wheedling. Mark smiled.

'Remember the 1987 manifesto, Gordon?'

'Before my time,' Gordon said instinctively, 'but yeah.'

'My daily task is to go through every detail of that document. Underline every portentous phrase, distil it down to its political essentials. Then I find the polar opposite of every promise and commitment…'

'Or threat,' mumbled Andy.

'The exact opposite. It's a mathematical exercise in a way. Or an artistic one. Finding the precise symmetry.'

'And?' Gordon prompted.

'And that becomes the basis for our new policy. The bedrock for '96. Or '97, as these bastards are already running scared and will cling on just long enough to line their pockets. The brilliant thing is, you feel you're building a new world from scratch. It feels a bit like the original punk rockers must have. You know, blowing away all the well-meaning hippy windbags. We've taught ourselves irreverence. Respect nothing, trust no-one. Saying the unsayable, thinking the unthinkable. You know what some of the hardcore boys have done? They've got little black badges of Smithy. They all wear them, and it looks like a sign of devout reverence for the great man, God rest his etcetera. But they have a little clique, a bit like the Monday Club. Meet on Mondays, strangely enough. Drink real ale, but in a sarcastic sort of fashion. Somebody says, 'May,' and they all stand to attention. And the toast is: "Smithy: if he hadn't kicked it, we'd have had to shoot him."'

'You started that club, Mark,' Andy pointed out. 'Only someone as tasteless as you would have dared.'

'It's about clearing away the past, great swathes of Soviet-style revisionism,' Mark went on. 'What do you think?'

'Fine by me. But all the old tankies aren't going to like it.'

'Exactly,' Mark said, sniffing his coffee. 'That's the beauty of it.'

'Talking of tankies,' Andy said, 'have you ever worn camouflage?'

'No,' Gordon said nonplussed. 'Why?'

'Defence junior,' Mark said. 'There's a job and we think you may be ideal.'

Gordon looked at the two of them but their faces weren't giving anything away.

'I know the job you mean,' Gordon said, 'but I was under the impression Russell Anderson had got it stitched up.'

Mark looked at Andy, Andy looked at Mark.

'This is true in a sense, but not empirically so,' said Mark.

Gordon just shook his head. He knew if he kept silent they would return to simple English.

'It's like this, Gordon. Anderson has been promised the job. He was elected in '87 so he's got five years solid background ahead of a Johnny-come-lately like you. He published a treatise on the changing role of NATO after the disintegration of the Warsaw Pact. He does radio interviews on advances in weapons technology. He makes a lot of salient points on the illogicality of the government's arms expenditure. I believe he is about to reveal some shocking facts about the sale of missiles to the Middle East.'

'Exactly,' Gordon said. 'I'm surprised he's only getting the junior post. He's a damned sight more qualified to be Shadow Defence Secretary than...'

'Gordon, Gordon, Gordon,' Mark sighed, 'you are *such* a slow learner.'

Andy stepped in.

'Anderson is a Cambridge sort. Slavic languages and modern politics. He was a member of CND from 1979 until 1992. 1992, for Christ's sake. We thought it was bad enough that Kinnock and bloody Glenys only handed in their cards in '91. Anderson, we know, is still very sympathetic, still has a hard-on for the unis, when the rest of us are all multis. He was a university lecturer. He has a beard.'

'So, he's still got far more experience and expertise than I have. I've got no chance.'

'Don't be defeatist, Gordon. The appointment won't be made until after Christmas. All we're looking for at this stage is a candidate, someone to offer a little comparison with smooth Mr Anderson. Sorry, Dr Anderson.'

'But I know next to nothing about defence.'

'Ah, but Gordon, what you have to remember is that innocence is the greatest selling point in the Labour Party these days.' Mark lifted his coffee cup up and pointed at its whiteness. 'It's the glory of the blank canvas. You have no history. That is your greatest strength. It's like in Eastern Europe at the moment. Any politician who steps forward without any trace of red on their hands is being swept into power with the kisses of the people all over their arse. We can learn from that. We have to lop off our diseased roots, cauterise them so the disease can't survive. We have to embrace post-industrial purity. We have to raise a new generation untainted by the old ideologies. People like you, who never joined anything in their life until the Labour Party found you. You're our creature, Gordon. You are the pure vision of the future. We love you.'

He paused. 'You can use some of that stuff in your speeches if you like, Andy.'

'Thanks,' Andy said, 'but we're steering away from the high-blown rhetoric after the Sheffield fiasco. Plain words for thick Brits is the line.'

'So you think I might have a chance?' Gordon said.

'Nah, not a hope,' Andy laughed.

'Every chance, Gordon, every chance,' Mark said, reaching out an arm to grip Gordon's elbow in one of the sensitive gestures he had been taught in Peter's presentation seminars, but wasn't quite comfortable with. 'A Christmas recess is a long time in politics.'

Three days before Christmas Gordon was fulfilling a promise. Richard had recently moved down to London, and Gordon had said he would take him for a drink at the Commons. They were sitting over their third pint of the day, and Gordon was leaning back in his armchair, trying to give the impression that this was his gentleman's club, trying to forget about that awkward business when the barman had asked to see his security pass.

They had played a brief game of understated one-upmanship, Richard being unimpressed with Gordon's verbatim account of a two-minute conversation with Robin Cook, Gordon being equally unmoved with Richard's blow-by-blow description of a tense encounter with Mark E Smith. Then Richard brought out the Christmas presents.

'Chocolates for Grainne, is it?' Gordon said, shaking the parcel. 'Same every year. I won't thank you for it, Rich. Grainne's not been doing much lately, and there's a fine line between voluptuous and fat, you know. Do you mind if I open mine now? I'm a big kid, I know, but I can't handle suspense.'

'Go ahead.'

'*The Prince*. Machiavelli. What is it? A play?'

'Gordon...'

'Yeah, yeah, I know, only kidding. Thanks.'

'Only, from what I've been reading, it's the set text in the Labour party these days. Thought you might need a survival manual.'

'I do all right.'

They were interrupted by a tall blonde man in his mid-thirties with round glasses and a wispy beard. Gordon looked up, expecting it to be one of his rather tight circle of parliamentary acquaintances, but the stranger was looking at Richard.

'Rich, what are you doing here?'

'Oh, hi... Er – just having a drink.'

'Strange place for an afternoon session. Still. Nice party the other day. Did you get back all right? Only you looked a little...'

'A little pissed out of my mind. Yeah. Vodka jellies do that to me. I've been sticking to the pints ever since, as you can see. Got back okay though, thanks. Autopilot is a wonderful thing.'

'Right, yeah, well see you again, Rich,' and the stranger headed off towards the door with a little laugh.

'Who was that?' Gordon said, looking up from *The Prince*, trying not to seem piqued that Richard hadn't introduced him.

'Russell Anderson. Didn't you recognise him? He's one of your lot. Let's face it, you don't have that many. Still, I suppose you move in different circles?'

'And how does he know you?'

'He doesn't. Well, not really. I met him at the party after the Pet

Shop Boys gig a couple of weeks ago. Oh, and he's rather grateful to our newspaper at the moment.'

'Why's that?' Gordon leant forward eagerly. Richard smiled.

'Bit of a secret, but seeing as you're on the same side. There was a spot of awkwardness with Anderson's boyfriend. Lover's tiff. Almost a punch-up in an Islington restaurant. We were going to do a piece, apparently, but the features editor has always been a pal of Anderson's and she persuaded the editor to leave it out. A nothing story anyway, if you ask me.'

'So Anderson's gay?'

'Christ, Gordon, do they keep you out of the party loop or what? Although I suppose it's not something he's going to publicise. After all, the Labour Party is still pretty Neanderthal about these sorts of things, isn't it?'

'Mmm, I suppose. Rich, another pint. Come on, it's Christmas.'

'Can't, I'm afraid. Have to go and write a think piece on new trends in Euro-techno coming our way in the New Year. It's a three-pint feature, maybe chased with a little speed and a black coffee. Have a good Christmas. Give my love to Grainne.'

Gordon was bereft for ten minutes, until Andy McInnes came along in the company of a small man who managed the tricky combination of being both weaselly and tubby, and who Gordon seemed to recognise.

'Gordon,' Andy said. 'Drinking alone? At Christmas? You sad fucker.'

'No, I was just with a ...'

'Three pints over here,' Andy called in a peremptory mock-Cockney twang. 'Gordon, this is Danny McBeth; Danny, Gordon Hendrie.'

'Danny McBeth. You're the one on the telly.'

'So they tell me.'

'With the sketch show. What is it, Channel 4?'

'BBC2, actually. So much nicer being paid out of the public purse rather than the tainted profits of international capitalist corporations. Sorry Gordon, only joking. I'm as much of a miserable money-grubbing hypocritical whore as the rest of them.' Danny took a large draught of his beer and settled back to look round at the austere surroundings. 'So which of these wankers is the coke-dealer?' he said loudly.

'Gordon, stop telling Danny his life-story, will you,' Andy said. 'He's hosting a fund-raiser in the New Year, and wanted to come in and have a look at where the establishment drinks.'

'Actually, it's not that different from the Groucho,' Danny said. 'Do you have a pool table?'

'Looking forward to Christmas with the missus, eh, Gordon?' Andy said. 'Away from all this nonsense?'

'Except I'll be spending it in the blighted north-east.' Gordon looked across at Danny. 'Oh, sorry, you're from around there, aren't you?'

'Where did you get that idea?' Danny said in broad Geordie. 'Yes, but don't apologise. What is it they say about us? Scots with their brains kicked out. Or is it the other way around? But one of our redeeming features is that we don't take offence. Or at least not once we've kicked seven shades of shite out of yis. Anyhow, I'm up in Morpeth with Maddy over Christmas, drinking brown ale, eating stottie cake, and giving each other Toon shirts for a laugh. We've got a place up there. We're having a bit of a party on Boxing Day if you want to come along. Here – I'll write down the address.'

'Brilliant, yeah, thanks, Danny. I'll look forward to it.' Gordon was feeling a little overawed. This was what they meant when they said politics was going to be the new showbiz. Danny leant in a little closer.

'My parties always go with a swing,' he whispered, and chuckled hoarsely. Then he tapped his breast pocket, looked around him and headed off towards the toilets. Gordon felt Andy looking at him, and turned to see the broad grin.

'Remember when you were a kid, Gordon,' Andy was saying, 'and you'd collect football cards from packets of bubble-gum?'

'Yeah,' Gordon lied.

'Remember how you'd always get a lot of duplicates. Loads of Sandy Jardine or Danny McGrain and no-one wanted to swap them? All anyone wanted was Kenny Dalglish, with the nice hair, crouching on the ball. Kids would swap anything for that.'

Gordon hadn't a clue who any of these people were, or what Andy was on about, but nodded anyway. Andy could do that to you. Make you agree with anything, just to make him think you understood, that you were in on the joke.

'Danny doesn't know it yet, but I think you may have Kenny Dalglish.'

This was far too cryptic for Gordon, especially after five pints. Behind the lager fug, though, there was something urgent he needed to convey.

'Listen, Andy. You know the Russell Anderson thing? I think I might have something useful to contribute.'

Richard

The sea was supposed to be relaxing, Richard thought. Supposed to put things into perspective, make you appreciate your own relative insignificance in the face of the inexorable tides, or something like that. Instead it had just added nausea to his general air of depression. Maybe he had needed a stretch with a little more cosmic significance than the North Channel of the Irish Sea.

They were on land now, speeding westward. 'The deal is,' Liam was saying, 'I drive this thing all the way to Donegal, you meet this beardy bastard, do your interview, then we get stuck into the black stuff. Which we could go at solid for eighteen hours or so if I turn on the brogue, then we puke up, get some kip, drink a lot of coffee and I drive us back. Sound plan?'

Richard briefly wondered why he had brought Liam on this trip. Then he remembered it was because he couldn't drive, and Liam could. Although, judging by the way they were weaving from lane to lane on the motorway west of Belfast, that was debatable.

Richard, labelled the folk expert on the magazine ever since he had given a half-decent review to a Christy Moore album, had been sent to Donegal to get an interview with an elusive songwriter who refused to meet the press anywhere that wasn't within sight of the crashing breakers of the Atlantic. 'He's difficult,' the editor said, a phrase that conjured up images of alcoholic belligerence that the cuttings file seemed to confirm. 'If he's sober, you might get a coherent half-hour out of it. If he's not – well, you can do a colour piece about the vivid physical influence of rural Ireland on his poignant ditties, some sort of shit along those lines.'

Richard had thought Liam might be an asset. Occasionally, Liam could remember his Hibernian antecedents enough to turn on a second-hand Celtic charm, and he might be able to deflect any hostility that might be directed against a gauche Englishman stumbling through Ireland. Or perhaps Richard was just tired of carrying around a solitary misery, and needed distraction.

The problem had been apparent, though, as soon as they boarded the ferry at Stranraer. Liam, denied the opportunity of drinking, had wanted to talk. Most of all, he had wanted to talk about Sarah. Richard wasn't sure he was ready for that.

Sarah had disappeared a year previously. Gone to Europe,

leaving behind her an old blue dressing-gown cord, a pair of worn-out tennis shoes, and a gaping crevasse in Richard's entire being. Sarah had found out a truth that Richard had hoped would remain concealed, had looked at Richard with a ferocious sense of betrayal, had packed her bags and taken a train south. He had seen the ticket. The fact that it was a return had inspired him with a brief flush of hope. Then he remembered that return tickets were cheaper than singles, and Sarah's thrift seemed a more believable constant than her love for him. 'She's gone to Europe,' friends had told him. 'There was something about a job ... Brussels, maybe Geneva. Or was it The Hague?' Sarah had made a point of leaving a cryptic trail. She hadn't wanted to be followed.

Since then he had heard nothing. She had disappeared into a continent, lost in Europe. Richard had to be content with the needles of memory, and a scorching regret. Otherwise there was the endless self-reproach. Not with the infidelity. A part of him still felt that had been inevitable, a part of his life that had just been awaiting its discrete timing. No, he reproached himself with his verbal impotence, with the memory that all his attempts to explain had found him staggering clumsily across a minefield of self-justification and excuses, when he had wanted the words to tell her the significance of love, to dismiss the notion that this was a betrayal. But he was no good with words, at least not when they needed to be marshalled swiftly and effectively with no chance to edit, rewrite, hit the backspace button and remove the inelegant phrases and the ambiguities. So, he told himself, he had lost her because he lacked the right language.

One summer afternoon, a year after she had gone, Richard came out of a rehearsal studio near Ladbroke Grove, and froze. Twenty yards up the street, coming towards him at a brisk pace, was Sarah's mother. He wondered briefly if it was a flash of speed-induced paranoia, but he ducked back into the doorway regardless. He hadn't seen her in two years, but she was immediately familiar to him: her slightly self-conscious way of walking, her quick glances to left and right, her pink cheeks with the ghost of Sarah lingering about her. Richard felt a foolish flush of panic, then felt himself swept back to the first time he had met this inoffensive woman.

It was one of those awkward, meet-the-parents weekends. In Norfolk, in her family's country cottage, he had made polite conversation about the state of the national press with Sarah's father, had talked about Scottish weather with her mother. There was an aunt there as well, a divorcee in her forties with a certain unsteadiness around the eyes, who had started on the red wine in mid-afternoon and was scattering mild expletives throughout her conversation – which tended towards a bitter sarcasm regarding men in general, and British men in particular.

'Should have got yourself an Italian, Sarah,' she slurred. 'So much more passionate. Or a Spaniard, although they can be brutal. Only joking, Richard; only joking. Don't mind me, I'm just the family embarrassment. Aren't I, Lizzie?' she said too loudly, looking over at Sarah's mother.

'Aren't you what, dear?'

'The family bloody embarrassment.'

'If you say so, dear.' And Sarah's mother had looked at Richard with a faint 'what can you do?' grimace. Richard had looked back at her. With some relief he had found her maternal, kindly. His only previous experience of other people's mothers had been Beatrice's, and before that, his adolescent yearnings for Martin's flamboyant Mum.

The aunt drank steadily throughout dinner, only Richard making an effort to keep up with her – from his own sense of awkwardness, and from an unwillingness to ask exactly what bulgar wheat couscous was. He pushed it around his plate, piling it up into large bundles which he washed down with a small lake of Pinot Noir. Towards eleven, the aunt who had been subdued in the last hour, nursing a balloon of brandy, sniffing occasionally, rose to retire.

'Must to bed,' she said dramatically. 'Alone, as usual. Talking of which –' and she directed a fierce gaze at Richard, who had been half-sleeping, anaesthetised '– if you are doing the foul business with my niece, I hope you are being careful. Well?' She seemed to expect a reply. Richard looked at her, confused.

'Meg, darling, please,' Sarah's mother said tentatively.

'I'm talking about condoms,' the aunt said and, gathering herself together, made a dignified exit. An awkward silence prevailed until Sarah's father said, 'Anyone mind if I put on *Newsnight*?'

Richard knew now that if he stepped out of that doorway he would be able to see that exact same expression. She would be civilised, would say 'Hello, so nice to see you again,' and look away, finding a sudden passionate interest in the denuded bushes of Blenheim Crescent, the boarded-up windows of Clarendon Road. Richard knew he would see the little edges of panic in those patrician eyes, the smouldering resentment that life could throw up these incidents. Half of him wanted to do it, to step out there with a jaunty wave and the confident swagger of the single man. The other half of him knew that Sarah would already have offered a few details by way of explaining the break-up, and he would have seen those details reflected back at him as a reproach, and an acknowledgement that it was no more than they had suspected all along, ever since that moment when they had first registered his earring, his dyed hair, the leather jacket, the flattened estuary accent. He couldn't bear that.

So he cowered in his West London doorway, pretending to be engrossed in his NME until the housewife in her fifties, with her woven basket and her sensible handbag, disappeared into the Bangladeshi delicatessen. Then he turned the other way, took a left towards Latimer Road underground station, and wondered for the seventeenth time that week how he had allowed his life to fracture so alarmingly.

'Tell me if I'm wrong, old son,' Liam said now, looking across grey-blue waters towards Campbelltown, 'but didn't she leave because she discovered that you had been involved in some high-scoring away fixtures with another bird in London?'

'That was part of it, yes,' Richard said reluctantly.

'The most important part, I'm prepared to bet,' Liam said. 'Women are unreasonable like that. For some reason, if they find out you've been planting seed elsewhere, they seem to think they can swan off and retain the moral high-ground. Can't tell you how many times it's happened to me.'

Richard didn't want to have this conversation, didn't want his mistakes reduced by Liam's bald, demotic summary. But at the same time he felt he deserved it, realised that this was the real reason Liam was here. It had been a year. He needed advice. Needed to crystallize his reaction to what had happened.

'What I don't understand, though,' Liam was saying, 'is why you're still moping around about her. It's been a year. And to put it cruelly but accurately, it seemed to have been you who tired of her first, or you wouldn't have been looking elsewhere.'

'Yeah, well that was a mistake. I realise that now.'

'What, were you pissed? That I could understand. In fact, it's pretty much obligatory after the eighth pint to find an unsuitable sort to drag into bed. But from what I gather, this thing of yours went on for a year or so. Now, not even I could be pissed for a year. So there must have been something about this other bird, whoever she was.'

'Where did you get all this information? Oh, right. Sally.'

'Yeah, unavoidable side-effect of going out with each other's best pals. Women have a very unpleasant habit of confiding each other's emotional secrets. Not something blokes do too often. So anyway, what happened to the bit of spare? You see, traditionally, if the number one leaves, you shuffle up the number two into the vacancy. It's like promotion, up from the Second Division. I take it she wasn't ready for the big league? Choked in the play-offs?'

'Not a possibility. It wasn't that sort of relationship, it was…'

'Just the occasional shag when you happened to be in the metropolis?'

'No. She was a bit mixed-up. She had gone through a bad time.'

'Oh, Christ, Rich. Not that. Not the shoulder-to-cry-on bit. I cannot believe it. So she's off the scene now, is she?'

'Yeah. She's in Italy.'

'Tell you what, Rich, you have a talent there. Sarah went off to Europe. This other sort went to Italy. It's like they can't trust themselves to stay on the same land-mass. What do you do to them? Sorry, sorry. Listen, why don't we have a pint? Or rather, you have a pint, I'll have a coke. And I'll shake it up so I get a bit of froth on top and can pretend it's Guinness. Why don't you learn to drive, you selfish bastard?'

Liam drove west past Lough Neagh, and Richard saw a querulous side to him he hadn't noticed before. Richard realised that he had never seen Liam more than half an hour away from his previous or next drink. Liam seemed a little sour.

'Ahh, the Lough, and the gorgeous vista of the mountains of Sperrin ahead of us,' Liam said sarcastically. 'I hope to fuck there isn't a road-block. I've calculated the exact time remaining until my first pint, and I believe that the merest of fifteen-minute delays will fracture my soul.'

'Do they still have road-blocks?' Richard said, not quite keeping the panic out of his voice.

'Occasionally, although it tends to be to discourage people driving over the border to buy cheap fags. Why? Oh Christ, you're not carrying? That's why Sarah dumped you, wasn't it? Your congenital stupidity.'

'No, well, not much. Just a little wrap of speed.'

'Oh, for fuck's sake,' Liam said, slowing down and pulling into a lay-by. 'Listen. They have no sense of humour about that here. If you were driving with six pints on board, they'll give you a wink and a smile at your roguishness, but a spliff or a couple of lines, trust me, they'll bang you up in a cell with a twenty-stone farm labourer with homo-erotic inclinations. Give it here.'

Richard passed over the foil wrap, and Liam emptied half the grey powder onto his palm and signalled for Richard to hold out his hand. He poured out the rest, threw the foil out the window, and started to rub the powder onto his gums.

'Er – this is quite pure stuff, you know,' Richard said, but started to do the same.

'Might as well get your money's worth. Besides, it'll keep us awake for that extended lock-in we're going to get at Paddy O'Riley's Bothy or wherever the fuck we find ourselves in Donegal tonight.'

They sped though into the Republic, Liam's eyes fixed ahead, disdaining picture-postcard scenery to the sides, his pinhole pupils fixed on the road ahead of him. 'Gives you a thirst, this stuff,' he said laconically. 'And I already had one.'

The interview was arranged for the following lunchtime. They checked into a B & B above a pub in the middle of Donegal ('Might as well be close to the beer pumps,' Liam suggested). Still buzzing from the speed, they had beef stew and mashed potatoes in a café run by a taciturn matriarch who looked at them with impatience as she swept the floors around them. 'Don't you just love the sparkling welcome of auld Ireland?' Liam whispered through a mouthful of pastry.

At seven, they took their places in a bar crowded with four generations of Donegal locals. Grubby-faced toddlers chased each other around the slot machine, scrubbed teenagers sipped cokes and tried to look sophisticated, middle-aged working men rolled up their sleeves in imitation of sepia-tinged advertising posters, and the elderly survivors clustered around the dominoes table. 'Has there been a wedding, or something?' Liam asked the barman, putting on a strangled accent of his own fabrication. 'No,' the barman said, looking surprised. 'S'always like this.'

'I hate Guinness,' Richard said, taking a draught of the thick black stuff, just to remind himself. 'It tastes like blood.'

'Exactly. That's what's so good about it,' Liam said. 'Tell you what. Drink four pints of it just to take the edge off the speed, then you can switch to lager.'

They stood for a while on the fringes of the bar, ignored by the milling crowds, which were increasing every minute as extended families drifted through for their Thursday night session.

'For Christ's sake, will you cheer up, man?' Liam said. 'The state of your face is causing a chill as far away as Sligo. What's the problem? We're in the pub, drinking on expenses. All you have to do is chat to some ginger dipso about his fiddle technique tomorrow, and we're away. Come on.'

'Yeah, I know. I was just thinking about the time I went to Dublin with Sarah.'

'Right. Sarah. Might have known. Listen – lovely girl, loved her to bits meself as you know, but she's gone, all right? She's off to foreign climes, and it was quite a while ago, and you're here, and if you look over there you'll see a couple of what I believe are known as colleens, and your one might not be quite as appealing as mine but they aren't in their twenties yet, and I suspect they've been waiting most of their lives for a couple of sophisticates from places where the potato doesn't provide eighty percent of the diet.'

Richard looked in the direction of Liam's nod, but all he saw were a couple of grannies sipping sweet stout and glaring at him.

'Don't be too obvious, mate,' Liam hissed. 'Remember, every bastard here is related, and they devote most of their spare time to preserving the virginity of any girl who looks vaguely attractive. Did I ever tell you about my cousin Shonagh?'

While Liam delivered a well-rehearsed story about Shonagh, the 'whore of Drogheda' as the family knew her, Richard was thinking about Sarah. Richard was thinking about the notion that you fell in love once, and that was supposed to be it. You had to make it work, or else you were forever chasing unsatisfactory substitutes, ersatz versions of the real thing. The solution was surely to fight for that one true love, not to let it slip away into an unfathomable continent. Even if their sundering (Richard spent a lot of time coming up with more poetic descriptions of their banal break-up) had been his fault, did that mean he had to accept it? His mind was racing, partly through the speed, partly from what Liam was saying. Liam's words seemed to be set up as pure devil's advocacy, there to be refuted. If he accepted the loss of Sarah, he was accepting his own ultimate defeat, succumbing to his own weakness, admitting that he was just part of the common herd, a faithless drone ready to be conquered by a glimpse of young flesh.

'Will you ever look at the one with the red hair, man,' Liam was saying. 'A Celtic princess if ever I've seen one. And you know what they are like in the sack ... ?'

Liam told him, but Richard was only half-listening. The black stuff was beginning to choke him. He headed off towards the toilets, aware that he was attracting the curious looks of the locals. It reminded him of going home in the summer breaks when he was a student, the constant hostility of strangers. He used to enjoy it; now it just felt another tiresome detail of a world that had lost its colour.

He came back, saw Liam chatting to a young girl at the bar, saw her tall, square-faced brother or cousin or boyfriend or uncle or protector approach and give Liam the universal signal of the sharply reversed thumb. Liam sloped back carrying another couple of pints.

'Ah, alas, we may have to look elsewhere for our entertainment tonight, old son. This town is a little too small, and its inhabitants a little too small-minded.'

Richard looked at Liam, took in the genial grin, watched the chins wobble as the first third of the pint went down. He saw the look in the eyes, the optimism tempered only a little by experience, and wondered if he could ever approach that complacent air of constant possibility.

He could go on like this, he thought. Holding himself together with scraps of vaguely entertaining work, making do with the occasional opportunities to jump into bed with women who offered spectral glimpses of what he had before. Or he could summon up his courage, reject what logic told him, and try to recover the past. He sipped his beer, listened to the occasional strain of music that could be heard above the cacophony of conversation. There was a half-familiar song on the juke-box. It was the singer he had the interview with the following day, his last single, which had sold millions in Ireland and America and was beginning to pick up airplay in Britain. It was a vaguely threatening ballad of obsessive love, as the singer listed a series of habits that made his lover irresistible, ending each verse with an impassioned cry of 'Wherever you are, I will find you.' It was the sort of song Richard wanted to loathe, but each time he heard it made a stronger impression.

Leaving Liam sighing over a full Irish breakfast the next day, Richard took a taxi out to the singer's house by the coast. He looked over Donegal Bay to Bundoran, to a land greener than the print used in a brand-new geographical atlas. He felt the wind coming in from the Atlantic, felt the edge of Europe under his feet.

He walked up the long drive. The record company PR was waiting for him, wrapped in a voguish suede coat with a headscarf tied around her neck. 'Hi, Richard,' she said calmly. 'I'm afraid the interview's off.'

Richard looked baffled. Cancelled interviews weren't unknown, but it didn't usually happen when the writer had travelled a few hundred miles to get there. The PR seemed a little embarrassed, but only a little.

'Really sorry, but Ryan's been taken to hospital.' She lowered her voice. 'Shouldn't really tell you this, but it seems the wife stabbed him with a pair of scissors. Accidentally, of course. He should be all right. Listen, if you hang on here for a few minutes, I'll give you a lift back into town.'

He walked back down the drive just as the rain began. He looked back out to sea then turned around, looked past the house to the wooded hills, the distant mountains, to the rest of Ireland, to Europe. He found himself singing a refrain under his breath. 'Wherever you are...'

Beatrice

There was something about the way the filthy river lapped against the land. Something about the grudging way your coffee was refilled. Something about the sheer physical disdain of the big black girl in the Washington Square Subway station when Beatrice bought a token with dimes. Beatrice knew she was supposed to, but that didn't stop her loving New York City.

She would spend mornings over coffee in the diner on the corner of her street, making mental lists of what she adored about living here. Riding the subway, squatting inside the spray-slashed aluminium, bouncing back the curious stares she would attract from middle-aged derelicts. Walking down a deserted Fifth Avenue on a rainy late Sunday afternoon when all the commuters were tucked up on Long Island and all the tourists huddled in Irish bars, and one of the world's busiest streets had become a silent backwater. Pushing past a crush of Japanese camera fanatics clustering around the Empire State, just feeling that tingle of a New Yorker's superiority. She lived here. She loved the fakery of the ethnic districts, the artificial Eastern bustle of Chinatown, the ersatz Naples ambience of the Little Italy cafés. Everything had been put through a New York filter, the city's melting pot reducing it all to a thick, thrilling brown.

She had given up nearly all stimulants. That little wrap of cocaine at Liam's party all that time ago had been her last dalliance, although people were always offering it to her. Half the writers she worked with spent the bulk of their salaries at their Lower East Side connections. Beatrice would sit in her apartment and sip an occasional beer.

Here, too, was an escape. Manhattan's intimacy, the closeness of those millions crushed onto the island made it possible to sink into a warm familial anonymity, the sort of discreet evasion she had never been able to accomplish in London. Edinburgh had been a tiny village by comparison, a place where you constantly ran into acquaintances who would ask the same questions, make the same judgements.

Here, her celebrity was minor, unimpressive, a three-storey affair in a land of skyscrapers. Beatrice would turn up for work, see people in the lift whose exploits she had just read about in the New York Times Metro section. Not that Beatrice was the sort to be overawed;

she just enjoyed the closeness of it all, that ability to look down a street and see locations, buildings that looked like film sets, to brush past people at the centre of their western world.

She laughed at New York's towering ego sometimes, but she enjoyed it because its very pomposity threw a few crumbs of importance her way. She fitted in here because she was strange. To survive in New York you needed an alien streak, hundreds of strangers had told her in different ways. They liked her here because she was English. They liked her because she was tall, graceful, beautiful, with a priceless accent, and because they thought it their right to laugh at her.

She stood by the water cooler on the nineteenth floor of the building on West 53rd street, looking through her notes. She was aware of the presence of Jay Absalom, a short New Jersey gag-writer whose job on the show was to 'inject the profane touches.' Jay was there to pretend he hadn't gone to Yale, to swear a lot, put up a token protest when a risqué line was rejected. She liked him, because his was an easy artifice. He didn't believe his own assigned image, unlike some of them, who would talk of the 'integrity of the narrative.'

Beatrice had been forbidden to write jokes. Her role had been defined as 'dreaming up single-woman-in-the-city scenarios, problems that require resolutions.' The producer had clarified this by saying she was 'the schoolmarm setting the questions that the other assholes had to answer.' She rather liked the description, although she was aware she was being judged on appearances.

'I love your *Bosom*,' Jay said beside her, almost yucking at his own line. Beatrice found it impossible not to put on an RSC tone of hauteur as she turned to him. It helped that she was five inches taller.

'Jay, you know what worries me?'

He was grinning.

'Tell me, Beatrice.'

'It worries me that I have a contract to work in a team of comedy writers, one of whom feels unashamed to use a line I must have heard three thousand times since I delivered the manuscript for that book two years ago.'

'*One of whom*. I love it when you talk grammatical. Sorry. But what makes you so sure I was referring to your book, Miss Smarty

191

Limey? Maybe I should just have said I like your tits.'

Beatrice laughed, which she never did in script meetings.

'No, but really, I liked the book. Which was unusual in itself.'

'Why's that?'

'Because I don't like books by women.'

'Mmm, right. I feel overwhelmed. The likes of Jane Austen, George Eliot, your own Edith Wharton, Virginia Woolf, any one of innumerable Brontës, have left you cold, and yet you warm to my work. Jay, I feel humbled.

'Yeah, well, you can write like a guy, I guess.'

'You're so kind. That's really the ultimate accolade.'

'Beatrice. A word of advice. Sarcasm don't play well in sitcom. The midwest don't get it, and if they don't get it they don't like it. So rein it in. Do you like beer?'

'What? Yes, I suppose so.'

'Yeah, yeah, I know, American beer is piss, except without the body and the complex flavour. But I know a decent micro-brewery in SoHo that does some pretty good brews, and they sell that Brit stuff. Bass, is it? I'll meet you after the rewrites tonight.'

Beatrice sat at the end of the table in the script conference and wondered if she wrote like a guy. She didn't think so, but thought it would be interesting to try. She looked around the executive producer's office. This was the grown-up room. The writers had a deliberately cluttered den where they would work, a masculine retreat with a model-car circuit, a basketball hoop, whole stacks of comic books, and piles of sweaty sports shirts hurled into corners. Beatrice liked to think of it as the bedroom of the brother she never had.

The producer's room had a long oak table, swivelling aluminium chairs, walls featuring glossy stills of the show's cast picking up awards for best supporting actor, best guest appearance, best coverage of a minority issue in a network comedy.

While the meeting preamble would go on, Beatrice would stare at these photographs. It was at her third meeting that she stumbled on what had seemed disconcerting. In each picture the very centre of the frame featured the star's white teeth, bared in a mixture of friendly pleasure and challenge. That was the heart of it, she realised. The rest just revolved around that whiteness, fading into insignificance around the purity of the dental grimace.

That was the secret of the show, she realised. America had to see itself reflected back off that perfect white surface; that brilliance had to stay at dead centre. Beatrice, the rest of the writers, the producers, even the actors were just so many technicians making sure the framing was mathematically perfect.

The smile wasn't one of pleasure, it was one of deep trepidation, the reflex response to the sudden fleeting thought that the world wasn't pristine. When the creeping, nagging attacks of belligerent doubt came in, America's response was to smile, a concerted growl of outward confidence. That was why, Beatrice realised, it was so important for them to keep on lying in this show and in all the others. The truth could only terrify.

'So, Beatrice, what are we going to do with Jamie?' The producer, one of about a dozen, looked over at Beatrice and in his bland, American media face Beatrice could see the constant fear of it all collapsing, the panic-levels kept just short of boiling point. She looked around and wondered how anything so definitively trivial could exert so much power. They looked at her as if she were their mother, waiting for her to feed them. She had to force herself not to sigh at their desperation. She stood, looked around, smiled the smile of consolation. It was going to be okay, it was all going to work. But she might as well screw a little with them first.

'Jamie gets commitment,' she said, and she felt a few faces drop. 'Jamie learns to suppress his own selfishness, to realise another's needs. Jamie gives up womanising, hanging around bars…' By now she could feel the heads shaking. '…Jamie becomes a caring, considerate human being. You see, we're in the fifth season now, I believe. Even by the standards of sitcom time, he's a little older. He's not the carefree boy of seasons one, two and three. He can hear time's winged chariot clattering at his heels.' She paused to register the nervous dismay in their faces. They liked it when she talked classy, but they didn't like where she was going with this. 'So Jamie has to grow up a little, start to act like a mature adult.' She held the pause cruelly, watching the fear begin to articulate itself in the nervous sag of their jaws. 'And all for the love of this little pooch he has to look after for a sick cousin. Or something. I'm thinking Jack Russell. Cute. Manly. Not too yappy.'

'A dog? Love it,' says the executive producer, sitting back in relief, but still looking at a couple of minions to see if he really loves it. They nod enthusiastically. 'It's brilliant. Because we get to see the soft, caring side of his nature, and yet we can still keep up his reputation as a babe-hound. Right?'

'Mmm,' Beatrice said quietly. 'Instead he's a hound-hound.'

'Hound-hound. Love it. Write that down. And we resolve the dog thing at the end, lose the mutt, only nice, and he goes back to the old ways, yeah? Same old Jamie? Same interests?'

'Same interests. No more dogs. Just pussy.'

'Write that down too. No, maybe not, advertisers would freak. But nothing changes, right?'

'Oh no,' Beatrice said, looking around at their pink, excited faces. 'Nothing changes.' They all nodded happily.

Then, the meeting over, Beatrice shuffled her notes and stepped outside to find Jay Absalom standing by the water-cooler, giving the impression he had been there all the time, although she had seen him snoozing through the meeting.

'Beer,' he said. 'Now.'

'You sound like an Englishman,' she said.

'Only not so faggy, right?'

Soon after, Beatrice found herself drinking Anchor Steam Beer in the Washington Tavern, watching stocky Wall Street anglophiles trying to play darts. She was listening to Jay, whose conversation followed a kind of Viennese waltz rhythm. He would offer an elongated, melodic description of a sad event in his life, then he would spit out a staccato question.

'You know there are divorce accountants now?' he was saying. 'Can you believe that? Number-crunchers whose entire vocation is devoted to making a financial post-mortem of people's misery. They come over, look at all your stuff, discuss your relative earnings, calculate your economic contribution to the partnership, tell you who gets the Joni Mitchell album, and then charge a couple of thousand bucks for their trouble. My ex, Alicia, was threatening to bring in one of these retards last year, so I said take it all, every goddam cent. Except I kept the coffee-machine. She only drank camomile. Yeah, I know, why did I ever think we had a future? That's my trouble. I refuse to see the evidence before my eyes. So what do you think of the show?'

'It's insane, Jay.'

'Tell me about it. You being a Brit, I guess you've got a problem with these single people being far too wealthy, beautiful, witty and smart for it to ring true. I've seen some of your British comedies. Man, those people are so ugly, poor and stupid. I was slitting my wrists by the first commercial, except there wasn't one, because this was the BBC. Where's that at? See – in America, you have to remember that the people watching the shows are the ugly poor fat bastards snarfing Cheez Whiz and belching. With one or two exceptions, they do not want to see that on their TV sets. They want mildly erotic, escapist stuff with some wisecracking guys and some cute chicks.'

'No, no, I was expecting that. It's just that the … what's the word I'm looking for … the *ethos* of it seems so conservative.'

'Tell me more.'

'Well, these three girls and these three guys. What is the summit of their ambition?'

'To get laid. To make money. To get laid some more.'

'Close, but you know it isn't true. When do we get our biggest ratings?'

'Yeah, I know, I get it: when we have the big love scenes, when the kids finally get it together after a season of misunderstandings. The wedding stormed. People love the smooch.'

'You see. The essential message we are putting out is "find yourself a partner, or happiness will forever elude you."'

'Shit, for a girl with a job on a sitcom, you can sure make stuff sound bleak.'

'But that's it, Jay. The essence of comedy is an understanding of bleakness. This is something the producers never tell you. All those smartass one-liners you guys come up with are underpinned by an awareness that they are staving off despair. Actually, Jay, with some of your best lines I think you really are actually embracing despair.'

'Hey, I try and throw a little dark into the mix. It's the frustrated playwright in me.'

'But what I'm saying is that in the end we have to bow down and make everybody kiss each other better in the season finale. I've seen you. All the alcoholics and coke-fiends and divorcees and misogynists, all of you sitting there with big dopey grins on your faces figuring out a way for Jennifer to realise that her secret admirer with the cryptic messages and the tulips has been Marty all along. That's the rule. Everyone accepts it. If we want to keep the viewers we have to tell them that everything is going to be fine, that everybody has their significant other just waiting to sink into their arms.'

'And they don't? I'm not hearing this. Listen, I've had two divorces already. It's only the prospect of pulling off a third and maybe a fourth that keeps me going.'

'You see, what would be truly adventurous would be for us to suggest that these people could be happy in themselves, that they might be able to put aside this endless quest for a mediated idea of love and start to find a little fulfilment in their own lives, rather than borrowing it from others.'

'You don't ever let the producers hear you talking like this, do you?'

'I'm not stupid, Jay. I like the money.'

'But you're ... what's that English word ... slumming, aren't you? The books are the real deal. All jokes aside, I liked *Bosom*, and maybe that's why. Because that chick was like a guy. You know, one look back at the bed, a little smile, and *click* – the door closes and it's back on the road. Is that the way you feel, Beatrice? How old are you, anyway?'

'I'm thirty-one years old, although in England it's considered rather vulgar to ask. Your real question is how come I'm not married. The thing is, you see, in England it's a bit different. Over here, if you meet someone who likes the same films as you, or has their eggs cooked the same way, you're married within months. You find a diner where you don't get short-changed and you marry the waitress. You get a husband or wife the same way you get a car. You pick the one you like at that moment because you know you'll be trading it in after three years maximum. It's because divorce holds no stigma. You tell a friend you got divorced, it's like telling them you bought a new TV.'

'Too cruel. Although pretty accurate in my case. Except I have the same TV I had five years ago, and I've never felt like running off Friday nights having a few bourbons and watching a saucy little Sony down the block. So how come you never ...'

'A couple of reasons. I've never met a man I've wanted to spend longer than, oh, an evening with. And my parents weren't the greatest advertisement for conjugal bliss.'

'So what happened? Forgive my asking, but I'm from Jersey. We have to know everybody's life history in case they turn out to be people we have vendettas with.'

'Oh, a long and really very sad story. But off the point. What I was talking about was the show, and its refusal to reflect modern realities. Which is that people, and not just me, are beginning to realise that the promise of fulfilling and rewarding love is actually a lie. And not a very seductive one any more.'

'You may be right,' Jay said, 'but hey – there are alternatives. Meaningless sex, for instance. With a half-Jewish comedy writer from the gritty suburbs of Trenton. Would that be so bad?'

'Jay, I like your Anchor Steam Beer, but it's not really that strong.'

'Sheesh, okay, okay. You wanna play some darts?'

'Sure. I'll whup your arse.'

'Beatrice, Beatrice, don't try and get American on me. It don't become you.'

So Beatrice, as she had for every one of the nights she had spent in New York up until then, went home alone. Sitting in that room, with the faintly comforting sound of the taxis changing ('shifting' she said internally, loving the word) gear as they turned into Canal Street, and the snapping lines of a late-night sitcom rerun on the TV going back and forth like an endless tennis rally, Beatrice felt more alone than she ever had in her life.

She would look out over the lights of the world's greatest city and make another list. The delights of New York comprised her morning list; this was her night list, the tallying of connections now sundered. A father, a mother, an Italian family she would hear from once a year. At least, she thought, until they read the Italian translation of *Bosom* that was coming out later that year, when they would realise that their little Beatrice had never come close to being a good Catholic girl.

What is it, she thought, standing in her hallway, looking at herself in her full-length mirror, in her black underwear, staring at her paleness and wondering about desire – about the look she had seen in the eyes of the men she had gone to bed with, and the same look in the ones that she hadn't. It was a hunger, and a corresponding resentment of her power. She remembered the look in the eyes of Jacqui Francis in Norwood Park as the 70s ended;

could smell the grass, taste the Babycham. She could look back as an adult and recognise it at last. That was love, she thought. That was love, and I have never felt it.

She thought of her father, chasing a love that would reconcile him to his family, to his riches, to his status as a man from the north of Italy. She thought of her mother, stranded for years in a south London flat, cast adrift from a love that had promised a more exotic existence. Love had led them to the sea and to a bottle of pills. Even Jacqui Francis's love had led to a council estate outside Croydon, three kids, a divorce and a new boyfriend with tattoos in interesting places.

Beatrice considered her love for books, for learning, felt a distant flicker of memory for the physical thrill she would feel at the age of thirteen, at the local library, on the corner of Robson Road and Norwood High Street. She had eight books, four on her own ticket, four on her mother's, and the assistant would always say 'Sure you can manage all these, dear?'

Books had freed her, she knew, but maybe they had imprisoned her as well. She looked down at her bare flesh, shivered a little, ran a hand over her own smoothness, and wondered if she had reached a cold middle-age, if intellect had strangled baser passions at birth. She realised her heart had never raced for a man the same way it would race for an eighteenth century Gothic novel, for *The Monk*, or for Zola, or Maupassant. She was back in that library briefly, back feeling the thrill of anticipation as her eye ran along familiar shelves, seeking out new names. Beatrice looked out towards Midtown, towards the centre of late-twentieth century western civilisation, saw New York refusing to sleep, and realised she had never felt that excited since.

A Party In 1996

R ichard and Liam were walking down Fifth Avenue, competing with each other to be the least impressed. Richard was in his early thirties, Liam approaching the end of them; neither of them quite ready to admit they were anywhere near middle-age, yet both wanted to seem like blasé sophisticates. Richard had seen a lot of Liam lately. When they were together they would each rely on elaborate verbal artifice to suggest that their lives were complex and troubling existences, although they knew each well enough to see through them – and what's more, each was aware of the fact.

'How come we haven't been shot yet? Or at least mugged by some crack fiend?' Liam said. 'I hadn't realised that New York was a place you came to get away from the grungey urban terrors of Glasgow.'

'It is pretty docile, isn't it?' Richard said, sparing a sideways glance at the Empire State, and the burly black street-traders lurking on the sidewalk. 'Listen, let's go and buy some pirated designer tee-shirts. They're three dollars a pop.'

'Ah, a tiny blow against the forces of Mammon,' Liam sighed. 'Do you think they do extra-large?'

'I think it's pretty likely. Look around you. America invented extra-large.'

The truth was that they were both a little overawed by the city. Richard kept being startled out of his habitual melancholic reverie by a street or a building or a district already familiar from some song. He stood on the Bowery staring at CBGB's with the reverence you would associate with art-lovers in the Louvre gazing at La Giaconda.

Liam wasn't a traveller; wasn't entirely sure what he was doing here. 'If we were meant to move around we wouldn't have arses to sit on,' was one of his favourite mottoes. The only thing that could have persuaded him was a party. Liam missed parties. Glasgow somehow didn't seem the right place for them: the population too orthodox, too homogenised to provide a satisfactory mix for Liam. Besides. Sally seemed to have granted herself the power of veto, and usually exercised it when Liam broached the idea of 'a bit of a bash.' So a party in New York City, coinciding with the arrival of a cheque to cover a summer-school that had been so unruly that

Liam had prepared himself for the organisers' refusal to pay him, had been sufficient persuasion. He had met Richard in London, dragged him round the bars of Soho. They had boarded the ten o' clock flight from Heathrow with stinging hangovers, which they'd topped off that night with a crawl round the Irish bars of Midtown. A day later, they were still disorientated.

They had three hours to kill before the private party. It might have been one of, say, forty-five prestigious private parties taking place in Manhattan that week in the September of 1996, but this one had been mentioned in The Village Voice, had been sardonically acknowledged in The New York Observer, and had even been advertised in the previous Sunday's New York Times, although that was because Beatrice's publisher had paid a civilised sum of money for the privilege.

Downtown, in a room above the Knitting Factory arts club, Beatrice was looking around at a room that had been cleaned-up and de-grunged – but not excessively so. The publisher had consulted a designer – nobody too expensive, but a useful contact – who had been happy to look around the room, move a table, frown at the wine-glasses, and smile at the picture of Beatrice looming over them, staring through them.

A few feet away from the huge photograph, Beatrice herself was frowning. She wasn't sure about all this urban anomie. But her agent and editor were pushing it as a selling point, a piece of voguishness that could take her off the dry literary pages into the fashion and music arenas. The main character of her book, *Greyhound*, the jacket of which decorated the camouflage green walls, came from Seattle, after all. Beatrice's third novel was the story of an American journey east: across a continent in reverse, starting in Washington State and ending up in New York City on the Lower East Side. Beatrice had made it the Lower East Side not because she was particularly enamoured of the district, but because she found poetry in that combination of four syllables.

Sometimes she would wander along Hudson or Mercer, half-looking in the expensive clothes shops, intoning the words as a private mantra. Beatrice had taken to wondering whether she was in danger of insanity, of disappearing so far inside her own head that some day she would be unable to recognise the outside world at all.

'We've got a promise of a mention in the *New Yorker*,' Beatrice's America agent Tina was saying, at the same time fanning out a pile of the books on a side-table. 'They wouldn't tell me what, exactly; you know how snooty they are. But if they're mentioning it, that usually promises something positive.' Beatrice smiled down at Tina, but was distracted.

'Is there going to be beer?'

'Beer?' Tina looked confused.

'As well as champagne?'

'No, Beatrice. It's a book launch. Usually we just have champagne. The literary crowd are not great beer-drinkers. These people are either style leaders, or else they're in their fifties and sixties. Either way, they don't feel comfortable chugging a Bud.'

'Only I've an English friend coming tonight, and he hates champagne.'

'Listen, that's not a problem. If he wants beer, he can just go to the bar downstairs. I'm sure they'll accommodate him. Are you all right?'

Tina looked at her with that slightly embarrassing gaze of all-American concern, the vague panic that occurs when someone is behaving outside of the socially conventional norm. Beatrice stared down at the jacket of her book and admired its chic, smooth design. She liked the pale blue background, liked the stylised aluminium sheen of the back of the Greyhound bus. The back of a bus. It was the way Gordon used to describe anyone ugly, but Beatrice looked at the design, ran her finger over the surface and thought it truly beautiful.

It was the best thing about the book, she thought. It was her shortest novel, her slim, stylised take on '90s Americana, her modernistic Kerouac thing, a stream of smart consciousness. Tina had told her it would appeal to the 'alt-crowd,' whatever that meant. She couldn't remember a word of it.

Not quite true. She knew that she'd called her hero Evan. It seemed a suitably bland North-West Pacific Coast name, a simple two-syllable hiss of alienation. *Evian*, she had found herself thinking of him halfway through the book, because he seemed so wet. Now she thought she must have stolen the name from a book or a film or a record. *Evan* was not a person she could ever imagine existing outside the frame of media conventions.

Tina had told her that a production company was already negotiating for the film rights to *Greyhound*, that critics were queuing up to describe it as 'cinematic.' Beatrice had looked at her as if she were mad. Beatrice didn't want to be cinematic, she wanted to be novelistic.

She looked around at the neat approximation of a '90s counterculture, at the sprayed-on edginess of the room. They had got to her, she thought. She had come here, stood tall and English and smiled at their colonial obsessions and thought she was untouchable, but they had beaten her. Two years of devising ever-more humiliating plotlines for her ageing but still perky sitcom *Manhattanites* had channelled her mind into thinking visually, into seeing everything flattened onto a screen. She hadn't worried about Evan's character because she had visualised him, borrowed him from one of the casting sessions she had seen on a trip to Los Angeles for the show. *Greyhound* was her own little road movie, with a soundtrack that already sounded dated.

'Nothing's wrong, Tina,' she said, 'except … do you think we could insert a slip into every copy of the book saying "Do not read after 1996"? Oh, and do you think we could open one of those bottles now? Only I'm gasping.'

Tina smiled back nervously. Brits, she thought. Smart, but losers. And most of them with no idea about how to control their drinking.

Liam and Richard were among the first to arrive. They were already a little drunk. They had discovered a suitable-looking bar on Houston and had attempted to get a couple of beers. 'Guys,' the barman had said in the reasonable manner of a business consultant, 'I could sell ya a couple of beers, nothing easier, but that's going to be seven bucks. Else I could sell you a pitcher of four beers and that's only nine bucks. Do the math. Now waddaya say? The pitcher? Good thinking, guys.'

They had respected his candour, although they weren't impressed by the beer. But in the interests of economy they had followed up with a second jug, and only Richard's sense of duty had prevented Liam ordering a third. Going up the stairs at the club, Liam had grabbed Richard's elbow urgently and pointed out the giant colour photograph of Beatrice. 'Look – that's her. Isn't it? Looks just like her.'

'Yeah, I know,' Richard said, laughing, pointing to the doorway, 'and so's that.' Beatrice was standing there with a glass in her hand, smoothing her black dress, shaking a silver bracelet down her wrist when she saw them. It was the warmest welcome Richard had ever had from Beatrice. She clung to his neck, and Richard, numbed as he was, had a more than slight rumble of memory of an old longing.

'Darlin',' Liam was bellowing warmly, 'you still going to give us the time of day now you're the big shot?'

'You smell of beer,' she said, more in delight than reproach. 'Did you find your hotel? Oh, look at the state of you. Did you sleep in those clothes? You look so bloody English I can't believe it.'

'What are you saying?' Liam bleated. 'We're not chic? We made such an effort, too. The hotel's fine, but what's with the shared room thing? What happens when I pull a sophisticated uptown publishing executive?'

'You'll just have to go back to her place,' Beatrice said, ushering them into the still-empty room. 'Except I should warn you that New York women are more fastidious than the types you're used to. Although that probably applies to all nationalities.'

'Is that a challenge?' Liam said, his eyes already scanning the sparsely populated room. 'If you don't mind me saying, there aren't many here. I heard you had a cult following but this is verging on the wilfully obscure.'

Over the next hour they began to arrive, and Liam gradually backed into a corner. It looked like one of his crowds, only the language was different, like a parallel universe assembly of the austere and the weird and the self-destructive. He felt lost without a kitchen, without a fridge full of tepid lager, an oven full of potatoes.

The crowd was mid-90s Lower-Manhattan-alternative, a group that could almost be pre-booked through an ad in Barnes and Noble or the right East Village deli. Tina's assistant Marsha had assembled them, ticking off the categories as they were filled. There were the bookstore managers, record company executives, script editors, cutting-room assistants, final year fashion students, collagists, video technicians, DJs, SoHo Grand receptionists, manicurists, freelance photographers, sushi chefs, comic-book artists, comedians, carpenters, architects, provocative academics, community action volunteers, coffee-shop baristas, unsigned rock singers, cartographers, Flamenco guitarists, ice-hockey goal-minders, a struggling Portuguese actor, a poet from an old Boston family, a body-piercer, an AIDS activist, two members of the Olympic bobsleigh team, an English film critic, a homicide detective, Tina's cousin Dave, Dave's landlord to whom he owed money, a well-known Canadian short story writer who Beatrice had slept with and an elderly fat man called Arthur in a stained dinner-jacket who used to be a gatecrasher, but had come to be a mascot, a lucky charm for any book launch on the island. He had been featured in a boxed profile in the back of Vanity Fair. Then, filling the tiny gaps in the room, were the rumours. David Byrne was supposed to turn up. Laurie Anderson (who might bring Lou) was on her way; a couple of TV producers had already been thrown out; wasn't that guy over there Johnny Depp; and Jay McInerney, if he was in town, was bound to be there.

'It's like a party, except nobody's drinking,' Liam yelled to Richard, grabbing his arm and using him to steer away from an academic who was regaling Liam with his opinions on Yeats and Irish Republicanism. 'And where did you get that pint, you bastard? This champagne is killing me.'

Richard led him downstairs to the bar and somehow, once they had found the comfortable stools and settled down to a fresh pint, and Richard had smiled at the music which he had identified to the uncaring Liam as Sebadoh, it seemed like too much of an effort to go back upstairs. They looked out into the blackness of New York, leaned on the bar, carved out a little spot of England to themselves.

Beatrice found them there half an hour later, creeping up behind them and slapping them on the back with an accusatory 'So ... ?' They both looked guilty.

'Look, we were heading back upstairs, honest,' Richard stammered. 'It's just that we fancied a pint and it was a bit crowded up there and ...'

'Don't worry,' Beatrice laughed. 'I know, it's like the annual Village Voice intellectual posing competition up there. What's that you're drinking?'

'Bass. The eternal British beer of foreign climes. Wherever an English traveller may venture, he'll find a thick pint of Bass awaits him. Disgusting stuff by any standards, but at least it's not

American.'

'Get us a pint, will you?'

Beatrice sipped her beer and looked at the two of them and grinned. 'Listen,' she said. 'I'm really glad you came over. In fact, you don't know how much it means to me to have a couple of friendly faces from back home. Sure, all this stuff is really exciting, and I should be grateful for all the attention, but just seeing you two drunken idiots coming up those stairs meant so much more to me.'

Liam and Richard looked at each other. 'Is she serious?' Richard said. 'Fuck,' said Liam. 'I think she is.' 'She's gone American,' said Richard. 'Most sincerely,' Liam continued in a grotesque American accent. 'You worked on that sitcom too long, Beatrice; you got sentiment. Doesn't suit you. I think she's got a tear in her eye, Rich.'

He looked and it was true, she had. Richard and Liam put down their pints to look at her. She seemed to be blushing. In the ten years he had known her, this was the first time Richard had seen her blush. The tear was still there.

'It's my party; I'll cry if I want to,' Beatrice said, smiling. 'Bastards.'

'Do they actually have that, then?' Liam asked.

'What?'

'The Village Voice Intellectual Posing Competition.'

'If they did, you could be the first overseas champion, dear.'

The three of them sat in a companionable line for a few moments.

'The thing is, this is all fictional,' Beatrice said. 'It took me a couple of years to realise it, but there's nothing remotely real about New York. The whole city is one huge two-dimensional film set. All the people are playing characters, all spitting out these tough one-liners. You know, you go into a deli and ask for a sandwich, and no-one ever says, right or okay or sure – there's always this third degree interrogation involved, as if they're getting paid by the line. So what you were saying about the sentiment thing – okay, very cruel, but you've got a point. I've been acting most of the time I've been here. They cast me as the smart English bitch, so I played that for a while. Then I was the tough cookie – I was good at that. Now I'm the brittle-exterior-conceals-a-heart-of-gold.'

'Are you trying to tell us something, Beatrice?' Liam said. 'Only I'm ready for another pint.'

'Only that the new book is shit. I probably don't need to tell you because if you read it you'll notice. But the really worrying thing is that I didn't notice until a few hours ago. Up until then I thought it was my breakthrough.'

'Everyone I spoke to thought it was really cool,' said Richard. 'Not that any of them had read it.'

'Maybe that's the secret,' Beatrice sighed. 'It can be my accessory book, the one to carry around on the subway, put on the table in coffee-shops, buy for your friends. Just so long as you never read the bloody thing. What was I thinking of?'

'Easily done, love,' Liam said, in between trying to attract the barman's attention. 'This place is seductive. It's easy to get carried away, especially if they're paying you hundreds of thousands of bucks and telling you you're the greatest thing since aerosol cheese. Whatever happened to that TV show, anyway? I don't believe it graces our screens any more? Bass. Yes. Three. Yeah, I know, we're English: we have to drink it.'

'I think it was when the cast demanded seven million dollars each upfront before they would have a preliminary meeting about doing a new series that the rot set in. But around that time I lost it. I couldn't take it seriously any more. I started to laugh in script conferences. Are you aware how these people look at you if you laugh when you're talking about the growth curve of a comedy series? They gave me a big cheque to go away. That was the only thing I loved about television. The more they wanted you out of their business, the more money they were prepared to give you.'

'Wish universities would think that way,' Liam said. 'Then I could afford to indulge some of my fantasies about the undergraduates.'

'How's Sally?' Beatrice asked, with a gleam in her eye.

'Love her to bits, of course. You know, the further away from her I am, the more affectionate I feel. Right now, with the whole expanse of the Atlantic separating us, I feel a strong glow of tenderness towards her. What can this mean?'

'Interesting, that. Perhaps it means the only way to take the relationship to the next level is to spend more time apart.'

'I see where you're going. Eventually we could not see each other at all, and reach a sort of erotic nirvana, flawless and pure. That would be something to aim for. Except … I think she would keep phoning, and that might ruin it.'

'What about you, Richard?' Beatrice asked.

'What about me?'

'Any developments?'

'No.'

'Hopeless case,' Liam said. 'Wouldn't even look at this glorious Mexican girl in the hotel lobby this morning.'

Richard threw him a look of disgust and reached for his pint.

'Sorry folks, I'm going to have to ask you to clear the bar,' the barman interrupted. 'Only we've got a band coming on in about half an hour, and we need to vacate the room. Unless you want to pay the cover.'

What's the band?' Richard asked.

'Teenage Fanclub. Irish or Scotch or something.'

'Scottish actually. From Bellshill. How much?'

'Twelve bucks.'

'Shall we?' Richard asked, and smiled a rare smile, and Beatrice paid for three tickets. An hour later, Liam stood on the sidelines guarding three pints. Richard and Beatrice bounced around at the front while the singer bellowed in paradoxically tuneful Glaswegian. Midway through, the group brought on a guest, garbling an incomprehensible introduction to a lank-haired tubby guy who sang back-up vocals in a nasal whine.

'Who's that?' Beatrice bellowed in Richard's ear.

'Evan Dando,' he screamed back.

'What?'

'Evan Dando. From The Lemonheads.'

Beatrice had never heard of him, but she looked up and realised she must nevertheless have absorbed him somehow – that corn-fed American blitheness, that spaced-out grin, that name. She realised she had just written a book about him. For a second she laughed at herself, then jumped up frantically, shaking her head to the music, the hair bouncing back into place precisely at every beat. Richard looked at her, wondering how America had changed her.

At the end, they drifted back in search of Liam. 'We're too old for this,' Richard said, looking down at his sweat-soaked blue shirt.

'I've always been too old for this,' Liam said, draining a last pint. 'You know what, though? And I think I may have read this somewhere, so it's not that original. I love New York.'

'I don't,' said Beatrice quietly. 'I've had enough. I'm leaving next month.'

As they were sitting at the bar, looking at their empty glasses, Tina's cousin Dave, arm-in-arm with a manicurist, stopped on his way out. 'Hey, writer lady,' he yelled. 'Great party!' He waved, tottered a little, steadied his grip on the manicurist, and disappeared out into the New York night.

'We should have asked him where he got her,' Liam said morosely. 'There might have been more of them.'

Faith

Grainne

L ooking out of the French windows, you could see all the way down that tight-mowed green sloping lawn to the edge of the lake. The lake always worried her. She could only occasionally remember why. Grainne would sit upright on one of those stiff, wooden chairs, resting her elbows on the table, watching the last of summer turn too quickly into mid-September autumn. She would watch the raindrops come in at an angle, hitting the surface of the lake like machine-gun fire.

She looked at the dark indigo water and remembered Perthshire fourteen years before: that first and last summer of freedom before going to university. She remembered the brutal, cold embrace of that loch, and shivered with a longing to have that day back again. Grainne could sit and stare at that water for an hour or so. She would be disturbed either by Abigail, bringing her a cup of lemon tea with a gentle smile, or by Marcia, sidling up to her and hissing, 'Don't eat the carrots. Don't ask why; just don't touch 'em. You'll thank me.'

Then she would remember. Abigail was a nurse, Marcia a patient, and this was a mental hospital. And really, wasn't it rather a bad idea to have a lake in the grounds of a mental hospital?

Of course, nobody ever admitted it was a mental hospital. *Sanatorium* was about as far as they would venture, conjuring up images of a bucolic 1920s escape, a mystical place of gentle caring, of shell-shocked officer poets starting at the thoughtless slamming of a door, of a fitful, sad coughing from the tuberculosis cases – doomed, all of them, but in a romantic, beauty-dies-young sort of a way. *Sanatorium* they would say sometimes, but usually they just called it The Grange.

Grainne wasn't fooled, and made a point of telling herself she wasn't mad either. She couldn't vouch for Marcia, a wispy aristocrat who had developed a peculiar phobia about food, each day selecting a different vegetable to be the object of her suspicions. Or for Graham, who would fold back the odd-numbered pages of the *Daily Mail* with an intense and touching determination. Or for Helen, a famous TV actress whose self-loathing seemed somehow connected with her diminishing level of celebrity. Or for Matt, a man whose anger seethed at a barely containable level, who shrieked 'Thanks, bitch' when Abigail brought him orange juice, although Abigail smiled at him just the same. Or for Abigail, who claimed to be a nurse.

Nobody had surnames at The Grange. Except for Dr Anderson. Grainne made a point of asking Dr Anderson why he was the only one entitled to this privilege. 'We don't want too much formality, do we now, Grainne?' he said. Dr Anderson had an East of Scotland burr that had the unfortunate effect of conjuring up an image of Grainne's father. 'Quite a lot of our clients like to preserve anonymity. In fact, your husband was quite firm in that regard. Understandably so.'

Understandably so. At times Grainne realised that being here was probably the worse thing she could have done to Gordon. A thought that would give her a tiny glow of pleasure.

Dr Anderson would ask her the usual questions in a seemingly uninterested, offhand tone. 'How much resentment do you feel towards your husband?' he had asked once. 'A little,' Grainne had replied, and he had been satisfied. Out of weariness rather than caution, Grainne didn't elaborate. Explaining it all would have been too arduous, and she didn't think it would help. She tried explaining it to Gordon, and had realised it was a mistake.

'I can't afford this,' Gordon had said on his first visit, taking in the gymnasium, the lake, the tennis courts. 'I really can't afford it, even taking into account how much we're saving on vodka.' It was a theme he returned to on each visit.

'It wasn't my idea,' Grainne would say, but Gordon would look at her and she would look back, and she would remember that Sunday morning when he had been woken by a particularly discordant racket, and had got up to look out the window and had seen Grainne, naked, lying on the estate green, screaming incoherently. He had rushed down, grabbed her arms and hauled her inside, with Grainne yelling, 'What's the matter? Embarrassed that other people might see me naked? Never seems to bother you other times, does it?'

Gordon had called Dr Andrews, another one of those hazily Scottish figures who seemed to have the monopoly in practicing medicine among the moneyed middle classes. Dr Andrews had registered an empty vodka bottle, vomit stains on the carpet, a state of hyper-excitement, and had administered a sedative injection.

Grainne had a vivid memory of slumping in an armchair with her colour spectrum dissolving, seeing the walls change from magnolia to grey, seeing the beige carpet turn white, seeing the florid pink face of Dr Andrews drain into the monochrome blankness of the Prime Minister. The doctor had been conversing cheerfully with Gordon, occasionally glancing with vague concern at Grainne, before writing down a number on a card and handing it over to Gordon with a consoling pat on the elbow.

Gordon would close the door behind him when he came to visit, but still spoke to her in such a whisper that she had to lean into him to hear the words. She felt self-conscious at the proximity, at a parody of the intimacy she used to feel.

'What do they do here?' Gordon said, with vague trepidation.

'How do you mean?'

'The treatment.'

'No electro-shock I'm afraid, Gordon, although if you paid extra and asked nicely, I'm sure they would oblige.'

'Grainne, please.'

'What you'd expect. You have a group session where you have to stand up and talk about yourself, about your dependency. Then there's lunch, all very healthy. Then individual sessions, for which read "cheap pop psychology;" recreation, exercise. It's like school, really. Except without the heavy drinking.'

'What did you say about yourself?' Gordon looked keenly at her.

Grainne looked back at him evenly.

'What do you expect?'

'I don't know, tell me.'

'My name is Grainne Hendrie, I'm the wife of a man who thinks he is going to be in the next government. I've taken to drinking a bottle of vodka every day. Why, I'm not entirely sure, although it may be connected to the fact that at weekends my husband likes to drive me out to country houses where we have sex with complete strangers. One time, I was expected to entertain four different men, two at a time, one of whom was at least sixty...'

'All right, all right,' Gordon hissed. 'You didn't...'

'No, of course I didn't. You know what they tell you on the first day here? That you have to surrender your shame; that you have to get past the stigma of being an alcoholic if you are going to start helping yourself. But there is some shame that I'm not quite ready to sidestep, Gordon. It's too much. It will always be too much.'

'You never said,' he murmured. 'I thought you were as keen…'

'As keen as you were? I don't think that would have been possible, would it, Gordon? Didn't you ever notice that I had to be semi-comatose before I could face those trips? Or didn't you care?'

'You never said anything.'

'We're married, Gordon. We're supposed to know each other well enough for things to be able to be unsaid. Things as basic as my not being entirely comfortable with the idea of having rough, non-consensual sex with a vicious cross-section of the English middle classes.'

But he was right, she thought. She had never said, and she had always known that Gordon was not the sort of man to read a facial expression. She should have said something the time when Dr Andrews came round to deliver their blood-test results. Gordon had told him it was for insurance purposes. The doctor had handed him a couple of slips of paper. 'I'll get these photocopied,' Gordon had said when the doctor had left. 'They're our entry ticket to a whole new circle.'

Circles, Grainne thought now. Wasn't that how they divided up hell? She remembered, through a haze, a long trip down to Dorset. She had taken the train down to London on the Friday night to meet Gordon. He had driven west on Saturday morning, whistling gently as they negotiated their path onto the motorway. In a service station, while Gordon had refuelled and bought his *Times* and *Telegraph*, Grainne had slipped into the ladies' toilets, taken a swing from her familiar vodka flask, and swallowed half a pill – one dove's wing. Saved the other half for later.

The houses were always big, discreet, off the main road, with electronically-controlled gates. Inside, the 'parties' seemed joyless affairs because the guests were so few. Any more than twelve was risking discretion, Gordon told her. Sometimes the faces would be familiar. Maddy and Danny would often be there. Maddy would kiss her cheek, smile at her as if they were intimates (which they were, Grainne supposed; it would be difficult to conceive how they could be more intimate). Danny would be cool, although he didn't mind if Grainne asked him for pills. He would smile at her, palm her a couple and say, 'Red, my rule is never twice with the same girl, but with you I might make an exception' – drawled in a fake Bogart voice. He never did, which was one of the few small mercies Grainne was grateful for.

There would be back rooms, four-poster beds, velvet drapes, handcuffs, silken ties, oils, lubricants, sweat, little cries of panic and exultation, and everywhere an aroma that would have made her sick even without the vodka, disguised in long glasses of orange juice. Grainne would look at the faces sometimes, even though it wasn't the done thing, and see a coldness, a desperation, and recognise it as the same expression Gordon wore when he was figuring out how to swing a committee around to his way of thinking.

Gordon would be looking around for the smallest, frailest women there: tiny, slim, breastless creatures, preferably blonde, the younger and quieter the better. When she had first noticed this, Grainne had wondered briefly what this said about his attitude to her own robustness, her curves, her strength. Then she had laughed at the indulgence of this small anxiety when there was so much more to panic about. She would slip down the other wing of the dove, make sure she had spares in case of a weak dose, and feel herself being led off by the wrist. The convention at orgies, she found, was that people held your wrist rather than your hand. Hands denoted affection. Affection wasn't invited. Grainne would cry to herself afterwards. To herself. She couldn't let Gordon see. That would be allowing herself to be conquered twice.

'So,' she said, looking out of the Grange's always-clean windows rather than at Gordon. 'Do you still go? Or aren't you invited without your little red-haired ticket? Single men aren't welcome, are they?'

'Grainne,' Gordon said impatiently. 'We have to forget all that. We were going to have to stop anyway. We couldn't take the risk...'

'No, no, of course not. Not with an election coming up. All forms of unorthodox recreation must be put on hold. Did Peter have a word, dear?'

'The thing is to get you out of here as soon as possible, before the press get hold of it. And before it bankrupts us, as well.'

'You'd have thought the Party might chip in. Fund for alcoholic degenerate wives. I'm sure the unions have cash for that sort of thing.'

'I find it impossible to talk to you these days, Grainne. I know you're ill, but you seem to have no sense of logic any more. Your mother was saying the same thing.'

'She is not my mother!' Grainne screamed the words, and Gordon winced.

'All right, all right. I'm sorry. Lynne. But she offered to have you up there in Scotland for a while. Just while you get your nerves back under control.'

'Do you think that would work?'

'It's worth a try.'

'You don't know me, Gordon. You should admit that. I don't know you, but I realised that a long while ago. The idea that I might get better with Lynne and my father is too ridiculous for words. I'd be on the first bus into Edinburgh, and straight into the first pub. You'd better go, Gordon. I need time to think.'

Gordon left, and she watched him go.

The Grange was forty miles from London, and Richard came to visit, bringing flowers and Belgian chocolates. 'The box is open,' he said. 'They searched them at reception. What's that all about?'

'Checking for alcohol.' Grainne smiled. 'You know, there are people here who could try to get pissed on a pound of kirsch liqueurs. I'm probably one of them.'

They went for a walk around the grounds; Grainne pointed out autumn foliage while Richard nodded politely.

'This is what happens in drying-out clinics, you know, Richard,' Grainne said. 'As soon as the first wave of toxins gets out of your system, you become hypersensitive to your surroundings. You go around in raptures over the pattern on a leaf, or the ripples on the lake.'

'That would explain a lot of Van Morrison's lyrics,' Richard said. 'So what have you been doing with yourself?'

'I've been thinking. I know it sounds ridiculous, but I never really had the chance before. Yeah, I know, I was in that house, on that bloody executive estate, and I didn't have a proper job, and I had plenty of time … but somehow I never really got around to questioning things. Now, part of that was because I had a couple of bottles of Stoli in the cabinet and started pouring around lunchtime, but part of it was just acceptance. I was the politician's wife, and I had to keep things in order for him. Gordon kept giving me these little time-scales, you know: January before the defence appointments are made, summer before the campaign committee, November '96 election ... although that doesn't seem to be happening, does it? But there were all these little markers that I had to keep in mind; that we had to use to measure out our lives. Now I don't have that, so I've been thinking about the past.'

'And?'

'Remember Joachim, the boy I used to work with in the coffee place?'

'Oh yeah, the speed freak, right?'

'Exactly. I never really thought about it, but every time I saw him after you pointed that out, I would think of him with this mixture of condescension and pity. You know, the way you feel about people you think of as weak. Quite funny really, that it's me who's ended up in detox.

'You know what else? I'm thirty-two, and I'm the youngest one here. I always thought these places would be full of teenage junkies. But it's not. It's bored housewives with too much money, except most of them manage to hold it together until they hit forty. I'm so pathetic I couldn't even last long enough to become a career alcoholic.'

'Actually, this place gets pop stars and footballers too,' Richard said in a consoling voice. 'It's just they check out at the end of the summer, once the university tour circuit and the football season start up.'

'Oh, right. Trust me to miss the celebrities. But you know what happens to people here? They come to believe in their own historics: they find something in the past to blame for their pain, or else they get religion. Nobody can ever just say they liked to get blitzed because they were bored or unhappy. It has to be their response to a trial, or their weakness in the face of a divine test.'

'What about you?' Richard asked.

'No visions of the Madonna just yet. But it made me think. It made me think about us, our little group. What happened to make us so faithless?'

'What do you mean by *faithless*?' Richard asked, nervously.

Grainne stopped, looked over the lake.

'Look at us. Beatrice is in America with her novels about bleak individualism, about the failure of understanding. You're closer to her than I am, but she is so, so solitary. Gordon just wants to feel important; he wants to have the next job title up the ladder, wants to feel that all that wheedling and persuasion he does makes him important. I can't believe he doesn't realise how much he's being used, how compliant all that eager ambition makes him. You? You haven't been the same since you split up with Sarah, and I don't know what that's about, except I do know it's unhealthy. And I am the subject of concerned meetings of Russian vodka importers wondering why their profits in the north-east have slumped alarmingly in the last quarter.'

'Where does the *faithless* bit come in, though?' Richard asked, piqued by what Grainne had said about him and trying (unsuccessfully) to hide it.

'None of us has had a family; none of us has even contemplated it. None of us is particularly happy. Gordon pretends to be, but he has too much anxiety to be content. None of us trusts ourselves. We're all hiding behind something. We have no faith in living.'

'Did you want to?'

'What?'

'Have children?'

Grainne laughed. 'With Gordon? What do you think? What kind of father would he make?'

They walked on a few more yards, then took the path back up towards the building. 'Come on,' Grainne said, 'I think it's starting to rain. I'm sorry about all that. I'm supposed to be the patient and you're the cheery visitor trying to make me snap out of it. Let's eat those chocolates. If we ask nicely they might give us some decaffeinated coffee. It tastes just like that Nicaraguan stuff I used to force on you all.'

Later, Grainne watched Richard head off down the path towards the front gate, the same way she had watched Gordon before, drifting away with the same slump in the shoulders.

Faithless.

October days drifted by, unusually calm, the Grange cooling unhurriedly. Grainne woke with a start around four in the morning, feeling hot – more than the usual night-sweats of alcohol memory. She wandered over to the window in her nightdress, looked out over the moonlit lawn, down the black slope to the tree-lined lake, saw the branches drifting a little in the breeze. She pressed herself against the window, felt the coldness of the glass though her nightdress.

Then she found herself creeping silently down the stairs, looking down the corridor towards the kitchen, turning towards the television room. She crossed the room, feeling the stiffness of the carpet under her feet, the moonlight slanting in through a crack in the curtains.

Grainne felt the catch of the French windows give, felt cold English air coming through the gap. Then she was through, stifling a gasp at the freezing dew on the lawn, the icy blast of the breeze catching her nightdress, pushing it tight against her shoulders. She walked steadily down the slope, keeping in a straight line, wanting directness, no deviation.

At the lake's edge she stepped into the water, found it warmer than the dew on the grass, looked down at its murkiness lapping over her toes. Into the water, she kept telling herself, wondering briefly if this was a dream. The water would be her blanket, she said to herself, and moved forwards into the lake, feeling resistance from grass and weeds at the edge. She moved on until the water was at her knees and there was a pleasant cool numbness around her ankles. Water would soak through and clean her, replace all the liquids she had lost, turn her back into the girl who had laughed at Perthshire rain, had lain naked under the skies.

The hem of her nightdress was soaked, clinging to her thighs, and Grainne went on, slightly off balance. She panicked briefly at the idea of falling. She wanted to stay upright until the last, to step purposefully under the surface staring ahead, letting the water quietly close above her.

But the water seemed unwilling. It started to retreat, as if cowed by her determination. It ebbed downwards, fled below her knees, and Grainne felt the breeze again, felt the air currents curve around her legs, battling the water, chilling and drying her. She looked down and saw her feet, muddy, scratched, but pulling her back up the gentle incline, through the reeds and the grass. Grainne looked back, saw the far bank, saw the lawn sloping up to the French windows, saw that she had crossed the entire lake and was emerging on the other side.

Waiting for her there was one of the nurses, Jake, tall, black and patient, with the moon beaming down behind his head, giving his cropped hair a vague halo. He was holding out his jacket, wrapping it around her shoulders, smiling.

'Good job that lake's only a couple of feet deep,' he said in a soft voice. 'You could have caught your death. Come on, Ophelia; back in the warm.'

Richard

aithless, Richard thought. That was the word. An inability to remain faithful to one ideal. He should have remained in love with Beatrice, he often thought, should have settled for that glorious impossibility. He remembered something Liam had said: 'When I was a kid and we used to sing that hymn, I would always wonder what *ineffable* meant. Now I look at Beatrice and know. It means unfuckable.'

That would have been fine, the serene knowledge that your goal could never be achieved. You could live with that, with the purity of failure. But Sarah had come along and supplanted Beatrice, and had embodied the lethal quality of being attainable. Now he still wanted Sarah and she was as impossible as Beatrice, only more so because she was lost, made unreachable because he had once held her.

Faithless. Hadn't he always been faithless, even then? He had no faith in his ability to keep Sarah, or at least no faith in his ability to be happy with just Sarah. That had been the problem. Now it was worse. Now he had no faith in music's ability to make him feel alive, in amphetamine's ability to keep his brain engaged, or in his oblique, sarcastic writing style's ability to keep making him a living.

He had a call asking him to drop into the newspaper office. That was unusual. He would rarely venture inside the riverside complex. Most of his commissions came over the phone via a terse conversation with Dave Simmonds, the arts editor. Richard was still writing about music, but had branched out into book reviews and television previews, into the unnoticed fillers of a bloated broadsheet. With the TV features he was at least assured of a warm afternoon in a Soho viewing facility, a few glasses of wine, and whatever the catering budget could provide in the way of food.

Faithless, Richard thought to himself: but more than that. He was aimless in a manner he recognised in the homeless people outside Tottenham Court Road tube station, drifting on through an irregular income, learning to prioritise those valuable little interludes of free food, drink, or entertainment. He had even started to dress like them, Richard thought, looking at the holes in his Fila trainers, the crumpled black jacket, the shirt stretching over a flabby waistline. He divided his days into segments: the hours of brief activity, the flurry of anxious chasing after money, punctuated by

221

meals, drinks and long stretches of waiting around for something to happen.

He had read in his *Big Issue* that a substantial proportion of the homeless had suffered one cataclysmic event in their life that had sapped their will to hold their social fabric together. This event – bereavement, abandonment, addiction, whatever – had made the usual imperatives of food, shelter and survival seem temporarily unimportant. By the time they had come around to the realities of their situation, it was too late.

Richard thought he knew the temptations of that hopelessness, thought he could appreciate the idea of waking up and just laughing at the pathetic obligation to survive. Sometimes, nearly always lately, Richard despised his own weakness when he answered the phone, when Dave Simmonds asked him to preview a new costume drama or write a potted profile of Chris Evans or Danny McBeth, hated himself for drawling back in his media-weary voice, 'Sure, how much do you need?' Some nagging instinct, though, told him he would need the money for some greater cause, had to keep himself afloat, just in case a rescue craft should come along.

Richard walked down towards the river, through a London he had started to hate. It was a city he blamed, along with himself, for losing Sarah. When he had started to come here regularly he had lost himself, lost his moorings.

It was its hugeness, its impersonality. Walking down through mid-afternoon crowds in Chelsea he still felt it: that idea that you were invisible in this city, that all your actions were unseen and so didn't need to be acknowledged. It was like the old Catholic Church, handing out indulgences. London was a place to hide your crimes. Except, somehow, they always emerged.

Richard signed a visitor's slip at the reception desk and tried to smile. The security guard was already looking at him as if he was a likely terrorist, and the forced, slightly manic smile didn't seem to reassure. Richard scurried off in search of the lifts.

Dave Simmonds was someone Richard had known for a while, a former music journalist who had scrabbled for a desk job as soon as his hairline had started to recede. One of the cruel truths of the music business is that 22-year-old musicians laugh at bald men sent to interview them.

Dave was on the phone, speaking in the clipped journo-speak

obligatory for anybody who wanted to be taken seriously on a London newspaper. Richard half-sat on a corner of the features desk, deflecting the gaze of the hostile sub-editors, trying to give the impression that he was a dangerous bohemian with access to all sorts of hard drugs. Though he knew that newspaper executives indulged in far better and more expensive narcotics than he ever would. Richard flicked through a copy of *The Face* that Dave was no doubt about to plunder for ideas. Dave came off the phone at last, and tried to fake up some bonhomie.

'Rich, good of you to come in.'

'Well, I found myself with a surprising amount of leisure time.'

'Yeah, sorry, only we've been told to cut back on the freelance stuff. Budget hell. News has been eating cash, sending all sorts of arseholes to the Balkans. For some reason BBC2's new drama strand has been pushed down the priority list. Anyhow, might have some good news for you. Jenny wants to meet you.'

Jenny was Jenny Wolseley, a famously elusive features executive whose existence Richard had always thought to be an unsubstantiated rumour. During one or two of his sporadic bouts of journalistic enthusiasm, Richard had tried to call her in order to float a few ideas. He would never get any further than her secretary's voice-mail. Dave had told him that Jenny was adept in the art of delegation, calling a meeting on Tuesdays to delineate the week's pages, and then spending large chunks of the subsequent days lunching in London's more voguish restaurants, visiting high-fashion outlets, or having meetings with travel companies to arrange free trips to the Caribbean.

She had a capacity for what her journalists called 'brilliant ignorance.' At meetings she would show a complete inability to understand the concept of, say, a by-election, or would wonder aloud whether it might be possible to fix up an interview with Edie Sedgwick. Her minions would blush for her, making it unnecessary for Jenny to feel in the slightest bit abashed. 'She's headed for the top,' the more cynical subs would say. 'She's just too thick to fail.'

Dave led Richard along the office to a partition. It was a pathetic piece of carpentry that reminded Richard of a set from an Australian soap opera. The late '80s and early '90s' vogue for open-plan newsrooms had been killed off by the burgeoning egos of the new executives, who felt they needed plywood and a glass-fronted door to shield them from the vulgar masses.

Jenny's desk was strewn with striking pictures of models in their underwear. She was punching keys on a mobile phone. 'Hang on a minute,' she said distractedly, 'I'm sending one of those text message things. Isn't that brilliant?' Then she looked up at Richard in vague irritation. Jenny had the kind of blonde hair that he had heard described as 'ashtray,' and a slightly protruding top set of teeth that gave her a vacant, vaguely aggressive look. She looked questioningly at Dave, then a gleam of realisation hit her.

'Ah, you must be ... ?'

'Richard. Richard Martin.'

'He's the one ...' Dave started to explain.

'Yes, yes. Sit down, Richard. Do you want some coffee? I could send Claire down to the canteen.'

'No thanks, I'm fine.' Richard could have killed for a cup of coffee, but for some reason he didn't want to witness Jenny sending Claire to the canteen to fetch some.

'So, I hear you're a friend of Beatrice Morelli?'

Richard was taken aback, and immediately suspicious.

'Well, I suppose, yes. I've known her for a while. We were at college together.' Richard always avoided saying university.

'Still in touch?'

'Yes. Except she lives in Italy now, so I don't see much of her.'

'Beautiful woman.' Jenny seemed to be talking to herself now. 'Wonder what moisturiser she uses.'

'Are you thinking of doing a piece? Only I know Beatrice doesn't like to do interviews.'

'Tell me about it. I've been on the phone to her snooty whore of an agent all bloody week. Didn't want to know. Then Dave here let slip that you were her bestest buddy, so I phoned up the tart and said Beatrice would be sure to talk to Richard ... Richard ...'

'Martin.'

Jenny's brow furrowed. 'I thought your name was Richard?'

'It is. Richard Martin.'

'Yeah, yeah, so I told her Beatrice couldn't refuse Richard bloody Martin, could she?'

'I don't think that'll work,' Richard said, 'and I'm not sure it was ...'

'Too bloody right it worked. She left a message on my voice-mail saying Beatrice Morelli would do it if you could fly to Italy at the weekend.'

'Oh. Right.'

'That's okay by you, is it? Nothing planned?'

'Er, no, nothing planned. But…'

'Not a books piece, though. We have to make it a bit broader. Celebrity profile kind of thing. It's for the magazine. Might even be a cover; see how the pictures work out. You'll have to ask her about the affair with the Yank actor, and the TV work, of course. Not too much droning on about literary stuff. I've been flicking through the cuts and it's mostly high-brow. Bit of a yawn, and quite surprising given that she looks like such a sex-bomb. You didn't, er, how shall I put this…'

'No.'

Only her mother, Richard thought, and wondered how much Jenny would have paid for that story.

'No. Shame. For you and for us. But still, you know her pretty well, so she might open up a bit more than she did to the … well, what the fuck does *TLS* stand for, anyway?'

'She'll only tell me what she doesn't mind being published. She knows I'm doing this as a journalist, not a friend.'

'Maybe. Maybe not. You'll be surprised how easily people forget there's a tape recorder running. Anyway, ask the questions, see what you get. She's not going to storm out on an old pal, is she?'

'You don't know Beatrice. How much do you want?'

'Well, that depends on the pictures. Actually, this is just a flier, but go with me. Seeing as it's Italy, do you think she would go for a fashion shoot? Quite tasteful. Autumn in Tuscany. Is it Tuscany? Doesn't matter, but Milan's up that way isn't it? Get some Versace, maybe…'

Richard was trying not to smile. Instinct told him that wouldn't be a good idea. 'I don't think Beatrice would go for that, Jenny. In fact, I know she wouldn't. She would hate it.'

'Really?' Jenny sounded amazed. 'Well, if you think so. But we'll get Mark Bowden to do the shots. He's great with cheek-bones. What about a make-up artist?'

'I don't think she'll need one.'

'No, she probably won't will she? The bitch.'

Jenny laughed, and Richard felt fear looking at those bared teeth, at Jenny's sudden manic eye-contact.

Two days later Richard was on a flight to Venice, watching West London, the terraces of Ruislip and Ealing, the Brentford football ground fading under the clouds scudding in from Berkshire. He read his paper, sipped his coffee, waited for an hour until he felt himself over Europe, then felt a familiar thrill of exultation, at another temporary escape.

He liked to listen to the captain running through the flight itinerary, found a certain poetry in Le Havre, Strasbourg, Milan. He felt as if he could scan the continent from his British Airways eyrie, look down at its polyglot patchwork and seek Sarah out, wherever she was.

From Venice he took a bus down the coast, following Beatrice's instructions. He had called her from the office, ready to drop the whole idea if she felt coerced. But she had thought it was funny. 'I thought it was a good idea, actually,' she'd said, her voice sounding as if was being gently warmed as it came down the line. 'You get to visit all expenses paid, and actually get paid for the piece. We can catch up, and my agent stops hassling me to do publicity stuff.'

'But what shall I write?' Richard had whispered. 'It'll feel ridiculous.'

'I'm sure it won't be a problem. I don't really have any secrets.'

That was funny, Richard thought, looking out the bus window at the grey-green waters of the Gulf of Venezia. Everything about Beatrice was one perfectly-preserved secret.

She met him in the town square. He saw her first, sitting at a café terrace, sunglasses sitting on the end of her nose, while she read an *International Herald Tribune*. She was sipping her Italian coffee, and Richard had a brief, warm memory of the first weeks he had known her, when she had leaned against the wall of that tiny Nicolson Street kitchen, sipping her Italian coffee, occasionally looking up and meeting his gaze and smiling, and Richard flushing hotly. She looked just the same, he thought, looking through the window at her until the bus's brakes squealed, Beatrice looked up, met his eyes, and Richard wondered if he was still blushing.

'I feel embarrassed,' she said an hour later, pointing out the swimming-pool, and the view over the Adriatic, and the vines heading off on their terraces up to the woods behind the villa. 'I hadn't thought about it before, but now I'm seeing it though your eyes. This seems so lavish somehow. But really it's very cheap to rent, because it's out of season, and I got a deal and...'

'And it doesn't matter because you're filthy rich anyway,' Richard said, and got a brief pang of pleasure from seeing Beatrice abashed.

'Just don't write in your bloody article that Beatrice Morelli reclined on her marble terrace sipping a decent *Chianti* counting her cash. The English really hate that sort of thing.'

'What shall I say? That you live in a high-rise in Turin, next door to a crack dealer and a couple of mafia enforcers?'

'Could you do that?'

'No.'

'Pity. A bit of image-massaging might not go amiss. But listen, how was Grainne?'

Richard told her at length, and Beatrice sat back and listened, and once more Richard felt that each detail was being stored up, allowed to soak and expand in some marinade of Beatrice's own devising.

'There's some mystery there, though,' Richard said. 'It's not just the drink. It's something else. Something to do with Gordon. The way she spoke about him sometimes suggested she really hated him.'

'She should never have married him.'

'You never said at the time.'

'Not my place. And I didn't know then. Retrospect is a writer's gift, you know.'

'She said something about us.'

'Us?'

'The four of us. She said we were all faithless. That we didn't believe in ourselves.'

'Really?' Beatrice looked intrigued. For a moment Richard thought she might go off and write it down.

'What do you think she meant?'

'She was talking about herself. Grainne always needed to believe in something. You remember the Nicaraguan coffee thing? Then she just transferred that to Gordon. She had hopes for him. She thought he might change things, become a big wheel in the party.'

'He still might. I read a piece that mentioned him as one of the bright prospects...'

'But we know better, don't we, Richard? We know him.'

'I suppose.'

'It just took Grainne a little longer. That's what I meant when I said she should never have married him. From a distance, she could have kept her faith a little longer. If you see someone every day, at that level of intimacy, you're going to get disillusioned pretty quickly. Especially if it's Gordon.'

'*Faithless*, though. It's a strange word to use.'

'Don't take it personally, Rich.'

'What?'

'I know you. I know that you were applying it to yourself. Which is why your habitually glum expression is beginning to verge on despair.'

Richard made himself smile.

'Tell me what happened again. Tell me about the exact moment, the decisive moment.'

'I thought I was here to interview you.'

'I think this will help. It'll help me, and it'll help you. I know I hate these people who say talking about things is the best therapy, but actually putting stuff into words and sentences helps you to make sense of it.'

'These things happen in a moment, you know. You just don't have the time for the considered judgement. Sure, you make all the wrong decisions in the build-up, but that's because you lie to yourself, tell yourself you'll always swing away from the final infidelity. It's like people who drive. They always believe that they can avoid a head-on smash, that their instincts will allow them to spin the steering wheel at the last moment and swerve out of danger. You lie to yourself, and this is the same. You get to that moment where there's an attractive and naked woman in front of you. Then, well, you don't weigh all the value of a love affair developed over weeks and months, you don't think about the accumulation of a singular language, you don't count all the signals and gestures and the traces of love, you don't put them up against a brief infatuation with a friendly and attractive girl from the West Country with a rather nice body. You just look. And once you look, you're lost.'

Beatrice was nodding. 'But you hate yourself in the morning.'

'No, that's the thing. You tell yourself it was inevitable. That's a function of the brain, the conscience-override. You tell yourself that this wasn't a sordid little fling, but something that had a meaning. However complex. That was in London. But it happened again, you know. In Bologna. We came there for a weekend, with another friend of mine. Stephen, remember him? He went off to Florence and the two of us were left alone.'

'Bologna. Nice place for infidelity. We could drive over tomorrow if you like, and we could revisit the scene of the crime.'

'You've got a cruel streak, haven't you?'

'I like to think so.'

'I regret it all, you know.'

'Not really. I don't think you regret the story. You're just not happy with the ending.'

'I want to change the ending.'

'You can't. I know. I write the beginning and the ending of a novel first. The ending is always there. You're just working towards it, eliminating all the cul-de-sacs and diversions that might lead away from it. Once the ending is there and the foundations are set, well after that, all I can change is the middle. Although you shouldn't underestimate the middle. The middle is the real story, after all. Maybe that's what you need. A different middle. You need to change your plot.'

Richard didn't know what she meant.

'What would you like to happen?' Beatrice asked.

'Really?'

'Really.'

'I'd like to get back with Sarah. To have things as they used to be.'

'That can't happen. You know that. But have you tried?'

'How can I try? I don't know where she is.'

' I thought you said she'd gone to Europe.'

'Europe is a pretty big place.'

'Is it? Not too big for someone who really thought that was the only solution.'

'So, what are you saying? That I should search all Europe until I find Sarah?'

'You think it's ridiculous, but that's because you have no faith in the idea. Now, I think you're right, I think it would be futile, but my viewpoint isn't the same as yours. Grainne might be right, though: you have no faith in yourself. You see, the beginning of the story is

London, and the fling with the naked girl and the inevitable break-up with the distraught Sarah. The end of the story is you getting over this whole thing and facing the future. All that's left is the middle, and at the moment you're not filling in those chapters.'

'I could never find her. It's been five years.'

Richard looked at Beatrice questioningly. She looked back, and she smiled, but he had rarely seen her as serious.

'Well,' Beatrice said, reaching for a bottle of wine. 'Shall we get this interview over with?'

Beatrice

Beatitude

Enigmatic, beautiful, successful. Beatrice Morelli cannot possibly be British. By the shores of the Adriatic the author talks about cultural dislocation, that TV show, and the joys of not looking for love in a warm climate. By Richard Martin. Pictures: Mark Bowden.

Just down the Adriatic coast, south of Venice but before you approach Ravenna, Beatrice Morelli is sitting on the patio of her tiled villa looking out over that ancient sea, and looking about as un-English as you can get.

Beatrice – let's call her Beatrice because she's in one of her informal moods today – is wearing one of those shift dresses that looks like it could be snipped out of a piece of raw fabric, but if you flip forward to the fashion pages, you'll probably find it well into the three-figure price bracket. Beatrice is sipping Campari, the bitter drink of Mediterranean grown-ups. Look at the pictures next to this feature, those pictures which took far too long to plan, set up and light, but which have ended up showing Beatrice Morelli exactly as she is. Look closely. Does she seem like the leader of the 'new Britishness' to you, a protectress of old-fashioned island virtues? Thought not.

Look away from those pictures now. You can go back to them later if you must. Consider the books. That awkward first novel, *Portico*: an academic whodunnit, half of which was set in Italy, not too far from here, over in Bologna, and maybe a quarter of which was set in the Middle Ages. In the course of our conversation Beatrice admits to me that she wanted to write a whole chapter of that book in Latin, but her agent dissuaded her. She asks me not to mention this in case it makes her sound pretentious, so I won't.

Then there was Beatrice's *Bosom*, a title she admits she chose as a whim because she liked the rhythm of the word, and that her agent reckons was worth an extra five thousand sales. It was a delayed rites-of-passage story about a young woman's search for a sexual identity and, apart from one flash-back chapter, entirely set in Italy.

Last year we had *Greyhound*, her American novel, another

road movie plot following a grungy anti-hero across America, with the twist that he got more urbane and sophisticated as the trip progressed. It is being made into one of those edgy American independent films as we speak, assorted guitar-noise outfits being corralled for the soundtrack, young Hollywood method actors preening their goatees. Beatrice is convincingly ignorant about the details of the film, and has never heard of any of the bands.

So you see, as oeuvres go, it's pretty determinedly un-English. So why does Beatrice Morelli crop up on all those lists with the Brit prefix? Why does her face peer out from Union Jack page designs (apart from the obvious fact that her face is rather more presentable than those of the usual suspects)? Beatrice takes another look at the Adriatic, clinks the ice in her glass, sips her Campari and gives us the definitive answer.

'I don't know. I really don't know.'

It's not really the bright explanation that we were hoping for.

'I'm sorry, but I've been out of Britain for a long time. I don't really know what is happening there. I've seen some of the stuff in the papers, but all the people I'm lumped in with? I've either never heard of them, or there seems to be no obvious connection at all. I can vaguely see how I might be connected to musicians or film-makers, but I've no idea what I'm supposed to have in common with a footballer.'

She is referring to a recent style magazine article that paralleled her life with that of a Chelsea full-back with the inclinations of an aesthete. The trouble is that Beatrice Morelli is impossible to categorise. She just doesn't fit into the pigeonholes. 'I never have,' she says – not proudly, just matter-of-factly. 'I'm not sure if that's good or bad.'

Beatrice Morelli was born in South London thirty-five years ago. She got the surname and perhaps those Mediterranean looks from her Italian father. He died when Beatrice was eight, her mother died when Beatrice was twenty-eight. Cheap psychological trick number one: perhaps Beatrice's fascination with the solitary is a result of being parentless at such an early age, perhaps ... ah, but she's interrupting here.

'I've heard all that before, and of course I've no way of arguing with it,' she says, in what is close to an argumentative tone of voice. 'All I will say is that my first book was written while my mother was still alive. I've never been conscious of being influenced by an absence of parents. None of the characters in any of my books are supposed to be autobiographical, but then all authors say that, don't they?'

Indeed all authors say that. And shameless critics attempt to contradict them. When it comes to the enjoyable game of identifying the characters with their creator, though, the most tempting connection is with Lucretia, the delightfully-named heroine of *Bosom*. You would love Beatrice to be like Lucretia, if only because the character has such a splendid time.

'Yeah, there was a bit of wish-fulfilment there,' Beatrice laughs. 'After that book came out people would look at me with a slightly more inquisitive eye, wondering if I'd done all that stuff. But actually that book is more about my impressions of the country of Italy than about the human aspect of the character. That was written before I knew Italy. Deliberately so, because I wanted to preserve my initial idea of it being a country of sensuousness.'

True enough, it's a book full of sensory detail, the smells and flavours of grapes, figs, olives, coffee, an olfactory overload. It's also a book full of erotic interludes, sharp vignettes of moderately joyful couplings along the *autostrada*.

'God, everyone still wants to talk about the sex in that book,' says Beatrice, who doesn't. 'I was embarrassed about it, of course. You're torn between the notion that writing about sex reveals far too much about your character, and realising that all writing should, in the end, be revealing about your character, or it'll have no vivacity at all. But again, I wanted that to be an expression of my hazy, romanticised notion of Italy. Says it all, really – that when I thought of Italy, I thought of bare flesh, and food.'

Beatrice lives in Italy now, in her rented villa with a view of the sea and a dusty track into one of those villages they always put on the covers of travel brochures. 'It makes me laugh,' she says, 'driving in there and seeing all the old peasants selling bread and olive oil and little jugs of wine. It's as if they've come straight out of casting for some dreadful EM Forster adaptation. But it's like a reproach. Because I wrote all that local colour stuff in *Bosom*, I feel like they're all there haunting me. Writers, you see. Terrible solipsists.'

I wondered if other aspects of Italy made her regret that novel, made her think she had got the country wrong. 'No, quite the opposite. You can be crippled as a writer by knowing too much. That can make you want to do justice to all the contradictions and compromises of reality. You get bogged down in ... what's the word ... *reportage*. I don't think that can work in fiction. You have to develop a kind of ... well, without sounding too indulgent, a kind of poetic truth that works for you, and doesn't necessarily reflect the real world.'

It's an approach that has attracted the rare criticisms that have occasionally surfaced in otherwise gushing reviews. She has been accused of being a 'stylist,' of fabricating exotic locales for essentially escapist stories. Put like that, it doesn't seem the most devastating dismissal, does it?

'I don't take any notice of reviews,' she says, although that's another thing that all authors say. 'Saying that, I suppose they may have had a point with *Greyhound*. That was written in America, and one thing about America is that it can saturate you. It's something about the way that country is so inward-looking. Americans barely acknowledge that there's a whole wide world beyond their shores. They laugh at Canadians and eat out at Mexican diners, but otherwise they don't do foreign. However well-meaning you might be, you end up absorbing part of that attitude. So I can read *Greyhound* now and not understand it, not recognise some of the references. But in a perverse kind of way I suppose that makes it the nearest of my books to realism, because it is so much a part of the place and time in which it was written.'

She says all this in such a detached way that I can't help asking if she hates it. She smiles and looks back out to sea, understandably, because a great ball of red sun is setting off westwards to guide fishermen home. She pauses for a long while. 'I'm told by my agent that being an author is just like being a mother,' she says. 'So I can't go hating one of my babies, can I?'

Cheap psychological trick number two: novels are her babies. Or as a *Daily Mail* profile put it, 'When is Beatrice Morelli going to find Mr Right?' She hadn't read that one, due to a commendable habit of avoiding that particular newspaper. I expect her to sigh with disdain when I tell her about it, but instead she breaks into a fit of very un-Beatrice-like giggles. 'Do people still believe in Mr Right?' she snorts.

A year or so ago, Beatrice was being mentally ushered up the aisle, in chic circles, on the arm of a New York friend whose critical lustre on their side of the Atlantic was the equal of Beatrice's on ours. Gabriel Stein, a Wooster Group actor who published a collection of short stories so hip and minimalist that you were left wondering if it was a literary or design event, squired (as they say in the gossip mags) Beatrice for a few months around the launch of *Greyhound*. There was a photograph or two in the edgier society pages. Then silence, the drying up of the trickle of lines in the hipster gossip columns.

'Well,' she says, painfully naïve in the art of personal revelation.

Well, what happened? Then she smiles again, a smile that suggests this isn't the most painful of memories.

'Oh, Gabriel met some girl who was in the new Robert Altman film, and was a bit more high-profile than an ageing Brit-lit chick.' Typing those words make them look a little bitter, but I have to report that Beatrice was still smiling all the time.

'Being single suits me,' she says more seriously. 'I know that every single person says that right up until the time they are signing the register, but I've seen friends get married. And however well-suited they seem, a few months after the marriage it's as if they've been diluted, as if their vital essence has been drained and replaced by something harmless. Marriage is very much associated with liquids for me. Make of that what you will.'

Her characters are as determinedly single as their creator. Isabella, Lucretia, Evan are driven on by their own urgencies, but rather unusually in contemporary literature, none of them seems that bothered about finding a significant other.

'You see, that's one area where my imagination couldn't stretch. I'm quite happy to make up long passages about an imaginary Italy, or Oregon farmsteads, or having oral sex in an abattoir (which I'm afraid to confess I didn't research) but when it comes to being obsessively in love, I'm a coward. I can't write about that yet, although I'm working up to it.'

A coward about being in love, or a coward about writing about it?

'Bit of both. As I said, I'm quite happy to make up descriptions of landscapes or accents or city streets I've never walked down, but I still shy away from describing emotions I can't recognise.'

Why?

'Well, because they might not exist.'

Love might not exist?

'Well, sure, I've seen my friends go through what looks very like being in love. But then my friends also believe in the privatisation of the railways, the probity of Daniel Ortega, or that the last minute of *Simply Thrilled Honey* by Orange Juice is a holy text. Doesn't mean they're right.'

There's a notion, put about by the sort of people who float these ideas, that love can stifle creativity, that the truly gifted writers need to have that emotional vacuum to fill with their words. Let's call them the 'Well, Jane Austen never got any' school.

'Oh, what a nice idea,' Beatrice says. 'Essentially misogynist of course, because they're only talking about women, aren't they? Actually, it just sounds like a variation on the idea that any woman with a successful career would secretly rather be lying on her back.'

She is living in Italy now. Because she can, because she has no close family to speak of (although her father's family lives not far away from here, in Emiglia Romagna). 'I need to soak America out of my system,' she says. 'If you go to the market here, you'll sometimes see the salt cod stall. To make the salt cod edible you have to soak it for about thirty-six hours, keep changing the water, or else it will be impossibly rancid. I feel a bit like that about America. I have to soak myself in Europe for a while before I'm ready to write again.'

It sounds like she regretted ever going there. 'No,' she says firmly. 'I really regret nothing. Oh, I don't know, perhaps nothing is a bit of an overstatement. But regret always seems a pointless emotion. You can't alter what happened in the past, so it's best to take as much profit as you can from the experience. America was about the experience, about seeing it all at first hand, knowing I could do it. Although, after working on that show for a couple of years, I realised I couldn't.'

The show you will know: that loveably life-affirming saga of six young New Yorkers who could never quite get their love-lives together despite being better-looking, wealthier and wittier than virtually all Americans ever. People watched it for a while, talked about it at work, and then they stopped. And it disappeared off our screens at just about the right moment.

'Bleakness killed it eventually,' Beatrice says. 'You know, after a few months of all that sunniness you reach a point where you stare straight back at someone who's trying to make you laugh, and the look in your eyes tells them that you want to kill them. It made me realise that I work best on my own, that collaboration would drive me insane after a while.'

I tell her that an Italian TV channel runs the series on repeats twice a week, and she smiles at me. 'I don't have a television. If I did I might watch it, because I think it would help me improve my Italian. All the American shows are dubbed here, and I think I would remember those scripts verbatim, so that might have worked. All those set-ups and one-liners in Italian. That would be fascinating. But…'

But it's a part of her life she obviously wants to put away in the store cupboard, tidily enough, but forgotten. History. She doesn't even keep any copies of her own books in the house, and certainly no videos of that show.

'Don't misinterpret me,' she says sternly. 'In New York, when I quit, there were a few snipey columns that said that the uppity Brit was leaving because she thought a sitcom was beneath her. I never thought that. In fact, I learned more about myself from doing that comedy show than from anything else I've written.'

Ah, now we're getting somewhere. How so?

'Because it was about optimism. About looking for the love inside of people, realising that after all the disappointments and let-downs it was all going to be all right. And I'm afraid I never really believed any of that.'

Do any of us? It sounds like a very American idea.

'Possibly. But I think it is in Europe, as well. I was walking around in Ferrara the other day, a bright Saturday afternoon. I started looking in a photographer's window. He had pictures from all the weddings he had taken. You know how people in wedding pictures always look deranged? Well, these were no exception, except they all seemed to have this odd radiance about their faces. At first glance you could pass it off as stupidity, but if you stood there for more than a minute, you had to admit it to yourself. They looked more than happy. They looked … hopeful. I must have stood staring at them for about twenty minutes, at all those teeth and gleaming eyes. It took me that long to remember where I'd seen those expressions before. It was in the publicity stills for the show. That really frightened me. Because, like you, I had dismissed it as an American thing. It's not. It's people. People all want to believe in a happy ending.'

So when did you stop believing in happy endings?

'I don't think I ever did believe. I always preferred books that had a gloomy conclusion. You know those CS Lewis books? *The Lion, the Witch and the Wardrobe*, all that stuff? Well, being a particularly atheistic little girl, I preferred to think all those kids just got killed off in the end, rather than going off to their white-bread, middle-class, English, High Church paradise. Then I moved on to *Anna Karenina* and that was more like it. Death by public transport. Was ever a book more likely to appeal to an adolescent suburban girl?'

Cheap psychological trick number three: Beatrice Morelli has read too much to fall in love. She would anticipate its approach from the hackneyed sighs, the too-familiar glances, the heavily-delineated overtures of rapture. Love has become another fictional device, a bit more widespread than metaphor, but equally prone to identification, analysis.

'Hmmm, I'm not sure I like that one any more than the idea that I'm just waiting for Mr Right to come along. Does it matter that much? We're a few years away from the next millennium. Surely we've come up with a more liberal interpretation of the correct way to live. We don't all have to walk along in tidy couples, do we?'

There's a first hint of exasperation there. There will always be the insidious pressure of the norm, though; an attendant suspicion of one who doesn't conform to its parameters. Or, in simpler words, Beatrice Morelli will always be regarded with a certain wariness until she finds a Nice Man.

'Oh yes, I know you're right. But I'm doomed here, you know, stuck out on the edge of the cliff, a mysterious *signora*. The delivery men try to flirt with me, but they would hate their mothers to know. Italian men go around in a permanent state of wondering what their mothers will think. It's a kind of personal version of the worship of the Madonna, an active conscience nagging away at them. And mysterious foreign women well into their thirties are distinctly off-limits.'

You sound almost wistful.

'Oh, do I? Well, I'll just have to resist temptation, because winter is on its way, and I have to get back to writing.'

The new book is another historical mystery, mostly set in the Byzantine and Turkish courts around the sixth century. Beatrice has been wandering around Ravenna, 'trying not to write down facts, because I don't like to have facts in my books. It leaves less room for impressions.'

She's already thinking one book ahead, though, and with a teasing smile she threatens that she might be contemplating writing a love story.

'If I do, I think it will be one with an unhappy ending. Or at least, unhappy by conventional standards. Boy might not get girl. I was talking earlier about not being able to write about obsessive love. Well, I might, but I think it will be in the third person. I'm thinking about writing a book about a friend of mine who fell in love. The affair went wrong, probably his fault, and since then he's been unable to move on. He is obsessed with this girl. It's fascinating, really, that level of single-mindedness. I think if I write a book about it, it will fictionalise the whole thing, make it too incredible to believe, and then he might snap out of it.'

If he reads it.

'Of course he'll bloody read it. Then he'll snap out of it.'

And just for a moment, with that sternly sensible second 'snap out of it' – just before that setting sun flashes some ancient Mediterranean magic off Beatrice Morelli's eyes – she looks and sounds very, very English.

Gordon

L ook at yourself in the mirror, he had been told. Look for the signs. Is there anything there that you might not trust, might not feel is worthy of a voter's faith? Gordon looked that morning and tried to smile, a smile that wouldn't seem smug or patronising or complacent, or simply shifty. He tried the frank and appraising gaze, the look of mild concern, the seriousness tinged with a hint of playfulness. He used to be so good at this, but he was finding it harder every day. Previously it hadn't all been acting. Now it was all hope, a desperation that he could carry it off, that nobody would be able to see past the mask.

Gordon thought he was too old to develop the art of introspection. It was too late to start ploughing away inside of himself and wondering if he liked the little flints and shards that he dredged up. The secret, he always thought, was to keep on going. You had to keep facing the front. If you started to look to the sides, started to hesitate, you were lost, overtaken, back in the chasing pack. But it was getting harder. He caught himself two or three times a day whispering to himself, 'Hold yourself together,' wandering around with a twitching vacuum sucking away inside of him.

Things weren't moving fast enough. He had his place on the defence committee, his suggestions were taken seriously, one or two of the Shadow Minister's entourage had even sought out his opinion or advice. Andy and Mark would make encouraging noises, suggesting his contributions were noted and would be rewarded. Still, every so often, Gordon would find himself succumbing to the notion that he was being taken for granted, that the action was happening elsewhere.

A couple of weekends already that summer, they had been corralled in groups of sixty (the MPs and the aspirants) to a house in the country. It was a Hertfordshire place, and as he swung into the driveway Gordon had experienced a brief cold flush of alarm that he might have been here before, with Grainne, to one of those parties. He got out of the car slowly, breathed deeply the way those magazine articles suggested, and looked around, trying to reassure himself. But the imminent panic attack was only dispelled when he saw the furnishings were relatively conventional. What was he going to do, anyway? Ask if they still had the leather-lined boudoir off the first-floor landing?

Gordon liked to think he was one of the seasoned campaigners, but he still enjoyed the whole attention to detail at these seminars. He felt like a commando being briefed before a covert mission, appreciated the fact that none of the party names were in attendance, that they kept themselves far from the front, like First World War generals. It had all been sub-contracted to professionals from the advertising or PR industries.

They would watch a video, a familiar reiteration of the usual points, hammering home the danger areas. Gordon knew them off by heart, because they seemed like a resumé of his own political career slope. Membership of extra-parliamentary pressure groups was discouraged, the verb being made to sound darkly minatory. Suits were to be restrained, dark grey or black. Brown jackets were suspect, coloured ones distinctly unwise. Facial hair was to be subject to a statute of limitations. If photographic evidence could be provided that the moustache or beard had a life span of more than ten years, then it could be considered a valid element of facial identity, and allowed to survive. Otherwise it was sending out all the wrong signals and should be terminated at the sharp end of a Bic.

Gordon knew all of this. Some of it had already been in operation in '92. What was new was the arrival of the image consultant. The man's name was Bennett, and he stood before them on the Saturday morning with the demeanour of a slightly camp sergeant-major, his cold blue eyes perusing the ranks with mild disgust. Then he had smiled and launched into a bantering peroration, calling on them to suppress their deep-rooted convictions and enjoy a temporary wallow in the shallow superficialities of appearance. 'Gentlemen, ladies, comrades,' he said with such over-arching sarcasm that they had all laughed on cue. 'Lend me your ears, eyes, hearts and minds, and I will deliver you the promised land.' Then he broke into a broad smile, and opened his palms apologetically. 'Sorry for the borrowed rhetoric, but what I want to show you this weekend is that words are to be our slaves. As opposed to the entire history of the Labour Party, where we were slaves of our words. I use the word 'we' facetiously, as I should admit that I am not a party member. That was a condition of my being employed for this task. There is no point to you being preached at by the converted. I am a sceptic – i.e. exactly the sort of person you will have to set about convincing.'

The speech had been deliberately couched to provoke any members still clinging to a red-blooded notion of socialism. Though Gordon had looked along the line of smooth pink faces, gleaming pastel eyes and eager notebooks, and had identified a uniform innocence there. They reminded him of himself, of a Gordon before the fall, when the smile had been as blithe, when his guts hadn't gripped him with panic every five minutes. Gordon envied them.

At coffee, Gordon had found himself sitting opposite Bennett. The image consultant had looked at him with a frankness that caused Gordon to feel uncomfortable. When he caught his eye, Bennett had smiled. 'I'm sorry, I should know this, but what is your name?'

'Gordon Hendrie.'

'Of course. Already in the House. A budding shoot. My apologies. Sorry for staring, as well. You're perfect, you know.'

'I'm sorry?'

'Perfect. Don't take this the wrong way, Gordon, if I may call you Gordon, but your face is devoid of any extremity of feature. You're almost like a PR company's ideal composite graphic of an electable young MP. Yours is the face of the future.'

'Er ... thank you.'

'Don't mention it.' Bennett screwed up his face into a mischievous grimace, and half-whispered, although he was surrounded by people who could hear him perfectly well. 'Pity about the rest of them. We've got our work cut out.

'Have you ever looked around those portraits in the House?' Bennett went on. Gordon hadn't. Gordon rarely noticed his surroundings. 'It seems that a prerequisite for getting elected in the nineteenth and early twentieth centuries was to have the features of a gargoyle, liberally flushed with claret. Admittedly, people only saw their MPs once every five years, and then the agents could probably do a few tricks with the lighting, but still ... you wonder why the electorate showed such a fondness for werewolves.'

Gordon laughed, but Bennett didn't seem to be joking. He gripped his water glass and gestured at Gordon. 'People talk about television and the cruelty of the close-up, but I believe that if people had enjoyed the opportunity earlier – say, candidates had to put their photographs next to the voting box on the ballot – then my evil art would not be quite such a young one. Done much telly?'

'No. Hardly any.'

'Yes. I suppose the TV channels might find the look a bit anodyne. But perfect from our point of view. I'll have a word. I like that accent too. It sounds almost Scottish at times.'

'I'm from Glasgow,' Gordon said.

'Really. Superb.'

In the afternoons they practiced speaking, Bennett wincing at dropped *h*s and flattened vowels, but getting angry when the abashed hopefuls tried to replace them with BBC plumminess. 'No, no,' he would yell, like a frustrated theatre director. 'Work with what you've got, but make it work for you. If you want to say 'appen, say it slowly, unapologetically, as if it's about to preface some profound insight.'

They watched videos of the Welshman on the campaign trail in '92. Every thirty seconds or so, Bennett would freeze the tape and point out the faults. The sixty of them looked at the screen, the red face stuck in an emotive death-pang, lines of interference flickering across the freckled features, staring at what they were being taught was the face of defeat. 'Passion, sure, but no message,' Bennett said, tapping the screen with his baton. 'Moving perhaps, but nobody's listening. People at home are giggling at the tear in the eye, at the way the words caught in his voice. We want you to be mediums for the message, faithful conduits.

'Look here, here and here,' he said, tapping the screen as if inflicting surgical incisions on it. 'He is stretched; the face contorts with the effort of conveying how much he wants you to hear him. That doesn't sell. If you go into a shop and the shopkeeper keeps telling you how fantastic his bacon is, in a rising voice of panicky conviction, do you say 'Great, give us half a pound'? No, you edge away, backing out the door, keeping a wary eye out in case he makes a sudden move. That's the British voter's instinctive response. They want an offhand, confident voice from a conventional-looking sort, saying 'Yeah, the bacon's all right', as if they weren't really sure whether you were discerning enough to appreciate it, and weren't entirely happy about selling it to you. That's the secret.'

Bennett paused, watched them all scribbling frantically, then drifted over towards a prospective parliamentary candidate with a shock of red hair.

'Plus, there was the Welsh accent,' he said. 'Didn't help, whatever the opinion polls might have suggested. What are you going to say if a pollster comes up and asks if you like Welsh accents? No, I'm a bigot with deep-rooted irrational prejudices? Of course not. But that's the real picture. That's what we have to address. Reality, rather than a rosy ideal. So, we speak with one voice now and we want that voice to be as orthodox as physically possible. I'm sorry Griffith, Finlay, and that lovely chap from the Black Country whose name I don't recall, but that's the way it has to be. It's worth it, isn't it?'

There had been a rough but chorused murmur of assent. Bennett had looked up and smiled at them all, and Gordon was back in the schoolroom in Partick, remembering the little rush of satisfaction he would get when he remembered a Latin conjugation correctly.

They had a subdued cocktail party that night, and Gordon ran into Andy McInnes.

'What do you think of the new intake?' Andy asked.

'They're all very young, aren't they?' Gordon said. In fact he was feeling a little piqued at no longer being the most youthful face.

'You know what they remind me of?' Andy said. 'Those little plastic Airfix soldiers I used to have as a kid. They'd always have some big plastic blob on their heads where you had to break them off the sprue. That's what this bunch are like. All shiny and polythene and marching forward with their guns pointed in the right direction.'

'That sounds a bit cynical, Andy. Which is like you.'

'But the great thing is, it doesn't matter. The Greeks have this word – *hubris* – but the bloody Greeks can keep it. We really are unstoppable now. Every day, I spend a half-hour doing various drafts of magnanimous victory speeches. I always have to cut out the line that goes, "Fuck you, losers – we creamed you."'

'You didn't think about trying to get a seat?'

'Not yet, not yet. It's a bit early for the ideological storm-troops. For the next four years after the election, most of the serious business is going to happen outside the House. A bunch of us will go in as a solid wave in 2001, then we'll have hardcore back-up in 2006 to build on the foundations of the thousand-year Reich.'

'A lot of people might think you were joking, Andy. What worries me is I know you're not.'

Andy smiled, then stopped suddenly, leaned forward and lowered his voice.

'Never mind me, Gordon. I've been hearing some troubling news. Friend of mine works in the press office at Strathclyde Constabulary. There's going to be a big story in the *Sunday Mail* tomorrow.'

Gordon looked confused.

'Apparently the boys in blue picked up a small-time dealer in Pollok. Big bag of what he called "jellies," but which innocents like you and I, Gordon, would be shocked to discover don't come in tangerine and lime flavour. So they administered a mild kicking and were just getting round to telling him he could expect a couple of years in Bar-L when he mentions, casually, that his big brother Gordon is a Member of Parliament.'

Gordon felt as if he had been stabbed.

'Fuck, Denis.'

'It would seem so. Did you know your brother was a drugs dealer, Gordon? And so small-time as well? Embarrassing, no?'

'No. I mean, I never see him. I've no idea what he gets up to. He's always been dodgy, but fuck, what am I going to do?'

'Nothing. I've taken the liberty of drawing up a prepared statement. The *Mail* boys have been in touch and I gave them a couple of lines as a quote. Here…'

Andy pulled out a sheet of greasy fax paper. Gordon looked at the smudged print and read the words, his lips moving along with them.

'Gordon Hendrie has been made aware of his brother's arrest. He is standing by his brother at this difficult time, and will be offering him his support in any way that might be required. As an MP he has seen at close-quarters the misery inflicted by drugs in working-class communities, and wholeheartedly condemns this kind of traffic. He is also aware of the difficulties and temptations he and his brothers faced growing up in an industrially demoralised city. He asks for understanding in this difficult time for his family, and has faith that the judicial system will treat his brother fairly.'

Andy looked across anxiously. 'Family loyalty, decent citizen stuff, and perhaps just a tiny hint that you are pretty cool about Class As. Play this right and you might get a tiny bit of street cred out of it. I'm officially concerned to admit that there is a small but influential section of the electorate that admires a man with a

245

dealer in the family.'

'How do you think it's going to work out?'

'Should be all right. He's got a bit of form, but nothing heavy. You'll pay for a slick, shiny super-lawyer, of course. Suspended sentence, I should imagine. I don't think the cops are going to push too hard to make him out to be a dangerous baddie. They don't want to mix it with a boy who might be in the Home Office inside a year, do they?'

'No, I meant for me, in any Shadow reshuffle. This doesn't look good, does it?'

'I love you, Gordon. Love the fact that you really don't give a shit about your brother.'

'Come on, I haven't seen him in three years and it's not like we ever got on. The lawyer's going to cost me, and I'm not exactly flush at the moment.'

'Ah, family. The ties that bind. But to answer your question. No, I don't think it will be a problem. You can't be held to account for little bro, and as I said, it gives you a slight edge. You know the sort of stuff: an intimate understanding of underclass activity without actually being afflicted yourself. That sort of thing is a nice counter-punch to the idea that we're all middle-class tossers straight out of the better class of uni. Plus, I've handled it with the usual degree of sureness and sensitivity. Plus, it's in the *Sunday Mail,* which is a paper for semi-literate scum who fell off the electoral roll when the poll tax kicked in. If you'd been on the front of the *Independent* or *Telegraph*, there may have been some awkward questions in Millbank. There'll be follow-ups in the dailies, but nothing too spectacular. Don't speak to anyone, though. The statement says it all, and from what you said just now, I'm not sure I can trust you not to sound heartless.'

'Look, Denis has always been...'

'What?'

'A bit dim.'

'Nothing dim about it. You know how much these guys can make out of a stolen batch of anti-depressants? Makes our little consultancy fees look like dry-roasted. Maybe he should buy his own lawyer. But that's not really the point. Our theatrical chum Michael Bennett is going to tell you all this tomorrow, and I know you've heard it before, but it pays to keep an eye on the old home hearths. Just in case something stirs and causes the bloody house to burn down. Are you with me?'

'Yes, yes,' Gordon said, 'but you think I'll get away with this one?'

'Out of the shite smelling like roses, I expect. But don't get complacent. Something else, on the same subject. How's Grainne?'

'Fine. Bit bored, maybe. But fine.' Gordon knew he was sounding defensive. With good reason. Andy's network of spies was broad and diverse and it was eminently possible he may have heard something. Gordon thought of Grainne, thought of her staring out of a window a thousand miles away, thought of the cold look of disdain she had treated him to the last time he had seen her. The lurch in the stomach came back again.

'Good. Only she was looking a little peaky last time I saw her.'

'You know Grainne. She's always been a bit pale. Makes a point of staying out of the sun. That holiday in the Canaries was a waste of money. Apparently we're going to the Tatras next year. No, I don't know either.'

'What about the parties? You think she might not be such an enthusiast on the scene as yourself? Every time I see her, she always looks a little bit out of it.'

Gordon shook his head. 'No. She loves them. But that's Grainne: she's a bit reserved at first, not too outgoing. But that whole thing has been a revelation. It's been really good for her. It's really opened her eyes.'

'And legs.'

Gordon and Andy laughed at each other over their Manhattans, then Andy stopped laughing. It was a habit he had picked up from a TV show. Gordon found it annoying.

'Be careful though, Gordon,' Andy said seriously. 'Those parties are very discreet; everybody's vetted in advance. Those houses don't even have cassette decks in the hi-fis. So nobody's going to talk. Unless it's one of you two.'

Gordon looked at him in astonishment and shook his head again.

As Andy had promised, on the Sunday evening they talked about family. Bennett stood at the podium, spot-lit from behind, declaiming in an amused, almost parodic fashion. 'We are the party of the family,' he said. 'Or at least that is what we have to become. And before that can happen we have to ask ourselves about our own families, our loved ones, our nearest-and-dearest, whatever cosy little sound-bite you need to use to describe them. And, without being too heartless, we have to ask ourselves whether they are an electoral asset or a liability. Are those husbands and wives fit to hold our hand on the podium, or should they be left at home watching the TV?'

He went on, and Gordon was leaning forward now. Everybody beside him was eager enough, but Gordon was engrossed. This is what he had been waiting for.

'By family, I'm not necessarily speaking in the old wife-and-two-kids nuclear sense, of course. All partnerships are equal in our eyes. So whether you have a wife, a husband, a live-in lover, or hire out rent boys by the hour – that's fine. Except for the last one, which might be a tad troubling. No, what I'm saying is that the exact legal status of the partner isn't the issue. It's just a question of whether they are … supportive.

'The problem is,' he went on, 'that they won't have had the benefit of these sessions, won't be alert to the possibility of a damaging slip. That's where you have to be on your guard. The important element is smoothness, keeping everything flowing in the same direction. It's like sanding down a boat. You have to make sure you don't go against the grain…'

Bennett, happy with his boat metaphor, took it out to sea, but Gordon sat back and began to think quick, urgent thoughts. Going against the grain. He needed to make a decision, and quickly. He needed to find the faith to act decisively. What was the expression they used? Damage limitation.

A Party In 1997

This wasn't what the end of an era was supposed to look like. Where were the portents in the sky, the seismic shifts of the old order, the terror, the panic, the gratifying misery of defeated overlords? A little blood on the streets couldn't have been too much to expect.

Instead, there was the pop of champagne corks, accompanied by the braying that had sound-tracked certain parts of the city for the last decade. London's music wasn't about to undergo any radical changes in its time signatures.

The speakers playing the background sounds hummed with the tuneful clatter of drums and guitars, and the classless voices of the English suburbs singing of a lost '60s idyll, all sun and meadows and quirky characters stealing smalls off washing-lines. Side-tables were strewn with over-designed election supplements, with their pull-out-and-fill-in sharply delineated wall-charts of the British electoral system. There were stylised poster portraits of Blair, Ashdown and Major; airbrushed pop art renditions of the expressions of power. There were a lot of people in square glasses; too many polo-necked jumpers for a summer evening. There were canapés, once-elegant arrays of puff pastry, salmon and drying cream cheese. There was no Bastille, no Finland Station.

It was another party, an end of the century affair three years too early, and people were celebrating stability, toasting 'no change,' huddling together for constant reassurance that this wouldn't really alter things, would it? People were grinning encouragement at each other. It would all be the same, except without the guilt. It was a party of common defence, an assertion that a change of government couldn't affect the daily detail of a metropolis that clung to the eternal verities of Moët and the air-kiss.

Back at the newspaper office, the sub-editors – the sort of people too earnest and troglodytic ever to grace a party anyway – were staring at their terminals and collating the final edition's results, chiselling in the tedious narrative of electoral cataclysm. The leaders and front pages were written already, the gap for the photograph of a tired but exultant new Premier sized and cropped and merely awaiting the actual event. The features pages had been finished by the morning, and the features writers had started drinking at lunch.

Jenny Wolseley had watched the television screen for half an hour as the early results came in, her teeth digging into her lower lip. Labour had won, she surmised. Her entire career had been spent under a Conservative government; it was one of her lodestones, her givens, that her readers were interested in money and its corollaries. She had a little flutter of panic at the idea of chasing a new trend, the same flutter she got before the Paris shows. She had asked anxious but gentle questions of the business writers as they passed, looked at them flirtatiously as they smiled down at her. Adam Bates touched her arm and smiled kindly as he gave a quick précis of Gordon Brown's economic approach. She didn't follow the details but she absorbed his sanguine tone.

Now she had rallied. This could be a shot in the arm, ideas-wise, she told Claire, her PA, who was the only one loyal enough to feel she had to listen to Jenny during a party. The rest of the features desk had gathered in a drunken cluster to swap Jenny stories and occasional guffaws. 'I love this new British thing, all Union Jacks and parkas and little mopeds,' Jenny said. 'Carnaby Street, and all that stuff. We could do something with that. Get a superchef involved. Or a fashion spread. Models in red, white and blue knickers, on their Vespas.'

'They're Italian, I think,' Claire said quietly.

'Even better. We'll do the Italian job. You know, minis and stuff. We'll get the chap from Blur. They're not American, are they?' Jenny looked back at the screen that was in the process of announcing another five Labour gains, and smiled nervously. 'This is exciting, isn't it?' Claire told her that yes, it was.

At the edge of the conference suite, over by the windows, Richard looked out over the grey Thames, lit by the white lights of Cheyne Walk. To any casual observer, it was apparent that Richard didn't fit into this party. He had a tidy haircut and wore a grey silk jacket over a black shirt. As everybody around him had begun to get more casual, Richard had gravitated towards formality. He had started to be self-conscious about being in his mid-thirties and still being expected to have opinions about popular culture. Instead, he had cultivated a cautious hostility to everything, a disdain for success and achievement. Surprisingly, it had proved a selling point, and he had been given an occasional column with which to gainsay all that was voguish. 'Our cute little curmudgeon,' Jenny called him, and would have chucked him under the chin every time she saw him had Richard not studiously avoided her.

Richard looked out at London and scowled at a city he had started to hate. Even through the dense glazing he could hear ribald cries of drunken celebration eight floors below. Why were they celebrating? he wondered. Surely Chelsea, Battersea and Fulham were the bastions of the enemy. Why weren't they hanging themselves along their tree-lined avenues? Fleeing the country for some tax-haven?

Richard looked back into the room at the flushed, cheery faces opening their maws sporadically to pour in more champagne. He saw the shuffle of networking executives attempting to make pithy and cynical observations to their immediate superiors, at the pinstriped chiefs looking comfortable with authority, at the assuredness of it all. He saw the eager arms reaching out to denude the passing trays, the eyes never condescending to acknowledge the waiters. Everybody seemed so comfortable with themselves. Where were the pique, the gloom, the angry recriminations, all the side-dishes of victory? Richard went over to the bar and grabbed another drink.

'Forgive me, because I'm just a freelance and might have missed a meeting,' he said to the man next to him, 'but my impression was that this paper was always slightly to the right of Michael Howard. So how come everyone is pretending to celebrate?'

Dave Simmonds laughed. 'Richard, come on. Newspapers can't afford to have rigid party affiliations these days. The way to thrive is to be on the winning side. It's like the French attitude to wars. If you'd have read the paper this morning, you'll have seen that we endorsed New Labour completely, after a bit of humming and ha-ing about fiscal responsibility.'

'That was the feature marked, "Don't dare try to cut our taxes or we'll call you dangerous Bolsheviks"?'

Dave laughed. 'We're all New Labour now. My brother works in the City, and there are whole gangs of investment bankers glowing at the very mention of Brown. This is probably the most ruthlessly successful election campaign of all time. Christ, have you seen some of the results? Apparently Michael Portillo is about to get beaten by some teenage pixie.'

The newspaper's election parties used to be dour affairs, Dave explained, but somehow they knew that 1997 would be the celebration of a new mood in the capital, a brassy indulgent gathering of London's new demotic leaders. Politics was the new rock 'n' roll, somebody had said, and the theme had caught on. The parliamentary sketch-writer was wandering around wearing an Oasis tee-shirt. The lobby correspondent had come back from the Kensington count wearing a leather jacket. 'The '90s were the new '60s,' somebody had said sarcastically, and half a dozen people had made a mental note to offer that as an idea at the next features conference.

'Look around,' Dave said. 'For every bald psephologist and party hack, there are three comedians and a pop star. Danny McBeth is dishing out freebie coke in the executive bathroom. That bloke from Blur was here a while ago.'

'The Boo Radleys,' Richard felt obliged to point out.

'Whatever.'

Jayne Holland-Patrick came up and grabbed Richard's elbow. In her other hand she held a half-empty bottle of champagne. 'Richard!' she exclaimed. 'They've pointed you out as the lovely man who did the piece on my Beatrice.'

Jayne stared at him with rabid intensity. She grinned, baring her teeth, and to Richard it seemed as if she was on the verge of biting him. Richard stepped back a little, but couldn't help looking at the half-inch platinum crop of her hair. 'Don't mind that, Richard dear,' she said. 'I'm a victim of fashion, not chemotherapy. I really should stop taking notice of the crap you people put in your weekend magazines. Listen, have you heard from my little darling? Only we need a new book from her soon, if I'm going to keep myself in this stuff.' Jayne waved the champagne bottle, and it frothed a little at the neck.

'She said she's going to be in Italy for a while. I think there's some family business to sort out.'

'Really? Funny, I never really think of Beatrice having family.'

'Well, there're aunts or something over there. Don't know exactly. But she did tell me she had ideas for the next two books, although I don't think she ever likes to write in the summer.'

'How very English of her. Although I suppose that means I have to adjust my cash-flow to fit in with...'

But they were interrupted by the rough approximation of a smooth drawl, still on the suave side of drunkenness. 'Richard. Going to introduce me to your lovely friend?'

Richard had managed to purloin an extra invitation, and Liam was there. He was in London on a visit to see Sally, who had been involved with the Labour campaign and was at the victory party. Liam's waistline and hairline were those of a man in his mid-forties, but somehow he preserved an irrepressible spark of optimism, a belief that each new person he met could bring brightness or at least entertainment into his life. Liam looked at Jayne with the glint of interest, and she looked back at him with a curiosity that wasn't entirely hostile. Richard left them talking to each other while he wandered off to catch up with some results. He still didn't quite trust all the prognoses.

When he returned, Jayne was just writing her phone-number on Liam's wrist in dark green lipstick. She fluttered her fingers girlishly, and blew Richard a kiss by way of farewell. Richard gave Liam an interrogative look.

'Mmm, interesting bird,' Liam said. 'Mutton dressed as punk. I like that. And is there an age limit on gamine? I don't think so.'

'How old are you, Liam?'

Liam thought about it. 'Old enough to know better. Old enough to know my limitations. Old enough to be careful. Old enough to start to feel the consequences in the morning. Old enough to realise that Canadians don't make the best whisky. Old enough to know that really young women are more trouble than they're worth. Old enough not to get caught the same way more than three times a year. Old enough.'

'All right. So don't forget to wash that off before Sally sees it,' Richard said. 'I don't know why you aren't with her at the Labour shindig anyway. It would be amazing. Eighteen years, and all that.'

'Yeah,' Liam said. 'Except I would've felt like a fraud. I didn't vote for the bastards, after all.'

'What?'

'Well as far as I can see, they're just the same as the Tories. I voted Lib Dem.'

'In Glasgow?'

'Yeah.'

253

'Did you tell Sally that?'

'Haven't got round to it yet. She might not understand.'

'I think she probably wouldn't.'

'Well, the truth was it was a protest, however futile. I grew up with a rosy notion of the Labour Party as being this kind of moral monolith, heroic protector of the working man and all that. Yeah, I know Harold Wilson was a smooth operator, the Blair of his day, but in the end they were underpinned by some sort of principles. I look at this crew and have to say that your pal Gordon is one of the more personable representatives. You see what I mean? There is simply no character to them. And until they get that back, they won't be getting my vote.'

'Doesn't look like they'll need it.'

'No, but still. Once you see what they're like in government, remember, you can't blame me.'

'For such a sleazy character, you've got a particularly selective moral streak, haven't you?'

Before he could protest, Liam stumbled forward under the weight of a slap on the back from a tall, drunk, black-haired man in a kilt. 'Scotland free by 2003!' he yelled. 'But don't hold us to that.'

'Richard, you remember Callum from Edinburgh?'

Richard did, if only vaguely.

'Shouldn't you be up in Scotland, getting ready for an Assembly?'

Callum leered at him blearily. 'All in good time. The real action is down here at the moment, watching Tories topple. Have you heard about Portillo?'

'Believe it when I see it.'

'I met a few boys from Edinburgh down at the Embankment. They're all on their mobiles figuring out when the referendum's happening, and what they have to do to line up a seat for Holyrood.'

'That's another pile of crap, as well,' said Liam. 'Scotland already has three tiers of government dominated by crooks, siphoning off funds and giving jobs to their cronies. Do they really need another, paid for at huge expense by poor mugs like me, just so a bunch of fat weegies can stuff their back pockets with cash?'

'Since when did you pay taxes?' Richard said.

'Aye,' said Callum, 'but they'll be our crooks. Good Scots villains.

About time we had a say in the way the country is run.'

'Hate to confound your logic, Cal,' Liam said, 'but as of tomorrow, the Prime Minister, Chancellor and Foreign Secretary are all Scots. Seems quite a vocal sort of representation to me.'

Richard had heard the argument several times before, and was looking around for another drink. Liam leaned over and slapped his palm onto Richard's shoulder. 'Richard, don't get excited, but guess who Sally was speaking to on the phone this morning?'

Richard knew instantly, and got excited. Sarah. 'Where is she? How is she?'

'No idea, because Sally made a point of not mentioning it. But I did something a little underhand, and all for you, because I love you dearly, and underneath this breezy exterior I'm a sentimental old fuck, and because you remembered me when you had a ticket for free booze. Although the food's not up to much ... a few baked tatties wouldn't have gone amiss.'

'What? What did you do?' Richard was shaking.

'You know Sally. Pretends to be the conscientious liberal, but secretly she's a yuppie, although she hates to admit it. So she's a sucker for all these technological advances. Christ, she's got an electronic filofax that makes up a whole lot of imaginary friends for you. Anyway, her phone has got this little screen. If you press a button it shows you the numbers of incoming calls.'

'So?'

'So, I waited for her to head off to the bog, because I know how long she spends in there, then I pressed the last number button, and wrote it down. I thought you might appreciate it.'

Liam handed over a scrap of a cigarette packet. 'It's a phone number, Richard. Only don't tell anyone I gave it to you. Sally would mince my balls up and sprinkle them on her pasta. Even if she is a vegetarian.'

'She's in London?' Richard tried and failed to keep the panic out of his voice.

'Only for a few days. And I suspect that she definitely doesn't want to speak to you. I still don't know exactly what you did there, but I think the Americans will be forgiven for carpet-bombing Cambodia sooner than you'll get a word out of her.'

But Richard was already heading off toward the telephone booths downstairs in the lobby, stumbling in his haste, side-stepping minor celebrities, research assistants, IT technicians, and the Keeper of the Queen's Paintings. He kept his eyes fixed on the blue ink of that phone number as if it might dissolve if he let it out of his sight.

Every detail began to be enhanced. He picked up the faux-bakelite telephone receiver, in the mock-retro red plastic phone cubicle. He looked past the revolving door at the front of the lobby, at the gilded sheen of the doorman's epaulettes glinting back from the riverside street lamps, past the ironic Union Jack panels in pink, cream and sky-blue, pastel patriotism. He could still hear the champagne bottles being popped. He felt a hum, the city buzz echoing by some strange acoustic trick off the surface of the river out there. He fumbled for his ten-pence pieces, throwing in three, and then adding a couple of twenty-pences as well. How long could this conversation last? He scrabbled in the pocket of his jacket and felt the reassuring chunkiness of three pound coins, ran his finger around the milled edges. That would be enough. If she was there. She had to be there.

He dialled the number slowly, punching the keys with fixed determination. It would have been just like Liam to copy it incorrectly, Richard thought. But what if she had been calling from a phone-box? But it was ringing. Richard felt icy, sick, his vision blurred. He tried to focus on the embankment opposite, but all he could hear was that two-beat tone. He could see it, a telephone, somewhere in London, in a hallway, could half-imagine her drifting slowly down the hallway with that irritated expression on her face. After eight rings and an eternity, the answer-machine clicked into action.

'Hi, this is Marsha. I'm not here right now, but you know what to do.'

Sarah's sister. Or at least, an older, confident, assured-sounding version of Sarah's sister. Richard held on to the receiver for what seemed like an hour, felt it cold against his palm, felt himself turning into the seventeen-year-old again, reduced to silence at the time when eloquence could have been his saviour. He needed the words to print a tiny, bitterly-comic haiku of regret and yearning onto something as banal as an answering-machine tape, to encapsulate longing and lamentations in a few pithy syllables. Phrases ran through his mind, and he remembered that *cliché* in its purest meaning meant a typographical imprint. He thought too long, and became aware that the immensity of his cerebral effort was making him breathe hard into the mouthpiece. Now he would have to speak. He stuttered into the receiver, 'Hi, hello, this is a message for Sarah. Well … isn't this brilliant?'

He had meant the election result, but as soon as he had hung up and shuffled away from the booth, he realised that he hadn't even identified himself, and the message had hardly been coherent. But she would get it, wouldn't she? She must recognise his voice, and understand him? Sarah had always been more enthusiastic about the Labour Party than he had. Now he came to think of it, he realised she was probably at the victory party with Sally, making use of Liam's unwanted ticket.

Richard wandered through the revolving doors, walked down the steps to the riverside. He looked east, downriver, watching the traffic heading over Chelsea Bridge, busloads of partygoers heading off to celebrate a new nation very much like the old nation. He looked further, beyond Vauxhall Bridge, trying to cast his mind out along the river all the way down to the estuary, to the mud-flats at the end of England, but he couldn't remember the details any more. They were muddled in with fragments of tunes, of bad television dramas. He was in danger of confusing his home with a bad sitcom set, his sister's boyfriends with characters from *Only Fools And Horses*, or the subject of a song on Parklife.

He took the lift back upstairs. Next time he called, Sarah would be gone again, swallowed up by Europe, and another little glimmer of hope would be extinguished.

'No dice,' Liam said, seeing his expression. Liam passed him a can of lager in mute consolation. 'Ah. There's a result coming in from the north-east.' Liam pointed at the television screen. 'This'll be our boy, the shite that he is. Any chance of him losing?'

'None,' Richard said. 'He'll have made sure of that.'

'Don't you have to admire the sheer steely ruthlessness of that bastard?' Liam asked, tipping over his lager can to confirm it was empty.

'No,' Richard said, looking blankly at the giant screen, watching Gordon's grin. He was taking in the detail of it, the cool, escapee's relief that formed the upturn of the lips, the liberty in the eyes, then he saw it spark and crack and fracture into a million pieces as a thin stream of amber beer trickled over the spliced plug connection and short-circuited the wiring.

'Er, sorry,' Liam muttered. 'Forgot I'd just got a fresh one.'

'Don't be. He deserves it.'

An hour or so later the party ended, and people headed off in their cabs, to wake up the next morning and look thick-headed but smiling into the sun of the same old England.

Hope

Grainne

E ngland in the spring of 1997 made Grainne smile. Leaves in the trees, birds on the bough, a watery sun glinting off the dew – it seemed like it only needed a thousand violins soaring bucolically in the background. Grainne woke up early these days. She awoke with a dryness in the throat, a raging thirst for (and she smiled at the thought) coffee and orange juice.

She would wander along to the kitchen and beg an early breakfast. She would sit by the windows, hearing the croaking chorus coming up from the water's edge, gaze out into the morning, and butter a croissant. On sunny mornings the solitude, the peace, the warmth, the melting butter, the slight smooth tang of that orange juice and the blandness of her milky decaffeinated coffee, would give her a sensation of almost painful happiness. She had an hour of it before the Grange bustled into distracting life. Sometimes she would try to read, but usually it was enough to look down that damp grass slope or up into a pale blue sky, and feel liberated. How did I ever get to be this happy? she would think, and look at the thick white bandages around her wrists, and the tiny brown coffee stain at the corner of the white linen.

She would sit and dream until woken from the reverie by Marcia hissing, 'I warned you about that coffee, but do you listen?' or Matt screaming, 'I bet you've used all the fucking butter!' Then the day took steady shape around her, and Grainne shook herself back into its demands.

In the afternoons she lay back on Dr Anderson's couch and waited for his quiet encouragement. He had suggested she just sit in an armchair, but she had insisted on the couch. 'I'm sorry, doctor, but I really couldn't take you seriously as an analyst unless there was a couch.'

'How are you, Grainne?' he would begin.

'You know, I really think that I couldn't be better. Spring is here. Although I can't remember spring ever making me this happy before. Are you from Scotland?'

Dr Anderson was taken aback. 'I'm sorry. Is this relevant?'

'No. Yes. Oh, it's a simple enough question. Are you?'

'From Dumfries.'

'Right. Well you'll know about Scottish spring. On the island this kind of weather didn't really arrive until May, by which time you'd built yourself up for the school holidays already, Easter was gone, and really it became a bit of a non-event of a season.'

'I don't remember it like that.'

'Ah, well, I suppose Dumfries is the Scottish tropics. But no. This is the first spring I've spent in the south, and it's only March, and the sun is in the sky, and for some reason these things are making me happy. Unless you've been giving me extra doses of happy pills?'

'No. On the contrary,' Dr Anderson said, looking at his notes, 'your medication is still quite strong, but we are softening it in gradual increments.'

'What a lovely word. So it's just the glories of the season, then?'

'Perhaps.'

'"Perhaps." Analyst-speak for "no".'

'How do you feel about your actions of five weeks ago, Grainne?'

'My actions of five weeks ago? Let me see. Oh. I suppose you're referring to the little incident in the bathroom. Is that the *action* you mean?'

Dr Anderson looked at his notes again.

'You broke a bathroom mirror and attempted to slash your wrists, Grainne.'

'That's one way of looking at it.'

'How do you feel about that now?'

The silence lasted three minutes this time.

'I feel embarrassed.'

'Embarrassed?'

'On three counts. First, I didn't lock the bathroom door, which makes it seem suspiciously like a feeble cry for help. Second, I did it around midday, when there were lots of people around, which makes it seem like ditto. Third, I didn't have any clothes on, which meant the orderlies carried me naked down the corridor, where Angry Matt had a good look and has smiled to himself every time he's seen me since. Can't you do a memory wipe on him, or something?'

'We wish.' Dr Anderson laughed, and its rarity made Grainne laugh too.

'Where's the nearest railway?' Grainne said suddenly.

'Main line to Scotland's about twelve miles to the west, Cambridge line is about fifteen miles east. I think there used to be a branch line went across towards St Albans, but Dr Beeching killed it off, I suppose. Why do you ask? Thinking of travelling somewhere?'

'No, but I always loved *Anna Karenina,* you know. So I thought the railways might be an option. Third time lucky, I thought. Although, with my record, there'd probably be a train strike and I'd be lying there all day.'

Dr Anderson stayed silent for a few moments, or for what Grainne now realised was the standard minute and a half. She had learned to enjoy the silence, to forget where she was, stare up at that dusty white ceiling and listening to the birds chirping down by what she'd come to call that fake lake.

'This is a good sign,' Dr Anderson said. 'That you can joke about it.'

'Who says I'm joking?'

'But it's good you can talk in this way, all the same. It shows a detachment from your situation. If you can visualise it, that means you're less likely to do it.'

'"Less likely?" You don't want to give any guarantees, do you?'

'Nothing is certain, Grainne. You know, with a lot of patients, it's just a matter of them coming to understand that nothing is certain. Uncertainty is precisely what they're afraid of.'

'I'm sure none of this is in your textbooks.'

'We can't get it all out of books.'

'I know,' Grainne said. 'Although there's an enormous amount in them and you could spend a lot of time trying. That would be something, though, wouldn't it? Lying there feeling the cold steel of the rails across your shoulder blades and the back of your knees. Just looking up at the clouds scudding across the sky. Waiting for the first tingle in the metal that tells you that the Edinburgh express is about a mile away and building up to top speed. Those few minutes as it approached would really be something, wouldn't they? A time to put all your affairs in order in your mind.'

Dr Anderson offered up the requisite ninety seconds.

'It's interesting, Grainne. You're something of a sensualist, aren't you?'

'So my husband would like to think.'

'You don't?'

'I like different things. My senses are more selective.'

'What kinds of things.'

'Cold dew on the soles of my feet. Black coffee. The warmth of the sun coming through the window. Melting butter. The little itch of healing skin. Velvet. I like your accent. It's unreal. The rather dirty white of your ceiling. Birds, although I couldn't tell a sparrow from a wren any more. Could do when I was a kid. The sea. I really miss the sea. I don't know, raindrops on roses and...'

'Spring makes you happy?'

'More than happy. Exultant. The same way I used to feel after the fourth vodka. No – that's a lie. Better, because with the fourth vodka I knew I was dancing at the edge of a cliff. Now, I don't know. I feel untouchable.'

'It's common enough.'

'You're very cruel. What's common enough?'

'Joy at surviving. Getting through the suicidal crisis. It puts things into some kind of perspective.'

'No, no, no.'

'Why don't you want to believe that?'

'Because I prefer to believe that my suicidal crisis, as you call it, was a logical and reasoned response to my mess of a life. That's the trouble with this place. It assumes that despair is a disease or at least an aberration, whereas it seems perfectly reasonable to me.'

'Is your life simpler, now?'

'Yes. No. Or at least, not outside of here. Maybe that's the explanation you're looking for: that I just want to be kept here a little longer. When I'm sitting looking out of that window it seems simpler. But I can't spend the rest of my life doing that, can I? Unless I decide to head out to those railway tracks one of these mornings.'

'Next time, Grainne...'

'Oh, you're getting rid of me, are you?'

'Next time, I want you to tell me about your mother.'

'Back to the textbooks, then?'

'The books have their uses, Grainne.'

Grainne didn't mind so much when her breakfasts were interrupted by Helen. She, at least, had a horde of stories about scurrilous goings-on on the fringes of the entertainment industry.

'Head of drama at one of the regions, won't tell you which one, but look – I seem to have written it down on this napkin – asked me to give him a blow-job to be considered for the part of a housekeeper in some Sunday afternoon piffle,' Helen began one morning, sloshing lemon tea over the tablecloth. 'To be *considered*, you'll notice, not necessarily to get the part. "It's set in the 1890s," I said. "There was no cock-sucking in Victorian times, so you're not telling me this is a proper audition?" I did it, though, and I got the job, although the funding never came through.' Helen ran her tongue round her mouth to dislodge a lump of bread roll.

'Helen, why are you in here?'

'I don't think you're supposed to ask that, dear.'

'No, that's prison. In a sanatorium it's a perfectly acceptable line of conversation.'

'Really? I'm glad to hear it. I'm in here because I suffer from pitiable delusions of adequacy.'

'What?'

'It's what some snide bastard of a critic wrote about my one-woman show. It was something I had big hopes for. Okay, it was on late on Channel 4. But it was sketches, monologues, and I got to sing a number with this really smooth band: a Julie London song, the sort of thing my mother would have loved. Nobody even noticed the show. It got tiny figures. And then this complete shit filled out a TV review with some really vicious stuff. Cheap lines. "She's the sort of torch singer you want to set light to." There was more. I remember every word, actually.'

'And you're in here because of one bad review?'

'Bad review, broken marriage, addiction to tranquillisers and three abortions when I was in my twenties. That doctor used a nice word. *Cumulative*. But I think it was the review that hurt most. I'll never forgive that bastard.'

'Who was it?'

'Richard Martin. Although that's probably a pseudonym. These bastards are always too cowardly to use their own names.'

'Mmm, probably,' Grainne said, thinking it was for the best that Richard hadn't been able to visit lately.

'Did I tell you about the time I was in an all-nude Chekhov production on the Edinburgh fringe?' Helen went on, more cheerful now. 'I got my period in the middle of the Wednesday matinée? We didn't win a Fringe First and they blamed me. Typical.'

'Tell me about your mother, Grainne,' Dr Anderson said one warm afternoon as March was getting ready to fade into a very Hertfordshire April.

'I know you've looked up my records, and I know you know that my mother died when I was a teenager. So what's to tell?'

'I want to know about your relationship with her. Can you remember the details of your childhood?'

'Of course I can remember. Why, are your drugs supposed to be killing my memory as well?'

'Tell me about your mother, Grainne.'

'My mother was called Mhairi. We had a romantic Celtic thing going on in our family – hence my name. She looked like me. I'll show you a picture if you don't believe me.'

'I'll take your word for it.'

'Most of my memories of her are about weather,' Grainne said, her voice softening. 'Probably one of my first memories is of a sudden squall blowing up on the harbour at Tobermory, and my mother tucking me under her coat as if I was some kind of baby kangaroo or something. I was three or four, and she just scooped me up and hoisted me under her coat and half ran towards a bus shelter. I remember her looking down at me, and I was struggling and she was laughing, and she said, "You weigh a ton, Grainne." I was four, I think. Before school, anyway.

'I remember the wooded hills above the town. The smell of them. Like mushrooms and hay and horses. We would go up there on afternoons, and I'd get out of breath, and she would look at me and laugh and tell me I needed the exercise. Then she would give me a toffee – I remember there was a little shop down by the harbour where they made their own, and they tasted like the condensed milk we had on our tinned fruit on Sunday afternoons.

'Then the rain would come down and we'd shelter under a tree, but it would creep in between the branches and soak us anyway. One time I remember I forgot my hat, and my hair got soaked. "Your hair looks much darker, wet," my mother said. For weeks afterwards I wondered if I could go around with wet hair all the time, just to stop the other kids yelling "ginger nut" at me.

'One Christmas, I remember, we went for a long hike in the hills with my Auntie Bryony and one of her little dogs. It started out white, but then rolled in all the icy mud and finished up a kind of dark grey. We were coming back around the south side of the town overlooking the harbour and my mother grabbed Bryony and put her hands over her eyes, and said "Okay: colours." Bryony laughed, and she said, "red, blue, black, black, pink, yellow, blue." She was listing the colours of the houses along the harbour front. After that I made my mother do the same to me. But it changed one day. I suppose someone must have painted one of the houses, which shouldn't have been allowed. The blue was always my favourite, because it was the colour that the sky or the sea should have been. But they were always grey or black.

'I remember the wind. Sometimes it would hit us full on in the face, when we were coming back from the Spar with the milk or the bread. I would walk behind my mother's knees and I would hold onto the tail of her coat, and she would pretend to be irritated but really she was laughing because I had my head down to the ground and was all hunched up to avoid the gale.

'I remember looking out the window, waiting for an ambulance for her, and seeing the rain pattering against the glass and the sky just darkening a shade or so every ten seconds – you know how it does when a storm is coming in. There were bits of blue and green and brown and red and they were all turning gradually black, as if someone had spilled black watercolour and it was trickling across the sky. When I saw that I thought that if I'd been superstitious, this would be full of portent. But I wasn't all that mystical. I saw her sitting on the sofa with her breathing mask, and her hair all dusty grey, and thought I didn't need to believe in myths and legends. It was all there in front of me. She never came back to the island after that. I'd visit her in Edinburgh and sit by her bed, and I'd say, "Red, blue, black, black, pink, yellow, blue."'

'Believe me, Grainne,' Dr Anderson whispered, 'you're a sensualist.'

Grainne liked the slow queue for medication. It made her feel her life was imitating *One Flew Over the Cuckoo's Nest*. Grainne would shuffle deliberately, look blank-eyed, as Abigail sorted out her pills. Abigail never tired of the joke.

'Not for you at the moment, Grainne,' Abigail said that morning.

'After dinner tonight.'

'You're changing my routine. I don't think that's good, is it?' Grainne asked.

'Just this once. Your husband called.'

'What's it got to do with him?'

'He asked if we could delay your medication. He's coming to see you this afternoon, and didn't want you to be drowsy.'

'And he gets to dictate my treatment, does he?'

'I'm sorry.' Abigail seemed genuinely distraught. 'But it is just the once. And it really won't do any harm.'

'I shall be the judge of that,' Grainne said, and strode off – but then had to smile at her own pomposity.

Gordon arrived at three with a nervous look on his face, not knowing where to put his hands.

'How are you?' he asked.

'Clinging desperately to life because I was refused medication at your request,' Grainne croaked.

'Come on,' Gordon said. 'It's just that I've got some important news and I wanted you to be alert.'

'I'm always alert. What news?'

Gordon was looking distinctly uncomfortable.

'Grainne. You know we can't go on like this.'

'Like what? You in the Commons, me in the mental institution? There's a certain ironic kind of symmetry, though, don't you think?'

'We have to face facts, Grainne. We're not the people we used to be.'

'What is it, Gordon? Are you going to start singing the theme tune to *Whatever Happened To The Likely Lads?*'

'What? What are you talking about?'

'What became of the people we used to be? Here's a clue. You became a power-crazed fetishist with a thing for submissive near-schoolgirls. I became a suicidal alcoholic whore.'

'Shut up, Grainne. Just shut up and listen.'

Grainne shut up. And looked at him. Gordon had lost control. He was trying not to look at her.

'In these situations you have to act quickly, do what's best; you don't have time for regrets and recriminations.'

'And what's best?'

'I'm coming to that. Look, this might seem a bad time, but I don't think we can delay it any longer. We need to face up to what is best for both of us. I don't think being with me is doing you any good.'

'Well, if being with you had been the end of it. But there were all the others. There were thirty-three in that marriage. As far as I know. There may of course have been more when I was too pissed to notice.'

'I'm getting the papers drawn up. It shouldn't take too long, as long as you don't make things difficult.'

'Papers?'

'Yes. The legal people …'

'You're divorcing me?' Grainne's voice was steady, cool, but with a slight interrogative rise at the end.

'I think it's …'

'You're divorcing me.' Grainne smiled. 'On what grounds? That I slept with thirty-three assorted men at parties to which you dragged me? Have the divorce laws become a lot more liberal since I was banged up in here?'

'I don't think it's necessary to bring all that up, Grainne. It'll only hurt both of us.'

'Of course. I get it. You've got an election coming up, and the Labour Party's rising prince cannot afford to have a vodka-swilling consort in the loony bin. A quickie divorce doesn't look too good either, but you've weighed it up as the lesser of two evils. It's a political decision, isn't it? Have you taken advice from your usual sources? Maybe you've taken an opinion poll. Dump the missus, or stick by her and risk embarrassing revelations further down the line?'

'Come on, Grainne. It's not like that. This is better for you. I think you'll be able to sort out your life a lot easier without the pressures of … well, you know. This will be the best option. It could have got much worse. It could have been necessary to have you committed. There are those who'll say that you're a danger to yourself. These two attempts to …'

'You didn't really need to threaten me, Gordon.'

'It's not a threat, Grainne. I'm just saying …'

'You're just saying, best not make any waves about the divorce, or you'll have me in a straightjacket before I can say teenage

269

nymphette…'

'You're not yourself, Grainne. You need some rest, some time for thought, to come to your senses.'

'This is a mental institution, Gordon. Coming to your senses isn't that straightforward.'

'That's another thing.' Gordon's tone was tentative.

'What?'

'You can only be here for another month at the tops. Obviously after the separation I'll make adequate financial provisions, but I'm afraid funds just won't run to the sort of fees they charge here. You know the rates go up in May, don't you? Apparently that's when all the pop stars and footballers check in. If you still need treatment, we'll have to look for somewhere public sector. Looks bad enough going private as it is.'

Gordon dropped an official-looking brown envelope on the chair beside Grainne's bed, picked up his jacket, and headed off down the corridor. Helen, coming the other way, saw his expression and raised an eyebrow.

'Husbands,' she said. 'The only reason we end up in places like this is because it's illegal to kill them in their sleep. At least, I think it's still illegal.'

'It's all right, Helen. I think I'm cured.'

'Just you keep believing that, darling. But there is no cure.'

Beatrice

B eatrice shook the wine bottle to check it was empty, then looked to her left and then to her right, wondering what particular cosmic joke had arranged this lunch party. Some malicious Riviera sprite had played a bittersweet joke on her. Surely one of those Rimini transsexuals must have smiled slyly and conjured up this Italian farce.

She liked this town, with its very un-Italian vulgarity, its brown-toothed grin of welcome stretching out along the promenade, gazing broadly and lewdly over the Adriatic. It reminded her of a sweatier Brighton, a slapdash seafront with a flash of flamboyance. Rimini was where she came when she tired of the view from her villa, when seclusion's comforts began to pall. She liked the subdued tinkle of English conversation, liked the way waiters looked at her and smiled at her passing, liked the screech of the brakes as buses edged up side-streets oblivious to oncoming traffic.

She liked the restaurant, too. Here she would indulge herself in the textures and subtleties of every detail of an Italian meal, mentally testing her own powers of description. There was the slight gritty resistance of her clams, the soft milled smoothness of ravioli, the tang of fresh tomato sauce, the wheezing accordion music flattened by the radio speakers, the background whirr of the ceiling fan, the sharp sudden snap of a fly hitting the electric coil hanging above the doorway. Beatrice tried to lose herself in the details again, tried to shelter from the two daunting presences on either side.

To her left was Theresa Beroto. Theresa had a mound of viciously blonde hair piled up like ice cream, thinning at the parting from too much Latin peroxide. It was hair that was supposed to sing of good times, of a happy-go-lucky adventuress – but Theresa's hair was as sad as the rest of her. Her black eyebrows formed the most immediate contradiction, arcing gloomily over indigo eyes that seemed to have been borrowed for the afternoon from the Adriatic: deep, wet and unfathomable. Theresa wore the thick make-up of an Italian woman who wasn't a mother. The hair and the lipstick were little lifelines back to her youth. Theresa must have been around forty, but seemed ten years older. Beatrice had started to think of her as a stepmother, and hated herself for doing it.

Beatrice's Aunt Ofelia had called. 'She wants to meet you. She telephoned,' she said, as if they were in the middle of a continuous conversation, although Beatrice hadn't heard from Ofelia for more than six months. Ofelia had a brusque intimacy that Beatrice admired, although it could be infuriating.

'Who wants to meet me? Who called?'

'Theresa. She lives in Rimini. She would.' Ofelia's voice dripped disdain.

Beatrice had to make an effort to remember who Theresa was. Then it came back to her. She was the bar girl. Her father's last girlfriend. The one responsible for the break-up of his second marriage.

'Why? What does she want to meet me for?'

'She has things to tell you. I told her you were a famous writer and had no time for such business. She seemed to accept that. You don't have to call her. She is not our problem.'

'I'll call her,' Beatrice had said eagerly – and for a moment she had been a teenaged Beatrice again, back at her grandmother's house, wincing at the *grappa* burn at the back of her throat, hungry for information, ardently needing to colour in all the grey areas of her family background.

Theresa worked as a housekeeper in one of the cheaper tourist hotels. Beatrice had waited in the cramped lobby for half an hour until Theresa came off duty. The receptionist had cast her a hostile look, but realising that Beatrice wasn't a prostitute, had smiled and left her alone. Theresa, hair piled under a brown cap, her breasts seemingly stuffed into a blue overall, had seized Beatrice's palms as if trying to pull her down to her own level. Beatrice had stared down at Theresa's thinning parting and then had been swept up in an embrace while Theresa stuttered out her thanks. 'You are so generous to come. You cannot know how important it was to see you.'

They had sat in a tiny smoky café, drinking milky coffees. Theresa had stared at Beatrice until Beatrice had just smiled back. Theresa had tears in her eyes. Beatrice did too, but that was from the smoke. She was used to sitting outdoors on terraces.

'You are like him. Perhaps a little stronger,' Theresa said.

'I am nothing like him,' Beatrice replied, and heard her mother's voice.

'He spoke about you. He always spoke about his Beatrice.'

Theresa pronounced it Bay-a-tree-chay, and Beatrice took a quick, scalding sip of her coffee and tried to smile again. It wasn't as easy, and the smoke seemed to be getting worse.

'I am sorry about all this,' Theresa said. 'But it was important to me. Your family do not want to know about me. They blame me, I think, for what happened to Vincenzo. I was not asked to the funeral.'

'No,' Beatrice said, not sure whether she was trying to reassure Theresa or to confirm her suspicions.

'It was a long time ago, and they think I will have forgotten it all, but I cannot forget Vincenzo. You see, I have never married. There could not have been another after him for me. But they think I was just the little bar whore who seduced him away from his wife. I think you will be kinder. I read your book. About the girl with all the lovers. I think you are not like your family. I think you understand a little about passion.'

'I'm not so sure,' Beatrice said, feeling uncomfortable. This seemed familiar. It seemed too much like her own last conversation with her father: the coffee, the music, the Italian menu, the tentative voice seeking her approval or at least a word of sympathy. Theresa looked at her inquiringly, hoping for some slight response.

'You do not mind me talking about him? I have nobody else who knows.'

Beatrice shook her head.

'It was too much for him,' Theresa was saying. 'He wasn't strong enough. He didn't think love could be an excuse.'

'An excuse?'

'Ah, you know what it is like in Italy. You have a duty. He already hated himself because he had left your mother and you behind in England. With Antonia, he'd thought he could not abandon another wife. It would make him nothing, a crawling creature in the dirt. But he loved me. He loved me more than he would admit, and I loved him back. I thought that should be enough, but then I was younger. I was twenty-two. When you are twenty-two, you think you can do anything in the world, and it will be a happy ending. Yes?'

'Yes,' Beatrice said, although she had never felt that way herself.

'He felt too bad about leaving you. With a wife, I suppose, you can always say that it was not your fault, that she was not the soul-mate you thought she would be. With a wife, you can justify yourself. With a daughter, she is only yours. You cannot deny her. Vincenzo would show me pictures. Pictures of you as a baby. Of course, you were in your mother's arms, or she was in the picture. Vincenzo would put his thumb over her as if I would not notice her in the picture. It made me laugh. I didn't care about her. She was in England far away and in the past. So I would take the picture and look at both of you, and I would understand why he hated himself for leaving you.'

'Did he really?' Beatrice said, and heard her mother again, the thin notes of English suspicion out of place in the aromatic air of a Rimini café.

'Of course. Don't you remember? He would write you letters. It would hurt him so much to write those letters, because he had to stop himself from saying everything he felt. He thought he had to be the strong, reserved English father so you would respect him. He would write a letter full of his love and his reproaches to himself, and how much he missed you, and then he would tear it up, and scatter all the pieces on the beach, and start another.'

Beatrice drank coffee and said nothing, but looked at Theresa's dark eyes, and remembered her father's as the same, as if her father and Theresa had been related – not lovers but family.

'Because you were beautiful, it made it harder. If you had been a big round blue-eyed English baby I think he would have thought it easier to leave you there on your own island. But every picture reminded him that you were part of him. He would torture himself with them.'

'What about Antonia?' she asked, because Beatrice felt a sudden urge to change the subject, to challenge Theresa's narrative, to look for an alternative thread.

'She is a cold woman. She has the pride. She is from the north, thinks civilisation stops at Prato or Forli on the railway line. She married Vincenzo because she was too proud to be alone, and because she thought she could use him. It is not love, I think. He was a possession, and Antonia was very jealous of her possessions. I hear she didn't shed a tear at the funeral, just arrived for half an hour and was driven away. She didn't say a word to your family. Why weren't you there? You were the one that mattered.'

'It happened quickly. My mother thought it best if I...' But

Beatrice felt the just sting of the accusation in Theresa's voice.

'I think you didn't know him as well as he wanted,' Theresa said. 'It cannot be helped. There is so much sadness about Vincenzo.

'I go out there each year. I walk out in the sea, I let it come up to my thighs and I throw the lilies on the water, and tell myself he is still there somehow. Your father liked flowers. Not like other men, who never notice them. He loved flowers, would bring me huge piles of them. So I go there and I feel the warm water and I sprinkle those flowers for him. The first couple of years, you know, I felt it would be easy to walk out a little further and just sink under those waves myself, with the flowers all around me. But that would have been stupid: a stupid, girlish piece of drama with no real meaning, the young woman dying for love. So I would laugh, and wade back to the beach, and go into a bar and drink Campari, and the old women would look at my wet skirts and whisper to each other. I would be happy then, you know, because I would imagine we had been together that day.'

Beatrice had drunk her coffee and ordered more, and Theresa asked her about her books. Beatrice ordered wine then, and the two women looked out the smoky café window at the streets of Rimini and a solitary white cloud floating in from somewhere over Dalmatia. They exchanged numbers and addresses and agreed to meet occasionally, to talk about Vincenzo.

'This is too much for me,' Theresa had said. 'I have seen you as a child in my mind, and then I saw the picture on your book and knew you had grown up with a part of Vincenzo inside of you. Do you think it bad that I think of you as my family?'

Beatrice had smiled. 'Bad? No.'

Theresa had kissed her, and Beatrice had felt a little history slipping away down the beach. They met occasionally after that, and sometimes Theresa would talk about Beatrice's father, but never with the same intensity. Instead she would mention details, the cigarettes he liked, how he preferred his steak, how fussy he was about his shoes and his ties.

Theresa sat there that day, looking intently at Beatrice, smiling when she smiled, waiting her turn. Theresa spoke no English, so sat patiently while Beatrice turned to her left to talk to Barbara Paterson.

Somehow it hadn't even been a shock to run into her on the

terrace of Pagliacci's. Rimini was a Barbara Paterson sort of place. And although it had been ten years since she had last seen her, Beatrice had recognised her immediately. She had heard the voice – not a shout, but a medium-level firm statement: 'Beatrice Morelli.' And, turning around, her mind had already placed it in context. There was Barbara, a very English Theresa, her chestnut curls in an expensive happily middle-aged style, a smartish suit making no concessions to the temperature.

'Barbara,' Beatrice had said, the name coming out of her mouth before it had fully formed in her mind. These were the three syllables she always associated with her time with Bryan: that blithe, regretted slide into sexual conformity that always made her laugh to think of it. Bryan had always mouthed 'Barbara' at inopportune moments, an alternative form of farewell. Looking at his watch, tying his shoes, roughly drying his hair on one of her towels, he would say the name with a steady panic.

Beatrice met her eyes, strong English blue, and the sort of face that had waited for its owner to grow into it. Barbara looked serene, confident, dauntless. Beatrice briefly worried that there might have been some unpleasantness. After all, she thought, with a stirring of vague shame that she felt so shameless, she had slept with the woman's husband.

'Join me for a drink, Beatrice,' Barbara said, patting a chair as if inviting a puppy to leap up and be petted. 'Englishwomen abroad, and all that.'

Beatrice sat down beside her, murmured a quiet thanks as Barbara poured out a generous splash of Chianti. Barbara looked over at her and laughed. 'Don't be nervous, dear,' she said. 'I know all about you having it away with Bryan. Don't worry, I'm not going to upbraid you and call you a whore. I'm just amazed that you could see anything in him.'

Barbara patted her arm and showed straight white teeth, only a little stained by lipstick and Chianti.

'We split up a few years ago, now. His student fetish became just a little too embarrassing. His standards dropped alarmingly after you ditched him. It tore him up not a little, I can tell you.'

'I'm sorry,' Beatrice said, and wondered if she was apologising for sleeping with Bryan or for ceasing to.

'Don't be. Oh, I hated you at the time. If I'd believed in voodoo there would have been a little Morelli doll with needles in all the most painful places. But really, I hated you just for being you, not for sleeping with poor old Bryan. For that, I almost pitied you. I know what it's like.

'His name was Brian with an *i*, you know. Named after his Dad, who was another Brian. My one hated his Dad, so he put in that *y* just to piss him off. Which it did. His Dad was this old trade unionist – a docker, or something. Thought changing his name, even that slightly, was bourgeois pretension. Which it was.'

Beatrice felt sick, a burst of retrospective nausea at the news that she had been to bed with a *Brian*, not helped by a sudden gulp of warm Chianti. The past seemed to be reaching out little daggers at her, making tiny, razored incisions in everything she had thought inviolate.

'I had thought I could make something of him,' Barbara said. 'He was kind-hearted, a bit shy when I met him. I thought he was promising material. But he decided to make something of himself instead, and it turned out to be something I didn't like that much.

'He read your books. He read them in secret; thought I might be offended if I found them. But I read them myself. I confronted him about them. Asked him what he thought. He didn't like them, and he wasn't just saying that to please me.'

'Didn't he?' Beatrice wasn't sure whether she cared.

'No. Because he wasn't in them. He scoured them all in the hope that some minor character might be based on him, but not a sentence, not a paragraph. Not even a bus driver with a Scouse accent. That was mean of you, Beatrice. I think he thought that was the cruellest rejection of all, that he had left not the slightest impression.'

'I'm sorry.'

'Don't be. He wrote a book himself, you know. Not a novel. A piece of pop academia about 1960s playwrights. He was quite excited about it, kept trying to think of a Beatles song to use as a title. It sold about four copies. A pity, or he might have been able to make some decent alimony payments.'

'You're divorced? I'm sorry.'

'I wish you'd stop saying that. It's not your fault. And I have enough to enjoy my *single English lady on the Italian Riviera* holiday. I went to Lake Como last year. This country is beautiful. Makes me wish I'd been born Italian, just so I could feel I belonged.'

The only time Beatrice felt Barbara give her a hard look of resentment was when she replied in Italian to an old lady who had asked the time.

'I love the sound of it,' Barbara said, 'but I'm hopeless with languages. Will you have lunch with me tomorrow?'

Beatrice had been about to demur. She had already arranged to meet Theresa, but then, on a whim, she invited Barbara. In the restaurant they sat beside her like bookends, dusty vestiges of her past, taking it in turns to engage her attention.

'What do you do here in Italy?' Theresa asked

'I sit looking out to sea, and I drink wine, and I wait for rain, and I look for fishing boats, and sometimes I go and write, but more often I think of the expression on the faces of the emperor Justinian and Theodora in the basilica of San Vitale in Ravenna. Theodora looks like the most indomitable bitch in history. That's who I want to be: tough, implacable, Empress of all she surveys. Justinian looks such a wimp alongside her.'

Theresa cackled with delight. 'He was a man,' she said. 'Of course he is looking weak.'

'I envy you living here,' Barbara said. 'What do you do with your time?'

'I sit on my balcony watching the sun falling into the Adriatic. Sometimes I drive my sports car south along the coast road for a few days, just keeping the sea on my left, heading down past Fano, or Ancona, or Civitanova, maybe as far as San Benedetto Del Tronto. I stay in chic little hotels, and very rarely I'll meet a businessman, a travelling wine merchant, or a Fiat executive, and we'll go to bed together, because Italians have become a lot more spontaneous lately. We have elaborate meals and we speak complicated Italian, and we order champagne for breakfast because we both have vulgar souls. But a few months ago I met a university literature professor called Luca Chinaglia, and for some reason he isn't married, and he would prefer me not to go on these little trips. So the sports car stays in the garage.'

'I love this. It is like one of your stories,' Theresa said.

'You're making it all up, you tart,' Barbara said, delighted.

She wasn't. It was the truth, or at least a stripped-down version. Beatrice enjoyed the telling, relished the chance to offer a few formulated thoughts about a life that still seemed unreal to her. She had the car, she had the sun falling into the sea, she had those hotel breakfasts, she could even have Luca Chinaglia if she said the right words. She had all this and felt as dark as Theresa's oceanic eyes.

'But you are happy?' Theresa said anxiously.

'Sounds like bliss,' Barbara said admiringly.

'Oh yes,' Beatrice lied, in two languages.

Barbara drank Asti Spumante that afternoon. She drank a lot of Asti Spumante. Filling their three glasses until the froth spilled over the top, Barbara tapped the tabletop with her teaspoon and said, 'A toast. To surviving.'

Theresa raised her glass and laughed. Beatrice held hers, felt sticky wine flowing over her fingernails, and realised this was defeat. That the joke was on her. She had brought them together thinking she could see her own escape in their expressions, take some cruel comfort in seeing them afflicted by the lost love of two men who hadn't been able to touch her, impermeable Beatrice Morelli. That sprite had been a malicious one, though, sandwiching her between these twinned spectres of her past, with their watery eyes and their wet lips, and their brave faces that whispered promises of her own doom. Defeat, all right.

Now she just had to identify what it was that she had lost.

Richard

The man in Riga had told him that time never heals, but hope can occasionally work. The accent, the way the consonants seemed to have been choked out of the throat coated in ancient Hanseatic phlegm, gave the words a certain authority. Richard would have believed him anyway, even without the laryngal inflections. Richard had decided to open his mind to all influences, to accept each casual conversation as a source of possible insight. You can sift through the sands of banal observations, he persuaded himself, and pick out the glittering little grains of gold. Collect enough of them, and you'll be rich.

Richard was in love. That was what he was trying to persuade himself at six in the morning on a damp side street off the Rue du Faubourg St Honoré. Love was his reward for a pilgrimage, he told himself, sipping a black coffee in an all-night Algerian café, watching a street-cleaning lorry spray water into the gutters outside. Strange that they were so industrious, and yet Paris was still so filthy.

Two months earlier, he had woken up in his bedroom in Stoke Newington and had felt unable to face an English sky. It would kill him to look out that window one more time, he had thought to himself, lying in his bed, looking up at the grey ceiling of his over-priced tiny flat, littered with its books and records, the collected evidence of a middle-aged man's determination to trawl through other's experiences.

It had been a physical phenomenon; a simple inability to look down the street towards the buses crawling down Stamford Hill, towards the kebab shop and off-licence on the corner, past the newspaper-sellers, the old lady walking her Jack Russell, the three black kids hanging out outside the Bangladeshi grocers. The very buzz of London oppressed him, that all-pervasive clamour that whispered threats of what would happen if you tried to relax or escape.

He had wondered if he could navigate his way to the railway station with his eyes closed, allowing instinct to guide him past the Irish theme pub, the Ladbrokes, the imprecise charity shop, help him sidestep the homeless teenager with the soft Northern accent and the apologetically outstretched hand.

It had been a late-winter Thursday in London, and he was supposed to be going down to Battersea to pick up some CDs to review in one hundred and fifty words or less, for a flat fee of forty pounds, which would allow him to buy some new shoes which he didn't really need. Instead he had found himself still in bed, turning to a page in his mini-encyclopaedia, tracing the lines of the roads and railways connecting the Baltic States, wondering about the lengths to which a credit card would stretch. Lately, the names of foreign towns had aspired to a kind of poetry in his head. He had found himself wondering about the old quarters of Angers or Norrkoping with a brooding discontent.

London had turned into a crumbling crime-scene, surrounded by dusty police tape. A couple of miles away from Stoke Newington, in his friend Stephen's flat all those years before, he had started his bizarre affair with Stephen's Gothic flatmate, the event that had eventually caused his break-up with Sarah. Richard liked to try to reduce it to the simplicity of words, because it made it more manageable. The streets and language of London were constant reminders of his own inconstancy, each new coffee-bar and sandwich emporium a new epitaph to his failure. What could you do with a city like this, that took history and built around it, making it ineradicable, rooted in concrete and stripped pine?

Richard rarely did anything on impulse, so he was a little disturbed to find himself at Stansted airport with his black and sky-blue holdall, clutching his passport and a copy of the *Rough Guide to Europe*, asking at the KLM booking desk about the next available flight. 'We have a flight to Amsterdam, leaving in eighty minutes,' the girl had said, leafing through her timetable. 'There are still seats available.' Three minutes later Richard had a one-way ticket and was heading towards a departure gate, crossing the broad stretches of echoing emptiness, there to make Stansted seem like a chilly, futuristic hub instead of a warehouse on the edge of Essex.

The pilgrim shall be spiritually rewarded, Richard told himself again, wincing at the sharp coolness of the coffee he had left to sit too long in its tiny cup. He had covered the miles, and had been rewarded, if that was the word, with a brown-eyed Slavic tour guide who had been haunting him across the roads and rails of the old continent. He could get himself lost in her, he thought. Lost again, after weeks of searching for another. 'You need another bird,' Liam had said. 'They get inside your head and go around tidying away all the traces of the old ones. Can't help it.' Even Liam's lines were beginning to stick.

He looked through the murky windows onto the wet streets of Paris, and felt a sudden surge of freedom. He was five months into a new century, adrift in the capital of the world, nobody knowing where he was, with another £600 or so before he reached his credit-card limit, with a strange and beautiful foreign woman, and of course he was in love. It would have been impossible not to be. 'You cannot fight fate. You must admit it to yourself,' a gloomy German had told him in a Munich bar, and Richard had folded it away and stored it, along with the rest of his wealth of words.

Back in March, he had arrived in Tallinn with a plan. It had been a plan formulated somewhere in the cafés of Amsterdam, the details sketched out in the skies over Europe, roughed-out in mid-air, a retrospective justification for jumping on board that plane at Stansted. He would scour Europe for Sarah. Starting with Russia he would work his way systematically westwards, looking in the obvious places. Beatrice had been right. He needed to make some effort, to prove to himself that he had tried. She was lost, but might yet be found. 'Where was she when you last saw her?' he had asked himself as the plane banked in over the Baltic and approached Tallinn. What worked with front-door keys might be applicable to lost lovers.

He had looked down at the land, at frosted fields and grey docks and it seemed to him that he could almost see her, could almost pick out her dark head bobbing about in Europe, waiting to be spotted.

From the shores of the Baltic, he had traced a path across the continent, not with any logic, but guided by instinct, railway timetables and the suggestions implicit in stranger's words. He would treat a conversation in a station bar as portentous, the glimpse of a destination board as a signal.

He had looked for her, and felt a pilgrim's justification from the search. Estonia, Latvia, Lithuania, Poland, the Czech Republic, Germany, Denmark, Holland, Belgium and France had been ticked off. With each one Richard had felt not the impossibility of his task, but its inevitability: that this was his only possible course of action, and one he should have pursued years earlier. Each morning he looked up at foreign skies, wandered along glimpsing headlines, instructions, imprecations in unfamiliar combinations of syllables, and felt the comfort of distance. England had been left behind, and Richard had left the unwanted part of himself there. Maybe this was why Sarah had gone to Europe in the first place, he thought: to hide away in its reassuring alienness. He had looked over the Oresund from Denmark, looked back from Sweden, and felt the satisfaction of the meticulous traveller, the secret joy of not belonging, of being a benign invader.

What had helped had been beginning with a half-promise, an olfactory hint of love. In a mad whirl of an evening in Tallinn's old town he had met Matya Lebinnen, who was a few years younger and only a little bit wiser than Richard. Matya had offered an intriguing piece of her history, and a lot of Estonian alcohol. Richard had offered less of himself, but still enough, it seemed.

Richard had changed. At Stansted he had shrugged off the old, diffident Richard, recast himself as a mysterious, melancholic traveller, receptive to all invitations. Matya seemed to have an ability to read volumes between his minimalist lines. In that, she reminded him of Beatrice – although in nothing else. Over vodka and strange dark meat Matya had laughed a lot, even cried a little, and Richard had looked at her bare, slender olive-skinned arm when she slipped off her cardigan, and had kept looking at it until he had felt the courage to look up into her round, brown, soft eyes and start to collect some more welcome memories.

With ice clinging to the dark streets and a Baltic gale tugging at her hat, Matya had packed him off on his European Odyssey at the Tallinn railway station, making a surprisingly firm arrangement to see him again in Amsterdam in May. Richard had been left with a retinal memory of her eyes, her soft lips smiling, a few loose strands of her dark hair being pulled in the breeze, and it had never left him as he crossed the continent.

By May, by Amsterdam, Richard had tortured himself with the thought that it would be forgotten, that the meeting in Tallinn had been a drunken dream. Crossing Europe he hadn't stopped looking for Sarah, but he had come to an appreciation that the looking was far more important than the finding. 'U2, man. *I Still Haven't Found What I'm Looking For* is the most joyful and celebratory song there is,' a stoned American had told him in Prague. 'You find what you're looking for, man, and your life is fucked. What that song is saying is "I am still alive."' Richard had bought him a beer, and kept the words as payment.

She had been there, in the rain, outside the Rijksmuseum, hair flattened against the angular cheeks, smiling. There was a moment, seeing her just before she saw him – that tiny little glimmer of time when he had seen her eyes casting around anxiously – when he had a second to appreciate that it mattered, that she mattered to him, and he to her. That was a priceless second. Not *anxiously*, he realised then, but *hopefully*. It was a moment of hope. Hope can occasionally work. There was a moment.

She was old enough to remember totalitarianism, young enough to find Holland's liberality attractive rather than disturbing. There had been a young summer's evening on the beach at Scheveningen, a peacefully passionate Dutch scene, with Richard glad that the North Sea's horizon dropped well short of English shores. There was nothing quite as deliciously foreign as the feel of Matya's lips on his own, the quiet lapping of the North Sea at the beginning of Europe, the lights of the promenade beer-houses reflected on the foamy water.

There had been moments and words that Richard collected and stitched together to form a mantle that he was pretty sure he wanted to describe as love. There had been hotel bedrooms and canal-side bars that he would press to his memory, words, half-promises, touches and sounds.

Matya Lebinnen was nothing if not eager. She wanted to see all of the west, wanted to drink it all in in generous gulps, fill her brown eyes with its wonders. They took a slow, clean train south from Amsterdam, watching the crowds pile on at Schiphol, past Den Haag, Rotterdam, the industrial sprawl of Antwerp, through Flemish farmlands to Lille, down towards the French capital, Matya staring out at the unfolding of Europe's western edge, impatient for the myths of Paris.

This was a gift, Richard had thought, as their train had pulled into the Gare du Nord. This woman has never seen Paris, and now she will see it in my company. Richard realised that even he couldn't squander this much of an opportunity.

With the set for their cinematic spring romance ready and primed, at first Richard had tried to avoid being obvious. He had booked them into a tiny hotel near the Place du Clichy; had taken her for walks in May rain through St Denis, to the Moulin Rouge, and across to Montmartre. They climbed the stairs to Sacré Coeur, and he had gasped for breath while Matya smiled at him. 'You are an old man,' she laughed, her arm entwined with his, and Richard felt twenty-two.

They looked at the view, Matya checking it against her memories of the tourist brochures back in the Tallinn office. 'We must go to Notre Dame, to the Eiffel Tower,' she pleaded in a little-girl voice. 'To Rouen Cathedral.'

'That's not here.'

'No?' she said, disappointed. 'Where is it?'

'Rouen, I suppose.'

Matya pouted at such perfidy.

They walked everywhere, Matya enthralled by the shops, the streets, by the head-scarved Parisiennes with their tiny dogs. She would seize Richard's arm and point gleefully at a particularly elegant femme d'un certain age. 'I want to be her,' she said.

'When you grow up.'

'No! I want to be her now.'

Richard and Matya sat down below Notre Dame and looked at the river. Matya pulled out her Marks and Spencer shopping bag. 'I have English sandwiches,' she said. 'From the English shop. Look.' She had bought Brie baguettes, and Richard didn't want to point out the mistake. They ate in silence for a while, and Richard noticed that their legs were swinging in unison, that they were the same height, that they were both wearing black, that they seemed to be symmetrical. Matya waved at a tourist boat speeding past the Ile de la Cité, and Richard realised with a start that Matya was perfectly relaxed, perfectly happy. It had never occurred to him until that moment. Perfect contentment was something thirty-six years of living had never shown him.

Matya could sleep forever. She would rarely wake before nine, and usually demanded the right to doze for another hour or so. Desire and uncertainty turned Richard into an insomniac. For those days in Paris, he would leave her in the hotel bed, departing with a silent kiss on her cheek, occasionally folding back the sheet a little to see her naked once more, then he would wander Paris, revelling in its emptiness.

Depending on his mood, he would choose different routes. He would head north-west up the Avenue de Clichy, peering down the side streets, the Rue Hélène, Rue le Chapelais, or Rue Jacquemont, watching for boulangeries or cafés cranking into dawn life. Then he would keep walking until he reached the highway, the junction where the cars sped into Bessières one way, Berthier the other, Napoléon's beaten marshals sharing la gloire of Parisian immortality. He could see the Périphérique half a kilometre away, feel the breeze and hear the roar of the morning lorries, and Richard would stamp out the boundary, feel at one edge of old Paris, then retrace his steps. His life had become a matter of marking territory, establishing a fleeting presence in these European marches.

The next morning he would head the other way, over the Boulevard de Batignolles, down the Rue de Clichy, taking the time to look up the Rue de Londres and confirm to his satisfaction that it looked nothing like Stoke Newington, that his luck was holding, and Europe was still binding him in its protective embrace. Reassured, Richard would pull himself towards the river, hurrying along the Boulevard Haussmann, down the Avenue de l'Opéra and the Rue de Rivoli, denuded of their panicky shoppers, stripped of their hustlers and buskers, through the Tuileries until he reached the Seine. Then he could stamp again at another boundary, and return to his Matya. She might be just beginning to dress, blinking those eyes in the May sun creeping through the hotel curtains, or she might still be sleeping, half-waking as he came back in the room with his croissants and his bad American coffee, the foamy stuff she loved, in its thick cardboard cups. Four mornings he went out, four mornings he returned with a little more European hope in his heart.

Richard tried to make himself realise that time was running out, but couldn't get away from the notion that this was a frozen idyll, that could last as long as he needed. They stood on the Champs Elysées and looked all the way upwards towards the Arc de Triomphe.

'When do you have to go back to work?' Matya asked, very quietly. Matya was supposed to be returning to Tallinn, to a job in a tourist office where she ushered Americans around the old town while they made generous and patronising references to winning the Cold War. Matya had one of the best jobs available in the new

Estonia, and hated it. Paris made her restless, made her want to keep moving, to pull herself constantly westward until the sea stopped her in her tracks.

'Not for a while,' Richard replied.

'I love your way of saying nothing with your words,' she said, laughing. 'But if we have some time, we must go further.'

Her eyes asked him how much time they had. He wasn't quite ready to tell her. Their last evening in Paris, they sat drinking Kronenbourg on an expensive brasserie terrace. The waiter had a tiny moustache, a way of flicking his white cloth and a half-amused, half-irritated glare that reminded Richard of all his country's prejudices against the French. 'Let's go,' he said, laying down the exact amount of francs with what he hoped was a baleful glance at the waiter.

They found a dirtier, cheaper, warmer Algerian bar up a side street, and sipped pressions while souk music drifted out of tinny speakers. Matya looked across the table.

'Remember in Tallinn, how I told you about my divorce?'

'Yes.'

'You remember what I said afterwards?'

'Yes, you looked at me, and raised your vodka glass in a toast and said "You too are divorced, I think."'

'Yes, and you said "Not exactly, but I know what you mean." How did you know what I mean?'

This was indeed the question, and in a way Richard was relieved that it had arrived. He looked around at the dusty bar, at the two old guys sipping pastis and coffee at the bar, at the young Algerian proprietor who glanced back at Richard with what seemed like a complicit half-smile. Richard sipped at his beer, and reminded himself that this wasn't the old Richard, this was the frank, easy European model. He asked himself how the new type would cope with this situation.

'I had a girlfriend called Sarah,' he began, 'who I loved a great deal and wanted to marry, and wanted to spend all my time with. But then one night, in a flat in North London, I met somebody else and went to bed with her, and my life took a turn for the worse after that.'

He told the story as flatly and dispassionately as he could, but still, halfway through, the old Richard made an attempt at a coup, slipped in explanations, apologies, half-excuses. There was a fight, a brief struggle, and then new Richard reasserted himself.

'I killed that love affair with my own weakness, I suppose, and I've refused to admit it. I've been wandering all over Europe telling myself that if I can just find Sarah again, everything will be all right.'

He looked up at Matya, met her brown eyes, and waited a while for her response. 'North London,' she said. 'I like the way those words sound. Perhaps one day I will go to North London, and South London too.'

Richard laughed. 'And West London and East London.'

'You are over this Sarah now, yes? She is in the history, like my Pyotr?'

Richard laughed again. 'History, yes.' When he heard the words coming from his own lips, with a little North African music as accompaniment, they even sounded possible to believe.

'Perhaps you might have found what you were looking for,' Matya said softly, and quickly picked up her glass.

They saw the Paris morning again under summer skies, Matya completing the tour of the places she needed to collect. On a Tuesday in late May, Richard stood on the Place de la Concorde with his arm entwined with Matya's, and looked at the Spanish football supporters waving their white and orange flag. 'Bah-lehn-thee-ya,' they yelled, staccato syllables of the south. 'I've never been to Spain,' Matya said. 'I've never been to lots of places. I think with all these people in Paris, their country might be empty. We should go there. Is it far?'

'Not too far,' Richard said. 'We could catch a train.'

'I hope you win,' Matya said to a little fat Spaniard with his face painted orange. He grinned back. '*Gracias, guapissima*,' he said, waving his flag.

Gordon

War would be good, he thought. Something more substantial than peace-keeping missions in the Balkans, skirmishes in Pristina. Some theatre of action where a junior defence nobody could raise his profile above the parapet, make his name memorable. Something to make him believe that being part of this government was worthwhile.

Gordon was unhappy with his lot. The problem was that there were too many like him; victory had been far too comfortable for him to be important. He had been more significant in opposition, he thought, with a pang of nostalgia. When winning the election was still faintly uncertain, he had enjoyed a modicum of status. People had asked his opinion occasionally.

Now it was difficult even to get his supposed friends to acknowledge him. 'What can I do for you?' Mark McGuire had said, not entirely pleasantly that morning, when Gordon had collared him at Westminster.

'Any chance you could arrange for there to be a war?' Gordon had said. Mark had looked into space for a while, as if pondering the possibilities. Then he had deigned to offer Gordon twenty minutes of his time over a cup of coffee.

'Are we not happy in defence, Gordon?'

'Come on, it's a backwater. All we do is send out little messages about the situation in Bosnia or Macedonia or wherever, and we have to double-check everything with the Americans and NATO, and there's just no scope there. I'm away from all the action.'

'Quite ironic, really,' Mark said, unsmiling. 'Join the army and see nothing. I can see your point. All the sexy stuff's happening in the Treasury and the Home Office at the moment, but I don't see what I can do. That's the path you took before the election. You can't just jump up and say "I'm bored." Wouldn't look good. Would make you seem like a little show-off.'

'Come on, people get shuffled.'

'True, but it's the people who make a name for themselves who get shuffled.'

'But I can't make a name for myself. Nothing's happening.'

'See your point again. I don't read novels, but I believe there's some American chap who …'

'*Catch 22*. Okay, I get it. So what do I do?'

Mark seemed to be considering a weighty issue. 'If you're so willing to swap around, there may be something...'

'What?' Gordon didn't even try to conceal his eagerness.

'What's your attitude towards the glorious homeland? The thistly land of the Saltire and widespread heart disease.'

'Scotland. Er ... I don't really have an attitude.'

'No, of course you don't. Silly question. Except, we're going to need the right sort of people up there soon, just to keep things on an even keel.'

Gordon shook his head. 'Come on. You couldn't stick me in the Scottish Office, Mark. I represent an English constituency, remember. That's the sort of stunt the Tories tried to pull. And look what happened to them.'

'No, no – nothing like that, Gordon. We're having enough problems as it is, trying to pretend the Scottish Office needs to exist at all. But there's an Assembly in Edinburgh these days. You may have heard of it. I believe they gather in a tent with a hamburger van outside, but it's an Assembly all the same. Debates football sectarianism, the price of chips, their own travelling expenses, that kind of thing.'

'Yeah, yeah I read *The Scotsman*,' Gordon said, although he didn't. 'I really don't get it, Mark. I'm in the Commons. I'm not an MSP.'

'For the time being. You'll have noticed that the more patriotic comrades and brothers, usually the ones whose accents meant that the Lady Speaker was reluctant to pick them out in the Commons because she couldn't understand a bloody word they said, have donned plaid and gone back to stoke the rather more socialistic fires of Caledonia. Now, cynics might suggest that this is merely because they can't be arsed with the travelling any more, and that they can get all sorts of cushy consultancies and the like in a Scotland which is still a little less fussy about extra-curricular earnings than Westminster. Or the genuine passion of Wallace may burn in their breasts. Who cares? The point is, as far as the Party hierarchy in London is concerned – and I speak advisedly, having spoken to both their majesties on this point – Edinburgh is both a blessing and a source of some concern.'

Gordon tried to look interested, although Scotland was not an issue that he had ever given any time to. It was something stored away in his history, like his childhood, his brothers, the filthy Clyde.

'On the one hand, having that assembly up in chilly Edinburgh has been like burning off the stubble. Some of the really awkward cusses have been shifted back north out of the way. On the other hand, it means that the Assembly might turn out to be a volatile affair, with a shortage of reliable safe-hands enforcers who can make sure that the line doesn't deviate from what enlightened people like myself recommend.'

'So?'

'So, Gordon, it means that the opportunities for smart young competent operatives like yourself are far more abundant in the new Scotland than they might be in the palace of Westminster. Tradition dictates that in our glorious homeland, our people are traditionally shagging each other senseless, lining their own nests, congenitally stupid or, more often, a combination of all three.'

'Forget it, Mark. I've just said I feel I'm in a backwater at Defence. I'm hardly going to be attracted by a provincial one, now, am I?'

'Gordon. Provincial? Is that any way to speak about the ancient capital of our proud nation? Look – the point is that the party up there is always just this side of being a laughing stock. If you had been a member for longer than the three and a half seconds it took you to get a seat, you'd know that yourself. It's all tough wee Glaswegians and Dundonians who've been arranging shady deals ever since they were fixers on the shipyards or doing whatever they do in jute mills. What the fuck is jute, anyway? The thing is that all that genial corruption has oiled the party's wheels up there for the best part of a century, but all those guys are old and complacent and happy that they've stashed away four decades worth of backhanders to soften the old age they won't get to enjoy because of their lifelong lard intake. They don't want to make waves. The executive up there is stuffed with mediocrities who can barely string a sentence together. Most of them are waiting to be caught out in some pathetic fiddle too. There are opportunities. Anyone with half a brain-cell can be King.'

'This may all be true, Mark, and it certainly sounds familiar, but it still sounds like the modern-day equivalent of those Roman tribunes sent off to patrol Hadrian's Wall.'

'You asked me for advice. That's all I'm giving. It's a big pool down here, Gordon, and there are a lot of sharks a hell of a lot bigger than you are. Just think – up there, in the midst of all those numpties, you'd be a great big deep-fried Scottish haddock.'

'Thanks, Mark, but I think I might stick where I am for the time being.'

'Your decision. Let me know if you change your mind.'

'It's a kind of cloth, I think. Textiles.'

'What?'

'Jute.'

'Really? Fascinating.'

Gordon's other problem required Andy McInnes's expertise. Gordon had learned to divide his attentions between Mark for political advancement, and Andy for more basic needs. Mark and Andy had fallen out, sundered by taking different sides in a Party controversy. To Gordon it had seemed a trivial affair, which meant, he knew, that the antipathy would last for a decade at least.

'Gordon, son. Long time and all that,' Andy said happily over a pint. It would be his only pint, Andy pointed out. He was on a strict health regime in order to be in acceptable physical shape for the next election. 'You could do with keeping an eye on that yourself, Gordon,' Andy said, prodding Gordon's midriff. 'You're beginning to look a tiny bit seedy. Plenty of time for that during the second term. That's when you're allowed to look decadent.'

'It's money, Andy. I'm in serious danger of being completely broke.'

'I could lend you a fiver until Friday,' Andy said, 'but don't make a habit of it.'

Gordon didn't laugh.

'I'm in a bad shape. Grainne's hospital bills nearly ruined me. I sold the house up north, and lost fifteen grand which I didn't have. I'm still paying off a mortgage on a house I don't own any more. Either I got stitched up or property prices have taken a real dive in my constituency.'

'Yeah, I know. I blame the government. Why don't you raise it in the House? It's a disturbing issue. About time you bobbed up out of your seat. Your faithful Geordie voters might remember that you're their MP then.'

'Listen, Andy: this is serious. I've got all these outgoings. The rent on the London flat is shooting up. Grainne's got me over a barrel with the alimony. It's not like I can try to negotiate, either, or we're straight into "junior minister stingy love-rat" headlines all over the local press, if not the nationals.'

'Oh, definitely the nationals. There's open season on any sniff of sleaze at the moment.'

'So what can I do?'

'Gordon. You worry too much. There are all sorts of ways of making money. You just have to decide which avenue is best for you. As it happens, you've come to me at exactly the right time. I can put a nice spot of business your way. Do you remember Callum Ferguson?'

'Never heard of him.'

'You know him, Gordon. He was at Edinburgh same time as us. Big nationalist. You used to take the piss out of him at parties. Stood in Glasgow in a by-election and gave our boy a bit of a scare. Then decided to get out of politics and make some cash. Runs a record label. Eivissa Records. Made a fortune out of Ibiza dance-music compilations. Banging sounds for spaced-out e-heads. All sounds the same to me, but then I'm an old fart who listens to Roxy Music. They sell half a million copies a time. It seemed to work for him, because from that and a computer games subsidiary he seems to have made an eight-figure nest-egg.'

'Yeah, yeah, I remember now. What about him?'

'He has to launder some of the cash spilling out of his back pockets. So he's got himself into the property business. Executive villas in Leicestershire.'

'Good for him. How is this relevant?'

'He needs investors.'

'Why? I thought you said he was loaded.'

'Because he's a pill-popping loon with a goatee beard and a couple of convictions for class Bs and a fondness for painting his face blue at the weekends. He needs to buy a little respect in the community.'

'What has this got to do with me?'

'I thought you could invest.'

'Fuck, Andy, have you not been listening? I can barely stump together my subscription to the gym. I'm hardly going to get into property speculation.'

'What gym? Anyway, there's no speculation about it. This is an earner. Callum won't need your cash, either. As I said, that's not his problem. He just needs a little cachet. Ministry of Defence notepaper should cut a lot of corners in planning departments.'

'I still don't get it. How does this work?'

'I'm not completely *au fait* with the details, but it's something like this. You sign up as a board member, quietly give your approval of our Callum being a top-class, all-round English gentleman, only Scottish. The places get built, you have something like a nine percent share for no initial outlay, and nothing on the payroll, so no awkward questions from the members' register. The places are sold or let, and the bank balance acquires a healthy glow. All this can happen within a year or eighteen months, top. Callum is all ready to roll, and builders don't mess around these days. God bless Maggie and all that.'

Gordon sat forward. 'What's the name of this company?' he asked.

'Rob Roy Properties. Yeah, I know. Want me to set up a meeting?'

Gordon nodded, and smiled for the first time in weeks.

The parties were getting wilder. Gordon wondered if he should worry. He would look around and see a crowd of forty or fifty people. This wasn't how it was supposed to be. What had happened to discretion? Then he would have a small drink, and reassure himself. These people probably had more to lose than he did. Danny had invited a game-show host, an internationally famous golfer, a couple of Maddy's actress friends, a soap opera villain. All of them were far more instantly recognisable than a junior from the Ministry of Defence. Gordon remembered Bennett's suggestion that he had no distinguishing features. Gordon thought, with a certain amount of bitterness, that he was the least famous person here. 'G, get undressed man,' Danny said, patting him on the shoulder. 'We're all getting in the whirlpool.'

Gordon had wondered whether, as Grainne had suggested, he wouldn't be invited to any more of Danny's parties without her. Instead, he had been introduced to a younger crowd. 'Good to get away from the old marrieds, eh, Gord?' Danny said. 'You always preferred the young girls, anyway.'

At a party in Norfolk that lasted a whole weekend, Gordon had drifted into the kitchen around midday on the Sunday. Sitting at the kitchen table was a member of the Cabinet. Gordon had briefly wondered whether some internal wall in his brain had collapsed and the various corners of his life had been knocked into some open-plan affair. Then the Cabinet Minister had smiled and said, 'Gordon Hendrie?' Gordon had nodded. 'Great not to meet you here.' The minister had smiled, beautifully, and Gordon had smiled back. 'Fantastic not to see you,' Gordon had replied. He had made coffee, and the two of them had an abstracted conversation about the future of Channel 4.

Danny had got him into cocaine as well, which had helped Gordon with his dwindling inhibitions, but seemed to have caused him serious financial problems. From a few chance remarks, he surmised that Danny charged over the odds as a kind of hidden cover charge to help with party expenses. Gordon half-approved, thought it the sort of indirect but effective tactic the Treasury would pull. Gordon learnt to be miserly with the little wraps Danny would proffer, heading off into one of the '70s-styled bathrooms so he wouldn't be obliged to carve out lines for the girl he was with.

Gordon would cough and sneeze, and laugh at himself. He would look in the mirror for a minute or so and wonder how he had got there. These were the only times Gordon allowed himself to think of Glasgow, to cast up a quick sepia image of late-'60s Partick, the grime-blackened Victorian buildings, the crumbling Clyde warehouses. Then he would pull aside the bathroom curtains, look out over a rolling lawn down to a landscaped wood or perhaps a little lake gouged out of the spacious grounds. Briefly, he would feel as if all this was his: earned. 'Fuck them, I made it,' he would tell himself, sniffing. He would wipe away the moisture from his eyes; wait for some of the red in his face to fade a little, and leave the bathroom, looking for the youngest girl at the party.

When it all happened, it wasn't even at one of the big parties. It was a quiet, late summer affair, somewhere in Wiltshire; one of what Danny liked to call his *comedowns*, when everybody sat around smoking Dutch grass and giggling before pairing off in a languorous fashion. There were only nine or ten of them invited, Danny's 'hardcore hard-core' as he called them. They had become Gordon's family, in a way, this crowd of people whose names he could barely remember. There was the gay chat-show host, the snooker player with the pale eyes, the classical violinist who had given up symphonies to play in a Britpop outfit, the woman who was a partner in a City investment bank. They were always there, in various combinations, assorted couplings.

'Shame about Grainne,' Maddy said, lying naked across a round bed. 'I liked her. Danny did too, or as close as he ever comes to liking anybody. When are you going to get married again? I thought MPs weren't allowed to be single.'

'I'm waiting for you and Danny to split up so we can get married, Maddy. When you've had the best, why accept poor substitutes?' He was lying with the proficiency he normally reserved for Westminster committees. Maddy was far too old and knowing to appeal to him. But he had arrived late, and she had been the only one available.

'Sweet,' she murmured, and reached for her bra.

At that moment Danny ran into the room naked, sweating, red in the face, and with a look of panic that Gordon had never seen before. Danny and panic were polar opposites. Gordon couldn't help staring at Danny's flabby white torso, the pudgy hands waving around, the words struggling to come out as he struggled for breath. It was distressing and obscene at the same time.

'Danny, what the fuck?' Maddy began, irritated.

'Mad Jane,' he garbled. 'Not good. Other room. Quick. For fuck's sake, come on.'

There was something in his face that suggested this wasn't one of his stunts. Maddy ran after him. Gordon stopped to pull on a shirt and trousers.

They were gathered in the large bedroom round the back of the house. The scene was like a tableau from some eighteenth century etching, sinners in the first stunned throes of regret. Only a couple of them had time to put on clothes. Gordon's gaze fell with mild repulsion on the skinny white body of the snooker player, studded with tiny bright red pimples. Gordon noticed in the half-light, the sportsman's millionaire hand clutching that of the chat-show host, thin white fingers intertwined. The violin player stood, contemptuously naked, hands on hips, long brown hair spilling down to her waist. Gordon thought briefly of Grainne, and wondered where she would be.

Danny and Maddy were leaning over a girl Gordon vaguely

recognised, the one they called Mad Jane. She was barely into her twenties; had piercings in most of the usual places and several unusual ones. Danny had introduced her to Gordon, several months previously, as a poet – but Gordon had never been able to envisage what kind of verse she would be likely to produce.

She was lying naked across the bed, eyes closed, face mottled white and blue, like mould on a cheese. There was a red mark around her neck, already beginning to turn dark purple in patches. Gordon saw a dressing-gown cord dangling over her bare arm.

'What the fuck have you done to her, Danny?' Maddy said, pulling a sheet round the girl.

Danny shook his head slowly. 'Bit of light asphyxiation. Never did anybody any harm. She loved it.'

'How long?'

'Not long.'

'How fucking long, Danny?'

'Shit. I don't know. Couple of minutes.'

Maddy was feeling the girl's wrists. 'I don't know what the fuck I'm doing,' she said. 'For Christ's sake, Danny, call an ambulance.'

'Wait,' Danny said, then he looked up at his audience. For a few seconds Gordon thought he was going to burst out laughing and Jane was going to leap to her feet with one of her demonic cackles. It didn't happen.

'Look, everybody,' Danny said, steadily. 'Get the fuck out of here. It was me, Maddy, Mad Jane. A suburban threesome. Nobody else here. Tragic accident. Fuck. I'll never work on BBC2 again, and I can kiss my chances of a Royal Variety goodbye, but there's no need for everybody else to get fucked up by this. We'll get through this, won't we, Maddy? Oh fuck, fuck, fuck. Look, everybody: fuck off. Now. I'm calling an ambulance in one minute.'

Unsurprisingly, nobody needed any further encouragement. Maddy started to slap Jane lightly across the cheeks, cursing softly.

Gordon gave a lift to the violinist, and hurtled up the driveway. It was fifteen minutes to the nearest town. They didn't speak, but caught each other's eye in the rear-view mirror. She was wearing a suede coat, seemed to be much smaller than the naked girl who had stood staring at Jane, and Gordon felt a strange tenderness towards her. They heard the siren of a speeding ambulance, and Gordon drove a little faster.

When they arrived at the railway station he reached over and pulled the door handle. The violinist looked at him and shook her head to acknowledge that she didn't know what to say.

'Do you think she's still…' Gordon began.

'What? Alive? I'm not sure. I think so. The ambulance people can revive her, surely?'

'Where there's life there's hope,' Gordon said, but he was talking to himself.

A Party In 2000

Y ou can never go back. That had been Liam's motto. 'Home, old
girlfriends or pubs where you've cashed a dodgy cheque,' he
would amplify if anyone asked. But Liam had gone back. Glasgow
had never agreed with him. There were too many others with
personalities of equivalent loudness. Liam had felt his grace notes
lost in the general racket. He was back in Edinburgh, easing his
way back into the party business, and if the flat was smaller, the
ambience was much the same.

Liam had found a new Edinburgh: a twenty-first century boom-
town, its customary austerity cheapening into a belated fiscal
vulgarity. George Street had become an eager pastiche of the City
of London, all wine-bars and franchised brasseries, polishing their
gilt, doubling their prices and playing host to an unhappy mix of
Edinburgh's old aristocracy and the financially blessed. You had to
move out of the centre to find a little peace these days.

Liam's was a diminished constituency, the bohemians of his era
settling into comfortable middle-age, with their galleries and craft
shops and record stores. The more interesting academics were in
the New Town apartments, nursing damaged livers or monitoring
their heart palpitations. There were enough survivors, though; all
was not yet lost.

There was still something about the city, too; still a vaguely illicit
promise lurking in the shadows of that formal skyline. It was still
a small enough place for the right sorts to find their way back to
Liam's door. On the last night of 2000 – which, for all the pedants'
arguments, was the first year of their new century – Edinburgh
froze itself into new shapes. You would walk past the braying
coming from doors of the George Street establishments, crunching
through the last snow of the old year. Head down Leith Walk, past
the roundabout at the top of Broughton Street, until you could see
the avenue stretching all the way down towards Leith. Turn right
at the Oddbins (its manager already witnessing a career upturn
since Liam moved into the neighbourhood) then up the anonymous
close to the top floor.

It's a small flat, but Liam's guests have spread themselves into
intimate pockets, tight-knit clusters of conversation and reminiscence.
They mill efficiently, shaping themselves into human corners, flowing

into restricted spaces with the adroitness of experience. His first party of his new start, of Liam's new millennium, has reached into his history with a greedy scoop, pulled out a thick fistful of familiarity. The fridge still groans at its hefty cargo of supermarket beer, the oven is still baking jacket potatoes, the kitchen table has the requisite bowl of crusting tuna mayonnaise.

Liam had pushed his supermarket trolley through a cloud of nostalgia along aisles of beers that were unfamiliar even to him: Korean, Indian, Japanese, Thai, the full global gamut of brewing. Liam felt old, gazing down the fecund shelves of five percent proof fluid. He fell upon the Tennents and the Stella like old friends. 'You've never let me down yet,' he said aloud, and smiled so winningly at the Edinburgh matron staring at him that she smiled back, almost flirtatiously.

Liam's hand still intervened occasionally to make otiose introductions; everybody knew each other, most of them shared complicated erotic histories. Liam looked about him, and thought, 'These are my people,' and wondered if they still were.

Plenty of the old crowd had reassembled. Next to the bookshelf, a bald man in his late thirties, Leonard – now relaxed about being called Lennie, although Liam is the only one who does so – was skimming his finger along the video collection, tutting to himself, until he found a director's cut of *Henry, Portrait Of a Serial Killer*, and flipped it neatly out of its row.

Behind him, a couple argued ritualistically. 'Listen, you've had nine of these, so I need to down two to catch up… So it was the same idea with that girl,' he was saying, waving a bottle of Sagres. Despite the words, he seemed to be smiling. 'Come on,' she said, 'you were never that interested in me, anyway.' 'Not true,' he murmured, looking around for fresh beer. Belinda and Gary. They were in their thirties, but neither wanted to believe it.

The American academic had tenure now, had published a not-completely-ignored volume about gender confusion in late twentieth-century women's literature, had lost Mel the poetess to a (male) literary agent who had promised to press her limpid stanzas between hard covers, had an eye that wandered over potential sexual partners that were not quite as young as in the glory days, but still had occasional flashes of rugged potential. She had been told Beatrice Morelli would be there, and was disappointed not to see her. Her gaze flicked over every tall dark woman in the room, lingering on one aloof creature too long, until she sidled off towards the kitchen.

There were Germans there, to keep the party quorate. They had found each other, had found the small exclusive supply of Becks, and were now amusing each other by practising their pronunciation of Hogmanay.

'Everything okay?' Sally said, reaching an arm around Liam's waist. Sally looked pleased with herself. She had been looking pleased with herself since May that year when three black teenagers had been acquitted of a manslaughter charge connected with the burning down of a Victorian terraced house in Camberwell. Police evidence had been discredited, which meant Sally's picture had appeared on page three of *The Guardian,* and because she had been standing on the top steps outside the High Court it made her look slim and elegant. With her career thriving and a little free time, Sally had decided to forgive, and to take Liam in hand.

Sally now weekended in Edinburgh, arriving on Friday night's shuttle just around the time that Liam's instincts were urging him towards mischief. Instead, they would sit in front of Channel 4 eating takeaway food, taking in repeated American comedies, nestling in a satisfying approximation of domesticity.

Liam had allowed himself to be taken in hand. Even this party had seen his leadership diminishing. Liam stood meekly by the fridge and sipped his beer and looked ... if not quite defeated, at least as if he was coming around to the idea of surrender. Liam was struggling to find the energy to maintain the necessary level of interest in the year's new intake of teenagers eager for borrowed wisdom. Liam was losing his glibness, as if by a joke of the ageing process he was being made to live out the tongue-tied adolescent unease he had never experienced.

He had cropped back the hair that had been in retreat for a decade, making a last stubbled stand above a furrowed brow. The waistline was growing, but amiably, into an academic's reassuring middle-aged spread. Liam had softened the old frenzy of the host, relaxed into a passive acceptance that not everybody's chemistry could be manipulated by his hand.

'I mind my own business these days,' he said to the tall, dark-haired woman who stood beside him, and when she smiled

301

disbelievingly, he protested. 'Come on, I do. I'm not even going to ask why you and Richard never patched up your differences and made a go of it.'

The dark-haired woman, whose name was Sarah, smiled again and sipped her wine. 'You're such a peace-maker, aren't you, Liam? You cannot be comfortable seeing any vestiges of bad feeling anywhere.'

Sarah looked French these days, in a manner that was difficult to attribute to any single detail, but more to the strangely Gallic combination of gesture and attire. She was half-smiling, but her words had a sad ring to them. Liam put what he thought was a comforting arm around her shoulders.

'The two of you were made for each other, though. Can you really say that you could never recapture that?'

'Of course I can say it. It's not enough just to fancy someone, Liam. It's not enough even to understand them. There has to be more than that. You know: trust, honesty, all that stuff.'

Liam looked dubious. 'He's still mad about you, you know. I heard a rumour that he's living in some log cabin in British Columbia. I wouldn't be surprised if the poor sod's gone and grown a beard.'

'Richard with a beard?' Sarah contemplated the notion for a while, as did Liam, and both weighed the horror of his words.

'It was a long time ago, you know, Liam,' Sarah said, looking down at his midriff. 'You can't try to go back in time. That all ended eight years ago. Too much has happened. We're different people. The world has moved on.'

'Not true, darling. We may look, in my own case, like a decrepit pile of shit, and we might be barely able to stumble up Broughton Street without coughing up half our lungs, but we're still the same confused kids we were. The problem is, the world is so much smaller. In the good old days, if you dumped somebody, you could go and live in the village on the other side of the valley and be pretty sure you'd never see them again in your life. Now all the circles interconnect. You can jet off to Katmandu, and you could still look at your email and find your ex had tracked you down. There is no escape. Eventually you're going to encounter each other again, and then who knows? Look at me and Sally, back together again. You just have to identify what it was you lost. Everything is retrievable.'

'Do you really believe that?'

'I certainly do.'

'How depressing. Now can you tell me why that American woman keeps staring at me?'

Gordon arrived around two in the morning. He had been at a night-club in the West End, at Callum's Eivissa Hogmanay party. Gordon had been short of invitations that New Year. Necessarily retired from the English party circuit, he had turned down a half-hearted offer to see Glasgow relatives. His mind had conjured up a brief vision of a Partick New Year, and he had shuddered with all his new English fastidiousness.

So he had gone along to the Edinburgh event with a half-formed idea of confronting Callum about the disappointing yield from his property deal, but it hadn't been the right time or place. Instead, Gordon had slumped in a corner, looking down at his sober suit, his buffed brown shoes, finding something pathetic about the way his laces were tied in a double knot, the way the hems of his trousers folded slightly above the insteps. His legs had always been just a little too short, Gordon thought. Maybe that was at the root of all his failures, that slight physical defect that was amplified into adult mediocrity.

The music was garage, although he couldn't have told you as much. He identified its repetitive beats only because that was a phrase he had heard in the House. He felt old, worn out; felt he had lost his ability to feel superior to these people. Instead, they had started to intimidate him.

Gordon looked around at the teenage girls – or, rather, he looked at teenage girls' midriffs as their crop-tops rode up, and wondered where the twenty-first century's abdomen fetish originated. He stared at little white bulges, hollowed navels, every other one adorned with a cheap gold ring bouncing and glinting in the pulsing lights. Normally, he enjoyed looking at teenage girls. Now he saw their faces lit by the strobes, saw the look of concentration on their hard young faces, the fixed grimace of thin lips, and began to panic. Gordon had slipped out just as Callum ripped off his headphones, added echo to his DJ mike and yelled 'Scotland free by 2003!'

Outside the Caledonian there was an endless queue for taxis, so Gordon had wandered east along a Princes Street strewn with debris, smashed champagne bottles littering the gutters, the occasional couple kissing in doorways, snow turning into slush. Drunks yelled 'Happy New Year' at him, but Gordon had just waved wearily, and walked on.

Liam answered the door. He seemed surprised. 'Gordon. Wasn't expecting you.'

'I know. I was in town. Is it all right?'

'Of course, come in, come in.' Liam had gripped Gordon in one of his unembarrassed embraces. 'Good to see you.'

'Yeah, you too,' Gordon mumbled, accepting a beer. 'Is … er … anybody here?'

'If you mean Grainne, she's supposed to coming along a little later with Beatrice. I thought she'd be here by now, actually. Must have got held up. That's not a problem, is it?'

'Problem? No. Well, not for me.' Gordon slumped onto a cushion in the corner of Liam's hallway. Liam sat down beside him and opened a beer.

'You know that song, *Let's meet up in the year 2000*?' Liam said.

'No.' Gordon knew nothing about pop music.

'Christ, you must do. It's never been off the radio for the last five years. Anyhow. I always thought it was the saddest piece of shit imaginable. Then it gets to the year 2000, and I thought we'd all meet up. Except we didn't.'

Gordon looked at him askance. 'Liam, I never had you figured for the sentimental type.'

'Comes with age, my boy.'

'I've got that to look forward to then.'

'You were a shit to Grainne, Gordon.'

'I know. It wasn't all my fault.'

'Most of it.'

'Okay, most of it. But it's not easy.'

'There's no excuse. Grainne is a beautiful girl, and you treated her like shit.'

'This is a bit of a single-themed line of yours, Liam.'

'But true.'

Gordon looked like he might be about to argue, but instead he slowly nodded his head.

'Look, what's done is done. It's a waste of time to start dwelling on regrets and whose fault it was.'

'Normally I'd agree with you. Having a record for behaving like a bit of an arsehole, I'm all for a strictly short-term statute of limitations. But at least you have to admit you were in the wrong. That would be a start.'

Gordon looked at Liam, took another hefty draught from his can.

'That's what I thought, Liam. That's what I thought three years ago. A start. It was exciting, you know. We were in government, we were doing things at last, and I was a part of it. The divorce from Grainne had come through and of course I felt guilty about it, but then I thought, I was still young, or at least I hadn't passed that thirty-fifth birthday – you know, the one that's supposed to be the halfway mark. So I thought I'd start afresh. The thing with Grainne was in the past and I'd made a mess of it, but there was time to sort things out. But it didn't quite work out like that. I wasn't being allowed to do anything in Westminster. Just as long as I filed through the right doors at votes, said the right things in committee, that was me. Fulfilling my function. They didn't even like me speaking unless it was something they had written for me.'

'Ha,' Liam said, pleased.

'Fuck off, Liam. You voted Lib Dem. Richard told me. You poser. But look – that wasn't the problem. I know the importance of party discipline and keeping a cohesive front in the first term, and all that. But the thing was that it had lost its thrill. You know, when I got there in '92, I'd run my hands over the seats, smell all the old oak, look at the mace, all that crap. I was in love with the place. And because we had the bastards on the run for five years, it was exciting. Now we're in charge, it isn't quite the same. It's become like an office job. You know: make sure you're efficient, and keep your nose down, and hope the boss notices.'

'And lick the right arses,' Liam suggested.

'There's a bit of that, yeah. The thing is, they don't need us. There's so many of us, the cabinet don't even know half our names. I'm sick of it.'

'You could always give it up. Aren't MPs supposed to walk into company directorships as soon as they fancy a rest?'

'I think you're supposed to have some vague influence first. Besides. I can't give it up. It's all I've ever wanted to do. I just need to sort myself out. It's not that easy, you know, starting again. I thought I could do it in '97 when we won. That didn't work. Then I thought last year – you know, the millennium. When I was a kid the year 2000 had always seemed like, you know, science-fiction. Never going to happen. But I always thought that by then I would be sorted out, you know? My life would be organised. I would be where I wanted to be. Then ... well, it wasn't, was it? So last year I tried to strip everything down, make a few decisions, get myself sorted out. I was divorced, I was an MP, I was broke, had to make some money. But things kept creeping back at me from the past. Stuff I'd done that I couldn't get rid of.'

'You know your problem, Gordon?'

'Which one?'

'You're not a Catholic. All my relatives in Dublin can get up to all sorts of shit, shag around, punch some bloke in a pub, drink-driving, incest, sodomy, pederasty, whatever they fancy. All they do is go to the priest, say sorry, three Hail Marys or whatever, and they're back on the streets with a clean licence.'

'Actually, I am.'

'What?'

'A Catholic. At least, I was until I was about twelve, when it really began to seem a little bit too ridiculous. Family supports Celtic and all that. I used to be able to do that, you know. Believe that if you repented of something it went away. Just disappeared. But you can't just rip everything up, can you? It's like those horror films you always used to make us watch. In the final scene the rotting hand always bursts out of the grave. Fuck. Okay. I was wrong. I made a lot of mistakes. Now can I please have another lager?'

'Stella or Tennents?'

'Stella, of course.'

'A fine choice. Now let the healing begin.'

Some time around the cusp of the years, the phone rang. Liam picked it up, heard a distant voice say 'Happy New Year' in a measured tone, with music booming in the background.

'Richard. Where the fuck are you, man?'

'In a little bar having eggs with ranchero sauce. I got hungry.'

'Fuck, you should be here. It's a great party. Like the old days.'

'Oh, it's pretty good here, Liam. You get refills for your coffee and everything.'

'Listen. Try to get over here, we'll be going on for a while ...'

But Richard's money rang out and the line went dead.

'Sarah's here...' Liam murmured.

Richard didn't arrive. It wouldn't have been practical. Richard's year still had eight hours left, and he looked out over the sound towards Vancouver Island, teeth chattering slightly in the gale blowing down from the Gulf of Alaska. Wrapped in three layers of thick plaid and a black woollen hat, he had wondered briefly about growing a beard, a real wilderness beard rather than a Seattle goatee. A beard would really show how low he had sunk. Looking back inland towards the mountains, he had wondered why he hadn't done this long before: disappeared off the map at the end of the year, floated away beyond civilisation. Then he heard the all-day party crowd in the bar thirty yards away down the ice-track, heard the bass-line from a Mudhoney single, and thought a drink wouldn't be an entirely bad idea. He listened to the snow and ice cracking under his feet as he walked, keeping in time with the bass, flexing his fingers to keep out the cold.

In Edinburgh the party went on, its rhythms slowing a little. These people weren't as young as they longed to be. A little amphetamine was being passed around, but most of them refused, citing babysitters, allergies, scorched septums or a belated sense of self-preservation. Instead, they gratefully grabbed Liam's baked potatoes, sitting in companionable clusters spooning up hot potato and butter.

Outside, Edinburgh was settling into the silence of 2001, broken by the occasional straggler still looking for the shelter of a party. Lost souls gathered in queues by the Deep Sea on Elm Row for the first fish and chips of the New Year, or the last of the old, depending on their temporal bearings. Snow was falling, settling over the trees in Gayfield Square, creating festive white caps on the mysterious black globes that ran down the middle of Leith Walk. Two women kicked up the snow as they walked down the hill, arm-in-arm.

The doorbell rang, and Liam swung open the door to two radiantly beautiful faces, reddened a little by the cold. They clutched orange juice cartons and flowers. 'Happy New Year!' they yelled, in a ragged but enthusiastic chorus, and Liam smiled back. 'At last,' he said. 'I'd given up on you.'

'Have we ever missed one of your parties?' the taller woman said.

'No, darling,' Liam said kissing her. 'I don't believe you have.'

Gordon

They all wrote books in the end, every last bastard he had ever met. He didn't mind when it was just Beatrice. That had even given him a little kudos among the Party's aesthetes, knowing the darling of the quality Sundays' literary pages. Then Richard told him that Grainne had published some of her poems. Richard emailed him one of them, called *Invasion:* an extended metaphor about sex with a stranger that Gordon had understood without his customary need for footnotes: 'The creeping occupation of the border villages, the punitive strike into the heartland...' and the rest of it.

'Where did she get the idea for this?' Richard had asked. 'Imagination and grain spirit,' Gordon had replied. 'Sadly, Stolichnaya is an unpredictable muse.' Poetry couldn't harm him.

This was different, though: this was the worst. Danny McBeth had been given a £100,000 advance to publish a memoir. By some sweet symmetry, most of it was written at the Grange, three rooms along the corridor from the one Grainne had occupied so expensively. He had called it *One Hundred Lines, McBeth*. It began with a few explanatory, exculpatory chapters about his miserable time at a minor public-school, went though his early successes as a comic, but really earned the publisher's money with the last seven chapters chronicling in some detail Danny's battle with cocaine addiction, and his sensational involvement with the 'death by misadventure' of the daughter of a Conservative peer. 'Dynamite,' the publishers were already crowing, four months ahead of publication.

Andy McInnes poured two large glasses of malt whisky, and shook his head. Andy was in a serious mood. 'This might be the last stand of the Hendrie tartan,' Andy said. 'It's looking bad. The proofs are waiting at the printers. At the moment there are nineteen names represented solely by codes. McBeth is the only one who can break the code, but right now he's doing deals with various showbiz pals and City types to see what it's worth to keep them out of the book. You know he's doing that chat show with the big queen who was always there at those parties? McBeth's getting half an hour to himself, apparently. This book was the greatest idea that clown ever had.'

'I'm in it, am I?'

'Yes. You're in it, all right. I've got pretty reliable information to that effect. Not a starring role, Gordon, but a cameo is damaging enough in the circumstances. There was a bigger name involved, a Cabinet chappie whom we both know and love, but his fist is substantially bigger than McBeth's balls so we can take it on trust that he won't be appearing. McBeth knows enough about self-preservation to make sure of that. It's already somewhat whiffy the way the DPP didn't go harder against him last year. The thing is, if our friend and colleague had any Party loyalty he would have made the little bastard pull your name out as well, but apparently it just didn't occur to him.'

Andy reached for his glass and took a large slug, and coughed slightly. When he looked back up, Gordon was looking at him and shaking his head.

'That's not true, is it, Andy?'

There was an awkward silence while Andy swirled the whisky in his glass. Gordon wondered whether it was just one of those theatrical pauses Andy enjoyed.

'Not quite, no.'

'He could have got my name taken out as easily as that, but chose not to.'

'Now, Gordon, let's not...'

'Chose not to, because they either want me to suffer the consequences, or they want to use it as a lever against me, to make me do something I'm not willing to do otherwise.'

'Gordon. Christ, to hear you speak, you'd think the Labour Party is a devious Machiavellian machine ready to use any unfortunate mischance that happens to befall a poor sod in order to further its own ends.'

'Just tell me the deal, Andy,' Gordon said wearily. 'And, more importantly, tell me what guarantee there is that I won't be stitched up even if I agree to it.'

'Hold on a minute, Gordon. It might be worthwhile me telling you exactly what sort of predicament you are in.'

'Go on.'

'The Honourable Jane Fitzmeadows.'

'What about her?' Gordon tried to sound neutral, but there was a wobble in his voice.

'Apparently you were there the night she and McBeth were experimenting with homicidal bondage. Might even have been involved.'

'That's rubbish.' Gordon was on his feet.

'Sit down. It's rubbish that might be available in numerous copies, couple of quid off, book of the month in your local Waterstones's by May. So get used to the idea. McBeth says you were there, along with a couple of other notables. He has some details that ring, if not true, then at least distinctly credible.'

'But I...'

'I don't care, Gordon. Don't want to know. I don't care about the truth. I know from personal experience that Mad Jane had enough of a maniacal streak for that coroner's court verdict to be on the money. I know what she was like. I know what McBeth's parties were like. I know the sort of people who went to them. I know that I stopped going three years ago for those reasons. I know that I wasn't there when Mad Jane croaked – quite literally, it seems. But we've got beyond what's known and what isn't. We're into the realms of association. What I'm trying to impress on you is that whether you were there or not, McBeth is confident enough to say you were, and I know the publishers are prepared to be ballsy about it. The rumour is, they're getting ten times what they've paid McBeth just for the serialisation rights. Which is what should really worry you. People don't read books, Gordon, but they read *The Daily Express.*'

'Okay. I get the point. So what do we do?'

'You remember the extent to which your knackers are in the wringer here, Gordon. Remember that when you have to weigh up a plan of action.'

'What plan?'

Andy set down his glass.

'I believe you had a conversation with that devious bastard McGuire not so long ago.'

'What about?'

'About Scotland. About the glorious Edinburgh Parliament, and our woeful shortage of suitable manpower.'

'Hold on a minute...'

'No, Gordon. You hold on a minute. People with rather more sway and more clout than me have decided that you would be a very valuable addition to our Scottish team. Relatively young, outwith all the corruption and sleaze in the Glasgow wing, and with a modicum of credibility from a junior government post. They believe you can do wonderful things back in porridge-land.'

'I'm an MP in England, Andy.'

'There's an election in the summer. The idea is that you won't be standing. The line is that family responsibilities and a sense of Scottish purpose are taking you back over the border to shoulder the broadsword of the Labour cause in Edinburgh.'

'You can't just parachute me into Holyrood.'

'Can't we? How long do you think we'll have to wait for a by-election? The great thing about the Scottish Parliament will be its constant state of flux. It used to take twenty years to kiss enough hairy Glaswegian arses to get into the sort of position where you were an acceptable candidate, and by then your good old Scottish life expectancy had kicked in, and before you know it there's a lethal mutton pie with your name on it. The sort of croneyism that meant all the candidates were pasty-faced West Coasters with a long spell as a shop steward under their belt, is coming home to roost in the form of the Grim Reaper. Apparently a survey done by an actuary reckons there'll be a vacancy every nine months or so. You'll be in Holyrood before Christmas.'

'If I don't do it?'

Andy reached for his whisky again.

'That would be your decision, Gordon, and we'd respect it.'

'It's "we" now, is it?'

'Let's look at the options. It might be okay. McBeth's book has bigger fish to throw in the deep-fryer than you. You'll get your column inches, but it might be page five stuff. Then again, maybe not. Any government sleaze is red-hot at the moment. The *Express* is one of ours, but the rest of the jackals will do the follow-ups. The media frenzy will blow over, but you'll be remembered in Number Ten. You won't get any promotions, and I suspect you may be shuffled out of the defence pack after the election. You're not back-bencher material really, are you, Gordon? Government is the whole point with you, not representing the poxy little interests of those flat-cappers up north.'

'How do I know until I try it?'

'Okay, Gordon, that was the best-case scenario. I think it might be more serious than that.'

'How?'

'Remember our pal Callum's property deal?'

'What about it? It was crap. I made about eight grand.'

'Our tartan chum has been messing with the VAT people. Said for a while that it was a political issue, that he refused to finance the corrupt English state – although I believe his lawyers are now working on a more astute line of defence. But the word *fraud* seems to be the likeliest upshot.'

'You put me on to that deal, Andy.'

'I merely suggested it as a possible way out of your financial difficulties. You should have checked all the fine print yourself. That was your responsibility.'

'So this is the back-up threat, is it?'

'Not at all. I just wanted to point out how complicated things could get down here over the next year. We're hyper-sensitive at the moment because of the election.'

'We've won the election already.'

'I know that, you know that, but you know what they're like at Number Ten. If they were 4-0 up with a minute to go, they'd send on a couple of extra defenders to shore up the back-line.'

'Let me get this straight. Unless I fuck off out of the way to Scotland, I'm going to be hung out to dry in the tabloids, and mentioned in a high-profile fraud case?'

'You see the difficulty, Gordon. Now I can see that you might be tempted to hang on in there, brazen it out. I know you're a fighter and I would admire you for doing that. But you're astute as well. That's how you got here in the first place. Sometimes the smartest move is the retreat.'

'Really?'

'It's your decision, Gordon. Don't take too long.' Andy raised his glass in what seemed peculiarly like a toast. 'Scotland isn't all bad, Gordon. It has its redeeming features.' They looked at each other for a minute or so, trying to think of one.

Five months later, they parted on the corner of Byers Road and Dumbarton Road. Gordon looked around at the grimy pubs, the precisely-named newsagents 'Mags n Fags,' and wondered if there was any tiny vestige of him that felt at home.

'I'll leave you here then, Gordon,' Andy McInnes said. 'Back home. My work is done. It's all up to you now.'

'You mean you won't even come and chap a few doors with

me?'

'That's the spirit, Gordon. The Glasgow accent will come back in time. You have to see your future here. You'll be fine. Well, this is it…' Andy was holding out his hand. Gordon looked at it, looked at Andy.

'What's this, dramatic farewell?'

Andy looked uneasy. 'Well, we won't be seeing so much of each other from now on. You'll be busy up here, and I'll be at Westminster, and – well, it's not seen as a good idea for fraternisation between the two Houses.'

'What is this crap you're talking now, Andy?'

'Look, I can't go into details. It's just that they want to gloss over our past relationship, you know.'

'You're getting a seat,' Gordon grinned. 'Congratulations, Andy. Where?'

'Well, it's not certain yet. It's all happened rather quickly.' Andy was the most ill-at-ease Gordon had ever seen him.

'Where?'

'Houghton Le-Fuck-Knows-Where. Makes sense, I know the territory, they know me. Some of them even know me in the Biblical sense.' Andy gave a hollow laugh, then looked a little more embarrassed. 'I'm sorry. They really should have told you, Gordon.'

Gordon turned away and headed west along Dumbarton Road, past Fags 'n' Mags, the Afghani kebab shop, the Corals. Going west, he thought, like his career – disappearing somewhere over the horizon where the motorway whipped past Partick.

Gordon walked quickly, putting space between himself and Andy, saying a silent goodbye to England and Westminster, looking ahead, walking into the guns. He looked down at his lapel, at the red rosette fluttering, at the yellow letters reading *Gordon Hendrie*. 'Politics are cyclical', Mark McGuire had told him, in a cool farewell over the telephone. 'We all get ploughed back into the earth eventually.'

Gordon walked steadily along Dumbarton Road and thought back over the last decade, wondering where he had faltered. That's what they always taught you at school about Shakespeare, wasn't it? That the tragic hero had one fatal flaw that eventually proved his undoing. Something more crucial than legs that were slightly too short.

He thought of Grainne, one afternoon in the summer of 1993. They had been sitting in a bar in a small town on the banks of the Rhine. It was their first holiday after the election. Grainne had only just managed to dissuade him from signing hotel registers as "Gordon Hendrie MP." They'd sat together in flat-bottomed boats, cruising down the river, staring obediently at schlosses pointed out by meticulous, multi-lingual guides. Eventually they'd decided to dispense with the schedule and find their own way around.

They found a small town between Koblenz and Bonn, a depressed place where the streets were full of cheap market stalls selling Bayern Munich raincoats and plastic Rhine siren souvenirs. 'I don't believe it,' Gordon said delightedly. 'We've found the downside of the German economic miracle.'

'It's like a scenic Paisley,' Grainne said.

They wandered around in search of a restaurant, but neither of them understood any German. They had gazed glumly at daunting combinations of harsh syllables, bolted together into threatening dishes.

'I just know we're going to end up with pig's knuckle with cabbage and dumplings,' Gordon said.

'Or calves brains stewed in cherry beer,' Grainne said, remembering one of the dishes on the hotel menu the first night.

'You can see why the Germans are prone to fits of depression, can't you? It's waking up every morning and worrying about what'll end up on their plate at dinner-time.'

'I know *würst* means sausages. Maybe we should just order those to be on the safe side.'

'Right. What's the würst that can happen?'

Grainne had laughed, and Gordon had realised with a shock of surprise that he never made those kinds of stupid jokes any more, that all his attempts at humour had been devoted to sarcastic or satirical jibes. Gordon had suffered a brief pang of self-knowledge, a sharp stab of recognition of what he was turning into. He ordered a lot of beer and Grainne laughed a lot, and her face got pinker as the night wore on.

They walked back along the Rhine, looked up at the hills on the opposite bank, and Gordon had entwined Grainne's arm in his and she'd looked at him fondly, and he had loved her, and a couple of passers-by had looked at them, the young British couple at the riverside, and smiled to see them go.

Maybe that was the beginning, Gordon thought now, staring into a Thresher's, looking at the vodka display, remembering a different Grainne. Had her drinking been his fault, after all? No, she'd always been a drinker. She liked the drama of it all, the way vodka could make her feel tragic, could let her scream and sob, and hurl her anger at the sky. That couldn't work. Anger had to be controlled, channelled, made to work for you, not spilled wastefully into the ether.

Gordon remembered the autumn of 1993. The start of new term, as he had thought of it then: the chance to impress the teachers. There was something about the smell of the place, the warm leather, the dust, the panelling, the serge of the suits in the rows opposite. At the start of a new Parliamentary session Gordon would be hyper-sensitive, savouring every sensation. He would dwell on the tiny, revealing details, the cracked veins in the flushed cheeks of the members opposite, the way their confident grins began to fracture with the passing of time, the dwindling of their reign.

He remembered getting to his feet, grinning boyishly at the acknowledgment of the Speaker, trying to catch her eye with the bold flirtatiousness he knew she loved. He couldn't remember a word of the question he had asked, or even what the debate had concerned, but everything else lived with him, and he could warm himself with the memory. The twitch of the Minister's mouth as Gordon's assiduously-prepared point struck home, the sudden glance to the side as the Minister looked for a rescuing prompt, then the look of grim boredom on the face of Gordon's victim, the longing to be somewhere away from the despatch box, hunting in Wiltshire perhaps, or sipping Pimms in Tuscany. Gordon remembered the crowing 'hear-hears' from his own ranks, remembered the smile on the face of his own party leader, remembered the warm pats on his shoulder from his colleagues behind as he sat down, steadily folding his notes in the manner of a prosecuting counsel resting an unanswerable case. Gordon remembered the sexual thrill he had felt at that moment, feeling the leather seat meeting him, seeing the eyes of the House lingering on him for a couple of seconds before the debate moved on.

Gordon looked over his shoulder, along Dumbarton Road,

towards the city centre, and wondered about which of his lost loves he missed the most. He didn't need to consider the question for too long.

'You'll be Gordon Hendrie, then,' the girl outside the campaign headquarters said. She was pale, about twenty-two, and looked at him with a look of faint distaste. 'I'm Vanessa Burns. I'll be showing you around the area.'

'I know the area. I grew up here, remember.'

'Yes, I've read the biography. But things have changed a little.'

'Really? Looks the same old shithole to me.'

Vanessa looked at him. 'Gordon – I can call you Gordon? – I should mention that there are a few of the local officials who are suspicious and not a little resentful of a Westminster MP quitting his London seat and within a few months leap-frogging the queue and getting the candidacy for a very safe Holyrood seat. Makes you wonder why they want to ship you in there so urgently.'

'Yes, well. I'm sorry, Vanessa, but that's politics. You can't anticipate these things. We just have to accept them as part of a grand strategy.'

Vanessa laughed.

'What's so funny?'

'They told me you were a pompous shite. We say *shite* up here, by the way, Gordon. Not shit. Also, best not call your constituency a shithole. We all know it is, but that's rather the point, isn't it? Oh, and by the way, I'm one of those suspicious and resentful sorts I was talking about a moment ago.'

'Fucking Scotland,' Gordon said to himself.

'Fucking Scotland, that's right,' Vanessa said. 'Now I've got a visit to some junkies and alkies lined up for tomorrow morning. Thought you'd like to touch base with your new constituents.'

'Thanks, Vanessa. I'll look forward to it.'

'Oh, and *The Times* have been on to me. They've got a picture opportunity they want you to do.'

'*The Times*, brilliant.'

'That's the *Glasgow Evening Times*, Gordon. Let's not get too excited.'

The picture appeared on page five of the *Evening Times*, under the headline *Back To His Roots*. The Hendrie brothers stood outside the pub – old Heraghty's still there, although the clientèle had been decimated – grinning at the camera, raising glasses of warm beer. The expressions should have told you the pecking order, but there was ambiguity there. Gordon, wavy brown hair swept back, stern blue eyes fixed ahead, had an arm over Denis's shoulder, a look that flirted with being authoritative and protective, but couldn't quite avoid seeming ill-at-ease above his tie, smart black jacket and rosette. Denis beside him, brown hair flopping greasily across his eyes, was smiling in a manner that could only be described as insolent, relaxed in his sweat-shirt, giving the impression that he was tolerating the picture but would prefer to get on with his pint. Paddy, wet-mouthed, freckled, ginger hair slipping backwards off his scalp, was casting a sideways glances at his brothers, clutching his pint as if he was afraid that one of them was about to take it off him.

The picture froze them there, and the photographer headed back to his car. 'Paddy,' Gordon said, patting his youngest brother on the shoulder. 'Thanks for coming along.'

'Aye, no problem Gords,' his brother said. 'Denis got *The Times* to give us fifty quid each.'

'Only fifty, Denis? Not very ambitious.'

'It was all you were worth, Gordie. And if you think we're voting for yis, you can go fuck yirsel. We're Nats.'

Beatrice

The flat was beautiful. It was difficult to argue with that. On clear days – and Edinburgh had them occasionally – Beatrice could look down beyond the green and brown sprawl of the Botanics, over the roofs of Trinity to the Forth and beyond. When she first moved in, that was what she would do. She would stand bare-footed on the polished floorboards on the top floor of her three-storey home, and look out towards what was almost the sea, willing herself to see into the coves and harbours of the East Neuk of Fife.

Now she had been here for a couple of months, her gaze had settled a little closer, down towards the high-water mark of the water of Leith, watching it meander under the looming sweep of the Queensferry Bridge. Beatrice would place her palms flat on the window-sill, watching the afternoon traffic heading up into town or out towards the suburbs or the Firth. She would look at the parapet and measure the distance below; look at the thick, tree-lined banks; pick out the footpath and the couple of craggy shelves of rock. It was a strangely comforting bridge. She began to think of it as her neighbour. It was the first thing she saw in the morning, its busy bustle outside her kitchen window.

She remembered adoring this building the first time she had crossed the bridge, in her first year as a student here. She had stared at its blackened stone walls, at its slightly curved lines, at the windows peering out into an early '80s Edinburgh autumn, and had said to Richard, 'Wouldn't mind living there.'

'When you've made a fortune from royalties from your first novel you can buy the place,' Richard had said matter-of-factly.

It had been the money from film rights rather than royalties, but Beatrice had bought the place. She had been sitting in a square in Padova one hot Tuesday in August, reading a copy of *The Sunday Times* that she had found next to *Die Welt* at the newsstand. There it was, pride of place in the Property section. Randolph Cliff, the photo showing it much the same as she remembered, slightly less black, still with the windows, still looking out proprietorially over Edinburgh. She had called Jayne; told her to make an immediate offer on her behalf. Buying property was still frighteningly swift in Scotland. Beatrice owned the place within a week.

'Randolph Cliff,' Liam had said, looking around the musty-smelling basement. 'It sounds like the lead actor in a 1940s propaganda film about out brave boys slaying jerries. *Bulldog Breed*, starring Randolph Cliff, with Drummond Place, and featuring Broughton Mews as the sergeant-major.'

Liam had been delighted to see Beatrice return to Edinburgh. He had finally managed to free himself from the grasp of Sally, who had quickly married a City lawyer. Liam was teaching in Edinburgh again, living in a small flat off Leith Walk, pining for a revival of his youth. 'This is the place for parties,' he said, pacing out the basement. 'We can crank up the music, maybe spill out the back on summer nights, get a little bonfire going, bake some tatties. It'll be brilliant.'

'I'm not sure I'm quite ready for parties,' Beatrice had said. She wanted to look out that window, to stare at that bridge, and measure the height from parapet to footpath, and imagine all that brilliant, icy Edinburgh air in between.

Around eight o'clock on the last day of 2000, Beatrice was sitting at her keyboard writing the last lines of the first love story she had ever written. With the last word, the final full stop, she briefly thought she had got it right: that love was like this, restless, unsatisfied, self-deluding. She had got it right, without ever quite knowing it herself. But that was the point, she thought; that was what being a writer meant: to see in others what she couldn't feel in herself.

Jayne had asked her about the new book. 'It's a kind of love story,' Beatrice had said. 'Written from a male perspective, and it turns into a travelogue at times, and it's really not very film-rights friendly.'

'We'll cross that bridge when we get to it,' Jayne had said. 'Just finish the bloody thing.'

She was finishing the bloody thing. She hit the "save" button, and ritually did a check of the word count. This was her work ethic, the reward, looking at the figure flash up to show that she had completed her requisite two thousand words that day, that these words had joined their predecessors in unending chain, a terracotta army of clauses, sentences, adjectives and simile, sent out to earn her the right to live here. It was a beautiful flat.

It was too dark tonight to see below, to look down at the grey water of that parody of a river. Instead, Beatrice looked over at the bridge, at the buses creeping along in New Year traffic, people coming into town for the huge street party that would close off Princes Street; at others heading away, back to their comfortable houses, surrounded by the frost and slush but warm inside, to New Year rituals of food and drink and coal and kisses and bad comedy on television and Helen singing jazzy old songs of desertion and madness with a little too much sentiment cloaking her strong voice.

Beatrice switched off the computer and thought of family. She thought of them in equal portions, by turn of their departure.

That summer she had driven down the coast road, from the Byzantine austerity of Ravenna to the tawdriness of Rimini. Her father had chosen a spot halfway between, a place where the spiritual and the secular were presumably in a state of uneasy mix. Beatrice had stood at the edge of the Adriatic and tried to imagine a cold December at the end of the '70s, the distant purr of a driver taking a coast road curve just a little too fast to be entirely safe, her father stepping out into the water, breasting the waves, ducking under for the first time, finding … what, under the water? Panic? Regret? Fear? Or comfort? Beatrice had stood at the sea's edge that day, but it was another century, too warm and peaceful and false. She put her cardigan down on the sand, tried to imagine that it was his clothes, his old suit, his polished shoes, his watch. She stood rooted in wet sand, but could imagine it only as a novelist, not as a daughter.

Half a year later, still half a mind on her book, she wondered if she was getting it all wrong. Beatrice was still looking at the bridge, trying to see that frost and slush as the same ice that gripped Landsdowne Hill in January 1980. Maybe imagination couldn't ever be enough. Maybe you had to feel everything first hand. But all she had was that meeting with her father in Parma; that last conversation, on a cold northern Italian December afternoon. Some novelist, she thought to herself; she could barely remember her central protagonist. What still lived most vividly was the smoky taste of her coffee, the exuberant syllables of stracciatella, the urgent radio warning that "London is drowning, and I live by the river."

Beatrice saw the maroon Lothians buses pulling away, and remembered that eleven years previously she had come out of the railway station at Tulse Hill, with Norwood Road blocked by three

321

double-deckers crawling to the edge of the suburb. She had gone there one last time to sort out her mother's belongings, to clear away the personal stuff before the auctioneers came.

The living-room was cold but still airless, still full of the lonely breathing of a decade, full of unsaid words, stifled stories. Beatrice had forced herself to look with a now-seeing eye, to take in the familiar arrangements, to acknowledge the shabby furniture, the clock, the dusty, never-used crystal in the corner cabinet.

In her mother's wardrobe she found a little leather trunk, the clasps rusted. Inside was Italy. A 1960s Italy of unfamiliar hairstyles, of Vincenzo smiling nervously, eyes wandering northwards as if trying to register the horror of a new haircut. Beatrice saw her mother as a foreigner, an insouciant *inglesa* under an Italian sun, looking radiantly free, clutching her husband's elbow in a mixture of possession and encouragement. There were other pictures, but they were beginning to show little traces of discontent, her mother and father staring off into opposite margins, or blinking in the sunlight. It was an age when photography was always conducted with the back to the sun, so the subjects squinted querulously at the lens.

There were letters. Three of them. Three, Beatrice had thought pityingly back then – but in later years she had realised that three was enough to make them priceless. She read a few paragraphs, recognised the florid Italian of her father's family, but her father had written with more serious intent. The words seemed ageless, and Beatrice couldn't allow herself to read them to their conclusion. In the intervening years she had read them all, but in tiny doses, never allowing herself to take them all in from start to finish. They were too rich, too unhealthy. She knew that with each paragraph she would read, she couldn't help but imagine that they were written to her. She was disturbed by the idea of her father calling her my "little white dove."

She kept them, along with her mother's faded green mini-skirt, a lilac scarf that featured in one of the photographs, a 1964 railway timetable for the routes between Torino and Udine, a tiny blackened tin of *tonno al olio*. There were times when Beatrice dearly wanted to take out a tin opener, rip into the can and spoon out the tuna. That would be an end to it, she thought.

She had gone back to the house four years later, had looked at it from the outside, barely recognisable after the modernising. She had taken a polystyrene cup of over-brewed coffee down to the West Norwood Cemetery and sat there, holding her lilies, allowing herself to think about it for the first time.

How did you start? she wondered, and it was the novelist's imagination that set to work. Turn up the gas fire until the heat blazes through the room, kills any cool pockets of escape, burns all the hope out of the air; turn down the television so that human voices become a blurred, background buzz, the stupid faces still there to remind you. What then? A couple of sips of sherry, followed by a whole glass, then another, then the first pill? What would it be like to count them, to decide on that crucial threshold with the last calculation of the sentient mind? She knew her mother; knew she would have taken them steadily, one by one. None of this dramatic hurling the bottle back and making a mess of it all. It would have been tidy, meticulous, until the heat of the gas fire and the warmth of the sherry and the dry air and the faint hum of the television set merged into one irresistible embrace. That's how it would have happened, with the empty bottles returned tidily to the coffee-table and the street-light outside blinking as it had for twenty years.

Looking around the house, Beatrice had thought about living, about the slow dripping torture of her mother's daily existence. She would wake to disappointment, look out at a London that had failed her, around a home that had atrophied in a past that was no longer even interesting. A life like this made suicide not so much daunting as a rather sensible attempt to galvanise your existence, to try something new. Life's a bit dull; let's see what death has to offer. It'll make a nice change, if nothing else.

Water, or pills? Beatrice had asked herself. Which? She had first asked the question – or, at least, allowed her conscious mind to couch it in those terms – the previous New Year's Eve, sitting on the freezing terrace overlooking the Adriatic, waiting for Luca to arrive to take her to dinner at some place that had demanded 100,000 lira merely to accept their reservation.

Grainne had called around 8 pm, the line from England crackly, confounding the telephone operator's boasts of their digital technology. 'All right, are we?' Grainne had said in a parody of matronly concern. 'I'm fine, Grainne, dear. What about you?' Grainne had seemed strangely solicitous on the phone. 'Well, Beatrice, I know this is a difficult time of year for you.'

Beatrice hadn't quite understood what she meant until Richard had called half an hour later. 'How are you? What are you doing?' he asked, too eagerly. 'Having a quiet drink.' 'On your own?' 'A friend's coming over.' Richard had recovered, had told her a little gossip about Gordon, wished her a Happy New Year and ended with a tentative, 'So, you're fine?'

Beatrice remembered then. There was a throwaway line in *Bosom* about the attractions of self-destruction, about the temptations of dates, Christmas, birthdays and anniversaries, about the urge to make their arbitrary significance into something darker. Richard would have read it with his assiduous critic's eye, and made a note. Beatrice had sipped her Chianti and smiled to herself. My father never made it into the '80s, my mother never made it into the '90s. Richard thinks I won't be able to drag myself into the new millennium. She had looked out at the swelling Adriatic and laughed at the notion.

Now she looked at the bridge and thought of water and pills. Of wading out into waves, feeling them break against ankles, thighs, waist, breasts, neck. Of the acrid taste of a white pill on the back of the throat, the rhythmic swallow, the flick of the neck, repeat until done. She could do neither, she realised. They belonged to her parents. Her father's was the water, forever; her mother had swallowed all the pills. They could not be part of her inheritance. She had taken nothing from her parents anyway, except perhaps her father's eyes and her mother's impatience.

In her second novel, after the passage Richard had remembered, she had made her heroine sit and consider the reasons for living. She had come down to three: the smell of the sea, the taste of coffee in the morning, and the possibility of love. Ah, Beatrice told herself, but my characters are nothing to do with me.

Beatrice didn't want to smell the sea any more. Since that trip along the coast from Ravenna to Rimini, she had lost the desire to be close to it. She preferred to look from a distance, to see the crests of the waves from a mile away when they seemed more benign. Close-up, they looked like killers. The view from her top floor was enough: the unthreatening Firth, fringed with its fishing harbours; the distant consolation that land was finite, but that it ended in a gradual and benign fashion.

Beatrice didn't drink much coffee any more. She was at an age

324

when she preferred sleep. She allowed herself one, maybe two cups in the morning. If she drank more, she started to feel a restlessness, a hollowness inside of her. That bitter tang reminded her of youth, and she didn't want to be young any more. She still bought the expensive imported brands, but she bought them for their Italian labels, for their crimson and blue foil. They sat in her cupboard in a state of aromatic decay.

Beatrice had never believed in the possibility of love. She had come close the previous summer. In that Volvo, on the road, with each day ending by typing the lines she had been forming in her head, she had felt close to understanding how love could drive you on, keep you moving. Perhaps they were right, she had thought resentfully: love was as much a functional life force as the pumping of the blood. That was why they always spoke of the actions of the heart. Outside a motel near Corigliano, with the low moon reflecting off the Gulf of Taranto, Beatrice had reached for her tiny, blue-lined notebook and written: 'Love, perhaps a rampant, passionate, erotic impulse, perhaps a slow-burn yearning, perhaps a tender pity; all cousins, although not alike. But the words come with their attendant small print that says love has its warranty, has its promise not to burn out within a week.' When she read the words back to herself, she wondered if that had been her loss: not to believe the worthless guarantees of words, but to see love as a short-lived affair, a temporal blip in the steady state of melancholy.

She didn't need love now, she thought. Like the sea and coffee, it had lost its ability to tempt. Now it would only trouble her, remind her of death, keep her awake at night. She thought of all the people she knew and counted their disappointments.

The traffic on the bridge was quieter now. Mostly pedestrians, heads down, marching with the steady directness you see during the Scottish winter. There was ice along the parapet of the bridge, brilliant ice glinting in the streetlight.

It would be cold up there, Beatrice thought; the cold of the metalwork on the palms of your hands, the cold of Edinburgh's wind coming in from the Forth and playing around the high exposed places. She looked for her black gloves: elegant Italian gloves, so smooth and supple that you could forget you were wearing them. She looked for her coat.

Beatrice remembered the four of them sitting around in Nicolson

Street in the spring of their first year, drinking Grainne's Russian vodka and getting maudlin and self-dramatising in a familiar and enjoyable way. Grainne had mentioned that it was her stepmother's fortieth birthday. 'Can't imagine ever being forty,' Richard had said. 'In fact, at present I'm planning to indulge in so much drunken and narcotic debauchery that by the age of thirty-nine I'll have the body of a man forty years older.' Grainne had said that she quite fancied the idea of being a consumptive poet, slipping away from existence after the publication of her first slim volume of brilliantly depressing verse. Beatrice rather fancied a plane crash, although it had to be somewhere exotic. 'Imagine hitting the runway at Luton or East Midlands,' she had said. 'How hilariously un-tragic would that be?' 'I intend to live to be a hundred and six,' Gordon had said. 'Just to piss off all the relatives who want to get their hands on my money.'

Beatrice looked in the mirror in the hall, and smiled. The hair was all in place, there was a slight pinkness about her cheeks, a tiny flush from the chill in the air. The collar of the coat framed her neck and made her look like a child. Or a heroine of a 1920s melodrama, all monochrome panic and panda eyes. In distress, waiting for a lover. A Randolph Cliff to rescue her. But she was thirty-eight, and thought she might be beyond rescue. She was still looking in the mirror when the doorbell rang. Beatrice started at the sheer cheerfulness of its peal.

Beatrice answered the door, looked out into city night.

'Bee. Great, you're ready. I've come to take you to the party. And I expect you to drink enough for the two of us.'

Beatrice looked at her, looked past her, as if expecting Grainne to be a spectre. Then she focused on the round, smiling face in front of her.

'Remember? Liam's party? I've got tickets for Princes Street first, then we're going to his afterwards.'

Beatrice kept looking at Grainne's face.

'I left a message on the answering-machine. I called again about an hour ago. Do you never answer your phone? I know you're never out. I suppose you were writing.'

Just at that moment, Grainne – pale, red-haired Grainne, with a big smile, and a middle-aged plumpness that suited her, and a cardboard carton of orange juice under her arm – Grainne was the most beautiful human being Beatrice had ever seen. She could smell her perfume, see the tiny line at the edge of Grainne's eye where the brown eye-liner had crossed its margins by a couple of millimetres, see the vapour around her mouth from the cold air. Grainne was looking at her with a fond glee. Beatrice smiled back.

'Since when have you called me Bee?'

'Since now. Do you mind?'

'I love it.' Beatrice took Grainne's arm, and they skipped out of the flat into the icy blast of twenty-first century Edinburgh. Beatrice looked back at the bridge, a good neighbour, almost empty now, an avenue of lights stretching away to the green suburbs, and off to the sea. She felt the arm in hers, was warmed by the touch.

They headed towards Princes Street, bent a little against the wind, purposeful, gripping each other with a tightness that had waited eighteen years. Grainne clutched her orange juice, Bee clutched Grainne, and they were on their way to be crushed together in the crowd, to kiss each other at midnight, and to find their party. Everyone they passed turned and looked, and smiled a little to see them go.

Grainne

Italian July scorched them, offering the occasional relief of a breeze
from the Ligurian Sea. Beatrice and Grainne stood happily in the
shade of the Cattedrale di San Lorenzo in Genoa, looking at the
Rubens, big splashes of salmon-coloured pigment.

'Gordon told me I was Rubenesque once,' Grainne murmured.

'The bastard,' Beatrice said sympathetically, staring critically at
the dusty canvas.

'That's what I thought. But now it just seems funny to me. What
I always hated about them, all those cherubic maidens, was the
stupid smile he put on their faces. I always thought that carrying
that much spare lard they should look a little depressed, or at least
guilty. But now I can see what it is.'

'What's that?'

'It's the "fuck you" smile. The smile of people who don't care
what you think of them because they've built a little private paradise
where they can swan around playing their harps and wolfing down
high-calorie ambrosia all day. They are oblivious to the world. All
those other artists were painstakingly painting earthly torments,
and Rubens was just bashing out all these contented gluttons. So
I am devoting my life these days to the development of the "fuck
you" smile.'

'Me too,' said Beatrice. Grainne laughed.

'Oh, Beatrice. You've always had the "fuck you" smile. You
were probably born with it.'

'But how do you know that this isn't just an outward expression?
Maybe all those plump angels are just burning up with doubt and
self-loathing inside.'

'Perhaps. But being able to look so serenely contented is half
the job done, I think. Appearances are more important than we
pretend to believe.'

Beatrice had shown Grainne around Genoa, taking her on the
funicular from the Piazza del Portello up to Sant'Anna to look out
over the city, pointing out the Riviera di Ponente stretching west
down the coast to San Remo. They stood on the exposed hill and
Grainne gazed down in the direction of Beatrice's airy wave.

'That's not the real sea,' she said. 'That's all serene and warm
and turquoise and luxuriant. The real sea is black and choppy with

oil slicks and dead seagulls floating on top, and smells of mackerel and Glasgow sewage.'

'So, Grainne,' Beatrice said. 'Tell me. Are you and the TV guy an item?' Beatrice said the words in her American TV producer's manner, all arch and playful.

Grainne looked back out towards the sea, smiled, and shook her head. 'Not at all,' she said, sounding very Scottish.

Grainne had met Joachim at the meeting in Hampstead. Grainne was living in North London, renting Richard's flat while he disappeared off the face of the earth. She paid a rent that was well below the going rate, on the condition that Richard could leave all his accumulated male junk lying around. Her nearest support group had been in Hampstead, and she had headed along there, reluctantly, one April evening.

They had recognised each other immediately. Grainne had spent sixteen years trying to forget the first time, but there couldn't be two like him. He had got beyond the leopardskin tee-shirts and the spiked hair. He had the convict crop that was compulsory in London that year. He was wearing the black tee-shirt, jeans and leather jacket that had become the uniform of the new middle-aged.

'What are you here for?' Joachim had said, still smiling, still looking at her almost possessively. It was as if they had been seeing each other every week in the interim, an immediate assumption of the kind of intimacy Grainne didn't mind.

'Oh, vodka mainly. Plus a bit of sherry. Nineteen counts of port taken into consideration.'

'Nice. I'm cocaine. And Valium. Amphetamines, a while back – but I grew out of them. Got too old.'

They fell into easy gossip that didn't dwell too much on the past or on the years in between, accepting their common present as somehow inevitable. 'Do you remember the first time?' Joachim asked her once, when a Pulp song had been playing in the café.

'Of course,' Grainne said.

'Shit, me too,' Joachim said, but it didn't matter as much. Grainne's first time now seemed almost idyllic to her by comparison with all the times there had been since then.

Grainne hated the meetings, but went because she found she enjoyed Joachim's company more now that they had something in common. She would find herself meeting his eyes when a particularly verbose addict would hit a confessional fast lane, and start dropping the names of Riviera resorts where he had scored with edgy celebrities.

She didn't know many people in London. All the people in her address book came from Gordon's parties. She threw it into the Thames that spring, watching it float for a minute or so by Vauxhall Bridge before sinking below the surface. Grainne stayed there for a while to make sure it didn't pop back up to the surface, and imagined she was disposing of all those bodies, weighting them and slipping them into the depths of the river. Danny and Maddy and Andy and Mark and the rest of them, choking for breath as the black Thames filled their lungs. She had smiled and walked away and bought herself a blank maroon notebook with clean white pages. She wrote in Beatrice's name first, in tiny handwriting as if to make a pre-emptive claim for all the new friends she would make and find space for.

Grainne liked the city, though; liked the anonymity it bestowed. Richard had left most of his possessions in the flat, and she browsed through his collection of obscure books and even more obscure records, nostalgically picking out the ones he used to play in Edinburgh. She listened to the Jesus and Mary Chain and hated them all over again.

Mostly she wandered the streets, pretending to be an innocent Oban girl again, counting her blessings in negatives. No husband, no job, no children, no house (Gordon had sold the place in the north after she had a laughing fit when he asked her if she wanted to go back there), no responsibilities, no seeing thirty-five again. People in London didn't look at her. She had grown an invisible bubble around her, a private cocoon that allowed her to wander around the city without making a ripple, never disturbing its choreographed flow.

Grainne ate in Lebanese cafés, sometimes pretended to be Polish, waved her arms around and yelled the occasional piece of Slavic nonsense, flirted with the tiny parodies of insanity, because they made her feel better about the real thing she had seen in the Grange.

Grainne took anti-depressants because the doctors had told her it was a good idea and because they helped her to sleep, but she had given herself a time limit. One more prescription and then gone. No more crutches, no more 'support mechanisms.' No more.

Sometimes she would look in the window of a Victoria Wine. There was a good one in Stoke Newington, a place that catered to a less exclusive clientele, an unprepossessing outlet for booze and its necessary accessories. It was always busy. Grainne would make herself stand outside, make herself scrutinise the cans of Special Brew piled into a confusing mock-pyramid. Standing there, she would remember her old mental picture of herself as a straggle-haired harridan lying in an alley cursing at passers-by. She remembered that it used to cheer her up. Now it seemed too attainable to be fun.

She told herself she was looking at a mirror, not a window display; that the glass showed a possible future. It wasn't quite one of the classic aversion therapies they spoke about at the Grange or at the meetings, but it worked for her. She needed to look through that glass, to see her problem written in the minatory typeface on a can of fortified lager.

She saw Helen occasionally. Helen was rebuilding her career with a two-hander in Islington, with no nudity and no singing but with a potentially heart-rending speech in Act Three. She brought round a couple of free tickets.

'I'd love to go, Helen, I would. But I really can't,' Grainne said.

The actress had looked affronted. 'I'm not that shit, honestly. I had a half-decent review in *Time Out*.'

'I'm sorry, I can't.'

'You're frightened I'll be embarrassing, aren't you? Scared I'll turn out to be the sad old talentless bitch after all?'

'It's not that, Helen. Really. I'm sure you're great.'

'Maybe you're right. I've lost it. If I ever had it in the first place. Maybe I'm fooling myself.'

'That theatre is in a pub, Helen.'

Helen bit her lip. 'Oh, I see.'

The meetings, she felt, were about blame. Grainne didn't want to start apportioning blame; she had too many candidates. Besides, what was the point of finding out who else was responsible for your urge to swallow a bottle of spirits a day? Although in Hampstead it was more often narcotics. After two or three meetings, Grainne realised that there was a certain level of competition in the addicts' weary claims of how much they had spent on cocaine. One literary agent would claim to have blown £40,000 in a year. The rest of the circle would nod respectfully. The following week, a record producer would double the stakes. When a photographer claimed to have been doing 'six-figure sums' annually, Grainne formulated a theory that they were addicted to the reckless expenditure rather than the drugs. She told Joachim. 'Let's go for a drink,' he said after the meeting, eagerly, quickly adding, '...of tea.' Grainne had laughed. Joachim was an independent TV producer, which impressed her vaguely because her imagination had always placed him as unemployable. But then she had thought Beatrice should be a nun, and Richard a waiter.

'Funnily enough, it really helped my career knowing where to score decent coke,' Joachim said. 'My rise up the media ladder has stalled a little since I decided to clean up. Cocaine is a kind of status adjuster as much as a mood adjuster in my business.'

'You know the problem I had with alcohol?' she said to Joachim one rainy afternoon over hot chocolate in a crowded Starbucks.

'I think so. I was at the meeting, remember.'

'No, not what I said there. I can't tell them the real truth there. They would all shout me down and tell me I was in denial.'

'Oh. What, then?'

'When I drank, it was because I thought it would remake me as someone else. I always drank vodka because I wanted to think of myself as a gloomy Russian princess. I read too much Turgenev and Tolstoy, and they were always knocking back a quick vodka. I came to think of it as this elixir of tragedy.'

'You drank to forget who you were, then?'

'No, not really. It didn't start like that. I drank for the usual childish reason that I thought it made me grown-up. Except the difference was that I didn't want to be a grown-up Grainne, I wanted to be a teenage Natasha, or sad Anna, or some cheek-boned *devushka* looking over the Nevsky Prospect. Isn't that sad?'

'Not as sad as some of the stories I've heard in those meetings.'

'The thing is, I should have started to realise that it wasn't working when I was bent over the toilet bowl throwing up the rice from the previous night's curry. You never got that kind of scene in *First Love.*'

After a couple of months of teas, coffees, orange juices and strangely addictive mint lassis in a Bangladeshi diner, Joachim asked Grainne to go to Genoa with him. 'It's the G8 summit; I'm doing a bit of filming for a documentary on globalisation. There's going to be a huge demonstration.'

'I know,' Grainne said. 'The vodka didn't entirely destroy my brain.'

'Sorry. But do you want to come?'

'How do you know I wasn't going anyway?' Grainne said, but she smiled.

In Genoa, the four of them had lunch in a discreetly tasteful restaurant close to the Palazzo Bianco. Beatrice was with a steel-grey-haired smiling professor called Luca Chinaglia, who wore Armani and a tiny gold lapel pin with an anti-globalisation logo. 'You should talk to Luca, Joachim,' Beatrice said, 'he's one of the *tutte bianchi* bigwigs.' Joachim was immediately impressed; Luca pretended to be annoyed at Beatrice for blowing his cover. After lunch, the two men disappeared to talk global politics and demonstration tactics.

'It's going to get quite violent, you know,' Beatrice said. 'Luca was at Prague, Seattle and Gothenburg. He says the mayhem is increasing every time.'

'I know,' Grainne said. 'Joachim is looking forward to it. It's men's latest alternative to war. I feel guilty because it doesn't worry me like it used to. Not like before, when the idea of injustice used to bring me to tears. I don't cry at anything any more. What a heartless old bitch I've become.'

'You've toughened up. It's hardly surprising.'

'Have I? Funny, I never think of it that way. I think I just learned to reason. Now I realise that there's very little I can do that's practical, and it's a waste of time and energy to feel hopeless in the face of my own powerlessness.'

'You've learned detachment. It comes with age. Like the "fuck you" smile.'

'Or you can be born with it, if you're lucky.'

'I'm not sure lucky is the right word,' Beatrice said.

'It is, I know,' Grainne said.

'I'm sorry I didn't come to visit.'

'What do you mean?'

'When you were…'

'In the loony bin? Don't worry about that. You weren't even in the country. And it's not the most pleasant of outings.'

'Richard told me about it. What did they do to you in there?'

'Not a lot. Or at least, nothing that was really useful. That's not true, actually. They gave me peace occasionally. I hadn't realised how important that was, having time to yourself without having to worry about how you appear to others.'

'It's the same thing.' Beatrice smiled, clutching the rail and looking at the domes of Genoa. 'It's detachment. So what about this Joachim, then?'

'He's a boy, Beatrice. They're all bloody boys. Gordon, for all his ridiculous committee meetings and his speeches and his points of order, was always a big kid who just happened to be fond of a very boring game. He needed diversion all the time. This Joachim – okay, he's rather more amiable, but he wants to play. He's hoping there's a huge punch-up tomorrow so he can run around filming it and be excited.'

'Luca has a doctorate in economics, two grown-up children, his wife died of a brain tumour six years ago, and he's been arrested three times on trumped-up charges because the government believe he's a threat to national security.'

'Oh, I see.'

'And he's a boy, too.' Beatrice laughed. 'We had dinner last night and he was using the oil and vinegar bottles to show me the way the protesters were going to break through the police cordon. The bread rolls turned into the *tutte bianchi*. You should have seen the look on his face. I suppose I should be happy for him. Enthusiasm is a beautiful thing, isn't it?'

Grainne looked at Beatrice and Beatrice looked back and they laughed, together.

'Do we have to walk down or can we get that funicular?' Grainne asked. 'I'm a fat middle-aged lady these days.'

The next day, the riot happened as expected. Joachim and his cameraman and sound-recordist had disappeared into a crowd of demonstrators. Beatrice had gone back to her hotel. She didn't like crowds, ones armed with bricks less so. She told Grainne to come with her, but Grainne had refused. 'I feel I've spent the last ten years missing things,' she said. 'I'll stay for a while.'

Grainne leant against the cool wall and looked. The noises, the screams of anger and fear seemed as if they had been muffled or as if they were underwater and had to struggle through the layers of the deep to reach her. Grainne stood and witnessed and it was as if she were looking through old glass, the greenish panes where you could see the slight tide of the glass tugged by gravity towards the bottom of the frame. Grainne looked out from her own spectator's gallery.

She saw the dustbins overturned, saw them being hurled towards the police lines and the riot shields. She looked down the Via Giuseppe Casareggi, saw the riot police forming into an assault squadron, and it seemed like a newsreel. She saw the bricks rebounding off their shields and bouncing off the cobbled street. From an upstairs window of a side street, what looked like a computer monitor sailed out and crashed against the road scattering glass and wires into the gutter.

Grainne saw the faces of onlookers and of the riot police, saw the grimaces of resolution, rage and panic, and they seemed artificial to her, the extremes of bad acting, forced passions. She felt her own face form into a calm half-smile, the non-committal expression of the unimpressed audience member. Masked demonstrators were hurling fire extinguishers at the side of a police van. She looked down the street towards the Palazzo Ducale, saw sheets of water slapping against the walls, rippling upwards like the breakers hitting the sea-wall at Tobermory. She saw soaked protestors, half-smiling as they dashed dripping down narrow side-streets.

Grainne saw it all though her own glass partition. That had always been her role, she thought: the onlooker. She remembered that afternoon in the hospital in Edinburgh, in a different age, staring though the glass as her mother and father mimed the final scenes of their fractured marriage. She could feel that nurse's arm across her shoulders still, feel the faint moistness of the glass on a summer afternoon. She could still see her father's hand gestures, pushing away his personal history, shoving it under the covers of that hospital bed, leaving it there to be buried with her mother.

She remembered the living-room on the Crawheaton Estate, remembered kneeling on that hideous carpet looking out over the central green to the windows opposite, four layers of thick glass separating her from others' lives. She'd been able to see the cold through her double-glazing, visualise the individual ice-crystals clinging to the well-tended grass-verges, feel their crispness reaching inside her then.

She thought of the polished glass of the Victoria Wine on the corner of Lynmouth Road, of the special offers scrawled in black marker pen, the cans of Special Brew marshalled into an unsuitably tidy diamond formation, not quite real there behind their glass. She felt the wary gaze of the regulars coming out with their eight-packs of Kronenbourg, their Australian Chardonnay, their forty Marlboro.

She had spent her time hating those barriers, wanting to be on the other side of the glass, hating the view from her side. Wasted her time complaining about her view, lamenting that she had been allocated a bad seat.

Now she looked and felt the bliss of detachment. The world was a few yards away, in all its noise and misguided passion, and Grainne was warm under the Genoa sun, and the noise was sidestepping her respectfully, observing her personal space, moving on towards others who might appreciate it. The squadron of riot police came by in their own diamond formation, forcing back the protesters with their batons and their stern Latinate shouts. A white-clad teenager with a slight tuft of a red goatee poking out under his face-bandanna tripped past her with a sharp exclamation of fear. The baton of the pursuing policeman swung in a smooth arc, like a baseball bat sundering the air in readiness to knock the ball high into the stand. It was a beautiful summer moment, brief hot stillness, then Grainne was cooled by its breeze, heard its faint whistling in the air by her right ear, felt it sail past her, inches away, before it swept off into its invisible future. She couldn't move an inch, and then they were all past her, the rioters, the police, the camera crews and all of them, ignoring her.

Something acrid was in the air, drifting over and settling in her eyes and nose. Tears streaming down her cheeks, eyes stinging, throat on fire, Grainne rested against cool old marble and started to laugh. This was the first time she had been able to cry in a year. She sniffed, gasped a little to catch her breath, and smiled back towards the protesters fleeing the batons of the riot police. She thought she saw Joachim being struck across the shoulder but it seemed at a distance, in slow motion. Grainne stood where she was, half-tapping her foot to the sound of the sirens. She thought she heard gunshots. She wasn't sure.

This was the happiest she had felt for years.

Richard

I f you knew how to look, you could see the end of the world from Stanley Park. Richard liked to think so, even if the park was full of smiling skaters, well-wrapped couples pushing prams, kids hurling Frisbees, all the cosy denizens of the cosseted West. This was where the sun went when it slipped below the horizon, hissing into the cold ocean. The last thing it looked at before it sank into the northern Pacific was this reassuring spot of Victorian civilisation, neat, liberal, prosperous and clean.

It was a tamed frontier, he would tell himself. Richard would wander along the wooded trails, kicking through the dead leaves from unfamiliar trees, imagining himself at the fringe of a wilderness, a cold and desolate edge of the world. A couple of minutes later he would emerge into a clearing where a gardener was whistling softly, trimming his immaculate rose-bushes, or a couple of lively pensioners were playing for fifty cents a hole on the pitch-and-putt green.

Richard would look out from the cliff path, down towards the rugged beaches stretching northwards out of the lee of Vancouver Island and the white-iced ridges of the North Shore Mountains, then turn around and take in the cheerful, modernist but accommodating skyline of Vancouver. In the same minute, he could stand in the shade of towering maple and red alder trees, gazing out at the grey-white waves of the northern Pacific, then turn about and see the comfortably familiar statues of Lord Stanley, Queen Victoria, and Robert Burns, gentle signifiers of his own old culture.

History was something you could escape, he had hoped, if you went far enough. He had started in the heat of a New York August and steadily ran away from summer, keeping it on his tail, a couple of road-blocks behind him to the east. He had hoped to lose his past in the same flight, throw it off his trail, leave it searching for him in an abandoned motel bedroom in Wyoming, no forwarding address.

He had run to a land where the streets had no connotations, where the language was his own but with the innocence of distance, the purifying force of an ocean and countless mountain ranges to separate it from the dismal dust of London.

Now, on the threshold of winter, he could see under those

spreading alders that history could follow you halfway round the world, tap you gently on the shoulder and whisper 'I'm still here.'

'When do you have to go back to work?' Matya Lebinnen had asked him in Spain, another lifetime ago, and it was a question he would ponder on the cold nights at fifty degree latitude, with the wind carrying ice in the air, sweeping down from the Queen Charlotte Islands. Soon he would have to go back to work, to face the vestiges of his old life, try to tidy them into the foundations for a new one. But not quite yet. He was still waiting for a signal that he would recognise when it came. Until then he could indulge himself, keep wandering the streets trying to lay a few last remaining ghosts.

Richard had taken a short-term lease on a dingy, damp flat in Hastings Street, on the edge of that chintzy, heritage-centre quarter of Vancouver called Gastown. The elderly tourists arrived in coach-parties and wandered around the restored nineteenth-century buildings of Gastown, cooing politely at its unremarkable antiqueness. But they stopped short of Hastings, where the refurbishers, the history fictionalisers had yet to extend their narratives.

In the letting agency, reticent Canadian realtors had made polite noises to suggest that Richard's flat, the cheapest property on their books, was in an area that wasn't entirely salubrious, and wouldn't he like to look at something in a somewhat leafier banlieu, maybe out by the University?

Richard preferred cheapness to tranquillity, and when he saw the area he realised with a smile that Vancouver's standards were a little higher than he was used to. The flat suited his purposes; the occasional noise, shout or pumped-up stereo nothing to what he had to put up with in London. A couple of Sikhs lived opposite, and would nod slowly and formally if they encountered him on the landing. Richard smiled a quick smile, and hustled onwards.

He asked himself what he was doing here, but could only answer that it was because he was unable to be anywhere else. In an afternoon outside a travel agent's in Santiago de Compostela, in Spanish summer, he had fought the sudden urge to cross the United States, chasing Sarah's spectre one more time. He had been unequal to the struggle. He had made himself look at Matya's face, and if that had not been enough to detain him, it was impossible to conceive of anything that could have managed it. A couple of days later he was at Madrid airport waiting for a flight to New York, Matya's reproaches silent but deafening.

The United States had been a less fulfilling trek than Europe, its vast homogeneity between the coasts blending into a month of Howard Johnsons, Taco Bells, strip malls, diners and Walmart outfits until Richard had lost track of his whereabouts, was forced to buy a local newspaper to find out where he was on the planet. Even then, it would take him an hour and four coffee refills, ploughing through reports of traffic violations, high-school spelling-bees, Little League results and dispensary opening hours before he would find a clue as to what state he was in. He had laughed aloud once, thinking he was in Topeka, only to discover from a confused waitress that he was just outside Sioux Falls. 'I'm not in Kansas any more?' he had asked in genuine confusion, and she shook her head and edged behind her formica counter.

In Europe he had felt an illogical certainty that he would find Sarah the next day. There she would be, he imagined, lurking, frozen in time in some European café, waiting at a table for him to walk through the door. She would have smiled at him, they would have clasped hands like eighteenth-century paramours, all would have been forgiven in Copenhagen, Utrecht, Soria, Europe's history embracing them and absorbing them into its weave. In the United States, the futility had been apparent the moment the Greyhound bus had pulled out of the Port Authority in New York and cranked its wrecked gears through the Midtown Tunnel. All he had to go on was a postcard Liam had received from San Francisco, a few jotted lines. What seemed inevitable in Europe became ludicrous in the USA.

On the interstate, he had seen that this was a place where nobody wanted to be found, where you could slip into anonymity in the vast, indistinguishable spaces of a continent-country. Richard felt lost in a delicatessen, ghosting up aisles filling a plastic container with Waldorf salad, staring for five or ten minutes at a time at a bewildering array of soft drinks.

Richard had deliberately gravitated towards towns with vaguely European connotations: Durham, North Carolina; Frankfort, Kentucky; Lincoln, Nebraska – trying to root himself in vaguely familiar names, until he reached Olympia in Washington State, felt the first chill of a Pacific autumn, and gave up. The USA had been unyielding, offering up no clues, just the up-tilted chin of a taciturn bar-tender looking at him questioningly, or the weary sigh of a waitress topping up his breakfast coffee.

Richard had listened to so much soft-country music creeping out of the tinny speakers of a Greyhound bus, that he sat in his motel room in Pierre, South Dakota and wrote a long discursive feature on abandonment, infidelity and independence in the new Nashville. In half-waking moments, when his prodigious coffee-intake did battle with the fine weariness of twelve hours on a bus, his lips would form notes and he'd find his subconscious throwing up lines at him. 'You can't depend on anything, really,' it sang. 'There's no promises, there's no point.' He faxed his article off to a music magazine in London, more out of hope than expectation. His money was running out, and he had to raise some funds to pay off the interest on his credit card balance.

He did most of his travelling by night to save money on hotel rooms, but couldn't sleep on the buses, so would try to read, or would stare out at the blackness of lost America, waiting for the occasional neon flash of an all-night gas station or diner, brief reassurances of human existence in-between the empty black stretches of infernal wilderness.

Richard tried to bury Sarah in America, leaving her behind in stages. Crossing Pennsylvania, he said goodbye to her flickering brown eyes, saw them close one last time. He kissed her lips farewell within sight of the Allegheny Mountains in West Virginia. They would try to creep back in his dreams in Kentucky, but he had to be strong. By Missouri, he could go a day without thinking of her; by the time he caught his first glimpse of the Rockies, he told himself he had made her name as meaningless a couple of syllables as Casper or Cheyenne.

He had conversations with himself. He had been doing that all across Europe: remixing old arguments with Sarah, inserting too-late refutations and justifications, laboriously rhetorical master-strokes. He still did that occasionally, but mostly he replayed that razor-slash dialogue with Matya Lebinnen at Barajas airport in Madrid, scalded himself with the look of distress in her brown eyes.

'It's something I have to do,' he had mumbled. 'It's unfinished as it is. I have to find out ... for my own good. We couldn't be happy together, unless I could exorcise this. That's what it is, an exorcism...'

He had stammered on, excuses, lies, meandering half-truths. Matya had looked at him, the moistness in her eyes glinting in the airport's harsh strip-lighting. 'It is silly, perhaps, but I think I shall not see you again.' He remembered trying to decipher that sentence, wondering whether its uncertain English signalled a decision or a foreboding.

He had told himself he would go back to reclaim Matya when this was over, but each time he thought of it his stomach lurched, his courage quailed at the thought of facing those eyes again, at summoning up the words and expressions to prove that he wouldn't fail her again. He didn't have the energy, he thought. That had always been his problem: a willingness to sink into silence, when the effort to assemble all the words, all the passion, all the promises that could save a love affair, just seemed too much.

He was too old for this, he kept telling himself; too old for one of these pilgrimages west. He should be smiling ironically over a dinner table, swapping middle-aged cynicisms with like-minded souls, squatting on the peripheries of twenty-first century culture, making a nice living, counting his white male blessings, not sweating next to a fat, nylon-suited Mormon on a cramped bus rolling west.

When he saw the ocean, he had thrown up in a motel room outside Olympia, sick of the road, his body rejecting America. Sitting by the quayside in Seattle, he had seen drifting maple leaves clogging up the drains and smiled at the cheap signals the late September weather offered him.

From Seattle he had taken a cool ferry over to Vancouver, to witness its conservative, old English welcome, the front for a confusingly cosmopolitan city.

On the boat over, he had sat next to an austere-looking Canadian businessman who hadn't said much, but looked across as Richard opened his travel book. 'Been to Vancouver before?' he had asked.

'No. First time.'

'It's not really Canada, you know. It's the first Japanese city in the West.'

'Really?'

His neighbour had laughed. 'Well, a few years back, in the '80s, there was a serious conspiracy theory going around that Vancouver was the starting of a creeping cultural colonisation by the Japanese; that they would begin there and eventually turn everywhere into these futuristic, techno-cities, all sushi and economic miracles. But I think we've held on, and it looks like the yen's gone belly-up. But don't let me spoil it for you. Find out for yourself.'

Richard found out for himself, walking the streets of a city that baffled him. Richard would wander around Hastings and Cordova Street, oblivious to the inquisitive stares of the locals. In Gastown Richard would hide behind a group of tourists, look up at the restored nineteenth-century frontier town, at its tidy lies about a chaotic past, and wonder how easy it was to clean up and order an ugly upsetting history into something so sweetly educational.

He would head down to South Vancouver, linger on 49th Street, or drop into one of the Punjabi restaurants to eat lentil curry and imagine for a few indulgent moments that he was back in North London, hiding in the multicultural capital.

Usually Richard preferred to eat in one of the Japanese places off Robson Street, because he enjoyed feeling like a fractured alien, and the Canadians made that difficult with their unassuming amiability. In the Japanese establishments you could feel a rosewater chill in the air, experience the awkwardness of being big and old and white and ignorant: a barbarian. He appreciated the slow formality of the service; the way his chopsticks were placed at an angle that he convinced himself was geometrically significant. He liked the black, lacquered dishes, the careful arrangement of sashimi and rice rolls, and the precise positioning of each grain. He asked for extra wasabi, enjoyed its punishing sting as an alternative to the sweet blandness of his Canadian breakfasts. Richard would look over at adjoining tables, see couples smiling tentatively at each other, feel like the ageing Briton, more blissfully alone than he had ever felt in his life. History was waiting outside the door, but for an hour and a half he had sanctuary, atonal music tinkling gently with what sounded like a waterfall providing percussion

Matya had been right. The further west you went, the more freedom you felt. Richard shovelled rice awkwardly around his plate and smiled to himself.

One night, in his first week in Vancouver, he found a nightclub called *Richard's* on Richards. Because it seemed irresistible he paid eight dollars, went in, and ordered a beer. It was early, only about ten-thirty, and hardly anybody was there, but he recognised the place immediately. It was the essence of the West: a bleak temple dedicated to erotic yearning. Dance music that was unerringly four years out of date bounced around the room, thudding bass under the soles of Richard's shoes taking him back home, back in time twenty years to establishments just like it, the taste of anodyne beer, embarrassment and glum determination unaltered by the years. A blonde Canadian woman about his own age looked across at him, let her eyes linger for maybe just more than a second before returning to the empty, red-lit vistas of the dance floor that, for a few moments, seemed to Richard as vast and mysterious as the American prairies. It seemed strangely satisfying that he should prove as unappealing to women across two decades and a whole continent. It offered him a little faith in human absolutes. The music swept up into an overwhelming cloud of deep bass and stabbing brass notes and crushed him against that bar, his hand closing against the cold confirmation of a Molson bottle.

Richard never went there again. He frequented a couple of quiet bars near Hastings, spoke only to bar staff. After a while Richard could go for weeks at a time without having a conversation with another human being. Instead, he ordered careful dialogues in his head with Sarah, Matya, Beatrice – even with his family. Tightly-scripted conversations, which he could alter subtly with each repetition. Richard wondered if this was a preliminary form of insanity, a slow retreat inside his own head. He remembered visiting Grainne at the Grange, remembered the strange woman Marcia who had sidled up to him and said, 'If you want to risk those chocolates, it's your lookout.'

Richard sat at one of the computer terminals in a cybercafé outside the Waterfront Station, a place milling with fresh young faces squinting at screens, green liquid crystal displays giving their faces an alien wash. He sent an email to Dave Simmonds on the newspaper, asking if he would be interested in a feature on the new North-West punk revival scene. 'What scene is this?' Dave had replied instantly. 'Give me a week and I'll start one,' Richard wrote.

Instead, he ended up being commissioned to write a piece about a comic-book artist who lived in Seattle. Richard gazed across the Sound and tried to summon up the will to cross back to the USA. 'When do you have to go back to work?' he asked himself.

Soon.

Soon became a month, became three months, became a thick white Canadian winter, then spring, then a red maple summer with the cries of migrating birds and a bright northern sun, and roads thick with tour buses and squadrons of Japanese holidaymakers. Richard would walk along the coast, watching the Asian waves break on the Vancouver shoreline, and wonder when he would be ready to return.

He moved out of Hastings when the weather got warm, found cheaper accommodation to the north, in a disused summer cottage. The rent he received from Grainne for his London flat, the occasional bizarre commission from Dave Simmonds and the odd music feature, were enough to keep him solvent. He listened to Seattle radio stations, minor-chord country laments blending in with atonal guitar noise, never saw a television. A war broke out in September, just as the birds were heading south and the maple leaves were beginning to drift. For a day or two Richard had the quick, thrilling belief that he would be stranded here, all escape routes cut off, the continents isolated once more by the oceans, the world retreating into self-contained communities. He could watch the end of the world from Stanley Park.

That would be satisfying, he thought; external forces making his decisions for him. His own indecision was having results. Sarah had disappeared over history's horizon, and he had left it too long to reclaim Matya. He remembered Beatrice telling him it might be an unhappy ending: boy might not get girl. He also remembered her saying that boy might snap out of it.

He was still waiting for some tentative touch from his past to come out and reclaim him. Ask for romantic asylum in Canada; that might be a plan. He thought if ever a nation could encourage erotic refugees it would be this cheery, chunky-knit, understanding retreat. It seemed a place where couples always held hands, where monogamy was akin to religion, where passion had been abandoned to an older, darker continent.

Instead, two days before his second Canadian Christmas, he was walking aimlessly around Kitsilano when he saw the window display in the Duthie's bookstore. It was a modest enough display, nothing like the lavish treatment they had given to Don DeLillo, Douglas Coupland or the Kurt Cobain photo-books. Just a smallish author photograph, a little pile of Euro notes fresh out of the colour photocopier, and a couple of book jackets. Beatrice Morelli's *Europa*. By the author of *Bosom* and *Greyhound*. Beatrice looked back through the slightly frosted shop window at him, and she was half-smiling – or was that a pensive gaze of intense sadness? You never knew with Beatrice. But she was looking at Richard, and if he had asked the question he was forming in his mind, he thought she would have nodded at him.

Richard went into the shop, picked up a copy and read the blurb on the back jacket. Feeling a chill of inevitability and a quick thrill of curiosity, he took the book to the counter and paid twenty-two Canadian dollars, silently.

Richard wasn't ready to go back yet. He had rented a cottage twenty miles up the coast for New Year. He was planning to take whisky, although he hated it; a handful of country music CDs, some warm clothes, and see what the difference was between the December of 2001 and the January of 2002. Lost in the frozen north-west, in the chasm between the years, Richard told himself that he would decide what to do with his life.

On December 28, with a bright damp northern sun beaming through the kitchen window, Richard sat down, propped the book up against the coffee-jug, sipped a little of his coffee and began to read his own story. In twenty chapters, with a prologue and epilogue. He resisted the temptation to read the ending first. He started at the beginning, on a brilliant afternoon in the summer of 2000, staring at a mosaic in the Roman museum of Merida.

A Party In 2001

G rainne drank orange juice, Beatrice drank champagne. They were in a small club in Soho in the late summer of 2001. It was a launch party for Beatrice's new novel, her love story without the happy ending. On the table between them sat a copy of *Europa*. Grainne had asked Beatrice to sign it for her, but Beatrice had laughed. 'Don't be ridiculous, dear.'

'Well, it's just that I thought it might be more valuable once they've all been pulped when Richard takes offence and launches a big court case.'

Beatrice laughed again. 'I told him I was going to write it. I told him years ago, before the events in the book had even happened.'

'What did he say?'

'I don't think he thought I was serious.'

'Has he read it?'

'Not yet. I can't get hold of him. He's still in Canada. I've sent him emails, but I think he lives out in the wilds somewhere.'

'He'll hate you.'

'Why?'

'Well, it's his story, isn't it? He wouldn't have told you all that stuff if he thought you were going to put it in a book.'

'Wouldn't he?'

'Of course not.'

'I'm not so sure. But really, most of it's my own invention. I've only used the outline of his story to frame my own ideas about a love affair.'

'It seems rather exact to me.'

'That's just detail, Grainne. Names and places give it veracity, but all the interpretation is my own work.'

'I still think he'll hate it. It's an invasion of privacy.'

'It's just a story.'

'It's his life.'

Beatrice sipped her champagne and looked across at Grainne, the grey eyes scanning Grainne's face, a little pink with excitement. It reminded Beatrice of when Grainne used to drink.

'It's still a story, Grainne.'

'Is that what we all are?' Grainne said a little sharply.

'Stories? Yes, I suppose. But is that so bad?'

Grainne wondered about herself, tried to remember how much she had told Beatrice about her life with Gordon, her time in the Grange. Beatrice shook her head.

'Don't worry, Grainne. You're not in the next one. Or the one after that.'

'I think you should write about your family,' Grainne said quietly. Beatrice thought about it for a moment or two.

'My family is history rather than fiction,' she said.

'What about yourself, though? You always say you are in none of your books. Why is that?'

'I'm in all of them. The words are all mine. This one is about me more than anybody else.'

'But it's written from a man's point of view.'

'Sometimes I have a man's point of view. Quite a lot of the time, actually.'

'Don't write about me,' Grainne said.

'How do you know I haven't already?' Beatrice asked, but seeing the panicky look in Grainne's eyes, she smiled. 'Tell you what. I'll agree not to write about you if you'll tell me something about yourself. Something you haven't told anybody else before.'

Grainne shook her head. 'Listen, that's tough. Remember, I was on a couch in that mental hospital for months. I had to tell them vast amounts. I started to make up stuff after a while.'

'I'm sure you held something back.'

'Nothing, really. I was disarmingly frank. Well, perhaps...'

'Go on then. This is what I'll put in the book instead of you.'

'I don't think you'll be able to.'

'We'll see.'

'I was in Russia. You know, it was the third year of my degree, and I'd been sent off to Leningrad. It was still Leningrad then. This was the Soviet Union, although it was on its last legs, black marketers everywhere. They had taken us off on a trip into the country, and we'd ended up in this town – Cherepovets, I think it was called, although they were quite cagey about telling us exactly where we were.

'The rest of them were looking at some museum devoted to the tractor or the industrial winnower or something like that, and somehow I managed to escape with this girl Paula. We had wandered off in this big square. They hated you doing it, and I was quite nervous, but it was a hot day even though this was October, and I was bored. We just walked down this shady street, and sat under this tree and we were eating apples, I don't remember where they came from.

'You know when you can feel you are being looked at? Well, I just felt this intense gaze on me. I looked up, and about thirty yards away there was this Russian boy. He could only have been about eighteen, and he had cropped hair, so I think he was probably in the army or something. He was standing at the door of this dark hall, and I think it was a bar because I could hear singing coming from inside – you know, that really sad Russian singing that they start off once they've had a few vodkas. This boy was just looking at me, and I looked back, and he smiled, and we stood there for what must have been a minute with the sun beating down and the only sound these tortured, drunken voices chanting this slow refrain, like a Mississippi work song or something.

'Anyway. After a minute, he made this tiny beckoning gesture with his head, just this little inclination to invite me into that hall. In that moment I conjured up a whole picture of me disappearing through that door and into another life. You know, just slipping away into Cherepovets and this Russian boy, and a new existence, and starting again. But then Paula saw him and she giggled, and he looked away and went inside, and I thought of Gordon back in Edinburgh waiting for me, and then the rest of the group found us and took us off to see the tractors or whatever it was. The sun went in, and we got back on the bus. But I still wonder.'

'I don't know if a book could be worthy of that,' Beatrice said softly, then looked around at the polite throng of London's literary set, the agents, publishers' assistants and critics. 'I've decided to get back to work,' she said. 'This was going to be the last one I wrote. I'd just finished it last year, you remember, when you arrived at the door to take me off to that party?'

'I remember. You were in a strange mood. Sort of happy and sad at the same moment.'

'That was because I thought this would be the last thing I wrote. Because it was quite personal. But then, well, what would be the point of that? It's not an ending, is it?

'The thing is, the writing is all that keeps me sane. Reality can kill you. Richard used to play this song to me, and it had the chorus,

Until you realise, it's just a story. I realised, eventually. It is just a story. You just have to make sure you write your own.'

Beatrice filled her glass. Grainne touched her arm.

'Smile, Beatrice: it's a party,' Grainne whispered.

'I am smiling,' Beatrice said. And she was.

Fiction from Two Ravens Press

Love Letters from my Death-bed
Cynthia Rogerson

There's something very strange going on in Fairfax, California. Joe Johnson is on the hunt for dying people while his wife stares into space and flies land on her nose; the Snelling kids fester in a hippie backwater and pretend that they haven't just killed their grandfather; and Morag, multi-bigamist from the Scottish Highlands, makes some rash decisions when diagnosed with terminal cancer by Manuel – who may or may not be a doctor.

Cynthia Rogerson's second novel is a funny and life-affirming tale about the courage to love in the face of death.

'*Witty, wise and on occasions laugh-aloud funny. A tonic for all those concerned with living more fully while we can.*' **Andrew Greig**
'*Her writing has a lovely spirit to it, an appealing mixture of the spiky and the warm.*' **Michel Faber**

£8.99. ISBN 978-1-906120-00-9. Published April 2007.

Nightingale
Peter Dorward

On the second of August 1980, at 1pm, a bomb placed under a chair in the second class waiting room of the international railway station in Bologna exploded, resulting in the deaths of eighty-five people. Despite indictments and arrests, no convictions were ever secured.

Exactly a year before the bombing, a young British couple disembarked at the station and walked into town. He – pale-blue eyes, white collarless shirt, baggy green army surplus trousers – and twenty yards behind him, the woman whom, in a couple of years he will marry, then eventually abandon. He is Don, she is Julia. Within twenty-four hours she'll leave for home, and he will wander into a bar called the *Nightingale* – and a labyrinthine world of extreme politics and terrorism.

More than twenty years later their daughter Rosie, as naïve as her father was before her, will return to the city, and both Don – and his past – will follow...

'*Nightingale is a gripping and intelligent novel; it takes an unsentimental and vivid look at the lives of a small group of Italian terrorists and the naive Scottish musician who finds himself*

in their midst in Bologna in 1980. Full of authentic detail and texture, Nightingale *is written with clarity and precision. Peter Dorward tells this tragic story with huge confidence and verve.'*
Kate Pullinger

£9.99. ISBN 978-1-906120-09-2. Published September 2007.

Prince Rupert's Teardrop
Lisa Glass

Mary undresses and wades into the boating lake. She dives and opens her eyes. In the blur, she perceives the outline of a head – she reaches... A dead bird. But she will keep searching. Because Mary's mother, Meghranoush – a ninety-four year-old survivor of the genocide of Armenians by the Turkish army early in the twentieth century – has vanished. Mary is already known to the police: a serial telephoner, a reporter of wrongdoing, a nuisance. Her doctor talks of mental illness. But what has happened is not just inside her head. A trail of glass birds mocks her. A silver thimble shines at the riverbed – a thimble that belonged to her mother. A glassblower burns a body in a furnace and uses the ash to colour a vase. Rumours circulate of a monster stalking the women of Plymouth. Has her mother simply left – trying to escape the ghosts of genocide in her mind – or has she been abducted? It is left to this most unreliable and unpredictable of daughters to try to find her, in this moving, lyrical, and very powerful work.

'Lisa Glass writes with dazzling linguistic exuberance and a fearless imagination.' **R.N. Morris**

£9.99. ISBN 978-1-906120-15-3. Published November 2007.

The Most Glorified Strip of Bunting
John McGill

The US North Polar expedition of 1871-73 was a disaster-strewn adventure that counts amongst the most bizarre and exciting in the annals of Arctic exploration. *The Most Glorified Strip of Bunting* is a fictionalised account of its events, based on the firsthand accounts of the participants. A recurring theme of the novel is the clash of two civilisations – Inuit and European – and the mutual misunderstanding and hostility that arise from it.

£9.99. ISBN 978-1-906120-12-2. Published November 2007.

Short Fiction

Highland Views: a collection of stories by David Ross.
£7.99. ISBN 978-1-906120-05-4. Published April 2007.

Riptide: an anthology of new prose and poetry from the Highlands
and Islands. Edited by Sharon Blackie & David Knowles.
£8.99. ISBN 978-1-906120-02-3. Published April 2007.

Types of Everlasting Rest: a collection of short stories by Scotsman-
Orange Prize winner Clio Gray.
£8.99. ISBN 978-1-906120-04-7. Published July 2007.

Poetry from Two Ravens Press

Castings: by Mandy Haggith.
£8.99. ISBN 978-1-906120-01-6. Published April 2007.

Leaving the Nest: by Dorothy Baird.
£8.99. ISBN 978-1-906120-06-1. Published July 2007.

The Zig Zag Woman: by Maggie Sawkins.
£8.99. ISBN 978-1-906120-08-5. Published September 2007.

In a Room Darkened: by Kevin Williamson.
£8.99. ISBN 978-1-906120-07-8. Published October 2007.

For more information on these and other titles, and for extracts
and author interviews, see our website.

Titles are available direct from the publisher at
www.tworavenspress.com
or from any good bookshop.